THE WORLD'S CLASSICS

FIRST LOVE
AND OTHER STORIES

IVAN SERGEEVICH TURGENEV (1818–83) was brought up on the estate of his mother at Spasskoye-Lutovinovo and educated at the universities of Moscow and St Petersburg. In 1838 he went to study in Germany and became a convinced believer in the West, or a Westernist (*Zapadnik*). On returning to Russia he gradually turned to literature, first as a poet, then as the author of the famous *Sketches* (*Zapiski okhotnika*, 1847–52), in which he exposed the evils of serfdom. He also began to make a name for himself as a playwright (*A Month in the Country*, 1850), but his life had already become dominated by his devotion to the famous singer, Pauline Viardot. Arrested in 1852 and exiled to Spasskoye, he turned to the larger genre of the short novel, publishing *Rudin* (1856), *Home of the Gentry* (1859), *On the Eve* (1860), and *Fathers and Sons* (1862). The hostile critical reaction to the nihilist hero of this last novel, Bazarov, and his own desire to live close to Pauline Viardot made him choose to live abroad, first in Baden-Baden, then, after the Franco-Prussian War, in Paris. Two further novels (*Smoke*, 1867, and *Virgin Soil*, 1877) followed, in addition to many short stories. By the end of his life his reputation had become overshadowed by his great compatriots, Tolstoy and Dostoevsky, but as the first Russian writer to gain recognition in Europe and America and as a master of the short socio-political novel and the lyrical love-story Turgenev still remains matchless among Russian writers.

RICHARD FREEBORN, Emeritus Professor of Russian Literature, University of London, has published several works on Turgenev and the Russian novel. His translations of Turgenev include *Sketches from a Hunter's Album*, *Rudin* and *Home of the Gentry*. He is also the author of several novels.

THE WORLD'S CLASSICS

IVAN TURGENEV

First Love
and other stories

Translated with an Introduction by
RICHARD FREEBORN

Oxford   New York
OXFORD UNIVERSITY PRESS
1989

Oxford University Press, Walton Street, Oxford OX2 6DP
Oxford New York Toronto
Delhi Bombay Calcutta Madras Karachi
Petaling Jaya Singapore Hong Kong Tokyo
Nairobi Dar es Salaam Cape Town
Melbourne Auckland
and associated companies in
Berlin Ibadan

Oxford is a trade mark of Oxford University Press

Introduction revised 1989
First published 1982 as Love and Death by the Folio Society
First issued as a World's Classics paperback 1989

British Library Cataloguing in Publication Data
Turgenev, I.S. (Ivan Sergeevich), 1818–1883
[Love and death]. First love and other
stories.—(The World's classics).
I. [Love and death] II. Title III. Freeborn, Richard, 1926–
891.73'3 [F]
ISBN 0–19–282591–7

Library of Congress Cataloging in Publication Data
Turgenev, Ivan Sergeevich, 1818–1883.
First love and other stories.
(The World's classics)
Bibliography: p.
1. Turgenev, Ivan Sergeevich, 1818–1883—
Translations, English. I. Freeborn, Richard.
II. Title. III. Series.
PG3421.A2F74 1989 891.73'3 88–26828
ISBN 0–19–282591–7

Printed in Great Britain
by Hazell Watson & Viney Ltd.
Aylesbury, Bucks

CONTENTS

INTRODUCTION

The stories chosen for this collection 'First Love and Other Stories' have several things in common. They are 'long' short stories – a literary form in which Turgenev usually worked successfully by expanding the significance of a single episode into a story capable of illustrating a whole life, even perhaps a whole age, certainly a whole relationship. His *Sketches*, particularly those which he assembled into his most renowned collection on rural Russian life and the peasantry (I have translated them under the title *Sketches from a Hunter's Album* in the Penguin Classics series), are brilliant in their finest examples, but in their weaker instances they are frequently rather formless and thin. His 'short' short stories are sometimes little more then expanded 'sketches' and provide little opportunity for the development of character and relationship at which he usually excelled. These 'long' short stories have therefore been chosen because they tend to suggest most of the strengths and perhaps few of the weaknesses of the form in which he was most successful of all, that of the short novel. They also have in common (with the obvious exception of the last of them) an autobiographical frame of reference, either being drawn directly from his own experience or being based largely on it. Yet they are not coloured by personal feeling to the exclusion of those social and political issues which reflected the problems of Turgenev's generation or his age. They have in common not only a realism of manner and purpose that vivifies or makes real, but also a sense of 'the body and pressure of time' (of sixteenth-century Italy as much as of nineteenth-century Russia). They have been chosen to illustrate the evolution of his skills and interests – from the diary form of his famous study of the 'superfluous man' (1850) through his poignant exposure of the tyranny of serfdom in his small masterpiece *Mumu* (1854), a work which ranks with the best of his early *Sketches*, to his two finest, most nostalgic evocations of love, *Asya* (1858) and *First Love* (1860). These are followed by the longest of the stories, *King Lear of the Steppes* (1870), which illustrates certain features common to Turgenev's mood during the 1860s, while the last, and shortest, of the stories is an example of his interest in the metaphysical and occult that became so marked in the last years of his life. Naturally, all the stories selected here have love as their theme in

7

one form or another. Turgenev's view of life entertained only two principal choices, the achievement of happiness in love or the recognition that man's only destiny was to die decently. Between the finality of these two choices many degrees of failure were possible. Each of these stories describes to a greater or lesser extent the failure of human beings to meet the challenge of love while simultaneously recognising that happiness must be sacrificed to death. As Turgenev grew older, the possibility of happiness grew both remoter and more precious, man's death and destiny more ennobling and somehow more awful. These stories explore, with subtle, often bitter, humour, with lyrical nostalgia, with profound human understanding and with all the elegant skills of his craft, Turgenev's lifelong commitment to the notion that mankind is balanced between love and death and cannot experience the one without the other.

His own life was remarkable for its balance between the differing heritages of his Russian birthright and his European education. In his public role as a Russian author, friend of so many celebrities and cultural ambassador of his country, he was famous and respected, but in his private role as a frequently introspective, despairing and pessimistic observer of life he proved to be a psychologically acute analyst of his own weaknesses and those of his own generation and people. Of large stature and strikingly masculine appearance, he was by nature a strange combination of masculine diffidence and feminine sensibility, Russian strength and bravura and European culture and refinement. Though he made the ecstasies of young love one of his principal themes, he liked to think of himself as prematurely old, disabled by life from any chance of re-experiencing the passions of youth. His emotional susceptibility nevertheless remained fresh and responsive to the end, just as he remained responsive to the younger generation's idealism and ardour, even if he did not always approve of their aims.

Being born in 1818 to wealth and privilege as a member of the Russian nobility, Ivan Sergeevich Turgenev knew his mother's estate of Spasskoye in the province of Oryol as both an oasis of culture and the boyhood home where his mother's arbitrary rule and capricious punishments affected him as much as they affected the servile peasantry. His father, his mother's junior by several years, was a handsome and accomplished man of the world (as the brilliant portrait in *First Love* attests) and on the whole kept himself apart from family life. He died in 1834. Although domination by his strong-minded mother was less marked after Turgenev went to university, he remained financially dependent on her and never entirely threw off her influence. In 1838 he left Russia to study in Germany, and this 'plunge into the German sea', as he called it, turned him into a keen advocate of the West, or a Westernist (*zapadnik*). When he returned to Russia in the early 1840s he attempted to find a university post and failed, did the usual things expected of a young member of the Russian nobility, such as entering the civil service and fathering an illegitimate child, and in 1843 did two quite unusual things by, firstly, publishing a long poem, *Parasha*, which attracted immediate attention, and, secondly, by meeting and falling in love with the famous singer Pauline Viardot to whom he was to remain devoted for the next forty years.

His career as a writer can be said to begin in 1847 when he published the first of his *Sketches*. Many of these were written while he was in Europe, engaged in following Pauline Viardot on her opera tours or, when he could not afford the expense, staying at the Viardot home outside Paris. At the same time he was busy trying to make his reputation as a dramatist, though his only major achievement for the theatre, the five-act play *A Month in the Country*, if completed in 1850, did not receive a proper production in a public theatre until almost thirty years later. When his *Sketches* were first published in a separate edition in 1852 he was arrested, and during the month of his imprisonment in St Petersburg he wrote *Mumu*. Afterwards he was exiled to his estate of Spasskoye until after the Crimean War. He was only one among several prominent literary figures in Russia who suffered at the hands of Nicholas I's government in the post-1848 period, but for Turgenev the enforced isolation was to make him reconsider his direction as a writer and he was consequently to turn away from the shorter form of his *Sketches* to the more elaborate form of the short novel. In doing so he amplified and developed in the hero of his novel *Rudin* (1856) the type of 'superfluous man' portrayed in *The Diary*. The poignancy of the love story in *Asya* is matched by the elegiac mood of his second novel, *Home of the Gentry* (1859), just as the themes of love and death in *First Love* find echoes in his third novel, *On the Eve* (1860). As for his work during the 1860s, after the criticism which greeted his finest novel *Fathers and Sons* (1862) and its nihilist hero Bazarov, he turned his back on Russia and made his home in Baden-Baden. The bitter criticism of his own countrymen which he expressed in his fifth novel, *Smoke* (1867), is reflected in the

INTRODUCTION

bitter and vengeful sense of hurt felt by Harlov at his daughters' ingratitude in *King Lear of the Steppes* (1870). In the 1870s, after the Franco-Prussian War, he settled in France and, though he remained unchanged in his liberalism, he became less censorious towards his own country and more conscious of the universality and agelessness of human problems. Many of his later stories are reflective and nostalgic, but his final novel, *Virgin Soil* (1877), blends scepticism at the younger generations' political aims with a respect for their devotion and self-sacrifice. It anticipates the technological future almost as realistically as it celebrates the rural tranquillity of the past. A similar realistic recognition of the apparent annihilation of human happiness and endeavour in the face of death is balanced by an exploration of themes concerning life after death in some stories towards the very end of his own life. Turgenev was always an agnostic, and that agonosticism is discernible even in such a *jeu d'esprit* as *The Song of Triumphant Love* (1881) in which love may perhaps be seen to confound death – or does it? The scepticism, lightened by humour and the elegance of his art, remained a constant in his work. He died in 1883 in Bougival, near Paris.

Turgenev's portrayal of love was not conventional. Nowhere in his work does love lead by easy stages to matrimony and happiness; it is rarely consummated and when it is the ensuing happiness is brief and crowned rather by death than by birth. The ideal life for Turgenev appears to have been what he identified in nature as 'a tranquil and slow animation, the leisureliness and restraint of its sensations and forces, a balance of health in each separate being – that is its very basis, its unalterable law, that is on what it rests.' Love, like death, represented an inevitable disturbance to this balance of health. As a result, love is frequently portrayed in his work either accompanied by illness – Asya, for example, falls ill, ostensibly of a headache (ch. 13) when it is clear she is in love with the hero, and Dr Lushin in *First Love* (ch. 10) talks of love as an infection – or literally as a disease, as the 'superfluous man' describes it in his diary entry for 25 March. This is not to say that Turgenev dwelt on the morbid aspects of love as an emotion; it simply means that he made painful but hard-headed acknowledgements of love as the most powerful of human emotions and one capable of changing human beings as profoundly as social or political upheaval or any kind of cataclysm. As he put it in *The Torrents of Spring*, his beautiful novella-length love story of 1872: 'First love is like a revolution; the uniformly correct ordering of life is

10

smashed and destroyed in an instant, youth takes to the barricades, its brighter banner raised on high, and no matter what awaits it in the future – death or a new life – it sends to all things its ecstatic greeting.' For if love at its first coming had this kind of destructive and transforming power, it was also an emotion that worked in mysterious ways and nowhere did Turgenev describe this better than in the words which he put into the mouth of his hero Rudin:

'Love!' he went on. 'Everything is mysterious about it: how it comes, how it grows, how it goes. It may appear suddenly, sure and radiant like the day; it may smoulder for ages, like fire beneath ashes, and burst into flame in the spirit when everything is already destroyed; or it may creep surreptitiously late into the heart like a snake, or it may suddenly slip away out of it . . . yes, yes, it's a question of the utmost importance. Who can love in our time? Who can dare to love?'

The question which Rudin poses here is one of that challenges not only his own resolve, as the relationship with Natalya clearly reveals, but also the resolve of many other Turgenevan heroes. The courage to love and to respond to love becomes the final measure of heroism in Turgenev's work. For the most part his heroes fail to meet the challenge by failing to exhibit the necessary courage at the appropriate moment. They appear to be not so much blameworthy for this failure as foredoomed by circumstances and their own weakness of will. Turgenev himself no doubt suffered from such a weakness or at least knew it well enough to be able to analyse and expose both the tragic and the comic aspects of it. What emerges as a kind of moral from his studies of this dilemma is the suggestion that all human aspiration is tinged with vanity, that even the expectation of happiness is vainglorious and that it is proper for man to regard life as uniquely precious and brief, always at the mercy of a deathward-moving process. The idea is stated at its clearest in *On the Eve*: 'Death is like a fisherman who has caught a fish in his net and leaves it for a time in the water: the fish still swims about, but the net surrounds it, and the fisherman will take it when he wishes.'

Love, for all its power to move and transform, cannot in the end outlast the brevity of human life, nor can it alter the fact that the individual human spirit is menaced by a surrounding darkness of nature. Even the most heroically proportioned of Turgenev's fictional portraits, that of Bazarov in *Fathers and Sons*, demonstrates his insistence that the ennobling tragedy of a potentially great human being laid low by sickness and death must be matched by an equivalent human awareness of mankind's comic smallness in relation to nature and eternity. His liberal distaste for the arrogant nihilism of the younger generation may have partly dictated such a death of a hero in his greatest work, but Turgenev, for all his commitment to his time, always believed – and this became increasingly marked – that there were eternal laws governing human existence and these did not give grounds for any gratuitous or shallow optimism about human changeability or progress. The final words of *Fathers and Sons* suggest a calm acceptance, a readiness to hope, even the possibility of faith. They do not suggest the triumph of love, simply a recognition of the need to reflect on the idea of eternity:

Can love, sacred, devoted love not be all-powerful? Oh, no! No matter how passionate, sinning, rebellious is the heart hidden in the grave, the flowers growing on it look at us serenely with their innocent faces; they speak to us not only of that eternal peace, of that great peace of 'impassive' nature; they speak to us also of eternal reconciliation and life everlasting . . .

Man, by this reckoning, may seem to be superfluous in life. Turgenev was the first Russian writer, perhaps the first ever, to isolate the problem of the 'superfluous man' – superfluous by virtue of his own failings as well as by virtue of the indifference of society to his personal inadequacy and his personal fate. In the disaster of his relationship with Liza the author of *The Diary* of course plays the role of the superfluous suitor, but it is less his superfluous role than his supposedly inherent redundancy as a human being that Turgenev emphasises. He is handicapped at the outset by an unimpressive name (Chulkaturin in transliteration, which I have preferred to translate as 'Mr Stocking' – hence the prince's reference to him as 'Mr Stucco') and a miserable family background of coldly virtuous mother and pathetically vice-ridden father. As a type, in the name given to his problem if not exactly in the diagnosis offered by Turgenev, he may seem to be of the same lineage as Pushkin's Eugene Onegin and Lermontov's Pechorin and several other 'superfluous' heroes in Turgenev's own work, and to achieve his apotheosis as a type in Goncharov's Oblomov. A member of the nobility impoverished by his father's profligacy, he could very easily be regarded as superfluous because he belonged to a superfluous class, but this was never Turgenev's principal intention. On the contrary, the 'superfluous man' seems superfluous to himself because there is always some obstacle between his feelings and his thoughts; he is hypersensitive, pitifully shy and bitterly introspective. Being led to feel that he is 'not like the rest' and therefore somehow singled out as superfluous in society, he regards himself as incapable of achieving happiness in any relationship, particularly with a member of the opposite sex. But the testimony of his own diary shows that he is a man of exceptional qualities of intelligence and sensibility. In some respects the sheer literary power exhibited by his diary, which we must naturally attribute to Turgenev himself, appears out of keeping with its author's supposed weakness of character. The self-scrutiny is devastating; the humour, no matter how unobtrusive, is sharp and original in its exposure of his own deficiencies and it verges on satire in its scorching comment on the triviality and pretentiousness of Russian small-town life. The portrait of Liza herself is by contrast unaffected by bitterness or malice. It is a wonderfully lucid, observant and sympathetic portrayal of an ordinary, attractive girl who suffers the misfortune of falling in love with the wrong man. The 'superfluous man' can discern the subtle changes in her to perfection and can hope vainly that he may be their cause. It is testimony to his own discernment, as it were, that we as readers care that much, but his own dilemma, his own seeking after self, absorbs us far more than the plight of the innocent Liza who has tasted misery for the first time.

As a confession *The Diary of a Superfluous Man* can appear to be an old-fashioned device for revelation of character. There will be occasions when the high-flown emotion seems maudlin, the anguish of the self-pity excessive to the point of caricature. Though this may have been intended as a feature of the characterisation, it must nowadays seem rather dated. Its obvious debt to a late-Romantic manner is set in relief by the cynically appraising, but realistic, eye of the 'superfluous man' in his analytical rather than his nostalgic mood. The wicked thumbnail sketches, the little sallies and the rancorous tone show us the fatuousness of the Ozhogin parents and the townspeople. The prince's portrait is a perfect replica of a well-known type, without any unnecessary warts. Coincidence plays its part too aptly, as it always does in Turgenev's work, in arranging a partner for Liza, but the final coincidence of the diarist's death on 1 April is accompanied by the ultimate ironic comicality of the doodlings and anonymous comments that occur at his diary's end. They offset the sentimental notes which creep into Stocking's last words. Whether or not we are saddened by his end, the single episode in his life which comprises his story is the pretext for a supremely ironic portrait, both saddening in its comic features and sardonically amusing in its exposure of so much talent gone to waste.

The censor took his toll of the work at its first appearance in print in 1850. All of the entry under 20 March describing the diarist's boyhood and his father's 'vice' was cut out, as was the satirical description of the town of O— under the entry for 23 March, and a great many other excisions were made. These were restored later, and in the process of restoration Turgenev seems to have reworked his text to some extent, so that it is likely that a final version of the story as we now have it was not in existence until 1856. Critical reception for the story was initially hostile, but it quickly acquired an acknowledged and influential place among Turgenev's stories, not least for the fact that it coined the term 'superfluous man'.

Mumu speaks for itself. Based on Andrey, a deaf and dumb peasant giant befriended by Turgenev's mother, the Gerasim of the story has Turgenev to articulate his otherwise inexpressible unhappiness. It seems that the real-life model remained devoted to his mistress despite the loss of his dog, but that is not exactly how Gerasim reacts. A distant relative of Turgenev to whom he read it before leaving St Petersburg after being ordered into exile on his estate reacted in the following way:

. . . All day I was under the impression of this artless tale. Yet what depth and sensitivity and understanding of spiritual experience it has! I have never encountered anything like it in other writers; even in my favourite, Dickens, I don't know of anything to equal *Mumu*. What a humane and good man one must be to understand and give expression to the experience and torments of another's heart in that way!

The mention of Dickens is very appropriate. Turgenev's story lacks the overt special pleading which so often accompanied attacks on social injustice in Dickens. Its effectiveness as a plea for social justice is all the more striking for its objectivity and unpretentiousness. Thomas Carlyle was reputedly driven to exclaim that it seemed to him the most touching story he had ever read; and John Galsworthy said of *Mumu* that 'no more stirring protest against tyrannical cruelty was ever penned in terms of art.' Despite the element of protest, the story has the power to move chiefly through its remarkable portrayal of dumb affection, of both man towards dog and dog towards man. The trivially selfish reason which eventually causes the animal's

14

INTRODUCTION

death simply underlines the servile nature of relationships in a serf society.

Asya and *First Love* can be regarded as Turgenev's finest love stories. If *First Love* is an undisputed masterpiece, *Asya* is very nearly its equal. Both are essentially reminiscences and nostalgic in tone, stories told by a narrator in the first person and therefore only thinly disguised forms of autobiography. The main difference between them lies in the ages of the respective heroes and heroines, and it is in large measure the age difference between the narrator-hero in *Asya* and Asya herself which accounts for that story's lesser appeal. The hero's failure to say the word 'love' at the right moment – perhaps, indeed, his failure to recognise the emotion at all, either in himself or in Asya, until it is too late – betrays his fallibility as a man, whereas the boy-hero of *First Love* is never faced by an equivalent predicament.

Asya was begun in Sinzig on the Rhine in July 1857 and completed in Rome in November of the same year. It may be that Turgenev's meeting with the Saburovs, brother and sister, in Sinzig in June and July 1857 provided a basis for the story; possibly, also, his meeting with the painter A. P. Nikitin at the same time and in the same place may have contributed something. One source quotes Turgenev as saying of the story's beginnings:

While travelling I stopped in a small town on the Rhine. One evening, having nothing to do, I thought I would go out in a boat. The evening was delightful. Thinking of nothing at all, I lay in the boat breathing the warm air and looking round. We were drifting past a small ruin; just beside the ruin was a small two-storey house. An old woman was looking out of the window on the lower floor and a pretty girl's face was peering out of the window on the upper floor. Suddenly I was overcome by a special kind of mood. I started thinking who the girl might be and why she was in the house, what her relations were to the old woman, and there and then in that very boat the whole plot of the story came to me.

Turgenev's friend and adviser, P. V. Annenkov, considered that 'such a poetic and at the same time realistic characterization of a heroine, of a kind not often encountered even in literatures a great deal richer than ours, should deserve greater development, the scope of a novel, for instance, which she would fill to the full.' Undoubtedly the story still has within it traces of the anecdotal form of its beginnings, and the characterisation of Asya is lacking in that fuller and consequently more successful development that Turgenev gave to Liza, the heroine of his second novel *Home of the Gentry* which he was to write the following year. Nevertheless, this charming love story, begun, so it seems, while Turgenev was drifting in a rowing boat on the Rhine, gave rise to one of the most extraordinary critical responses of any that occurred in nineteenth-century Russia. Even before the story was published the scene of the final meeting between Asya and the hero in Frau Louise's house caused dissent among those who had heard it or been privy to its composition. At the time of writing it, Turgenev was seriously disturbed by his own apparent lack of real achievement as a writer (it should be remembered that at this point, not far short of his fortieth birthday, he had only published one novel). He had criticised Leo Tolstoy, whom he had befriended immediately after the Crimean War, in 1855 and 1856, for his dilettante approach to his art and felt the same charge could be made against himself. The weakness of Asya's brother, Gagin, as an aspiring painter is no doubt a reflection of Turgenev's own temporary sense of inadequacy, a fact expressed in his own words: 'There are turning points in life, points when the past dies and something new is born; woe to the man who doesn't know how to sense these turning points and either holds on stubbornly to a dead past or seeks prematurely to summon to life what has not yet fully ripened.' The writing of the story involved him consequently in numerous alterations and reworkings. Still, neither Turgenev's doubts nor his hero's indecisiveness need have given rise to the critical storm that broke over the story on its first appearance.

Turgenev, a writer of liberal political views, did not court literary polemics, but his reaction to the views on aesthetics and the function of literature expressed by N. G. Chernyshevsky, the leading radical publicist of the post-Crimean period, was hostile in the extreme. He disliked Chernyshevsky's utilitarian view of literature and he took exception to his view of aesthetics as inevitably inferior to life. Until 1857 and the publication of *Asya* the mutual hostility of their attitudes had been confined to private remarks, it seems, but in his review of the story Chernyshevsky attacked the indecisiveness of the hero as typical of so many other 'superfluous men' in Russian literature and clearly attributed such weakness to class causes. He also implied that the historical role of such representatives of the Russian nobility was already over and a new class and a new generation – the 'men of the sixties', the nihilists, the revolutionary democrats, as they came to be known – should replace them. Annenkov came to the defence of the hero in an article which argued that Russian life did not need active revolutionaries, as might be the case in the West, but progress of a kind which could be supplied by a squirearchal liberalism.

It is hard to appreciate nowadays how such an innocent and evidently a-political love story could be the pretext for such socio-political dissent. In fact, the critical storm was merely the beginning of much fiercer polemics between liberalism and radicalism within the ranks of the Russian intelligentsia or between those whom Turgenev was to regard as the 'fathers' (his own, the senior, generation of the intelligentsia) and the 'sons' (roughly speaking, the following of Chernyshevsky). To this extent, *Asya* can claim to be of historical interest. Of perhaps more relevance now to our understanding of the story is that Asya's experience as a child was very probably based in part on the experiences of the illegitimate daughter of one of Turgenev's uncles and in part on those of his own illegitimate daughter Polina. Yet her characterisation obviously has something in it deriving from Turgenev's own experience as a young man in Germany, just as it reflects in unobtrusive though quite specific ways his interest in the type of religiously inclined, morally pure heroine whom he was to portray more elaborately in his second and third novels. *Asya* may therefore be said to be related to Turgenev's past as well as to the period of the story's composition, to the polemics of the day as well as to Turgenev's personal concerns.

Seen as she is, almost entirely through the storyteller's eyes, Asya's moodiness and changeability appear unmotivated to start with, and even after her brother has explained the circumstances of her birth and upbringing her portrayal seems coloured by the glow of the hero's feelings for her in ways which suggest that he is not as observant or understanding a portraitist as he might be. The reader may find it hard to believe that she should fall in love with him. He is hardly the hero whom she needs, it would seem. His way to her heart would appear to be through that appeal to higher things which for other heroines has an overtly religious meaning, but is given only a faint suggestion of religious commitment in Asya's case. Her desire to join the pilgrims, 'to do something difficult and heroic', quickly yields to an acknowledgement, as the hero puts it, that 'there are feelings which can lift you above the earth' – feelings, in other words, which can come to her on the wings of love. Her fascination, however, not only in her artlessness and vivacity, but also in the unusualness, the rarity of her charm, comes delightfully through the portrayal and is the magic at the story's centre. The hero is attracted to her perhaps less by

17

her strangeness than by his eventual realisation that she is Russian, though the paradox of this discovery is that it implicitly reveals his real ignorance of her true feelings and thus virtually ensures his failure at their last meeting. If the story has any theme apart from its principal concern with the heroine's portrayal, it is the theme of happiness so nearly found and then so irrecoverably lost. But in this sense it is no more than the story of a moment, a brief encounter, scarcely begun before it ended, for, as the hero reminds us: 'Happiness has no tomorrow. It has no yesterday. It does not remember the past, it does not think of the future.'

The emotional range of the story is literally signalled by its topography. The small Rhineland town of its setting, so beautifully summoned to life in all its summery romance and mystery, is like the very brevity of the story itself in its quality of stillness beside the eternally flowing Rhine that finally carries Asya and her brother out of the hero's life forever. For all its romantic appeal, the town represents life at a level of practical realities, whereas the place high up in the vineyard where the Gagins live is the site of higher things – the place where the waltz music not only sounds romantic but is the supreme moment of the hero's happiness as he dances with Asya, the place where he can literally feel that he can grow wings and fly, where he can be above the earth and know love as the free flight of a bird. The practicalities of the relationship, of his attainment of happiness, are finally constrained by the river level of the story with its portentous Lorelei rock and those obvious intimations of sadness, the pierced madonna sheltering beneath its ash tree and the tears of Hannchen. Of course, the clearest portent of unhappiness is the strange bird-shaped house where Frau Louise lives. In its grotesque wingless rootedness, it totally symbolises the place where the hero has to acknowledge his own earth-bound inability to rise above the petty constraints of propriety. Perhaps if he had said the one word which Asya had hoped to hear from him he might have been able to preserve forever the hope of happiness which the relationship offered, but that contingency seems so unlikely as to be practically unthinkable. The main lesson of the story is that life yields such riches very sparingly and that there is a very real distance between the promise of the heights and the choices which face man at the level of reality.

First Love traces the gestation of love in subtler, brighter and more lucid ways. Based on autobiographical experiences, the story was written between January and March 1860 and its dedication to P. V.

Annenkov was a recognition both of the latter's decision to give up bachelorhood (he married in September) and of Turgenev's devotion to the memory of 'first love', after which there can be no other, strictly speaking, as so many of his novels and stories tell us. He said of this story towards the end of his life: 'It is the only thing that still gives me pleasure, because it is life itself, it was not made up . . . *First Love* is part of my experience.' It is a startlingly fresh work despite the bitter-sweet air of nostalgia which serves to give it a frame, and its freshness is mostly due to the total recall of adolescent love through its many phases. It is also about an age – not only of youth, but specifically of Romanticism – which had long since given way to Realism and, for Turgenev's generation, to a bitter, even recriminatory, reappraisal of their own heritage. In 1863, for the French translation of the story, Turgenev added an ending which never appeared in the Russian version (though the German translation was to have a similar ending) and in this final section reference is made to this heritage. The scene recalls the opening of the story – the three men gathered together to hear Vladimir Petrovich's 'confession' – and it falls to the host to pass a final verdict on the significance of what they have heard. After a brief exchange in which Sergey Nikolaevich expresses the opinion that the story could only have occurred in Russia, the following lines ensue:

Vladimir Petrovich said nothing. 'What's your opinion?' he asked, turning to his host.

'I agree with Sergey Nikolaevich,' he answered, also without raising his eyes. 'But don't worry, we don't mean to suggest you're a bad man. Not at all. We mean that the conditions under which we were all educated and grew up were formed in a special way, that was unprecedented and unlikely to be repeated. We were appalled by your simple and artless tale – not because we were struck by any immorality in it. Here there's something profounder and darker than immorality pure and simple. You yourself are not to blame at all, but one senses here some overall, national guilt, something akin to crime.'

'What an exaggeration!' remarked Vladimir Petrovich.

'Perhaps. But I repeat the words from *Hamlet*:
  Something is rotten in the state of Denmark!
But we will hope our children won't have to tell such stories from their childhoods.'

'Yes,' said Vladimir Petrovich thoughtfully, 'that'll depend on what their childhoods are filled with.'

'We will hope,' their host repeated, and the guests went their several ways in silence.

19

Such an ending evidently added little to the story itself and proved to be the occasion for critical comment, especially in Germany. Its pessimistic verdict on the heritage of Turgenev's generation is the most noteworthy feature of it. In this respect it echoes Turgenev's feelings in the wake of the critical reception given to his most famous novel, *Fathers and Sons*, in 1862 and is clearly at odds with the spirit in which he actually wrote *First Love* early in 1860 when he was still hopeful that the forthcoming reformative measures, particularly the emancipation of the serfs, would be genuinely beneficial to Russia. This is not to suggest that any political meaning can be ascribed to *First Love*. It is simply to reassert that for Turgenev 'first love' was fundamentally transforming, like revolution, and that the hope of change which Turgenev looked for politically in the government's reformative measures had its parallel for him in personal experience in the beautifully evoked story of his own first love.

The story harks back, then, to romantic experience and is pervaded by Romantic feeling. Zinaida's dreams are the purest stuff of Romanticism, Wagnerian in their scale and tonality while also having about them a barbaric, even Dionysian quality of ruthlessness and, conversely, of deliberate readiness for sacrifice. Zinaida is simultaneously temptress and victim, though she does not consciously seek either role, so far as one can judge. It is in the nature of love that both poles of feeling should be necessary, and if they exist separately in father and son – in one as the will to dominate and overmaster, in the other as a readiness to sacrifice and submit – then in Zinaida herself, the object of both poles of feeling, they are combined in a complex blend of love-the-pleasure and love-the-sacrifice. It is something of a formula in Turgenev for two men to be in love with the same woman – a formula that, after all, dominated his life in the sense that for nearly forty years he was rivalled in his love for Pauline Viardot by her husband Louis – and *First Love* may perhaps provide the autobiographical basis for the formula.

The fascination of the story rests entirely on the fascination of Zinaida. If her portrayal had failed in the slightest facet, the success of the story would have been imperilled to that precise extent. It is a measure of the story's claim to be a masterpiece that her portrayal is virtually faultless. The boy sees her from a peerlessly fresh viewpoint and so illumines her portrait that, no matter how she may seem to fall short of the ideal which he had conceived for her, her image is always lucidly projected to the reader. Her louche background and circumstances undoubtedly provide some of the fascination for the boy. The mother, with her legacy of bad debts and poor spelling, typifies this background of seediness and vulgarity. It is probably this aspect of Zinaida which the boy never fully understands, for it is this aspect, the coquettish, as it were, which the father sees and which, as a womaniser, he presumably exploits in order to exert his mastery over her. The boy sees Zinaida in her ideal aspect and worships her as an ideal, ready at a word to hurl himself down to the ground from his favourite high point or to accept without demur the doubtful privilege of being her pageboy. The fresh, instantaneous responsiveness of his love dignifies and ennobles its object. When, after his final glimpse of her, the boy stares senselessly at the river with tears pouring down his cheeks and has the thought: 'They're whipping her . . . whipping her . . . whipping her . . .' it is as though one can feel the weals being made on his own heart.

In the boy's eyes, the father's blows exemplify the extent to which true love involves sacrifice. They also reveal that his own boyish love could only seem small and childish by comparison with Zinaida's. She embodied for him that 'image of a woman and the vision [the Russian literally suggests a ghost: *prizrak*] of a woman's love' which, though indefinite, involved a half-conscious, shameful or conscience-stricken anticipation of 'something new and inexpressively sweet and feminine'. 'This anticipation,' he admitted (ch. 1), 'this foreboding permeated every bit of me and I breathed it in with each breath, it was pumped through my veins in each drop of blood.' His 'first love' for Zinaida was eventually to seem, as he puts it enigmatically at the end of his story, 'a fugitive and momentary ghost' to which he said goodbye 'with no more than a sigh, a nagging sense of loss' (ch. 22). Simultaneously Zinaida – or his memory of her – represented something more universal, a recognition of the wanton ephemerality of youth and the way in which it 'disappears like wax, like snow in the heat of the sun.'

The work is the most densely textured of all Turgenev's stories. This is apparent in all its parts, though most obviously in the characterisation. The little court of admirers over whom Zinaida presides is a marvellous ensemble creation. As for the boy's parents, we can easily recognise Turgenev's very sparing but effective use of distancing technique in presenting them from the boy's point of view. Their exchanges appear full of reverberations of meaning that suggest only obliquely the real hostility at the heart of their relationship. As for the boy himself, he is boy-hero and adult narrator combined and what one admires is the absolutely sure touch which unites the two in such images as the one describing his anticipation of love (ch. 1):

'My imaginings played and darted continually about one and the same thing, like martins at twilight around a bell-tower'

Or the sight of the summer lightning after the revels in the Zasyekin household:

'It was simply that the sky was ceaselessly filled with dull flashes and long, forking streaks of lightning. They did not flash so much as tremble and quiver like the wing of a dying bird.'

In this commingling of the exultant, mysterious and sad an epiphany seems to be suggested, as if the boy as much as the man recognised that his feelings, reflected as they appear to be by the flashes of the inaudible storm, contained both excitement and intimations of mortality. Despite the summeriness of the story's atmosphere and the rich feel of total recall which pervades it, *First Love* is in the end more concerned with the coming to dust of golden lads and girls than with their joys and sorrows. It cannot fail in this respect to elicit a sense of regret from the reader.

It may even leave behind it a *frisson* of horror at the stark reminder, as Shakespeare puts it in *King Lear*:

As flies to wanton boys, are we to the gods:
They kill us for their sport.

In the ten years following the writing of *First Love* Turgenev appears to have accepted as his model the pessimistic bitterness which Shakespeare showed for human folly. His own version of the Lear story owes more to this bitterness than it does to the detail of the story itself, though it respects the main features. He first conceived the story in February 1869 but he did not complete it until about eighteen months later. In the meantime he wrote to his estate manager in Russia asking for details of the legal conditions to be observed in arranging the transfer of an estate from one owner to another in the first owner's lifetime. He also researched other details by inquiring of correspondents what parts of the roof were called. All of this evidence suggests what the story itself fairly clearly demonstrates: a certain unsureness about the background details and consequently greater emphasis on the dramatic or theatrical form of the work.

To some extent this may have been due to the Shakespearean

model, but Turgenev's own absence from Russia must also be held accountable in part. The English connection was important to Turgenev for more than one reason, it seems, though exactly what he intended when, according to a draft copy, he gave Harlov a resemblance to Oliver Cromwell is debatable. In his final version of the story Harlov-Lear emerges as an eighteenth-century figure proud rather of his reason than of his remarkable physical stature and strength, and flawed chiefly by his exceptionally morbid fear of death. The scale of his folly was of course much less grandiose than was that of the Shakespearean Lear, and yet under conditions of serfdom it showed up the bizarre nature of the system and the arbitrary nature of power almost as frankly as did King Lear's division of his kingdom. Harlov has no fool to console him, only a brother-in-law (Souvenir) to taunt and needle him. He has a sort of Goneril in Anna, but the softness of Yevlampiya's heart does not match Cordelia's and is only apparent for a brief moment at the climax of Harlov's revenge. The drama of Harlov's foolishness has no catharsis, only a tragic and bitter finality.

Harlov did not know *King Lear*. Had he done so he might have discovered that:

> *Men must endure*
> *Their going hence, even as their coming hither:*
> *Ripeness is all.*

He wished to anticipate his going hence and forgot the need for ripeness. There is an animalistic, instinctive strength and vulnerability about Harlov that gives his characterisation a certain appeal, but it is hardly sufficient to make him into a tragic figure. His story is racy, told to us in a series of dialogue scenes witnessed by a narrator who frequently effaces himself; and when the narrator comments he seems to be motivated rather by curiosity than by a desire to judge. In its reliance on dialogue *King Lear of the Steppes* differs from the manner of most of Turgenev's earlier stories and must seem thinner by comparison. The chief difference, however, is that the full ripeness of nostalgic recollection is not so obviously discernible at its centre. It has many skilfully done portraits and on the whole a brisk pace. Harlov's revenge provides an exciting and dramatic climax. What is missing is precisely what was so conspicuous in the earlier stories: the nostalgia for lost love. Here the dominant sentiment is ingratitude, and the iciness of this feeling seems to have turned the hearts of both

Harlov's daughters to stone. Monumental creatures as they appear to be, especially in Yevlampiya's case, they are unlikeable and unlikely recipients of earthly bounty, and when at the end we learn of their success, respectively as landowner and religious cult leader, their unyielding hardness and authority seem to reject all love and to respect only an unqualified devotion.

The Song of Triumphant Love demonstrates the inadequacy of love as well as its hypnotic and consuming power. It has all the polished stylishness of a beautiful artefact, but it has none of the natural, unforced loveliness of *First Love*. In this respect it is an incomplete gem cut from some greater whole, and in this, as in its manner, it is a deliberate concession to Turgenev's close friend, Gustave Flaubert, who died in 1880. Charcot's experiments with hypnosis no doubt helped to supply one theme in the story, but equally important was the respect for historical atmosphere, if not absolute faithfulness to historical detail, that Turgenev found in Flaubert. This story also has about it that striving for quintessential perfection, usually allegorical or symbolical in character, which we find in Turgenev's last works, his *Poems in Prose*. The realism of mundane experience with all its emphasis upon *realia* and social relevance has been replaced by a willingness to acknowledge a higher reality or a degree of supernatural in the supposedly real. Together with this it must be admitted that there is an element of the morbid associated with the idea of love. Similarly, if life is little more than the conjurings of a hypnotist, what worth is it?

One reading of the story may argue that it is really about the power of love as an emotion which cannot be thrown off no matter how far its victim – in this case, Muzzio – may travel. Or it may be that this is a love triumphant only as sexual lust, a debased feeling which attains its seduction through hypnosis. Or it may be love triumphant in the sense of being procreative – in which case the issue of fatherhood is tantalisingly left either as a triumph of virtue or as the hypnotist's last laugh. Not that it really matters, for the whole story can be regarded as a lightly sardonic piece in which the themes of love and death familiar to us from other Turgenevan stories are neatly woven into a stylish Italianate pattern.

The one feature which most obviously distinguishes this story from practically all others by Turgenev is the incursion of the East into the West, not in the form of a meeting of Russian and European but in the form of a mysteriously potent East, embodied by the tongueless Malay, exercising sinister power over a Christian West. If all the actions of Muzzio after his return are attributable to the Malay's hypnotic or extraterrestrial power, then he is merely his servant's puppet, love is merely the exercise of the black arts and death can be overcome by the galvanising forces of an occult alchemy. These may be construed as travesties of concepts of individuality, of love as the supreme happiness and of death as the final tragic end of human endeavour which Turgenev illustrated so finely in other works, but of course one may set against such a pessimistic interpretation the affirmative role given to marital happiness and the final affirmation – unusual in Turgenev's works as a whole – that marital love should be crowned by procreation and birth. In this affirmation, as in so many others by Turgenev, the three dots at the end, the incompleteness of the manuscript, leave room for doubt and beg the indulgence of all readers wise enough to know that life very rarely offers ultimate solutions.

In translating these six stories I have tried to be as faithful as possible to the original Russian without making too many concessions to modern tastes in English style and phraseology. Some modernising has been necessary to make the stories fully comprehensible to readers in the last quarter of the twentieth century. I hope I have avoided distortions of the original in the process of updating, though I have grown increasingly conscious of the very narrow line separating such updating from the perils of inaccuracy and all vulgarising or popularising tendencies. Only in punctuation have certain deliberate changes been made. These have mostly involved substituting full stops for Turgenev's favourite semi-colons and thus producing shorter, more modern-looking sentences where these seemed appropriate. A translator's task cannot be accomplished without a sense of great humility, and I am deeply conscious of my own humility in offering these translations to the reader, knowing as I do how easily mistakes are made and how hard it is to capture in translation the clarity, expressiveness and dignity of the original. A section of explanatory notes, referenced by asterisks, is included at the end of the text, p. 294.

RICHARD FREEBORN

The Diary of a Superfluous Man

Sheepwater, 20 March 18—

The doctor has just left me. I've finally got some sense out of him! Try as he might, he finally had to come clean. Yes, I'll soon die, very soon. The rivers'll thaw out and I'll probably float away with the last snow ... Where to? God only knows! Also into the sea – well, if one must die, one might as well die in the spring! But doesn't it seem comic to be beginning one's diary with perhaps only two more weeks to live? What of it? What makes fourteen days any less a time than fourteen years or fourteen centuries? In the face of eternity, they say, all things are as nothing; but in that case eternity itself is a mere nothing. It seems I'm falling prey to philosophical musings, which is a bad sign – am I perhaps getting cold feet? I'd better start telling my story. Outside it's bitterly damp and windy and I've been forbidden to go out. So what's there to tell? A decent man doesn't speak of his ill health; and it's not my business to go rattling off yarns; and I haven't the capacity for deliberating on elevated matters; and descriptions of the surrounding scene would bore even me, just as I'm bored by doing nothing and I'm too apathetic to read. Hey-ho, then, I'll tell myself the story of my own life. What a splendid idea! With death approaching that's a respectable thing to do and un-likely to cause offence to anyone. I am starting now.

I was born about thirty years ago of reasonably wealthy landowners. My father was a passionate gambler; my mother was a woman of charac-ter – a woman full of good works. Except that I've never known another woman whose good works gave her less pleasure. She fell down under the weight of virtues and was a torment to everyone, not least herself. Throughout the fifty years of her life she never once rested, never once folded her hands; she was forever rushing to and fro like an ant – and to no good purpose, which is not true of an ant. Day and night there was some restless worm gnawing at her. Once only did I see her completely quiet and that was on the day after her death, in her coffin. Looking at her, I felt that her face expressed a quiet astonishment; the half-opened lips, sunken cheeks and patiently motionless eyes literally said out loud: 'How lovely to be still at last!' Yes, lovely it is to be parted from the tedious awareness of life, from the importunate and disturbing consciousness of existence! But I'm not concerned with that.

I grew up in bad circumstances and without joy. My father and mother were both fond of me, but that did not make it any better for me. In his own home my father had no authority and no significance as a person through his manifest subservience to a shameful and ruinous vice. He acknowledged his failing and, not having the strength to abandon his favourite passion, he strove by his constantly ingratiating and modest expression and by his submissive humility at least to earn the indulgence of his exemplary wife. My dear Mama certainly did endure her unhappiness with that majestic and sumptuous long suffering of the virtuous in which there is always so much self-regarding pride. She never once reproached my father, silently surrendered to him her last farthing and paid all his debts. He lauded her to the skies both to her face and behind her back, but he disliked staying at home and would express his fondness for me furtively, as though frightened of infecting me with his presence. But at such moments his distorted features breathed such goodness, the feverish grin on his lips would yield to such a touching smile, his brown eyes, surrounded by such fine delicate lines, would light up with such love that I couldn't help myself, I would press my cheek to his cheek warm and damp from tears. I would wipe these tears away with a handkerchief and they would again flow down effortlessly just like water from a brimming glass. I would start crying myself and he would comfort me, stroking my back and covering my face with kisses from his quivering lips. Even now, more than twenty years after his death, whenever I think of my poor father I find dumb tears rising in my throat and my heart starts beating so fiercely and bitterly, it pines with such melancholy regret, as if it really did have a long time yet to go on beating, as if it really did have something to regret!

My mother, on the other hand, behaved towards me always in exactly the same way, amiably but coldly. Such mothers, edifying and just, are frequently to be found in children's books. She was fond of me, but I wasn't fond of her. Yes, I kept at a distance from my virtuous mother and was passionately devoted to my vice-ridden father!

But that's enough for today. A beginning's been made, and as for the ending, whatever that will be, I needn't worry. That'll depend on my illness.

21 March

Astonishing weather today. Warm and clear; sunlight is playing joyfully on melting snow; everything glitters, steams, drips; sparrows chatter like mad on the moist dark fences; the moist air plagues my chest both sweetly and terribly. Spring, O spring! I sit by the window and gaze across the river into the fields. Nature, O nature! I love you so, and yet I emerged from your wellsprings incapable even of life. There, look, a sparrow hops about with outspread wings; it chatters away and each sound it utters, each ruffled feather on its little body exudes health and strength . . .

So what? Nothing at all. The bird is healthy and has every right to chatter away and preen; while I'm sick and must die – that's all. There's no point in saying more. All tearful invocations to nature are killingly funny. Let's get back to my story.

I grew up, as I've already said, in bad circumstances and without joy. I had no brother or sisters. I received my education at home. Can you imagine what my dear mother would have done with herself if I'd been sent off to a boarding-school or some official place of learning? To keep parents from being bored is what children are for. For the most part we lived in the country, making the occasional visit to Moscow. I had tutors and teachers, as is customary; I recall in particular one dried-up and tearful German, Rickmann, an unusually sad creature, maltreated by fate and vainly burning with a melancholy longing for his distant homeland. There were many good times when my unshaven old man-servant Vasily, known as The Goose, would be sitting beside the stove in his blue-dyed, sackcloth coat as old as time itself, in the foul stuffiness of the narrow ante-room filled with the sour stench of old bread-cider – would sit there playing cards with the coachman Potap all decked out in a renovated sheepskin coat, white as water on the boil, and indestructible greased boots, while Rickmann would sing on the other side of the partition:

Herz, mein Herz, warum so traurig?
Was bekümmert dich so sehr?

THE DIARY OF A SUPERFLUOUS MAN

S'ist ja schön in fremden Lande.
Herz, mein Herz, was willst du mehr?

[Heart, O my heart, why are you so sad?/What distresses you so?/
Everything's fine in a foreign country./Heart, O my heart, what more
do you want?]

After my father's death we moved finally to Moscow to live. I was
twelve. My father died at night, from a stroke. I will never forget that
night. I was sleeping soundly, like all children, but I remember that even
through my sleeping I seemed to hear a heavy and regular snoring noise.
Suddenly I felt someone was holding me by the shoulder and shaking
me. I opened my eyes and saw my tutor. 'What is it?' 'Get up, get up,
Aleksey Mikhaylych is dying . . .' Like a mad thing I jump out of bed
and dash to the bedroom. I see my father lying with his head thrown back,
all red in the face and wheezing painfully. The doorway is full of people
with frightened faces and in the passageway someone asks in a hissing
whisper: 'Has a doctor been sent for?' Horses are led out into the yard,
gates creak open, a tallow candle burns on the floor of the room and my
mother then and there sheds her tears, without, however, any loss of
decorum or sense of personal dignity. I flung myself on my father's
bosom, embraced him and babbled 'Daddy, daddy . . .' He lay motionless and screwed up his eyes in a strange way. I glanced in his face and
an unendurable horror constricted my breathing; I squawked from fear,
like a bird seized by clumsy fingers, and was dragged back and away.
Only the day before, as if he had had a premonition of his coming death,
he had shown his fondness for me so fervently and gloomily. Some
sleepy and unkempt doctor was brought, smelling strongly of herbal
vodka. My father died under his lancet and the next day, completely
stupefied with grief, I stood with a candle in my hand before the table
on which he lay and listened uncomprehendingly to the deep intoning
of the deacon occasionally interrupted by the feeble voice of the priest;
tears all the while streamed down my cheeks, over my lips, over my collar
and the front of my shirt. The tears poured out of me as I gazed ceaselessly, gazed fixedly at my father's motionless face, just as if I were
waiting for something from him. Meanwhile, my mother made slow
bows down to the ground, slowly rose and, in crossing herself, pressed
her fingers firmly to her lips, her shoulders and her stomach. I did not
have a single thought in my head, I was oppressed with grief, but I felt

that something awful had happened to me ... Death had glanced in my face at that moment and taken note of me.

We transferred to Moscow after my father's death for one very simple reason: our entire estate had to be sold to cover his debts – literally everything except one small village, the very one in which I'm now living out my splendid existence. I confess that, young though I was, I grieved over the sale of our estate, our nest – that's to say I grieved in earnest only for our garden. Practically my only bright memories were associated with that garden. It was there, one calm spring evening, that I buried my best friend, an old dog with a docked tail and crooked paws called Trixie. There, hidden in the tall grass, I used to eat stolen apples – red, sweet, Novgorod apples. There, finally, I saw for the first time among the bushes of ripe raspberry the servant girl Claudia who, despite her snub nose and habit of laughing into a handkerchief, aroused in me such tender passion that I could scarcely breathe in her presence, would be completely at a loss what to do or say and once, at Easter, when it came to her turn to kiss my outstretched, lordly little hand, I almost flung myself down and kissed her worn, goatskin shoes. My God! Was it all of twenty years ago? Was it so long ago that I used to ride my shaggy chestnut pony along the old wattle fence of our garden and, standing up in the stirrups, pull down the two-coloured leaves of poplars? So long as a man is living he is unaware of his own life; like a sound, it only becomes audible to him some time later.

O my garden, O the overgrown paths beside the shallow pond! O the sandy spot by the dilapidated weir where I used to fish for gudgeon and perch! And you, tall birches, with your long branches hanging down, beyond which, from the nearby track, there used often to be heard a melancholy peasant's song unevenly broken by the joltings of a cart – to you I send my last farewell! In parting from life it is to you alone that I stretch out my arms. I long once again to breathe the bitter freshness of wormwood, to smell the sweet fragrance of mown buckwheat in the fields of my homeland; I long to hear again from afar the modest tinkling of the cracked bell in our parish church; I long to lie again in the cool shade of an oak on the slope of a familiar ravine; I long again to follow with my eyes the moving shadow of the wind running like a dark stream through the golden grasslands of our meadow ...

Ah, what's the good of it? I can write no more today. Till tomorrow.

Today it's again cold and overcast. Such weather's more suitable. It's in tune with my work. Yesterday quite improperly aroused in me a mass of unnecessary feelings and memories. It won't happen again. Sentimental outpourings are like liquorice – when you first suck it it's not bad, but it leaves a very unpleasant aftertaste in the mouth. I'll start telling the story of my life simply and calmly.

And so we moved to Moscow . . .

But I keep on thinking: is it really worth telling the story of my life?

No, it's definitely not worth it . . . My life's been no different from the lives of masses of others. Parental home, university, service in the lower ranks, retirement, a small circle of acquaintances, unsullied poverty, modest pleasures, run-of-the-mill pursuits, moderate desires – tell me, what's original about that? So I won't tell the story of my life, all the more because I'm writing for my own entertainment. And since even to me my past life has nothing very joyful in it, nor even anything very sad, it seems there's really nothing in it worthy of attention. It would be better if I tried to define to myself my own character.

What sort of a man am I? People may retort that no one's asking – I agree. But I'm going to die after all, I'm going to *die*, and in face of death it's surely forgivable to want to know what sort of chap I was, isn't it?

Having given this important issue a good deal of thought and not having, by the way, any need to express myself too bitterly on my own account, as people may do who are firmly convinced of their own worth, I have to confess one thing: I've been completely superfluous in this world of ours or, to put it another way, a bird of no account. And I intend to prove this tomorrow, since today I'm coughing like an old sheep, and my dear old nurse Terent'yevna won't let me have any peace with her: 'Lie down, good sir, and have a drink of tea . . .' I know why she goes on and on like this – she wants a drink of tea herself. All right, then! Why not let a poor old woman get as much as she can from her master in the last resort? So long as there's still time left.

Winter again. Snow is falling in large flakes.

Superfluous, superfluous . . . I've invented an excellent term. The deeper I peer into myself, the closer I survey my past life, the more convinced I am of the stern truth of this expression. Superfluous – precisely.

THE DIARY OF A SUPERFLUOUS MAN

The word is not applicable to others. People are bad, good, clever, stupid, pleasant and unpleasant; but superfluous ... no. That's to say, if you want to understand me: the universe could get along without such people ... of course; but uselessness is not their chief quality, not their distinctive characteristic, and when you talk about them the word 'superfluous' is not the first one that springs to óne's tongue. But in my case, nothing else can be said about me: I'm superfluous and that's all there is to it. Redundant – nothing else. Nature evidently did not count on my appearance and therefore treated me like an unexpected and un-bidden guest. One joker has said of me not inappropriately, keen on cards as he was, that I was the throwaway card in my mother's hand. I talk about myself now calmly, with no bitterness ... The game's long over! During the course of my life I constantly found my place already occupied, perhaps because I looked for it in the wrong place. I was highly strung, pitifully shy, extremely irritable, like all ill people; in addition, perhaps through excessive self-regard or generally through the un-successful structure of my personality, there existed between my feelings and my thoughts – and the expression of these feelings and thoughts – some senseless, incomprehensible and impregnable obstacle. And when I tried to overcome this obstacle by force, to smash this barrier, my move-ments, my facial expression, my whole being acquired a look of intense effort: I not only looked, but I actually became unnatural and over-wrought. I felt this myself and hastened to return to what I was. Then a frightful panic would arise in me. I used to analyse myself down to the last thread, used to compare myself with others, recalled all the smallest glances, smiles and words of those to whom I'd tried to be frank, inter-preted everything in a bad light, laughed viciously at my attempts 'to be like the rest' – and suddenly, in the midst of my laughing, I'd give way to sadness, fall into ludicrous despondency and once again start the whole process all over again – in short, I went round and round like a squirrel on a wheel. Whole days went by in this tormenting, fruitless activity. Well, now just you tell me, to whom and for what is such a man neces-sary? Who knows and who will say why this happened to me, what was the cause of this nitpicking concern with myself?

I remember I was once travelling away from Moscow in a diligence. The road was good, but the driver hitched up a fifth horse to the four already in harness. This unfortúnate fifth horse, completely useless, tied somehow to the shaft by a short, stout rope which mercilessly cut its haunch, rubbed its tail and forced it to run in the most unnatural fashion, lending its whole body the shape of a comma, always aroused in me profound pity. I remarked to the driver that on this occasion one could get by without a fifth horse . . . He said nothing, shook his head, lashed the horse ten times with his whip across its thin back and distended stomach – and muttered, not without a grin: 'Look, it's dragged itself along right enough! Devil knows why, eh?'

And I've dragged myself along just like that . . . though, thank heavens, the post-station's not far off now.

Superfluous . . . I promised to prove the correctness of my opinion and I will. I don't consider it necessary to mention the thousand trivial things, daily happenings and occurrences which, in the eyes of any thinking man, could serve as incontrovertible evidence on my behalf – on behalf, that's to say, of my opinion. It would be better if I began straightaway with one fairly important instance, after which there'll probably be no doubt about the accuracy of the term: superfluous. I repeat that I do not intend to go into details, but I cannot pass over in silence one rather curious and remarkable fact, namely my friends' strange behaviour towards me (I also had friends) every time I met them or paid them a visit. They would literally be embarrassed. Coming towards me, they would smile in a quite unnatural way, look not into my eyes or down at my feet as most people do but at my cheeks, would hurriedly press my hand and hurriedly say: 'Hello, Stocking!' (fate had endowed me with that honoured name) or: 'Ah there you are, Stocking,' and at once turn aside and even remain motionless for a short while, literally as if they were trying to make themselves remember something. I would notice all this, for I'm not without perspicacity and the gift of observation; on the whole I'm no fool; I even find sometimes that I have rather droll ideas, ideas that are a bit out of the ordinary; but because I'm a superfluous man and all locked up inside, I'm frightened of expressing my ideas, all the more so since I know beforehand that I'll express them very badly. I sometimes find it odd how people can talk, and talk so simply and freely . . . There's such a lot of fast chatter, when you come to think about it. Truth to tell, despite being so locked up inside, I've more than once done a bit of tongue-wagging; but it was only in my youth that I actually pronounced words, in my more mature years I almost always succeeded in mastering the impulse. I would say in a low voice: 'Perhaps we should be quiet a moment,' and then I'd be content.

THE DIARY OF A SUPERFLUOUS MAN

We're all adept at being silent; our womenfolk are especially good at it. Some high and mighty Russian ladies maintain such a strong silence that even in one prepared for it the very sight of them can produce a slight shivering and a cold sweat. But that's not my business, and it's not for me to criticise others. I am embarking on my promised story.

Several years ago, thanks to the confluence of very trivial, but for me very important, circumstances, I had to spend six months or so in the county town of O—. This town is built on a slope, and very uncomfortably built there. It has about eight hundred inhabitants, in unusual poverty. The little houses look like nothing at all. On the main street, on the pretext of providing a paved surface, frightful white slabs of rough-hewn lime are to be found, as a consequence of which even carts make a detour to avoid it. In the middle of an astonishingly untidy square there stands a diminutive yellowish structure with dark holes in it, and in the holes sit people in large hats pretending to engage in trade. There also is an exceptionally tall post, painted in different colours, and beside the post, for the sake of public order, on the instructions of the authorities, stands a load of yellow hay and one government hen walks about. In a word, in the town of O— life is really something. During my first days in the town I almost went out of my mind from boredom. I have to say of myself that, though I am of course a superfluous man, it is not through any personal wish to be one. I am myself sick and I can't stand sickness . . . I'm also not averse to happiness and have even made tentative approaches to it from right and left . . . And so it's not surprising that I can be bored like any other human being. I was in the town of O— for reasons connected with government service . . .

Terent'yevna is resolutely set upon making my life a misery. Here's an example of our conversation:

Terent'yevna: Oh, sir, why d'you go on writing and writing? It's unhealthy all this writing.

I: Terent'yevna, I'm bored!

She: You'd better 'ave a drink o' tea and a lie down, sir. God grant you'll sweat it out an' sleep a wee bit.

I: But I don't want to sleep.

She: Oh, sir, why d'you say that? The good Lord be with you! Just you lie down, sir, just you lie down, then you'll feel better.

I: I'm going to die without that, Terent'yevna!

She: Oh, the good Lord preserve you and forgive you ... Won't you have some tea anyhow?

I: I won't live another week, Terent'yevna!

She: Oh, sir, why d'you go on so? I'll go and put the samovar on in that case.

O decrepit, yellow, toothless creature! And I'm not a man even to you!

24 March

A hard frost

On the day of my arrival in the town of O— the reasons connected with government service (mentioned above) obliged me to call on a certain Ozhogin, Kirilla Matveich, one of the chief officials of the county; but I became acquainted with him or got on familiar terms with him, as they say, about two weeks later. His house was on the main street and was distinguished from all the rest by virtue of its size, its painted roof and the two lions on its gates – lions of that special breed, resembling failed dogs, whose place of origin is Moscow. Judging by these lions alone one could conclude that Ozhogin was a man of substance. And this was actually so: he had about four hundred peasants; he made a habit of receiving the cream of the society of O— and passed for one of hospitable manner. The mayor would visit him in a wide ginger-coloured droshky drawn by a pair of horses – a vehicle suitable for such an unusually large man who looked as if he had been made out of geological deposits. Other officials visited him: the attorney, a yellowish, malicious creature; the wisecracking surveyor, of German extraction with a Tartar face; the officer in charge of roads, a gentle soul and a singer, but a gossip; the former marshal of nobility in the county – a gentleman with dyed hair, crumpled shirt-front, close-fitting trousers and that excessively dignified expression of the face which is so common in those who have been taken before the courts. He was also visited by two landowners who were inseparable friends, both no longer young and even a bit worse for wear, of whom the younger was continually snubbing the older and shutting him up with one and the same reproach: 'Not a word out of you, Sergey Sergeyich! And so where are you off to now? You're always spelling the word "stopper" with two *b*'s. Yes, gentlemen,' he would continue with all the zeal of his conviction, turning to those round him, 'Sergey Sergeyich always writes "stobber", not "stopper".' And all those round him would laugh, although not a single one of them was particularly outstanding at spelling; and the unfortunate Sergey Sergeyich would say not a word and bow low his head with a dying smile. But I'm forgetting that my days are numbered, and I'm going into far too many details. And so, without further ado: Ozhogin was married, he had a daughter, Elizaveta Kirillovna, and I fell in love with her.

Ozhogin himself was an ordinary enough fellow, neither ugly nor handsome; his wife had the looks of a superannuated hen; but the daughter took after neither. She was not at all bad looking, and of lively and gentle temperament. Her bright grey eyes gazed warmly and directly from beneath childishly arched brows; there was almost always a smile on her face and she also laughed fairly often. Her fresh voice had a very pleasant resonance; she was agile and quick – and would blush happily. She did not dress too elegantly; simple dresses suited her best. In general I did not make friends easily, and if I did happen to get on well with someone from the start – which was almost never the case – it said a great deal, I confess, for my new acquaintance. With women I had no idea how to behave at all and in their presence either frowned and assumed a truculent air, or grinned in the most idiotic fashion and moved my tongue round in my mouth in embarrassment. With Elizaveta Kirillovna, by contrast, I felt myself at home from the start. This is how it happened. I went to see Ozhogin one day just before dinner and I asked whether he was at home. 'He's at home,' I was informed, 'but dressing; please go into the drawing-room.' I went into the drawing-room and saw by the window, with her back to me, a girl in a white dress with a cage in her hands. As usual, I was slightly put out; but, no matter, I simply coughed out of politeness. The girl turned round quickly, so quickly that her curls struck her in the face, saw me, bowed and with a smile showed me a little box half filled with seeds. 'You will allow me?' It goes without saying that, as is customary in such circumstances, I first bowed my head and at the same time rapidly bent and then straightened my knees (as if someone had literally struck me on the back of the legs), which, as is well known, serves as a mark of an excellent education and pleasing informality in one's behaviour, then smiled, raised my hand and once or twice cautiously and softly gestured with it. The girl at once turned away from me, took a small piece of board out of the cage, began scraping it vigorously with a knife and suddenly, without altering her position, uttered the following words: 'This is Daddy's bullfinch. Do you like bullfinches?' 'I prefer goldfinches,' I answered, not without some effort. 'Oh! I also like goldfinches! But just look at him, isn't he handsome! Look, he's not at all frightened.' (I was also astonished that I wasn't at all frightened.) 'Come closer. He's called Popka.' I came closer and bent down. 'He's really lovely, isn't he?' She turned her face towards me, but we were so close together that she had to raise her head back a little in order to glance at me with her bright eyes. I glanced back at her: the whole of her young, rosy face was smiling so warmly that I smiled as well and almost burst out laughing with pleasure. The door opened and Mr Ozhogin came in. I at once went up to him and began speaking to him in a very free-and-easy way; without knowing how, I stayed to dinner and spent the entire evening there; and the next day Ozhogin's footman, a tall, thin, short-sighted fellow, already smiled at me as a friend of the house when he took my overcoat from me.

To find a haven, make a nest for myself, even a temporary one, know the delight of day-by-day relationships and habits – such a happiness I, superfluous as I was, without family recollections, had so far not experienced. If there had been something of a flower about me, and if such a comparison weren't so shopworn, I would resolve to say that from that day forward I blossomed in my soul. Everything within me and around me changed in a flash! My whole life was radiated with love, every part of it down to the smallest detail, as if it had been a dark box-room into which a candle had been brought. I went to sleep and woke up, dressed, breakfasted and smoked a pipe quite differently from before; even while walking along I would give little jumps as if I had grown wings on my shoulders. I recall that I was never for a moment in any uncertainty about the feeling aroused in me by Elizaveta Kirillovna: I fell in love with her passionately on the very first day and from the very first day I knew I was in love with her. For three weeks I saw her every day. Those three weeks were the happiest in my life. But the recollection of them is oppressive to me. I cannot think of them by themselves. Despite myself, I have to think of what followed after them, and then a poisonous anguish slowly seizes hold of my recently softened heart.

When a man is very happy, it is common knowledge that his mind works slowly. A calm and joyous feeling, a feeling of satisfaction, pervades his entire being; he is consumed by it; his awareness of self vanishes – he is bathed in bliss, as badly educated poets are prone to say.

But when this enchantment is over, a man often feels annoyed and sad that in the midst of happiness he had observed so little about himself, that by thought or recollection he had not redoubled or prolonged his pleasure . . . as if one who is 'bathed in bliss' ever had the time to think about his feelings: a happy man is like a fly in sunlight. So whenever I recall those three weeks, I find it almost impossible to keep in my mind an exact, clearly defined impression of them, the more so since, in the course of that time, nothing particularly remarkable happened between us . . . Those twenty days are to me like something warm, youthful and fragrant, like a bright band of light in my grey and faded life. My memory suddenly becomes implacably true and clear only at the very moment when, in the words of the same badly educated scribblers, the blows of fate rained down on me.

Yes, those three weeks . . . As a matter of fact it isn't true to say they left nothing behind them. Sometimes, when I happen to think of that time, certain memories float unexpectedly out of the darkness of the past – in just the same way that stars appear unexpectedly in an evening sky when your eyes are watching attentively for them. Particularly memorable was a walk in some woodland outside the town. There were four of us: Mrs Ozhogin, Liza and I and a certain Bizmyonkov, a petty. official of the town of O—, a fairish-haired, kindly-ish, quietish chap I will have more to say about him later. Mr. Ozhogin had stayed at home: he had a headache from too much sleeping. It was a wonderful day, warm and quiet. I ought to remark that pleasure gardens and social promenades are not in the spirit of things Russian. In provincial towns, in the so-called public gardens, never at any season will you come across a living soul; save that some old woman, groaning to herself, may sit awhile on some green sunwarmed bench beside some unhappy-looking sapling – and then only if there's no greasy little booth by the gate. But if there happens to be a miserable clump of birches in the environs of the town, merchants, and sometimes even officials, gladly go there on Sundays and holidays with samovars, pies and watermelons, set down everything in the dusty grass beside the road, seat themselves around it and eat and drink tea in the sweat of their brows until evening. A wood of precisely this kind existed at that time a mile or so from the town of O—. We travelled out there after dinner, had some tea to drink in the proper way and then all four of us set out on a stroll through the woodland. Bizmyonkov took Mrs Ozhogin by the arm, I took Liza. Evening was approaching. I was then at the very height of first love (no more than two weeks had passed since our first meeting), in that state of passionate and attentive adoration when one's whole soul innocently and spontaneously follows every movement of one's beloved, when one can never have enough of her presence or of hearing her voice, when one is all smiles and looks just like a child recovered from an illness, and when someone with only slight experience of these things can tell at first glance from a hundred paces what's happened to you. Before that day I'd never had the chance of taking Liza by the arm. We walked along side by side, quietly stepping through the green grass. A light breeze literally danced around us and among the white trunks of the birches, occasionally blowing in my face a ribbon from her hat. I ceaselessly sought her look, until she finally turned happily towards me, and then we both smiled at each other. Birds chirruped appreciatively above us and a blue sky flickered kindly at us through the thin foliage. My head was spinning from an excess of pleasure. I hasten to point out that Liza was not in the least in love with me. She liked me; she was generally on friendly terms with everyone and I was not destined to be the one to upset her childish peace of mind. She held my arm as if she were walking beside her brother. At that time she was seventeen years old . . . And yet, on that very evening, in my presence, there began within her that calm inner ferment which anticipates the transformation of a child into a woman . . . I was witness to this change in her whole being, this innocent confusion, this anxious thoughtfulness; I was the first to notice the sudden softening of the gaze, the ringing nervousness of the voice – and, O fool! O superfluous man! for the length of a whole week I didn't even feel ashamed of supposing that I, *I* was the cause of this change.

This is how it came about.

We strolled a fairly long time, until evening came on, and we talked little. I was tongue-tied, like all inexperienced lovers, and she more than likely had nothing to say to me; but she was deep in thought about something and gave significant nods of the head, pensively biting a torn leaf. Sometimes she started walking ahead, so resolutely . . . and then she would suddenly stop, wait for me and glance round her with raised eyebrows and a confused smile. The previous day we had been reading *The Prisoner of the Caucasus** together. With what a hungry look she had listened to me reading, her face supported by both hands and her bosom

* See Notes at end of text p. 294.

pressed to the table! I tried to remind her of yesterday's reading; she blushed and then asked me whether I'd given the bullfinch any hemp seed before leaving, started singing a loud snatch of song and at once fell quiet. On one side the woodland ended in a fairly high and steep ravine; below us flowed a winding stream and beyond it there stretched as far as the eye could see, either slightly rising like waves or spread out flat as table-cloths, endless meadowlands interspersed here and there by gullies. Liza and I were the first to come out of the woodland; Bizmyonkov remained behind with the old lady. We came out, stopped and were both forced to screw up our eyes, for directly ahead of us, in a molten mist, an enormous blood-red sun was setting. Half the sky was aflame and glowing red; red rays of light struck out across the meadows, casting crimson reflections even into the shadowy sides of the gullies, and lay like a fiery lead on the surface of the stream (where it wasn't hidden by overhanging bushes) and literally pressed themselves into the very bosom of the ravine and the woodland. We stood there inundated by the fierce radiance. I am incapable of conveying all the impassioned majesty of this scene. They say that to a blind man the colour red is like a trumpet voluntary; I have no idea how correct this analogy is, but there was definitely some kind of invocation in the burning gold of the evening air, in the purple brilliance of the sky and the earth. I cried out in excitement and turned instantly to Liza. She was gazing directly at the sun. I remember how the conflagration of the sunset was reflected in her eyes in tiny spots of burning fire. She was overwhelmed and deeply moved. She made no response to my cry and stayed motionless for a long while, her head lowered . . . I stretched out my hand to her; she turned away from me and suddenly burst into tears. I watched with secret, almost delighted bewilderment . . . Then Bizmyonkov's voice resounded a couple of paces behind us. Liza hastily wiped away her tears and looked at me with an indecisive smile. Her elderly mother emerged from the woodland, leaning on the arm of her fair-haired guide; they in their turn admired the view. The old woman asked Liza something and gave a start, I remember, when in response to her there came the broken sound of her daughter's small voice like a cracked glass. Meanwhile, the sun had set and its rays began to die. We turned back. I again took Liza by the arm. The light was still bright in the wood and I could clearly make out her features. She was in a state of confusion and did not raise her eyes. The blush pervading her face did not vanish, just as if she were still standing in the rays of the dying sun . . . Her arm scarcely touched mine. For a long time I couldn't make myself say anything, because my heart was beating so strongly. Through the trees the carriage came into view in the distance and the coachman drove at a walking pace towards us along the dry sandy road.

'Lizaveta Kirillovna,' I asked at last, 'why did you cry?'

'I don't know,' she replied after a short silence and looked at me with her shy eyes that were still wet from tears (their expression seemed to me altered) and again fell silent.

'I see you love nature,' I continued, '. . .'

I had no desire to say that at all and my tongue was hardly able to complete the final phrase. She shook her head. I couldn't bring myself to continue, I was waiting for something more – not a confession of love (out of the question!), but simply a trustful look or a query . . . Liza continued to gaze at the ground and was silent. I again repeated in a low voice: 'Why?' and received no answer. I saw that she felt awkward and almost ashamed.

A quarter of an hour later we were already sitting in the carriage and driving towards the town. The horses went at a uniform trot; we rushed along through the dark, moist air. I suddenly began talking, turning the whole time first to Bizmyonkov, then to Mrs Ozhogin, without looking at Liza, but I could tell that her gaze never once lighted on me from the corner of the carriage. Once at home she shook herself out of her mood, but declined to read with me and soon went off to bed.

That change, that fundamental change which I have mentioned, had taken place in her. She had ceased being a girl, she was also expectant for something, as I was. She did not have long to wait.

But I returned that night to my apartment in a completely charmed state. A vague feeling – not quite a presentiment, not quite a suspicion – which had been on the point of arising in me now vanished. The sudden constraint in Liza's behaviour towards me I attributed to girlish reticence and shyness . . . Hadn't I read a thousand times in many stories that the first appearance of love always excites and frightens a girl? I felt myself extremely happy and even made certain plans in my mind . . .

If only someone had whispered in my ear at that time: 'What nonsense, my dear chap! None of that's for you, you know — all you've got to wait for is dying alone in some miserable little hovel to the sound of unbearable complaints from an old hag who can't wait for you to die in order to sell off your boots for a pittance . . .'

Yes, one can only repeat the words of a Russian philosopher: 'How can one know what one doesn't?' Until tomorrow.

25 March

A white winter's day

I've read through what I wrote yesterday and almost torn my whole diary to pieces. I feel that I'm telling my story too expansively and too sweetly. However, since what remains to be told of that time contains nothing joyful, save that special kind of joy which Lermontov had in mind when he said he always derived joy as well as pain from opening the wounds of old hurts* why shouldn't I indulge myself? But one has to be decorous in such matters. And so I will continue without any added sweetness.

For a whole week after our out-of-town trip my situation did not improve in any essential way, although the change in Liza grew daily more marked. As I've already said, I interpreted this change as being very much in my favour . . . The misfortune of all solitary and bashful people – bashful, of course, from ambition – is precisely that, though they have eyes to see and even keep them wide open, they see nothing at all or see everything in a false light, just as if they were looking at the world through tinted spectacles. Their own personal thoughts and observations get in their way at every turn. At the beginning of our friendship Liza treated me trustingly and naturally like a child; perhaps there had even been in her attitude towards me something more than simple childish attraction . . . But when that strange, almost instantaneous, change had occurred in her, she felt herself, after a brief moment of confusion, embarrassed in my presence; she involuntarily turned from me and at the same time grew tearful and thoughtful . . . She waited expectantly for something – but what? She herself had no idea, whereas I . . . I . . . , as I've already said, I was overjoyed at this change, I – dear God! – I damn near died of ecstasy, as they say. However, I'm prepared to agree that another in my place could have been deceived . . . Is there anyone entirely without some vain ambition or other? It goes without saying that this has all become clear to me only in the fullness of time, since I've been obliged to fold my hurt and by no means very powerful wings.

The misunderstanding which had arisen between me and Liza

lasted a whole week – and there was nothing very remarkable in that: I've seen some misunderstandings that have lasted for years. And who was it said that only truth is real? Falsehood can be just as alive as truth, even more so. I remember quite distinctly that in the course of that week there stirred within me some worm or other . . . but solitary men, such as we are, I will say again, are just as incapable of understanding what's going on inside them as of understanding what's going on before their very eyes. And what's more – is love really a natural feeling? Is it natural for a man to fall in love? Love is a disease and disease knows no laws. Granted that my heart was squeezed uncomfortably at times and everything within me was turned upside down. How can one be sure in a case like this what's right and what's wrong, what's the cause or what's the significance of each separate feeling?

But all such considerations apart, all these misunderstandings, presentiments and hopes were resolved in the following way.

One day – it was in the morning, about eleven o'clock – I'd scarcely entered Mr Ozhogin's hallway when an unfamiliar, resonant voice came from the drawing-room, the door opened and, accompanied by the host, there appeared a tall, elegant man of about twenty-five who briskly threw a military overcoat round his shoulders (it had been lying on a bench), cordially took leave of Kirilla Matveich, strode past me negligently touching his hand to his cap – and then disappeared, his spurs ringing loudly.

'Who's that?' I asked Ozhogin.

'Prince N—,' he answered with a worried face, 'sent from Petersburg to levy recruits. Where have all the servants gone to?' he continued with annoyance. 'There was no one here to hand him his overcoat.'

We went into the drawing-room.

'Has he been here long?' I asked.

'Since yesterday evening apparently. I offered him a room with us, but he refused. However, he seems a very nice chap.'

'Did he spend long with you?'

'About an hour. He begged me to present him to Olimpiada Nikitichna.'

'And you did?'

'Of course.'

'And with Lizaveta Kirillovna he . . .'

'He became acquainted with her as well.'

I paused before asking:

'Is he spending long here, do you know?'

'I think he'll be spending no more than a couple of weeks here.'

And Kirilla Matveich dashed off to change.

I walked several times to and fro in the drawing-room. I can't remember whether the arrival of Prince N— left any particular impression on me at that time, apart from that feeling of enmity which usually assails us at the appearance of a new face in our domestic circle. Perhaps there was mixed in with this feeling something in the way of envy on the part of a bashful and obscure Muscovite towards a brilliant officer from Petersburg. 'The prince', I thought, 'is a toff from the capital, he'll be bound to look down on us . . .' Although I'd only seen him for a moment, I'd managed to notice that he was good-looking, urbane and without shyness. After pacing about the room for a while I finally stopped before the mirror, took a comb out of my pocket, gave my hair a look of picturesque informality and, as sometimes happens, suddenly fell to wondering at my own face. I recall that my attention was worryingly concentrated on my nose. The oversoft and indeterminate characteristics of this member were affording me no particular pleasure when suddenly, in the dark depths of the tilted glass which reflected almost the whole room, I saw the door open and the elegant figure of Liza appeared. I don't know why I did nothing at that moment and kept the same expression on my face. Liza raised her head, looked attentively at me and with a lift of the eyebrows, biting her lip and holding her breath, like someone who's glad not to have been seen, cautiously stepped back and quietly drew the door towards her. The door squeaked slightly. Liza shuddered and froze to the spot . . . I still did nothing at all . . . She turned the doorknob again and vanished. There was no doubt about it: the expression on Liza's face at the sight of me was one which betrayed nothing save a desire to escape safely away and avoid an unpleasant meeting, while the quick flash of pleasure which I noted in her eyes when she thought she'd succeeded in escaping unnoticed – all this said one thing only too clearly: this girl doesn't love me. For a long, long time I couldn't tear my eyes away from the motionless, silent door, which once more resembled a white blur in the depths of the mirror. I would like to have smiled at my own strained pose, but instead I lowered my head, returned home and threw myself on my divan. I was extraordinarily depressed, so depressed I couldn't even cry . . . And what was there to cry about, after all? 'Could it be . . .?' I muttered to myself end-lessly, lying on my back like one dead, with my hands folded on my chest. 'Could it be . . .? Could it be . . .?' How do you like that, eh?

26 March
Thaw

When the next day, after lengthy hesitations and inwardly despairing, I entered the Ozhogins' familiar drawing-room, I was no longer the same man that I had been in the course of the previous three weeks. All my former ways, to which I had grown accustomed under the influence of my new feelings, suddenly returned and took possession of me like pro-prietors returning to their rightful dwelling-place. People like me are generally governed not so much by positive facts as by their own impressions. Only the previous day having been dreaming about 'the ecstasies of mutual love', I was today in no doubt at all about my 'un-happiness' and was completely despairing although I was in no condition to seek out any sort of rational reason for my despair. I couldn't feel envious towards Prince N— and, no matter the qualities attributable to him, his appearance alone was insufficient reason for the radical change in Liza's attitude towards me . . . But what in fact was that attitude? I recalled the past. 'The stroll in the wood?' I asked myself. 'The ex-pression on her face in the mirror? But,' I continued, 'the stroll in the wood, surely it was . . . Oh, my God! What a total nonentity I am!' I exclaimed aloud at last. It was such incomplete, such ill-considered thoughts, coming back to me thousands of times, that went whirling through my head like a monotonous whirlwind. I repeat that I re-turned to the Ozhogins the very same nervous, suspicious and highly strung person that I had been since childhood . . .

I found the entire family in the drawing-room: and Bizmyonkov was also sitting there, in a corner. They all seemed in a good mood, particu-larly Ozhogin, who literally beamed and from the first word told me that Prince N— had spent the whole of the last evening with them. Liza greeted me calmly. 'Well,' I told myself, 'now I understand why you're in such a good mood.' I confess that a second visit by the prin e had taken me aback. I had not expected it. In general people like me anticipate all kinds of things, except the very thing that must happen in the normal course of events. I became huffy and put on the look of one who has been insulted but is being magnanimous; I wanted to punish Liza with my disapproval – by which of course, it may be thought, I'd still not entirely abandoned my chances. They say that in some cases, when someone really loves you, it is even useful to torment the beloved, but in my position that was inexpressibly silly: in the most innocent way Liza simply did not pay any attention to me. Only her elderly mother noticed my solemn silence and inquired anxiously about my health. I replied, naturally, with a bitter smile that I was perfectly well, thank God! Ozhogin continued to hold forth about his guest but, noting that I responded to him unwillingly, he addressed himself more frequently to Bizmyonkov who listened to him with great attention, when suddenly a footman entered and announced the arrival of Prince N—. Our host jumped up and ran to meet him. Liza, on whom I was at that moment keeping an eagle eye, reddened with pleasure and fidgeted in her chair. The prince entered, exuding perfume, gaiety and charm . . .

Since I am not composing a story for a well-disposed reader but simply writing for my own pleasure, it is not for me to resort to the usual contrivances of literary gentlemen. I will say right away, without further delay, that from the very start Liza fell passionately in love with the prince and the prince fell in love with her – partly out of nothing better to do, partly because he had a habit of turning ladies' heads, but also because Liza was an extremely charming creature. The fact that they fell in love with each other was not at all surprising. He no doubt had not anticipated finding such a jewel in such a miserable setting (I am referring to the God-forsaken town of O—), while she till that time even in a dream had not seen anything faintly resembling this brilliant, clever and captivating aristocrat.

After the first greetings Ozhogin presented me to the prince, who behaved very politely towards me. He was generally very polite with everyone and, despite the immeasurable distance lying between him and our obscure provincial circle, he contrived not only not to embarrass anyone but even to give the impression that he was one of us and happened only by chance to live in St Petersburg.

That first evening . . . Oh, that first evening! In the happy days of our childhood teachers would describe to us and offer as an example the manly courage of the young Spartan who, having stolen a vixen and hidden it under his cloak, made not a sound when he allowed it to eat his entrails and in such fashion preferred to die rather than admit his disgrace . . . I can find no better way of expressing my unspeakable sufferings in the course of that evening when I saw the prince and Liza together for the first time. My perpetually strained smile, agonising awareness of everything, stupid silence and fretful and vain desire to leave – all this was probably very remarkable of its kind. There was more than one vixen gnawing my guts: envy, jealousy, a feeling of personal worthlessness and helpless malice were also tearing me apart. I couldn't fail to see that the prince was really a very charming young man . . . I devoured him with my eyes; true, I think I even forgot to blink while looking at him. He did not talk only with Liza, but of course everything he said was intended only for her. I must have bored him stiff . . . He probably guessed quickly enough that he was dealing with a discarded lover, but out of consideration for me, and also out of a profound sense of my complete harmlessness, he behaved towards me with extraordinary deference. You can just imagine how humiliating that was to me! In the course of the evening I remember that I tried to even out my sense of guilt – (Don't laugh at me, whoever you are reading these lines, the more so since this was my last hope!) – I suddenly imagined, heavens above, amid my different torments that Liza wanted to get her own back on me for my haughty coldness at the beginning of my visit, that she was annoyed with me and was flirting with the prince only out of annoyance. I chose my time and, approaching her with a restrained but kindly smile, murmured: 'Enough, forgive me . . . of course, it's not that I have anything to fear,' and suddenly, without waiting for her reaction, gave my face an unusually vivacious and expansive expression, grinned crookedly, stretched my hand above my head in the direction of the ceiling (I recall that I'd wanted to put my necktie right) and was even about to turn on my heel, as if wanting to express the idea: 'Everything's over, but I'm happy, let's all be happy!' but I didn't turn for fear of an unnatural stiffness in the knees . . . Liza simply had no idea what I was on about, looked me in the face with astonishment, smiled hurriedly, as if wishing to escape as quickly as possible, and once more went up to the prince. No matter how blind or deaf I may have been, I couldn't fail to admit to myself that she'd clearly not been annoyed with me in the very least: she'd simply not given me a single thought. That blow was decisive. My last hopes crashed to the ground just like a block of ice which is caught in the spring sunshine and suddenly disintegrates. I had been felled by the very first blow and, like the Prussians at Jena on the first day, had lost everything at a stroke. No, she had not been annoyed with me!

To the contrary! She was – I saw this myself – being carried along on the crest of a wave. Like a young tree, already half torn from the bank, she was bending greedily over the torrent, ready to surrender to it forever both the first bloom of her springtime and her entire life. Someone who has happened to be a witness of such an infatuation will have experienced moments of deep bitterness if he has himself loved and not been loved in return. I will remember for all eternity that consuming attention, that gentle gaiety, that innocent forgetfulness of self, that gaze, still childish, yet already womanly, that happy, literally blossoming smile which never left the half-opened lips and flushed cheeks . . . Everything that Liza had vaguely anticipated during our walk in the wood had now come to pass – and she, giving herself completely to love, had at the same time become completely still and bright like a young wine that has ceased fermenting because its time has come . . .

I had the patience to sit out that first evening and those that followed – each one to the end! I had nothing to hope for. Day by day Liza and the prince grew more attracted to each other . . . But I had completely lost any feeling of personal dignity and couldn't tear myself away from the spectacle of my misfortune. I remember that I once tried not to go, gave myself a promise to remain at home – and at eight o'clock in the evening (I usually went out at seven) jumped up like a madman, put on my hat and ran panting for breath into Kirilla Matveich's drawing-room. My position was unusually ridiculous: I was stubbornly silent and sometimes would make not a sound for days at a time. As I've already mentioned, I was never outstanding for eloquence, but now everything in my mind literally took wing in the presence of the prince and I was left bare as a coot. Besides, when I was alone I forced my unhappy brain to work so hard slowly reconsidering all the things that I'd noticed or suspected in the course of the previous day that on returning to the Ozhogins I scarcely had any strength left to do any more observing. They treated me like one who was ill, I could see that. Every morning I made anew a final decision which had mostly been reached very painfully during a sleepless night: I would prepare to have it out with Liza and give her some friendly advice . . . but every time I chanced to be alone with her my tongue would suddenly stop working, it would get stuck, and we would both wait impatiently for the arrival of a third person. Then I wanted to run away – forever, it goes without saying –

leaving behind for my loved one a letter full of reproaches, and I once even started such a letter, but my sense of justice had not yet vanished completely: I realised I'd no right to reproach anyone and threw my *billet-doux* in the fire. Then I would suddenly and magnanimously offer my whole self up as a sacrifice, hoping for Liza that she would be happy ever after in love and smiling fondly and meekly at the prince out of my own little corner. But the hard-hearted lovers not only didn't thank me for my sacrifice, they didn't even notice it and evidently didn't need either my fond hopes or my fond smiles . . . Then in annoyance I suddenly fell into an entirely different mood. I promised myself that, wrapped in a cloak in the Spanish fashion, I'd spring out of my corner and cut my happy rival's throat and then imagine Liza's despair with tigerish relish . . . But, to start with, there were very few suitable corners in the town of O— and, on second thoughts – a fence made of planks, a street-lamp, a policeman down the road . . . No, far better sell buns on a corner like that than try shedding human blood there! I must confess that among other means of escape, as I vaguely called it when talking to myself, I'd thought of turning to Ozhogin and directing this gentleman's attention to the dangerous situation facing his daughter and the sad consequences of her frivolity . . . Once I even began talking to him on this ticklish subject, but spoke so subtly and vaguely that he went on listening and listening – and suddenly, literally as if he'd just woken up, drew the palm of his hand briskly and powerfully across his face without even sparing his nose, snorted and left me. It goes without saying that, once I'd decided on this course, I kept telling myself that I was acting from the most selfless of motives, wishing only to serve the common good and doing what would be expected of a friend of the family . . . But I'm bold enough to think that if Kirilla Matveich hadn't cut short my outpourings I'd still have lacked the courage to bring my monologue to an end. I sometimes took it upon myself, with the solemnity of some sage of antiquity, to weigh up the prince's qualities: sometimes I comforted myself with the hope that none of it mattered, Liza would come to her senses and her love would not be real love after all . . . Oh no! In short, I don't know a single idea that I didn't mull over at that time. Only one resource, I candidly confess, never occurred to me: I never once thought of taking my life. I have no idea why I didn't think of this. Perhaps I was already aware at that time that I didn't have long to live.

THE DIARY OF A SUPERFLUOUS MAN

It's understandable that in view of such unfavourable facts my behaviour and my attitude to people were more than usually characterised by unnaturalness and tension. Even old Mrs Ozhogin – that congenitally stupid creature – began to be wary of me and at times had no idea how to deal with me. Bizmyonkov, always polite and ready to be of service, avoided me. I'd already begun to think that I had a fellow sufferer in him, that he was also in love with Liza. But he never responded to any of my hints and in general was unwilling to talk to me. The prince was very friendly with him; it may even be said that he respected him. Neither Bizmyonkov nor I imposed ourselves on the prince and Liza; but he did not avoid them as I did, he did not look like a wolf or a victim – and he readily joined them when they wanted his company. True, on those occasions he was not noted for his special high spirits, but in all his gaiety in the past there had always been something subdued.

About two weeks passed in this way. Not only was the prince handsome and intelligent, he could play the piano, sing, draw fairly well and he knew how to tell stories. His anecdotes, always culled from the upper circles of the capital's society, always made a strong impression on his listeners, the more so since he appeared to give them no particular significance . . .

A consequence of this simple subterfuge, if you like, of the prince's was that in the course of his brief stay in the town of O— he utterly charmed the whole of local society. It is always very easy for someone from high society to charm provincials like us. The prince's frequent visits to the Ozhogins (he spent every evening there) naturally aroused the envy of other officials and members of the local nobility; but the prince, like a man with good social sense, did not overlook a single one of them, paid visits on them all, had a kind word for all the ladies and their daughters and allowed himself to be dined with their elaborately heavy food and wined with their wretched wines with grandiose titles – in short, he behaved discreetly, urbanely and splendidly. Prince N— was in general a man of happy disposition, sociable and amiable by inclination and – and, yes, by design: in which case he could hardly fail to succeed in everything, could he?

From the moment of his arrival everyone in the house found time flying by with extraordinary speed; everything went beautifully; old Ozhogin, though pretending not to notice anything, no doubt in secret rubbed his hands at the thought of having such a son-in-law; the prince himself conducted the whole matter in a very calm and gentlemanly way, when suddenly something unexpected happened . . .

Until tomorrow. Today I'm tired. Remembering all these things gets me worked up even at the edge of the grave. Terent'yevna has just remarked that my nose is becoming pointed – and they say that's a bad sign.

27 March

The thaw continues

Matters were as stated above: the prince and Liza were in love and the old Ozhogins were waiting for something to happen: Bizmyonkov was always about the place – one can't say more about him; I was kicking up a fuss like a fish struggling against ice and observing as much as I could – I recall I'd given myself at that time the task of at least preventing Liza from being snared in the net of her seducer and consequently began devoting a lot of attention to the maidservants and that fateful thing, the world of 'downstairs' – although, on the other hand, I sometimes spent whole nights dreaming of the touching magnanimity with which in due course I would stretch out my hand to the victim of the deception and say: 'The cad has let you down; but I'm your true friend . . . Let's forget the past and be happy!' – when suddenly there spread through the whole town the glad tidings that the local marshal of nobility intended to give a large ball, in honour of the esteemed visitor, on his very own estate of Gornostaevka. All the officials and powers-that-be in the town of O— received invitations, from the mayor right down to the local medical dispenser, an extraordinarily self-regarding German with frightful pretensions to being the purest of Russian speakers, on account of which he ceaselessly and wholly inappropriately used such strong expressions as: 'My Gott, blutty hell, devil take me, today I'm completely a blutty fool . . .' As happens, the most awful preparations were set afoot. One seller of cosmetics sold sixteen dark-blue jars of cold cream labelled *à la jesmin.* Young ladies strapped on their armour of tight dresses drawn in painfully round the waist and jutting out like promontories over the stomach; mothers erected on their heads dreadful decorations on the pretext of wearing caps; fathers caught up in the bustle fell flat on their proverbial backs . . . The long-awaited day finally arrived. I was among those invited. Gornostaevka was seven or so miles from the town. Kirilla Matveich offered me a place in his carriage, but I refused – just in the way that children who have been punished, in wanting to avenge themselves on their parents, refuse to eat their favourite meal. In any case, I felt that my presence would embarrass Liza. Bizmyonkov took my place. The prince travelled in his own carriage, I travelled in a wretched droshky hired by me very expensively for this important occasion. I will not try to describe the ball. Everything was exactly as it should have been: a gallery full of musicians playing trumpets out of tune, dumb-struck local gentry with elderly families, mauve ices, sticky cordials, servants in down-at-heel shoes and fishnet cotton gloves, social lions of the provinces with spasmodically contorted faces, and so on, and so on. And the whole of this little world went spinning round its sun – the prince. Lost in the crowd, disregarded even by the forty-eight-year-old maiden ladies with red pimples on their foreheads and pale blue flowers perched on top of their heads, I kept my eyes all the time either on the prince or on Liza. She was extremely charmingly dressed and very good-looking that evening. They danced together only twice (true, he danced the mazurka with her!), but at least it seemed to *me* that there was some secret and incessant communication going on between them. He, not even looking at her, not even speaking to her, addressed himself to her, to her alone; he was handsome and brilliant and affable with everyone – only for her sake. She evidently sensed that she was queen of the ball and that she was loved: her face glowed at one and the same time with childish joy and innocent pride, and then suddenly shone with another, much deeper feeling. She exuded happiness on all around her. I took note of it all ... It wasn't the first time I'd kept my eyes on them ... At first I was extremely annoyed, then I was touched by it, finally I was infuriated. I suddenly felt I'd become unusually malicious, and I remember I was unusually delighted by this new sensation and even upheld myself in my own eyes. 'We'll show 'em we're not done for yet!' I told myself. When the first summoning notes of the mazurka resounded loudly, I looked calmly round me, coldly and negligently approached a long-faced young lady with a red and shiny nose, a mouth hanging wide open as if it hadn't been properly done up and a scrawny neck resembling the handle of a contra-bass – approached her and, drily clicking my heels, invited her to dance. She was wearing a rose-coloured dress that looked as if it had only recently recovered from an illness – and was not yet in the pink of health; above her head quivered some washed-out, melancholy-looking thing shaped like a fly on a bronze spring of outsize thickness, and all in all the poor girl, if I may so express it, was steeped in sour-tasting boredom and chronic failure. She'd not moved all evening; no one had thought of inviting her to dance. One fair-haired sixteen-year-old youth, for want of anyone else, had been on the point of inviting her and had even taken a step in her direction, but had thought better of it, given her one glance and hurriedly vanished into the crowd. You can imagine with what astonishment and delight she agreed to my proposal! I led her solemnly the length of the room, found two chairs and sat down with her in the circle of the mazurka, among ten couples, almost directly opposite the prince, who had of course been offered the first place. The prince, as I've said, was dancing with Liza. Neither I nor my partner was troubled by invitations, so we had ample time for conversation. Truth to tell, my partner was not remarkable for her ability to utter words in logical order: she tended to use her mouth for the execution of some strange kind of downward smiling I'd never seen before; at the same time she'd raise her eyes upwards, as if some invisible force were stretching her face from end to end; but I really didn't need any eloquence from her. I enjoyed feeling malicious and my partner didn't make me feel shy of it. I embarked on criticising everything and everyone, particularly venting my malice on city cads and Petersburg show-offs, and was so carried away in the end that my partner began to lose her smile little by little and instead of lifting up her eyes started to squint – from astonishment, no doubt – and to squint in the strangest way possible, as if it were the first time she'd noticed there was a nose on her face; and my neighbour, one of those aforementioned social lions, stared at me and even turned to me, looking like an actor who has just woken up on stage at an unfamiliar place, as though about to say: 'What are you going on about?' However, singing away though I was, like a proverbial nightingale, I still managed to keep my eye on the prince and Liza. Each of them received constant invitations to dance, but I suffered less when they danced together and even when they sat together, talking together and smiling the fond smiles which never leave the faces of happy lovers – still, I did not fret all that much. But when Liza danced about the room with some prancing show-off of a hussar and the prince, with her sky-blue gauze scarf lying on his knees, followed her thoughtfully with his eyes as if he were literally gloating over his victory, then, oh then I experienced unbearable torment and in sheer anger said such malicious things that my partner's eyes became completely pressed together against her nose!

The mazurka meanwhile drew to a close . . . They were beginning the figure known as *la confidente*. In this figure the lady sits in the centre of the circle, chooses another lady as her confidante and whispers in her ear the name of the gentleman with whom she wishes to dance. Her partner conducts the dancers to her one by one and the confidante refuses them all until the appearance of the fortunate gentleman who has been named. Liza sat in the middle of the circle and chose as her confidante the host's daughter, one of those girls of whom it's said: 'God help her!' The prince set about finding the gentleman of her choice. Having offered about a dozen young men (the host's daughter turned them all down with the pleasantest of smiles), he finally turned to me. Something out of the ordinary occurred inside me at that moment: I blinked with my whole body, as it were, and was about to refuse, but I stood up and walked towards him. The prince led me to Liza . . . She didn't even look at me. The host's daughter shook her head, the prince turned to me and, spurred on no doubt by the fact that I looked a complete goose, gave me a deep bow. This facetious bow, this rejection made to me by a triumphant rival, his careless smile and Liza's indifference – all this made me explode. I went up to the prince and whispered in a fury:

'You appear to be laughing at me, eh?'

The prince glanced at me with contemptuous surprise, again took my hand and, giving every appearance of accompanying me back to my place, answered coldly: 'Who? Me?'

'Yes, you!' I continued in a whisper, though submitting to him – following him, that is to say, to my place: 'You! But I do not intend to let some worthless St Petersburg upstart . . .'

The prince grinned calmly, almost condescendingly, pressed my hand and whispered: 'I understand, but this is hardly the place. We'll talk about it,' and turned away from me, went up to Bizmyonkov and led him to Liza. The pale-faced, insignificant little official turned out to be the chosen one. Liza rose to meet him.

Taking a seat beside the lady with the melancholy-looking fly-shaped thing on her head, I felt as if I were almost a hero. My heart beat fast and my chest rose nobly beneath my starched shirt as I breathed deeply and quickly – and I suddenly looked so grandly at the local lion that his foot gave an involuntary jerk in my direction. Having dealt with that chap, I surveyed the entire circle of dancers. I sensed that two or three gentlemen were gazing at me not without a certain bewilderment, but in general the conversation with the prince had passed unnoticed. My rival was already sitting in his chair quite calmly and with his former smile on his face. Bizmyonkov led Liza back to her place. She gave him a friendly bow and at once turned to the prince with what seemed to me to be a certain alarm, but he gave a laugh, graciously waved his hand and then undoubtedly said something very pleasant to her, because she blushed with pleasure, lowered her eyes and then directed them up at him again with a look of fond reproach.

The heroic mood which had suddenly arisen in me did not vanish until the end of the mazurka. But I made no more jokes and refrained from being 'critical', simply looking now and then sombrely and severely at my partner, who had now evidently grown frightened of me and completely tongue-tied and did nothing but blink unceasingly as I led her back to the protection of her mother, a very stout woman wearing a red cap. Having left the frightened girl where she belonged, I retreated to the window, folded my arms and waited for what would happen next. I had a fairly long wait. The prince was all the time surrounded by mine host, literally surrounded, just as England is surrounded by sea; not to mention the other members of the marshal's family and the remaining guests. What is more, without causing general astonishment, he couldn't come up to such an insignificant person as me and start a conversation. My very insignificance, I remember, delighted me at that moment. 'Go on pretending!' I thought, watching how he politely addressed himself first to one, then to another respectable gentleman who sought the honour to be noticed 'if for a moment only', as poets are inclined to put it. 'Go on pretending, my dear fellow . . . You'll come to me sooner or later. After all, I've insulted you.' At last, rather awkwardly freeing himself from the crowd of admirers, the prince walked past me, glanced not exactly at the window and not exactly at my hair, was on the point of turning away and then suddenly stopped, as if he'd just remembered something.

'Oh, yes,' he said, turning to me with a smile, 'there's a little matter we have to discuss.'

Two local landowners, among the most persistent of those pursuing the prince, probably thought that the 'little matter' was an official one and respectfully stepped back. The prince took me by the arm and drew me aside. My heart was thumping in my breast.

'You, it seems,' he began, elongating the word *You* and gazing at my chin with a contemptuous expression which, strange to say, went very well with his fresh and handsome face, 'you called me a name, didn't you?'

'I said what I thought,' I replied, my voice raised.

'Quiet, quiet,' he remarked. 'Respectable people don't shout. Perhaps you feel you'd like to pick a fight with me?'

'That's your affair,' I answered, stiffening.

'I will be obliged to challenge you to a duel,' he said negligently, 'if you don't refrain from using such expressions . . .'

'I don't intend to refrain from anything,' I retorted with pride.

'Is that so?' he remarked, not without a condescending smile. 'In that case,' he added after a pause, 'I will have the honour tomorrow to send you my second.'

'Very good,' I said in a voice that could not have been more unconcerned.

The prince gave a slight bow.

'I cannot prevent you from finding me worthless,' he added, arrogantly narrowing his eyes, 'but the princes of the house of N— cannot be upstarts. Until tomorrow, Mr . . . Mr Stucco.'

He rapidly turned his back on me and again went up to mine host, who was already beginning to get worried.

Mr Stucco, indeed! My name's Stocking . . . I could find nothing to say to him in response to this final insult and simply glared at his back in a fury. 'Until tomorrow,' I whispered, gritting my teeth, and at once went in search of an officer friend of mine, a captain in the Uhlans called Koloberdyaev, the wickedest of rakes and a splendid fellow, told him in a few words of my quarrel with the prince and asked him to be my second. It goes without saying that he agreed immediately, and I went home.

I could not sleep the entire night – out of excitement, not cowardice. I am no coward. I even gave very little thought to the possibility of losing my life, that highest of earth's blessings, as the Germans assure us. My thoughts were all concerned with Liza and my perished hopes and what I ought to do. 'Should I try to kill the prince?' I asked myself again and again and, naturally, I wanted to kill the prince, not in a spirit of revenge but out of a desire to do the best thing for Liza. 'But she wouldn't survive the blow,' I went on thinking. 'No, it'd be better if he killed me!' I confess I found it pleasant to think that I, an obscure provincial, was obliging such an important person to fight a duel.

Morning found me preoccupied with such thoughts, and not long after dawn Koloberdyaev appeared.

'Well,' he asked, stumbling noisily into my bedroom, 'where's the prince's second?'

'Look,' I answered in annoyance, 'it's only seven o'clock in the morning. The prince is probably still asleep.'

'In that case,' said the irrepressible captain, 'give me some tea. My head's aching from last night and I haven't changed my clothes. Besides,' he added, yawning, 'I don't often change them.'

Tea was brought. He drank six glasses laced with rum, smoked four pipes, told me that the day before he'd bought for a song a horse rejected by the coachmen and intended to drive out with her with one of her forelegs bandaged – and fell asleep, without undressing, on the divan, the pipe still in his mouth. I got up and put my papers in order. An invitation from Liza, the only note I'd ever received from her, seemed destined to be placed next to my heart, but I thought a moment and then threw it away. Koloberdyaev snored faintly, his head hanging over the leather pillow . . . I remember I gazed a long while at his dishevelled, bold, careless and warm-hearted face. At ten o'clock my servant announced the arrival of Bizmyonkov. The prince had chosen him as his second!

The two of us woke up the soundly sleeping captain. He rose up, looked at us with sleepy eyes, asked hoarsely for vodka, came to his senses and, after exchanging a bow with Bizmyonkov, retired to consult with him in another room. The consultation between the seconds did not last long. A quarter of an hour later they both came into my bedroom and Koloberdyaev informed me that 'we will fight today, at three o'clock, with pistols'. I gave a silent nod of agreement. Bizmyonkov at once took leave of us and drove away. He was slightly pale and inwardly excited, like any man unaccustomed to dealing with such matters, but apart from that he was very polite and cold in his manner. I felt uneasy in his presence and didn't dare look him in the eyes. Koloberdyaev once again started telling me about his horse. Such talk was not at all to my taste. I was frightened that he might mention Liza, but the good captain was not a gossip and, in any case, despised all women, describing them,

God knows why, as so much green lettuce. At two o'clock we had something to eat and at three we were at the chosen place – in the very same wood where Liza and I had once walked, within a couple of paces of the ravine.

We arrived first. But the prince and Bizmyonkov didn't make us wait long. The prince, without exaggeration, was as fresh as a daisy: his chestnut eyes looked out extremely brightly from beneath the peak of his cap. He was smoking a cigar and, seeing Koloberdyaev, shook him warmly by the hand. Even to me he bowed very charmingly. By contrast, I felt I was looking pale and my hands, to my awful annoyance, were shaking slightly, my throat was dry . . . This was my first duel. 'Oh, God,' I thought, 'don't let this contemptuous fellow mistake my excitement for timidity!' I inwardly cursed my nerves, but glancing finally straight in the prince's face and catching an almost imperceptible smile on his lips I was once again infuriated and immediately grew calmer. Meanwhile our seconds were fixing the barrier, measuring out the paces and loading the pistols. Koloberdyaev did most of it, while Bizmyonkov watched him. It was a beautiful day, no less fine than the day of that unforgettable walk. The thick blue of the sky shone as before through the gilded green of the leaves. Their rustling irritated me. The prince went on smoking his cigar as he leaned with one shoulder against the trunk of a young lime . . .

'To your places, gentlemen: everything is ready,' said Koloberdyaev at last, handing us our pistols.

The prince walked off several paces, stopped and, turning his head, said to me over his shoulder: 'Do you still refuse to take back your words?' I tried to answer him but my voice failed me, and I contented myself with a contemptuous wave of the hand. The prince grinned again and took up his position. We began to walk towards each other. I raised my pistol and took aim at my enemy's chest – for at that moment he really was my enemy – but then suddenly raised the barrel, as if someone had jerked my elbow, and fired. The prince staggered backwards, brought his left hand up to his left temple and a trickle of blood ran down his cheek from beneath the white chamois glove. Bizmyonkov dashed towards him.

'It's nothing,' he said, removing the cap through which the shot had passed. 'If I've been struck in the head and not fallen down, that means it's just a scratch.'

He calmly extracted from his pocket a cambric handkerchief and pressed it to his blood-stained curls. I stared at him as if paralysed and did not move from my place.

'Approach the barrier!' Koloberdyaev remarked sternly to me.

I obeyed.

'Is the duel to continue?' he added, turning to Bizmyonkov.

Bizmyonkov did not reply, but the prince, without removing the handkerchief from the wound and without giving himself the pleasure of torturing me at the barrier, answered with a smile: 'The duel's over!' – and fired in the air. I almost cried with annoyance and fury. With his magnanimity this man had finally stamped me into the ground and done for me. I was on the point of objecting and demanding that he should fire at me, but he came up to me and held out his hand.

'Shall we forget what's happened between us, do you think?' he murmured in a gentle voice.

I looked at his white face, at his blood-stained handkerchief and, completely losing control of myself, shamefaced and crushed, I took his hand . . .

'Gentlemen!' he added, addressing the seconds. 'I trust everything will be kept a secret, eh?'

'Of course!' exclaimed Koloberdyaev. 'But, Prince, allow me . . .'

And he set about bandaging his head.

On leaving, the prince once again gave me a bow, but Bizmyonkov didn't even glance at me. Destroyed, morally destroyed, I returned home with Koloberdyaev.

'What's the matter with you?' the captain asked me. 'You don't have to worry, it wasn't a dangerous wound. He'll be able to go dancing tomorrow if he wants to. Or are you sorry you didn't kill him? In that case, don't bother: he's an excellent chap.'

'Why did he spare me?' I muttered eventually.

'So that's it!' the captain remarked quietly. 'Oh, you chaps who like to make up stories!'

I have no idea why he should have called me that.

I resolutely refuse to describe the torments I suffered the evening after that unfortunate duel. My opinion of myself suffered indescribably. It wasn't my conscience that tormented me, but my awareness of my foolishness – that crushed me. 'It was I, I, who inflicted on myself the final, crushing blow!' I kept on insisting to myself as I strode backwards and forwards in my room. 'The prince, wounded by me and yet forgiving me . . . Liza is his now. There's nothing now can save her, nothing can stop her from falling.' I knew only too well that our duel wouldn't remain a secret, notwithstanding the prince's words; and in any case it wouldn't remain a secret for Liza. 'The prince is not such a fool', I whispered in a fury, 'that he won't make use . . .' But I was wrong: the whole town knew of the duel and its cause the next day of course, but it wasn't due to anything said by the prince; on the contrary, when, with his bandaged head and his made-up pretext, he appeared before Liza, she already knew everything . . . Whether Bizmyonkov had given me away, or the news had reached her by some other means, I can't say. And after all, how is it possible to hide anything in a small town? You can just imagine how Liza and the whole Ozhogin family received him! As for me, I suddenly became the object of general disapproval and revulsion, a monster crazed by jealousy and blood-lust. My few acquaintances treated me like a leper. The authorities of the town at once turned to the prince with the proposal that I should be given a severe and exemplary punishment, and only the insistent and unwavering appeals of the prince himself averted the misfortune hanging over my head. It was left to this man to humiliate me in every way. By his magnanimity he had literally banged a coffin lid down on me. It goes without saying that the Ozhogin house was instantly closed to me. Kirilla Matveich even returned me a simple pencil I'd once forgotten. In fact, he was precisely the one who had no cause to be angry with me. My 'crazy' jealousy (as the town expressed it) had served to define and clarify the relations between the prince and Liza. The Ozhogin parents and other townspeople began to regard him almost as a fiancé. Naturally, this couldn't have been wholly pleasant for him, but he liked Liza very much and of course he hadn't yet achieved what he'd set out for . . . With all the cleverness of an intelligent and worldly man he adapted himself to his new position and at once, as they say, entered into the spirit of his new role.

But I! . . . I for my part waved goodbye to my future. When sufferings reach the point of making everything inside us rattle and creak like an overladen cart, they should stop seeming funny . . . But no! Laughter not only accompanies tears to the bitter end, to the point of exhaustion, to the impossible point of not being able to shed any more of them, but beyond, for it goes on ringing and resounding even after the tongue has fallen silent and the last piteous cry has died ... And because, firstly, I do not intend to seem laughable even to myself and, secondly, I am horribly tired, I am postponing the continuation of my story and, if God wills, its conclusion until tomorrow ...

29 March

Slight frost; yesterday it thawed

Yesterday I wasn't strong enough to continue my diary: like Poprishchin*, I lay most of the time on my bed and talked to Terent'yevna. What a woman! Sixty years ago she lost her first fiancé from the plague, has outlived all her children, is herself unforgivably ancient, drinks tea to her heart's content, is well fed and warmly clothed – and yet what do you think she spent the whole day yesterday talking to me about? I'd given orders that another, completely destitute old woman should have the collar off an old suit of livery, a half moth-eaten thing, for her vest (she wore chest-bands in the form of a vest) – so why hadn't she been given it? 'I'm your nurse, aren't I? O-o-oh, you should be ashamed, sir, you should ... And after all I've done for you, sir!' and so on. The merciless old crone completely wore me out with her reproaches. But I must get back to my story.

Well, I suffered like a dog whose rear parts have been crushed by a wheel. It was only after I had been expelled from the Ozhogins' house that I finally realised how much pleasure a man can take in being aware of his own misfortune. O, human beings, what a pitiful species you are! ... Enough of such philosophising, however ... I spent whole days in complete isolation and only by the most roundabout and underhand means learned what was happening in the Ozhogin household and what the prince was doing, for my servant was friendly with his coachman's wife's cousin. This brought me some relief and my servant quickly guessed from my hints and little presents what he should talk about with his master when he took off his boots at night. Sometimes I happened to meet on the street someone from the Ozhogin family – Bizmyonkov, perhaps – or the prince, and I exchanged bows with them but did not enter into conversation. I saw Liza only three times: once with her mother in a dress shop, once in an open carriage with her father, mother and the prince, and once in church. Naturally, I dared not approach her and simply looked at her from afar. In the shop she was extremely preoccupied but happy ... She was ordering something and busily comparing ribbons. Her mother watched her, her arms folded over her stomach, her nose raised and that kind of foolish and devoted smile on her face which is only permitted to loving mothers. With the prince in the carriage Liza was . . . I will never forget that encounter! The Ozhogin parents were sitting in the back seats, the prince and Liza in the front. She was looking paler than usual. Two red patches were just visible on her cheeks. She was half-turned to the prince. Leaning on her straight right arm (in her left she held her parasol) and languidly bending her head, she was gazing directly into his face with her expressive eyes. At that instant she was surrendering herself to him completely, irretrievably entrusting herself to him. I wasn't able to see his face clearly – the carriage went past too quickly – but it seemed to me that he was deeply moved.

The third time I saw her was in church. No more than ten days had passed since I had seen her in the carriage with the prince, and it was no more than three weeks since my duel. The business which had brought the prince to O— was already done with, but he still delayed his departure by professing sickness to St Petersburg. Every day the town waited for his formal marriage proposal to Kirilla Matveich. I was only waiting for this final blow in order to be gone for good. The town of O— had become repugnant to me. I couldn't stay home and from morning till evening wandered about in the surrounding areas. One grey, overcast day, returning from a stroll that had been interrupted by rain, I stepped into the church. The evening service was just beginning and there were very few people. I looked around and suddenly noticed a familiar profile by the window. I didn't recognise it at first: the pale face, the burnt-out look in the eyes, the sunken cheeks – could this really be the same Liza I had seen two weeks before? Wrapped in a cape, hatless, illuminated from one side by the cold light falling from the wide white window, she gazed motionless at the icon screen and seemed to be trying to pray, to force herself out of some kind of gloomy trance. A fat, red-cheeked little servant boy with yellow embroidery on his chest was standing behind her, his hands clasped in the small of his back, and gazing at his mistress with sleepy amazement. I shuddered, was on the point of going up to her, but stopped. A tormenting premonition seized my heart. Liza did not stir until the service was over. All the people had left, the verger started sweeping out the church, yet she remained where she was. The servant boy approached, said something to her and touched her dress. She looked round, ran her hand across her face and left.

From a distance I followed her to her house and then returned to my room. 'She is finished!' I exclaimed as I entered.

On my honour I don't know to this day what my feelings were at that moment. I remember that, with my hands clasped, I flung myself on the divan and stared at the floor. But, I don't know, even in the midst of my sadness I was glad in some way . . . I would never have confessed this if I hadn't been writing for myself alone . . . True, I was tormented by frightful, anguishing premonitions . . . and, who knows, I might have been extremely annoyed if they hadn't come true! 'Such is the heart of man!' some middle-aged Russian teacher would doubtless exclaim now in an expressive voice, raising aloft a fat index finger decorated with a cornelian ring. But why should the opinion of a Russian teacher with an expressive voice and a cornelian ring be any business of ours?

No matter, my premonitions were justified. News spread suddenly through the town that the prince had left after receiving orders from St Petersburg, that he had left without having made any formal proposal either to Kirilla Matveich or to his wife, and that Liza would have to lament his betrayal until the end of her days. The prince's departure had been completely unexpected, because even the day before his coachman, so my servant assured me, had not had an inkling of his master's intentions. This news threw me into a white heat of excitement and I at once dressed and intended to rush to the Ozhogins, but, having thought it over, considered it polite to wait until the next day. Besides, I didn't lose anything by staying home. That evening I had a visit from a certain Pandopipopulo, a peripatetic Greek who'd accidentally been stranded in the town of O—, a gossip of the first magnitude, the one who'd boiled with indignation at my duel with the prince more than all the rest. He didn't even give my servant time to announce him, but *literally* burst into my room, firmly squeezed my hand, made me a thousand apologies and called me a model of magnanimity and valour, painted the prince in the blackest colours, did not spare the Ozhogins, whom, in his opinion, fate had punished fairly and squarely, and, *en passant*, referred slightingly to Liza – and then left, having planted a kiss on my shoulder. Among other things I learned from him that the prince, *en vrai grand seigneur*, on the eve of his departure, in response to a delicate hint by Kirilla Matveich had coldly answered that he had no intention of deceiving anyone and was not thinking of marriage, had risen, bowed and left . . .

The next day I went to the Ozhogins. The short-sighted footman jumped up at my appearance with the speed of lightning and I ordered him to announce me. He dashed off and returned instantly: 'Please, they say, do come in.' I went into Kirilla Matveich's study . . . Until tomorrow.

30 March
Frost

So I went into Kirilla Matveich's study. I would pay dearly anyone who could show me now my own face at that moment, as the esteemed official, hurriedly wrapping his Bokhara dressing-gown round him, came towards me with outstretched arms. I must have exuded modest triumph, sympathetic condescension and unlimited magnanimity . . . I felt myself as magnanimous as Scipio. Ozhogin was visibly embarrassed and saddened, avoided my eyes and fidgeted uneasily. I also noticed that he spoke unnaturally loudly and in general expressed himself very vaguely; vaguely but fervently he asked for my forgiveness, vaguely referred to his departed guest, made a few general and vague observations on the deceitfulness and inconstancy of worldly blessings and suddenly, aware of tears in his eyes, hurried to take some snuff in order to confuse me as to the reason for his tearfulness . . . He used Russian green snuff and it is well known that this plant makes even veteran snuff-takers shed tears, through which the human eye looks dully and senselessly for several instants. Naturally I behaved very cautiously with the old man, asked after his wife's health and his daughter's and then artfully directed the conversation to the interesting question of crop rotation. I was quite normally dressed, but the feeling of gentle *politesse* and mild condescension which filled me gave a fresh and festive sensation just as if I'd been wearing a white tie and tails. One thing alone worried me: the thought of meeting Liza . . . Ozhogin at last suggested taking me to see his wife. The kind but silly woman was frightfully confused on first seeing me, but her brain was incapable of retaining one and the same impression for long and she soon grew quiet. Then I saw Liza . . . She came into the room . . .

I expected that I would find in her a shame-filled and remorseful sinner and had already given my face a fond, appreciative expression . . . Why tell lies? I was genuinely in love with her and longed for the pleasure of forgiving her and extending a helping hand. But to my unspeakable astonishment she responded to my significant bow with a cold laugh and the casual remark: 'Oh, it's you, is it?' and at once turned away. True, her laugh sounded forced and in any case was ill-suited to her terribly thin face. Still, I had not anticipated this kind of greeting. I stared at her in amazement: what a change had occurred in her! There was nothing in common between this woman and the child she had been formerly. She had grown up, as it were, grown straighter. All her facial features, particularly her lips, were more clearly defined. Her eyes were deeper, firmer and darker. I stayed at the Ozhogins' till dinner and all the time she rose, left the room and returned, calmly answered questions and deliberately paid no attention to me. I saw that she wanted me to feel I did not even deserve her anger, although it was only by a hair's breadth that I had avoided killing the one she loved. Finally, I lost all patience and an acid hint escaped my lips . . . She gave a shudder, glanced swiftly at me, rose and, going to the window, said in a slightly unsteady voice: 'You may say what you like, but you must know that I love that man and will always love him, and I in no way consider him to be to blame on my account; on the contrary . . .'

Her voice broke, she stopped. She tried to overcome her feelings but couldn't, burst into tears and dashed from the room. Her parents were upset. I shook them both by the hand, sighed, lifted my eyes to heaven and left.

I am too weak and there is too little time remaining for me to describe with all the previous detail the new series of tormenting considerations, firm intentions and other fruits of so-called inner struggle which arose in me after the renewal of my acquaintance with the Ozhogins. I did not doubt that Liza still loved and would go on loving the prince for a long time, but as a man humbled by circumstances and reconciled to my own self I did not even dream of love: I desired only her friendship, I desired only to acquire her trust and respect which, I am assured by those with experience, are accounted the surest basis of happiness in marriage . . . Unfortunately I left out of account one fairly important circumstance – the fact that from the day of the duel Liza had despised me. I discovered this too late. I began visiting the Ozhogins as I had done formerly. Kirilla Matveich was more affectionate and affable than ever. I even have reason to think that he would gladly have given his daughter to me at that time, although I was not an enviable choice as fiancé; but the fact was that public opinion had it in for him and Liza, while I by contrast was being praised to the skies. Liza's attitude towards me did not change.

She said nothing for the most part, was obedient to her parents' requests to eat, gave no outward signs of grief, but, together with all this, melted as surely as a candle. One must do justice to Kirilla Matveich: he spared her in every way; the mother simply got herself all flustered whenever she looked at her poor dear child. There was only one person whom Liza did not avoid, though she did not talk much to him, and that was Bizmyonkov. The Ozhogin parents treated him severely, even rudely, because they couldn't forgive him for having been a second, but he continued with his visits, as if he did not notice their disfavour. He was extremely cold with me and – strange though it may seem! – I was literally terrified of him. This continued about two weeks. At last, after a sleepless night, I decided to have it out with Liza, to open my heart to her and tell her that, notwithstanding the past and all manner of gossip and talk, I would consider myself only too happy if she would deign to give me her hand and return to me the confidence that I reposed in her. In all seriousness I imagined that I would be displaying, as school text-books express it, an ineffable example of magnanimity and she would agree out of sheer astonishment. In any case, I wanted an explanation from her and to be finally released from ignorance.

At the back of the Ozhogin house there was a fairly large garden which ended in a small grove of lime-trees that was neglected and over-grown. In the middle of this grove stood an old summer-house of Chinese design; a wooden fence separated the garden from a narrow pathway. Liza would sometimes spend whole hours walking alone in this garden. Kirilla Matveich knew this and forbade her to be disturbed or followed on the pretext that such walks would disperse her grief. Whenever she was not to be found in the house, they had only to ring a bell on the steps before dinner and she would at once appear, her lips stubbornly sealed as ever, like her gaze, with some crumpled leaf or other in her hand. On one occasion, noticing she was not in the house I gave the impression of leaving, said goodbye to Kirilla Matveich, found my hat and went out of the front door into the yard, and from the yard into the street, but then shot back through the gates with unusual speed and made my way past the kitchen into the back garden. Happily, no one noticed me. Without taking much time for thought, I entered the grove with hurried steps. Right in front of me on the path stood Liza. My heart beat violently. I stopped, took in a deep breath and was just on the point of approaching her when she suddenly lifted her hand without turning and started listening. From beyond the trees, in the direction of the narrow path, came the clear sound of two knocks as though someone were hitting the fence. Liza clapped her hands, the wicket-gate gave a faint creak and Bizmyonkov appeared out of the bushes. I quickly hid behind a tree. Liza turned to him without a word. He silently took her by the arm and they both went quietly along the path. I watched them in amazement. They stopped, looked round, seemed to disappear behind some bushes, then reappeared and, finally, entered the summer-house. This summer-house was a diminutive, round structure with one door and one small window. In the middle of it stood an old one-legged table covered in a thin green moss. Two plain wood divans stood either side of it, at some distance from the damp and discoloured walls. Here on unusually hot days, and then only once a year and in times long past, tea would be served. The door did not close, the frame of the window had fallen out and, secured by only one corner, hung down sadly like a broken bird's wing. I crept up to the summer-house and glanced cautiously through a chink in the window. Liza sat on one of the divans, hanging her head; her right hand lay in her lap, her left was being held by Bizmyonkov in his own two hands. He gazed at her with compassion.

'How are you feeling today?' he asked her softly.

'The same as usual,' she answered. 'No better and no worse. The emptiness, the terrible emptiness!' she added, despondently raising her eyes.

Bizmyonkov did not respond.

'What do you think?' she went on. 'Will he write to me again?'

'I don't think so, Lizaveta Kirillovna.'

She was silent.

'And, really, what is there for him to write? He told me everything in his first letter. I couldn't become his wife. But I was happy . . . for a short time . . . I was happy.'

Bizmyonkov lowered his eyes.

'Oh,' she went on excitedly, 'if only you knew how hateful that Stocking is . . . I keep on thinking I can see blood on his hands – *his* blood.' (I winced in my hiding-place.) 'And yet,' she added thoughtfully, 'who knows, if it hadn't been for that duel . . . Oh, when I saw him wounded, I felt at once that I was entirely his!'

'Stocking's in love with you,' Bizmyonkov remarked.

'What's that to me? Do I need anyone's love?' She stopped and added slowly: 'Apart from yours. Yes, my friend, I need your love. Without you I would've perished. You've helped me to endure awful times . . .'

She fell silent. Bizmyonkov began to stroke her hand with paternal tenderness.

'I don't know what's to be done, what's to be done, Lizaveta Kirillovna!' he repeated several times in a row.

'And I think', she murmured faintly, 'I'd have died now without you. You're the only one who's given me any help. Besides, you remind me of him . . . And you knew everything, didn't you? You remember how fine he looked that day . . . But forgive me, it must be painful for you . . .'

'Go on, go on! Don't bother about me! For heaven's sake!' interposed Bizmyonkov.

She pressed his hand.

'You're very kind, Bizmyonkov,' she continued, 'kind as an angel. But what's to be done about it? I feel I'll go on loving him till I die. I've forgiven him, I'm grateful to him. God grant him happiness! God give him a wife after his heart!' And her eyes filled with tears. 'Just so long as he doesn't forget me, just so long as he should think occasionally about his Liza . . . Let's go,' she added after a short pause.

Bizmyonkov raised her hand to his lips.

'I know', she said fervently, 'they all blame me now, they're all throwing stones at me. Let them! I wouldn't exchange my unhappiness for their happiness . . . No! No! . . . He didn't love me for long, but he loved me! He never pretended, he never told me I would be his wife and I never thought about it. It was only my poor father who had such hopes. And even now I'm not completely miserable, because I have my memories and no matter how awful the consequences . . . It's stuffy in here . . . This was where we had our last meeting . . . Let's go out in the fresh air.'

They rose. I scarcely had time to jump aside and hide behind a thick lime. They came out of the summer-house and, so far as I could judge from the sound of their footsteps, they entered the grove. I don't know how long I remained standing there without moving, consumed by some ridiculous bewilderment, when suddenly I heard footsteps again. I was startled and peered cautiously out of my hiding-place. Bizmyonkov and Liza were returning along the same path. Both were very excited, particularly Bizmyonkov. He seemed to be crying. Liza stopped, looked at him and clearly uttered the following words: 'I agree to it, Bizmyonkov. I wouldn't have agreed if you'd only wanted to save me and get me out of my awful position. But you're in love with me — you know everything and you're in love with me: I'll never find a better, a truer friend. I'll be your wife.'

Bizmyonkov kissed her hand. She gave him a wan smile and walked off towards the house. Bizmyonkov rushed off into the grove and I made my own way home. Since Bizmyonkov had no doubt told Liza what I had intended to tell her, and since she had given him precisely the answer I had wanted to hear from her, I had no more need to worry over the matter. In two weeks she was married to him. The Ozhogin parents were happy to have any husband for her.

Well, tell me now, am I or am I not a superfluous man? Throughout the whole business haven't I played the role of someone who was quite superfluous? The role of the prince — that needs no explaining, and Bizmyonkov's role is also quite understandable . . . But what about me? Why did I get mixed up in it? What a stupid fifth wheel I've been! Oh, it all tastes so bitter, so bitter! But then, as the wretches hauling the barges on the Volga say: 'Heave away! And again!' — so there'll be one short day more, then another, and after that I won't need to bother if it's bitter or sweet.

31 March

I'm poorly. I'm writing in bed. Since yesterday evening the weather's changed suddenly. It's warm today, almost like summer. Everything's melting, cracking up, flowing. The air's full of the smell of newly dug earth — pungent, strong, intense. Everything's steaming. The sun literally beats down, literally scorches. I feel I'm disintegrating.

I wanted to write my diary, but in place of that what've I done? I've recounted one episode from my life. I got carried away and all the sleeping memories were awakened and distracted me. I wrote slowly, detail by detail, as if I had years ahead of me, and now there's no time left. Death, death is on its way. I can already hear its threatening *crescendo* . . . Time's up . . . Time's up!

It doesn't matter a damn! Does it matter what I write? In sight of death earth's last vanities vanish away. I feel I'm growing calmer and becoming simpler, more lucid. How late in the day to get wise to things! Oh, it's strange, here I am growing calmer and yet at the same time I'm terrified! Yes, literally terrified! Leaning half out over the yawning abyss of silence, I shudder and turn away and look around me with greedy interest. Every item is doubly dear to me. I gloat over my poor, sombre room and say goodbye to every little mark on its walls. I say to my eyes: have your fill of these things for the last time! Life is slipping away; it runs away from me smoothly and quietly, just as the shore slips from a sailor's sight. The ancient, yellow face of my nurse tied in a dark scarf, the hissing samovar on the table, the pot of geraniums in the window and you, my poor dog Treasure, the pen with which I write these lines, my very own hand, everything I now see . . . you're there, I can see you . . . But can it be that, perhaps this very day, I'll never see you again? How hard it is for a living creature to part with life! Why are you fawning on me, you poor dog? Why do you press your chest against my bed, frenziedly wagging your short tail and looking at me fixedly with your kind, sad eyes? Do you feel pity for me? Or perhaps you already know your master'll soon die? Oh, if only I could mentally look through all my memories as easily as my eyes can look at all the things in my room! I know the memories would be unhappy and unimportant, but I have no others. The emptiness, the terrible emptiness! as Liza called it.

O my God, my God! I know I'm dying . . . My heart, so ready and willing to love, will soon stop beating. Will it fall quiet forever without once having known happiness or once having expanded under a sweet burden of joy? Alas, that's impossible, impossible, I'm certain . . . If now at least, on the verge of death – for death, surely, is a holy thing, it uplifts all creation – if now some dear, sad, friendly voice would sing me some song of farewell, a song of my very own grief, then perhaps I'd be reconciled to it. But to die unmourned, stupidly . . .

I think I'm becoming delirious.

Farewell, life! Farewell, my garden, and you, my lime-trees! When summer comes, be sure you're full of flowers, so that people will be glad to lie on the fresh grass in your fragrant shade, under the lisping chatter of your leaves stirred so lightly by the wind. Farewell, farewell! Goodbye to you all for ever and always!

Farewell, Liza! I've just written these two words and almost burst out laughing. They sound so bookish. It's as if I were composing some sentimental story or ending a letter of despair . . .

Tomorrow is 1 April. Will I die tomorrow? That would be really rather indecent. And yet in my case appropriate . . .

How the doctor did go on and on today!

2 April

It's finished . . . Life's finished. I'll die today. It's hot outside . . . almost stuffy . . . or is it that I can't breathe properly? My little comedy's over. The curtain is falling.

In my obliteration I'll cease to be superfluous . . .

Oh, how hot the sun is! Its powerful rays have the breath of eternity . . .

Goodbye, Terent'yevna! . . . This morning, sitting in the window, she started crying . . . perhaps over me . . . or perhaps over the fact that she'll soon have to die herself. I've made her promise not to have my dog Treasure put down.

I find it hard to write . . . I'm going to lay down my pen . . . Time's up! Death doesn't approach with an increasing rumble, like a carriage approaching over cobbles at night, but it's here, dancing all round me, like the spirit that passed before the prophet's face and made the hair of his flesh stand up . . .*

> *I am dying . . . Live on, O living!*
> *And at the entrance to the grave*
> *May young life play and sing,*
> *And let indifferent nature save*
> *Its radiant beauty everlasting!**

Editor's Note. Under this last line was a head in profile with a large tuft of hair and a moustache, an eye *en face* surrounded by rays of eyelashes; and above the head someone had written the following words:

'The foregoing MS. Was Read
And the Contents Not Approved
By Pyotr Zudotyeshin Esq.
M M M M
My Good Sir
Pyotr Zudotyeshin.
Sir.'

But since the handwriting of these lines is in no way similar to the handwriting in the remaining part of the text, the editor regards himself as justified in concluding that the above lines were subsequently added by another person, more especially as it has come to his (the editor's) attention that Mr Stocking actually did pass away during the night of 1 and 2 April 18— in his native estate of Sheepwater.

Mumu

In one of the outer streets of Moscow, in a grey house with white columns, mezzanine and crooked balcony, there lived at one time a noblewoman, a widow, surrounded by a multitude of servants. Her sons were in government service in St Petersburg and her daughters had married; she rarely went out and was solitarily living through the final years of avaricious and boring old age. Her own day, cheerless and unpleasant, had long since passed; but the evening of her days was blacker than night.

Among all her house servants the most remarkable was the yardman Gerasim, a man of more than six feet in height, built like one of the legendary heroes of old and deaf and dumb from birth. The lady of the house had brought him from his village where he lived alone, in a small hut, apart from his brothers, and was, on the whole, considered the most correct of her peasant serfs in the fulfilment of his servile obligations. Endowed with extraordinary strength, he could do the work of four men – everything went well as soon as he touched it, and it was a joy to watch him whether he was ploughing, when, laying the enormous palms of his hands to the plough, it seemed that he alone, without the aid of the horse, was cutting a furrow through the softly yielding bosom of the land; or on St Peter's day wielding his scythe so devastatingly that he could as well have mown a small birch wood right down to the roots; or vigorously and ceaselessly threshing with a three-yard-long chain, the square, firm muscles of his shoulders rising and falling like levers. The constant silence lent a solemn significance to his tireless work. He was an excellent peasant, and had it not been for his misfortune any girl would willingly have married him . . . But, as it turned out, Gerasim was brought to Moscow, boots were purchased for him, he was given a caftan for the summer and a sheepskin coat for the winter, a brush and spade were supplied and he was made a yardman.

He took a strong dislike to his new way of life at first. From childhood he had been used to working in the fields and to country life. Alienated by his misfortune from other people's company, he grew up dumb and powerful like a tree growing in fertile soil ... Transported to the city, he couldn't understand what was happening to him, and he grew homesick and perplexed like a young and healthy bull that has just been taken from the pasture where the succulent grass grows as high as his stomach – has been taken and put in a railway wagon, his full round body at the mercy of spark-filled smoke and waves of steam, and is being rushed along with a great clanging and whistling, rushed along – God knows where! Gerasim's duties in his new work seemed to him laughable after his heavy peasant labours; in half an hour everything had been done, and then he would stop in the middle of the yard and stare open-mouthed at all the passers-by, as though wanting somehow to elicit from them a solution to his mysterious new state, or suddenly he would go off somewhere into a corner and, hurling the brush and spade from him, he would fling himself face down on the ground and lie motionless on his chest for hours at a time like a captive beast. But men can get used to anything and Gerasim finally grew used to city life. He had very little to do; his job consisted of keeping the yard clean, carrying water in twice a day, bringing in and hewing logs for the kitchen and the house, not allowing strangers in and keeping watch at night. And it has to be said that he did his job conscientiously: there was never so much as a wood-chip lying about his yard and never any rubbish; should the broken-down old nag of a horse which had been given to him for water-hauling get stuck in the mud during wet weather, he would simply apply his shoulder – and not only the water-cart but the horse itself would get shoved on its way; should he be hewing logs, his axe would ring out pure as glass and splinters and sticks would fly in all directions; and as for strangers, once at night, after having caught a couple of thieves, he knocked their heads together so forcefully that even though he'd not told the police afterwards, everyone in the neighbourhood became very respectful towards him: even passers-by in the daytime who were in no sense rascals, but simply strangers, waved at the sight of the awesome yardman and shouted at him as though he was able to hear their shouts. With the rest of the servants Gerasim was not on friendly (they were frightened of him) so much as familiar terms, and yet he considered them his own people. They communicated with him by signs and he understood them, doing everything he was ordered, but he also knew his own rights and no one dared sit in his place at the servants' table. In general Gerasim was a man of stern and serious disposition and liked things kept in order. Woe to any cocks that dared start fighting in his presence! As soon as he'd seen them he'd seize them by the legs, swing them round his head a dozen times and fling them from him. The lady of the house also kept geese in the yard, but the goose, as is well known, is a dignified and thoughtful creature and Gerasim felt respectful towards them, looked after them and fed them; and he also had something of the stately gander about him. He was given a small room above the kitchen and there he fixed himself up according to his own tastes, made a bed for himself out of oak planks set on four wooden blocks – a veritably heroic bed which would carry almost two tons without bending; beneath it was kept a hefty trunk; and in the corner stood a small table of the same hefty character and by it a three-legged stool so durable and thickset that Gerasim used himself to lift it, let it fall and break into a grin. The room was locked with a padlock as large as a small loaf, except that it was black; Gerasim always carried the key around with him on a little belt. He didn't like people dropping in.

In this fashion a year passed, at the end of which something happened to Gerasim.

The old lady for whom he worked as a yardman was old-fashioned in all her ways and maintained numerous servants. Her household had not only laundresses, seamstresses, joiners, tailors and dressmakers, there was even a saddler who acted as a veterinary surgeon and as a physician for the servants, there was a private physician for the lady of the house and there was finally a shoemaker, by name Kapiton Klimov, who was an inveterate drunkard. Klimov regarded himself as one who had been humiliated and underestimated, a man of education and urbanity who shouldn't be living in Moscow in some backwater with nothing to do, and if he drank, as he expressed it, spelling out each word and tapping himself on the breast-bone, then he drank out of bitterness. One day the lady of the house chanced to mention him in talking to her steward, Gavrila, a man whom, judging by his small yellow eyes and beak of a nose, fate itself, it seemed, had ordained to be a leader of men. The lady of the house expressed her regret at Kapiton's moral degradation after he'd been found somewhere on the street the day before.

'Gavrila,' she said suddenly, 'what do you think? Shouldn't we marry him off? Perhaps that'd make him settle down.'

'Why, let's marry him off, ma'am! It's possible,' answered Gavrila, 'an' it'd even be a very good thing, ma'am.'

'Yes, but to whom?'

'Of course, ma'am. Besides, it's as you'll see fit, ma'am. He can still be good for something, so to speak. There's no throwing him away just yet.'

'Isn't Tatyana rather fond of him?'

Gavrila was about to object but pursed his lips.

'Yes! Let him have Tatyana,' the lady of the house decided, enjoying a pinch of snuff. 'Do you hear me?'

'Yes, ma'am,' said Gavrila, and withdrew.

After returning to his room (it was situated in one of the wings of the house and was almost entirely occupied by leather-bound trunks) Gavrila first of all shooed his wife out and then sat down by the window and thought. The unexpected order issued by the lady of the house had evidently perplexed him. Finally he stood up and ordered Kapiton to be brought to him. Kapiton appeared . . . . But before we let the reader know about their conversation we consider it relevant to say a few words about this Tatyana, whom Kapiton was to marry, and why the order of the lady of the house had caused the steward such trouble.

Tatyana, who was employed as a laundress (as a clever and expert worker she was given only the finest pieces to launder), was a woman of about twenty-eight, small, thin, fair-haired, with a birth-mark on her left cheek. Birth-marks on the left cheek are considered in Russia to be a bad sign and foretell an unhappy life. Tatyana could hardly boast of her good fortune. From early youth she had been kept in drudgery; she did the work of two and never saw a moment's kindness; they dressed her in poor clothes and she received the meanest of wages; of relatives she had scarcely any: one elderly locksmith, left in the country on account of his worthlessness, passed as an uncle of hers, and there were other uncles among the other peasants – that was the sum total. At one time she had been something of a beauty, but her beauty had very quickly gone. She had an extremely submissive, or, to put it more accurately, an apprehensive character, was wholly indifferent to herself but mortally frightened of others; gave thought only to how to complete her work on time, never spoke to anyone and trembled at the very name of the lady of the house although the latter hardly ever knew her by sight. When Gerasim had been brought from his village, she had almost fainted with horror at his enormous figure and endeavoured in every way possible to avoid meeting him, screwing up her eyes tightly whenever she had to run past him as she hurried from the house to the laundry.

At first Gerasim paid her no particular attention, then he began to chuckle when he saw her, then he began to watch out for her, and finally he couldn't take his eyes off her. He fell in love with her, whether captivated by the submissiveness of her expression or the timidity of her movements God knows! Once when she was making her way across the yard, carefully holding up with outspread fingers a starched blouse belonging to the lady of the house, someone suddenly seized her by the elbow. She turned round and literally screamed: it was Gerasim standing behind her. Laughing foolishly and softly moaning, he extended towards her a gingerbread cockerel with sugary gold on its tail and wings. She tried to refuse it, but he forcibly thrust it into her hand, gave a nod of the head, walked off and then, turning round, once again moaned something particularly friendly at her. From that day he gave her no peace: no matter where she went he would be there, coming up to her with a smile, giving a moan, waving, suddenly drawing a ribbon out of his shirt and thrusting it at her or using his broom to brush away the dust in her path. The poor woman simply had no idea what to do with herself. Soon the whole house knew what the dumb yardman was up to; jokes, giggles and jibes poured down on Tatyana. Not everyone decided, however, to make fun of Gerasim: he was not fond of jokes and in his presence they left her alone. Willy-nilly she found herself subject to his protection. Like all who are deaf and dumb he was very sensitive and could understand very well when someone was laughing at him or her. Once at dinner the linen maid, Tatyana's superior, started poking fun at her, as they say, and brought her to such a pitch that she, poor thing, did not know where to turn her eyes and was almost on the verge of tears. Gerasim suddenly stood up, extended his enormous hand, placed it on the linen maid's head and glared with such baleful ferocity into her face that she literally cowered down to table level. Everyone fell silent. Gerasim then took up his spoon and continued eating his cabbage soup. 'The deaf devil, did you see that?' they muttered to each other, while the linen maid rose and marched off to her quarters. On another occasion, noting that Kapiton – the very same Kapiton who has just been mentioned – was chatting to her much too familiarly, he beckoned to him with his finger, took him into the carriage-house, seized hold of the end of a shaft standing in one corner and gently but meaningfully threatened him with it. From that moment no one dared strike up a conversation with Tatyana. And everything seemed to be going well for him. True, the linen maid had no sooner reached her quarters than she had collapsed in a faint and done it so well that by next day she had succeeded in telling the lady of the house of Gerasim's rudeness; but the eccentric old woman had merely burst out laughing and more than once, to the linen maid's extreme chagrin, made her repeat how he had forced her to cower down to table level under the pressure of his weighty hand, and the next day she sent Gerasim a rouble coin. She cherished him as a strong and loyal guardian of her property. Gerasim was thoroughly afraid of her, but he hoped to keep on good terms with her and was planning to approach her with a request to be allowed to marry Tatyana. He was only waiting for the new caftan promised by the steward, so that he could appear before his mistress appropriately dressed, when this very mistress took it into her head to arrange for Tatyana to be married to Kapiton.

The reader will now readily appreciate the reason for Gavrila's embarrassment after his conversation with the lady of the house. 'The mistress', he had thought as he sat by the window, 'is of course considerate of Gerasim' (Gavrila knew this well enough and was therefore deferential to him for his own part), 'since he is unable to speak, and yet there's no telling the mistress that Gerasim's been courting Tatyana. After all, would it be right, what sort of a husband would he make? But, on the other hand, God forbid he should find out that Tatyana's being given to Kapiton or he'll kick up a hell of a row! There's no way of talking sense into him. Sinner that I am, I've got no way of talking him round . . . no way!'

The appearance of Kapiton broke the thread of Gavrila's cogitations. The feckless shoemaker entered, thrust his arms behind him and, leaning idly against the projecting corner of the wall beside the door, placed his right foot in the shape of a cross in front of his left and shook his head as much as to say: 'Here I am, then, so what do you want me for?'

Gavrila looked at Kapiton and tapped his fingers on the frame of the window. Kapiton did no more than screw up his small, tin-coloured eyes a little, but he did not lower them, he even gave a slight grin and ran his hand through his whitish hair, which was in any case sticking up in all directions, as much as to say: 'Yes, it's me, it's me, why are you staring like that?'

'What a sight,' said Gavrila, and fell silent. 'What a sight and no mistake!'

Kapiton simply shrugged his shoulders. 'And do you consider yourself any better?' he said to himself.

'Just take a look at yourself, just take a look,' went on Gavrila reproachfully. 'What on earth do you look like?'

Kapiton calmly surveyed his worn and ragged jacket, his patched trousers, and then looked particularly carefully at the holes in his shoes, especially the toe of the one against which his right foot was leaning so foppishly, and once more stared back at the steward.

'What's wrong?'

'What's wrong?' repeated Gavrila. 'What's wrong? You ask: what's wrong? What's wrong is you look like the devil himself – the Lord forgive me, sinner that I am – that's what you look like!'

Kapiton quickly blinked his little eyes.

'Swear if you want to, swear away, Gavrila Andreich,' he said to himself.

'You were drunk again,' began Gavrila, 'isn't that so? Well? Answer me.'

'Due to the poorness of my health I've actually been obliged to resort to alcoholic beverages,' responded Kapiton.

'Due to the poorness of your health! You're not punished enough, that's what's wrong with you. And in St Petersburg you were given some education . . . A lot of you learned from your education! All you do is eat and give nothing in return.'

'In this instance, Gavrila Andreich, there is but one judge – the good Lord Himself – and no one else. He alone knows what sort of a man I am and whether I eat and give nothing in return. As for the consideration of drunkenness, in this instance I'm not the one to blame, but a friend of mine. He it was who led me astray, talked politics and then went off, while I . . .'

'While you were left on the street, you goose! Oh, you're a right idiot, you are! Well, that's not what I want to talk about,' the steward continued, 'but this: the mistress . . .' He stopped a moment. 'The mistress feels you should be married. Do you hear? Her ladyship thinks you'd pull yourself together if you were married. Do you understand?'

'Why shouldn't I understand?'

'Well, of course you do. In my opinion it'd be better to take you properly in hand. But, anyhow, it's her affair. Well, do you agree?'

Kapiton grinned. 'Marriage is a good thing for a man, Gavrila Andreich. And for my part I agree with the greatest of pleasure.'

'Well, of course you would,' said Gavrila, and thought: 'There's no getting away from it, he's got a fine line of talk has this chap. Except there's just one thing,' he continued aloud, 'They've chosen a fiancée for you who's not quite right.'

'Who's that, may I inquire?'

'Tatyana.'

'Tatyana?'

And Kapiton screwed up his eyes and peeled himself away from the wall.

'Well, what are you so excited about? Doesn't she suit you?'

'Doesn't suit me, Gavrila Andreich! She's all right, she works hard, she's quiet . . . But you know yourself, Gavrila Andreich, that fellow, that brute, the wild man of the steppes, he's after her . . .'

'I know that, lad, I know all about it,' the steward interrupted in annoyance, 'but there it is . . .'

'For heaven's sake, Gavrila Andreich, he'll surely kill me, he'll kill me, he'll squash me like a fly! You've seen his hand, you know what it's like – it's as big as the Minin and Pozharsky hand!* I mean, he's deaf, he'll hit me and he won't hear himself hitting me! It'll be just as if he's waving his fists about in his sleep. And there's not a chance of saying something soothing to him. Why? Because as you yourself know, Gavrila Andreich, he's deaf and in addition he's stupid, he's thick as the heel of a boot. He's some kind of wild animal, you know, he's a block-head, Gavrila Andreich – worse than a blockhead, he's got a sting . . . So why must I suffer from him now? Of course, it's nothing at all to me now, I'm someone who's been overlooked, overdone, overgreased like a kitchen pot – and still I'm a man, not some rubbishy pot.'

'I know, I know, don't carry on so . . .'

'My God!' the shoemaker went on fiercely. 'When is it all going to end? In God's name, when? An unfortunate wretch is what I am! My fate, my fate, just think of it! When I was young I got beaten by my

MUMU

German master, in the best years of my life I got beaten by my brother, finally, in my mature years, I've done my job to the point where I . . .'

'Oh, you'd try the patience of an angel!' said Gavrila. 'There's no point in going on and on!'

'No point, Gavrila Andreich! It's not the beatings I'm frightened of, Gavrila Andreich. A gentleman can beat me in the four walls of his house but greet me in public and I still remain a man, but when you think who it'd be in this case . . .'

'All right, be off with you!' Gavrila interrupted him impatiently.

Kapiton turned round and shuffled off.

'What if he didn't exist,' shouted the steward after him, 'would you agree in that case?'

'I'd consent,' replied Kapiton, and disappeared. His rhetorical manner remained with him even in extreme cases.

The steward walked several times up and down in his room.

'Well, send in Tatyana now,' he declared at last.

In a few moments Tatyana entered barely audibly and stopped in the doorway.

'What is your wish, Gavrila Andreich?' she asked in a quiet voice.

The steward looked fixedly at her.

'Well,' he said, 'Tatyana, my dear, do you want to get married? The lady of the house has found a husband for you.'

'I see, Gavrila Andreich. And who has been chosen as my husband?' she added hesitantly.

'Kapiton, the shoemaker.'

'I see, sir.'

'He's a feckless chap, that's for sure. But your mistress has high hopes of you in this case.'

'I see, sir.'

'There's one problem – that deaf and dumb fellow, Gerasim, he's been making advances to you. What's it you've been doing to him to get him in such a state? Well, anyhow, he'll most likely kill you, that bear will . . .'

'He'll kill me, Gavrila Andreich, he's bound to.'

'So he will, will he? Well, we'll see. What d'you mean when you say he'll kill you? Has he a sound reason for killing you, ask yourself that.'

'I don't know, Gavrila Andreich, whether he has or not.'

'For heaven's sake! Surely you must know if you promised him something . . .'

✎ 81 ✍

'Promised him what, sir?'

The steward fell silent and thought: 'She truly is one of the meek! All right, then,' he added, 'we'll talk about this later, but off you go now, Tatyana, my dear. I can see you're truly one of the meek and mild.'

Tatyana turned, steadied herself slightly on the lintel and went out.

'Maybe the mistress'll have forgotten all about this marriage tomorrow,' thought the steward, 'so what am I getting all worked up about? We'll fix that layabout of a shoemaker and if necessary let the police know . . . Ustinya Fyodorovna!' he shouted loudly to his wife. 'Put on the samovar, there's a dear!'

Tatyana hardly left the laundry the whole of that day. At first she burst into tears, then wiped them away and started on her work as usual. Kapiton sat in a tavern until late at night with a sombre-looking acquaintance and told him in detail how he'd once worked for a gentleman in St Petersburg who had everything in hand and was a stickler for the rules, but had one little weakness which he permitted himself: he'd take a bit too much drink and when it came to women he'd simply go the whole hog . . . The sombre-looking acquaintance just nodded his head; but when Kapiton announced at last that, on account of a particular matter, he'd have to lay a hand on himself tomorrow the sombre-looking acquaintance remarked that it was time to go to bed. And they parted boorishly and without another word.

Meanwhile, the steward's expectations came to nothing. The lady of the house was so preoccupied by the thought of Kapiton's marriage that at night she could talk about nothing else with one of her lady companions who was kept in the house solely on account of the mistress's insomnia and slept during the day like a night-time cabby. When Gavrila came to report to her after her morning tea, her first question was about the marriage and how the arrangements were going. He naturally answered that things couldn't be going better and that this very day Kapiton would be coming to see her with a request. The lady of the house was out of sorts and didn't spend long discussing the matter. The steward returned to his own room and summoned a council. The case demanded special discussion. Tatyana, of course, made no objections; but Kapiton announced to all and sundry that he had only one head, not two and not three . . . Gerasim kept on looking severely and rapidly at everyone without leaving the shelter of the entrance to the maids' workroom, but it seemed he had guessed that something was afoot which would be unpleasant for him. Those who gathered together to form the council (they included an old bartender, nicknamed Uncle Ragtail, to whom everyone turned respectfully for advice, although all they ever heard from him was: 'Yes, that's it, yes, yes, yes, yes') started by locking Kapiton in the store-room with the water-purifying machine for safekeeping, come what might, and then put their thinking caps on. Of course, it would have been easy enough to resort to brute force, but then – heaven forbid! – there would have been a row, the mistress would have been disturbed and that would've been that! So how should they go about it? They thought and thought and finally came up with an idea. It had often been noticed that Gerasim couldn't tolerate drunkards . . . Sitting behind the gates, he had a habit of turning away in disgust whenever someone who'd taken too much on board came by with unsure footsteps and the peak of his cap hanging over one ear. They decided to teach Tatyana how to act drunk and pass by Gerasim stumbling and swaying. The poor woman took a long time to agree, but she was finally persuaded; in any case she saw that there was no other way of escaping from her admirer's clutches. She walked off. Kapiton was let out of the store-room, for it concerned him as much as anyone. Gerasim sat on a little mound by the gate sticking his spade into the ground, and from all corners and through window-shutters people watched him . . .

The cunning plan could not have succeeded better. Catching sight of Tatyana he first of all started wagging his head and moaning softly as was his habit. Then he looked more closely, dropped his spade, jumped up, went to her, pushed his face right up to hers . . . In terror she started falling about all the more and closed her eyes . . . he seized her by the hand, rushed her across the yard and, going into the room where the council was meeting, thrust her straight at Kapiton. Tatyana literally collapsed in a faint. Gerasim stopped a moment, looked at her, gave a wave of the hand, grinned and then went off heavy-footed to his room . . .

For a whole twenty-four hours he stayed there. Antipka the postilion used to say afterwards that he had observed through a crack how Gerasim, sitting on the bed with his hand pressed to his cheek, quietly, evenly, with only occasional moanings, sang to himself – that is to say, he rocked slightly to and fro, closing his eyes and shaking his head like cabbies or bargees when they chant their melancholy songs. Antipka found the sight horrifying and stopped peeping. When Gerasim left his little room the next day, there was no particular change in him. He simply appeared a little more sombre and paid not the slightest attention to either Tatyana or Kapiton. On that evening they both went to the lady of the house with a goose under their arm and in a week were married. On the day of the wedding Gerasim did not change his behaviour at all, save that he did not bring water from the river; somehow or other en route he broke the water-barrel and at night, in the stables, he was so assiduous in cleaning and brushing his horse that the animal shook like a blade of grass in the wind and tumbled about from one leg to the other under his iron fists.

All this occurred in the spring. Another year passed, during which Kapiton finally drank himself out of a job and, like a man who has shown himself good for nothing, was despatched in one of the convoys to a distant village along with his wife. On the day of his departure he began by putting on a very brave face and declaring that no matter where he was sent, even if it was where women wash shirts and behave like lumberjacks, he'd still get by; but later his spirits dropped and he started complaining that he was being taken away to live with a lot of uneducated folk, and ended by becoming so feeble that he couldn't even put his own cap on and some compassionate soul stuck it on his temples, put the peak in the right place and then smartly pushed the cap down on his head. When everything was ready and the peasant drivers already had the reins in their hands and were simply awaiting the words 'God be with you!', Gerasim emerged from his little room, went up to Tatyana and gave her a going-away present of a red cotton kerchief which he had bought for her a year before. Tatyana who until that moment had endured all the degradations of her life with a great show of outward indifference broke down at this, burst into tears and, sitting in the cart, kissed Gerasim three times with true Christian affection. He had wanted to accompany her to the city limits and began by walking beside her cart, but suddenly stopped at the Crimean ford, waved his hand and set off walking alongside the river.

Evening was approaching. He walked quietly and gazed at the water. Suddenly he noticed something floundering in the slime by the bank. He went down and saw a small puppy, white with black spots, which, despite all its efforts, couldn't get out of the water, struggled, slid back and shivered with every inch of its wretchedly thin, wet body. Gerasim looked at the miserable little dog, seized it with one hand, thrust it inside his shirt and set off home with giant steps. He went to his room, set the rescued pup down on his bed, covered it with his heavy coat and then dashed off first to the stables to get some straw and afterwards to the kitchen to get a bowl of milk. Carefully removing the heavy coat and spreading out the straw, he placed the bowl of milk on the bed. The puppy, poor thing, was only three weeks old and its eyes had only fully opened quite recently. One eye even seemed slightly larger than the other. It didn't know how to drink out of the bowl and simply shivered and puckered its eyes. Gerasim took it very gently by the head, using two fingers, and drew its little mouth down towards the milk. The puppy suddenly began drinking thirstily, snorting, shaking and lapping busily. Gerasim watched and watched and then suddenly laughed . . . All night long he tended the puppy, laying it down and rubbing it, and finally he fell asleep beside it, succumbing to quiet and blissful slumber.

No mother looked after her child more than Gerasim cared for his puppy. (It turned out to be a bitch.) To start with it was very feeble, puny and ugly, but gradually it recovered and grew to its right size, and after eight months or so, due to the tireless attentions of its saviour, it had turned into a very fine spaniel bitch, with long ears, a full, flowing tail and large expressive eyes. She grew passionately devoted to Gerasim and never left him for a moment, following him wherever he went with wagging tail. He even gave her a name – the dumb know that their moaning sounds attract people's attention – and he called his dog Mumu. Everyone in the house fell in love with the dog and also called her Mumu. She was extraordinarily intelligent and friendly with everyone, but it was Gerasim alone whom she loved. Gerasim himself loved her to distraction . . . and he was unhappy when others stroked her, though whether he was fearful what might happen to her or jealous of her God knows! She would wake him in the morning, pulling at the hem of his coat, and by pulling the reins in her mouth, would bring him the old horse used for water-carrying, with whom she lived on very friendly terms. She would accompany Gerasim down to the river with an important look on her face, stand guard over his brooms and spades and allow no one into his little room. He made an opening for her in his door, and she somehow understood that she was completely mistress of her surroundings only in Gerasim's room and therefore whenever she entered she at once jumped on to the bed with a look of satisfaction. At night she did not sleep at all, but she never barked without good reason, not like some stupid mongrels that sit on their hind legs with muzzle raised and eyes half-shut barking at the stars out of sheer boredom – and usually barking three times in a row! No, Mumu's delicate little bark never resounded for nothing: either it was a stranger close to the fence or some suspicious noise or rustling . . . In a word, she was an excellent guard-dog. True, apart from her there was another dog in the yard, an old yellow cur with brown markings called Wolf, but he was never let off the chain even at night and, due to his feebleness, made no demands to be set free – he just lay curled up in his kennel and only occasionally emitted a drowsy, almost noiseless bark, which he would cut short at once, as if he himself knew how useless it was. Mumu did not go into the main house and when Gerasim used to carry the logs into the rooms she always remained behind and impatiently waited for him at the door, pricking up her ears and turning her head to left and right at the slightest sound on the other side.

In this way a year passed. Gerasim continued his activities as yardman and was quite content with his lot, when suddenly something unexpected happened . . .

One fine summer day the lady of the house was walking round her drawing-room with her lady companions. She was in good spirits, laughing and joking; her companions joined in without feeling any particular joy: they were never fond of the times when the mistress was in a good mood because, firstly, she insisted on everyone instantly joining in to the full and was annoyed if someone's face did not show radiant pleasure and, secondly, these moments of elation did not last long and were usually replaced by a sombre and sour frame of mind. That day she had risen in a happy mood; four jacks, meaning the fulfilment of desires, had turned up in her card-telling (she told cards each morning) and her morning tea had seemed to her particularly tasty, for which her maid had received praise by word of mouth and ten copecks by way of financial reward. With a sweet smile on her wrinkled lips the lady of the house walked round her drawing-room and went up to the window. In front of the window a garden had been made and in the middle flower-bed, under a rose bush, Mumu was lying and busily gnawing at a bone. The lady of the house saw her.

'My God,' she cried suddenly, 'what's that dog doing there?'
The lady companion to whom these words were addressed became

flustered, poor thing, with that very same sense of panic which seizes hold of any subordinate who does not know exactly how to take the exclamation of a superior.

'N . . . n . . . no idea, ma'am,' she muttered. 'It looks like the dumb man's.'

'My God!' the lady of the house broke in. 'But such a nice little dog! Have her brought here! Has he had her long? Why haven't I seen her before? Have her brought here.'

The lady companion at once dashed into the hall.

'Boy! Boy!' she cried. 'Fetch Mumu in here! She's in the garden.'

'So she's called Mumu,' said the lady of the house. 'A very good name.'

'Oh, very, ma'am!' responded the lady companion. 'As quick as you can, Stepan!'

Stepan, a sturdy lad employed as a footman, rushed headlong into the garden and was on the point of seizing Mumu, but she skilfully slipped through his fingers and, tail high, raced away to find Gerasim who was at that time engaged in the kitchen in knocking out and shaking out a barrel, turning it this way and that in his hands like a child's drum. Stepan dashed after her and began trying to catch hold of her by her master's very feet, but the nimble little dog would not submit to a stranger's hands, jumped and evaded capture. Gerasim observed all this fuss and bother with a grin. Finally Stepan got to his feet in annoyance and hurriedly explained by signs that the lady of the house was asking for his dog. Gerasim was slightly astonished, but nevertheless called Mumu, lifted her up and handed her to Stepan. Stepan took her into the drawing-room and set her down on the parquet floor. The lady of the house began coaxing the dog towards her. Mumu, who had never in her life been in such a magnificent room, was absolutely terrified and tried dashing to the door but, cut off by the obedient Stepan, started quivering and pressing herself to the wall.

'Mumu, Mumu, come to me, come to your mistress,' said the lady of the house, 'come on, you silly thing . . . don't be frightened . . .'

'Go on, Mumu, go to your mistress,' the lady companions reiterated. 'Go on.'

But Mumu looked miserably round her and would not budge.

'Bring her something to eat,' said the lady of the house. 'What a silly thing she is! She won't come to her mistress. What's she afraid of?'

'She's not used to it yet,' said one of the companions in a small and ingratiating voice.

Stepan brought a saucer of milk and set it in front of Mumu, but Mumu did not even sniff at it and continued shivering and looking round her.

'Ah, you're a one!' said the lady of the house, approaching her, and bent down intending to stroke her, but Mumu jerked her head round and bared her teeth. The lady quickly withdrew her hand.

There was a momentary silence. Mumu whined softly as if appealing and apologising. The lady stepped back and frowned. The dog's sudden movement had frightened her.

'Oh!' the lady companions cried all at once. 'She hasn't bitten you, has she, God preserve us?' (Mumu had never bitten anyone in her life.) 'Oh, oh!'

'Take her away!' ordered the old woman in an entirely different voice. 'A disgusting little dog! What a nasty animal she is!'

And, slowly turning on her heel, she went off to her boudoir. The lady companions timidly exchanged looks and were on the point of following her, but she stopped, looked coldly at them, said abruptly: 'Why are you following? I didn't ask you to,' and left.

The ladies made desperate signs to Stepan; he seized Mumu and cast her quickly out through the door, right at the feet of Gerasim – and half an hour later profound silence reigned in the house, and the elderly mistress sat on her divan looking more sombre than a thunder-cloud.

Just think, what silly little things can sometimes upset a person!

Until evening the lady of the house was out of sorts, talked to no one, did not play cards and had a bad night. She was sure the eau-de-cologne she was given was not the usual kind, that her pillow had a soapy smell, and she made the linen maid sniff through all the linen – in short, she was in a state and very 'worked up'. The following morning she ordered Gavrila to her an hour sooner than usual.

'Tell me, please,' she began as soon as the latter, not without a certain inner trepidation, had entered her boudoir, 'what dog is it in the yard that barks all night? I couldn't get a wink of sleep!'

'A dog, ma'am ... which one, ma'am? .. perhaps it's the dumb man's,' he said in a voice that was not quite firm.

'I don't know whether it's the dumb man's or somebody else's, it simply doesn't let me sleep. It surprises me we have such a mass of dogs! I'd like to know why. We have a yard dog, don't we?'

'Yes, ma'am, that's so, ma'am. Wolf, ma'am.'

'Well, why should we need to have another dog? It only causes more trouble. There's no one really in charge in the house, that's what's wrong. Why should that dumb man have a dog? Who allowed him to keep a dog out in my yard? Yesterday I went to the window and I saw her lying in the garden, she'd brought some filthy thing in with her and was gnawing it – and that's where my roses are planted!'

The lady of the house was silent a moment.

'See to it that the dog is got rid of this very day – do you hear?'

'Yes, ma'am.'

'This very day. Now see to it. I'll want to hear your report later on.'

Gavrila left.

As he went through the drawing-room, the steward moved a little bell from one table to the other for the sake of appearances, very discreetly blew his duckbill of a nose in the hall and went out into the porch. In the porch Stepan was asleep on a shelf, in the pose of a slain warrior in a war painting with his naked legs stuck grotesquely out from beneath a coat that served him as a bed-cover. The steward poked him and gave him an order in a low voice to which Stepan responded with a mixture of a yawn and a laugh. The steward went on his way and Stepan jumped up, pulled on a caftan and shoes and then went and stood by the steps. Before five minutes were out Gerasim had appeared with an enormous bundle of logs on his back, accompanied by the ever faithful Mumu. The lady of the house had ordered her bedroom and boudoir to be kept heated even during the summer. Gerasim leaned against the door, gave it a heave with his shoulder and staggered into the house with his load. As usual, Mumu stayed outside to await his return. It was then that Stepan, choosing a suitable moment, suddenly sprang on her, like a kite swooping on a chicken, wrestled her to the ground, grabbed her in his arms and without even putting on his cap dashed into the yard, hired the first cab that came by and galloped to Hunters Row. There he quickly found a purchaser to whom he sold her for a small coin on condition she was kept on a leash for at least a week, and then he at once returned home; but before reaching the house he got out of the cab and, circling the yard from the outside, jumped over the fence by a back way, for he was frightened of going in by the front gate since he might have met Gerasim.

In any case, his apprehensions were groundless: Gerasim wasn't in the yard. As soon as he had come out of the house he missed Mumu. He couldn't recall a time when she hadn't waited for him to return and he immediately started running about, searching for her and calling her after his fashion – rushing to his own room, looking in the hay-loft, darting out into the street, to and fro . . . She was lost! He turned frantically to the servants, in desperate sign-language asked after her, indicated her height from the ground, drew her in the air with his hands . . . Some of them simply had no idea where Mumu had gone and could only shake their heads, others knew and giggled at him, and the steward adopted a particularly self-important expression and started shouting at the coachmen. At that Gerasim ran right out of the yard.

It was already growing dark when he returned. Judging by his exhausted appearance, his unsteady walk and the dust on his clothes, one might have supposed that he had managed to run round half of Moscow. He stopped in front of the windows of the lady of the house, his eyes swept over the steps on which more than half-a-dozen of the servants had gathered, he turned round and once more moaned: 'Mumu!' Mumu didn't answer. He went away. They all watched him go, but no one smiled, no one said a word . . . And the ever inquisitive postilion Antipka narrated in the kitchen the next day how the dumb man had spent the night sighing and groaning.

The whole of the following day Gerasim did not appear, so that the coachman Potap had to go for the water in place of him, with which the coachman Potap was very dissatisfied. The lady of the house asked Gavrila whether her orders had been carried out. Gavrila said they had. The next morning Gerasim came out of his room to go to work. He appeared at dinner, ate and went away, greeting no one. His face, lifeless at best, as are the faces of all deaf and dumb people, had now literally turned to stone. After dinner he again left the yard for a while, but not for long, came back and at once disappeared into the hay-loft. It was a clear, moonlit night. Sighing heavily and ceaselessly turning from side to side, Gerasim lay there – and suddenly he felt something pulling at the hem of his coat; he started quivering all over, but he did not raise his head, even frowned; but again there came the pulling, stronger than before; he jumped up . . . Right in front of him, with a bit of cord round her neck, was Mumu twisting round and round. A strangled cry of joy was torn from his wordless breast; he seized Mumu

MUMU

and hugged her tightly; while she in one instant licked his nose, eyes, whiskers and beard . . . He stood still a moment, thought, carefully slid down from the hay, looked around him and, having made certain that no one had seen him, safely made his way to his own room. Gerasim had already guessed that the dog had not got lost of her own accord but had been taken away on the mistress's orders; the servants had made it known to him through signs how his Mumu had snapped at her – and he decided to take his own steps. First of all he fed Mumu some bread, fondled her and laid her down to sleep, and then he began to think over – and spent the whole night thinking over – how best to keep her hidden. Finally he hit upon the idea of leaving her all day in his room and visiting her from time to time, while at night he would take her out. He blocked up the hole in the door with his old sheepskin coat and as soon as it was daylight had gone into the yard as if nothing had happened, even pre- serving (such innocent cunning!) the former stony look of despondency on his face. The poor deaf and dumb man couldn't conceive that Mumu would give herself away with her whining: in fact, everyone in the house soon knew that the dumb man's dog had returned and was locked up in his room, but out of compassion for her and perhaps partly out of fear of him they did not let on to him that they knew his secret. The steward was the only one to scratch the back of his neck and then dismiss the matter with a wave of the hand as if to say: 'Well, the good Lord be with him! Just so long as the lady of the house doesn't get to hear it!' In any case, the dumb man was never so assiduous in his work as he was that day: he cleaned and raked the whole yard, pulled out all the weeds, pulled up by hand all the fencing surrounding the flower- garden to see if the stakes were strong enough and then personally knocked them back into place – in a word, he busied himself and made such a big thing of his work that even the lady of the house noticed his zeal. In the course of the day Gerasim made one or two stealthy visits to see his prisoner; and when night came he lay down to sleep with her in his own room, not in the hay-loft, and only after one o'clock in the morning took her out into the open air. Having walked her round the yard for a while he was on the point of returning to his room when there was suddenly a rustling sound from the other side of the fence that backed on to a side street. Mumu pricked up her ears, growled, ap- proached the fence, sniffed and emitted a series of loud and penetrating barks. Some drunk or other had chosen that place to spend the night.

At that very moment the lady of the house had only just fallen asleep after prolonged 'nervous excitement': these excitements always occurred after she had had a particularly substantial dinner. The sudden barking awoke her; her heart beat violently and she started to sink away. 'Girls, girls!' she cried out. 'Girls!' The frightened girls dashed into her bedroom. 'Oh, oh, I'm dying!' she declared, waving her arms in desperation. 'It's that dog again! Oh, send for the doctor! They're trying to kill me . . . That dog, that dog again! Oh!' and she threw back her head in a way which made it seem she had fainted. They dashed for the doctor, that is to say for Khariton, the household's private physician. This physician, whose entire expertise consisted in wearing boots with soft soles, knew how to take her pulse delicately, slept fourteen hours out of the twenty-four and spent the rest of the time sighing and plying his mistress with laurel water – this physician instantly came to her aid, fumigated the room with burnt feathers and, when the lady of the house opened her eyes, quickly brought her a wine-glass of the hallowed laurel water on a silver tray. The lady took the glass, but at once started complaining in a tearful voice about the dog, about Gavrila, about her fate, about the fact that everyone had abandoned her, poor old woman that she was, that no one had any pity for her and everyone was trying to kill her. Meanwhile, the unfortunate Mumu went on barking and Gerasim tried in vain to summon her away from the fence. 'There it is, there it is again,' babbled the lady of the house, and again rolled up her eyes. The physician whispered to one of the girls, who rushed to the porch, awakened Stepan, who ran to wake up Gavrila and Gavrila gave the alarm throughout the entire house.

Gerasim turned round, saw lights flashing and shadows in the windows and, sensing in his heart that misfortune was on the way, seized Mumu under his arm, ran to his room and locked himself in. In a few seconds five men were banging against his door but stopped when they found it was tightly bolted. Gavrila rushed up in frightful excitement, ordered the men to stay there until morning and keep guard, while he himself bolted into the maids' quarters and through an elderly lady-companion, Lyubov Lyubimova, with whom he used to steal tea, sugar and other groceries and then adjust the accounts, ordered the lady of the house to be told that the dog had unfortunately come back again from somewhere, but that tomorrow she would be got rid of for good and all and would the lady of the house, please, be gracious and not be angry and go back to sleep. The lady of the house would, no doubt, hardly have gone back to sleep so quickly had not the physician poured her not her usual twelve but a full forty drops, with the result that the laurel water did its job – in a quarter of an hour the lady of the house was soundly and peacefully asleep; and Gerasim lay white-faced on his bed with a firm grip over Mumu's muzzle.

The next morning the lady of the house awoke fairly late. Gavrila waited for her to wake up in order to give the order for a decisive assault on Gerasim's hide-out and meanwhile prepared himself to endure the thunderstorm of her rage. But no thunderstorm occurred. Lying in bed, the lady of the house ordered her elderly lady-companion to be brought to her.

'Lyubov Lyubimova,' she began in a soft and feeble voice; she sometimes enjoyed playing the role of a persecuted and solitary martyr to misfortune; whenever this happened, it scarcely needs saying, everyone in the house became extremely nervous; 'Lyubov Lyubimova, you see the state I'm in. Go to Gavrila Andreich, my dear, and ask him whether some good-for-nothing little dog is dearer to him than the peace of mind and the very life of his mistress. I wouldn't want to believe that it was,' she added with a look of deep feeling. 'Go on, my dear, be so good as to go to Gavrila Andreich.'

Lyubov Lyubimova went to Gavrila's room. It is not known what conversation occurred between them; but after a certain time a whole crowd of people moved across the yard in the direction of Gerasim's room, led by Gavrila holding his cap on his head, although there was no wind, and surrounded by footmen and cooks. Uncle Ragtail peered out of a window and gave them directions, that is to say he simply waved his arms about. At the back of the crowd came jumping and running a lot of small boys, half of whom were strangers. On the narrow stairway leading to the room one guard was sitting and two more were stationed by the door with sticks. The crowd began climbing the stairway and soon occupied its entire length. Gavrila approached the door, banged on it with his fist and called out:

'Open up!'

There came the sound of smothered barking; but no answer.

'I'm telling you to open up!' he repeated.

'Gavrila Andreich,' remarked Stepan from below, 'he's deaf, he doesn't hear.'

Everyone burst out laughing.

'So what?' said Gavrila from above.

'He's got a hole in the door,' answered Stepan. 'Poke a stick in and waggle it about.'

Gavrila bent down.

'He's stuck a coat in it, he's stuffed up the hole.'

'Then you push the coat in.'

There was another smothered bark.

'See, see – she speaks for herself,' someone remarked in the crowd, and again there was a roar of laughter.

Gavrila scratched himself behind the ear.

'No, my good fellow,' he went on at last, 'you can come and poke in the coat yourself if you want to.'

'Right, just let me!'

And Stepan scrambled up the stairway, took hold of a stick, poked the coat in and began waggling the stick about in the opening and shouting: 'Come out, come out!' He was still waggling the stick about when the door of the room suddenly opened wide – and the entire crowd dashed head over heels down the stairway, Gavrila faster than any. Uncle Ragtail locked his window.

'Hey, hey, hey, hey,' shouted Gavrila from the yard, 'just you look what you're doing, just you mind out!'

Gerasim stood motionless in the doorway. The crowd gathered at the foot of the stairs. Gerasim gazed down at all these little people in German caftans gathered below him, his hands resting lightly on his waist; in his red peasant shirt he looked like some giant by comparison. Gavrila took a step forward.

'Look here, my good fellow,' he said, 'don't play the fool with me.'

And he began by signs to explain to him that the lady of the house had said, 'I want your dog dealt with at once; give her to me now or there'll be trouble.'

Gerasim looked at him, indicated the dog, made a gesture with his hand at his neck as though tightening a noose and glanced with a questioning face at the steward.

'Yes, yes,' the other replied, nodding his head, 'yes, at once.'

Gerasim lowered his eyes, then suddenly shook himself, again pointed at Mumu, who had been standing beside him all the while innocently wagging her tail and pricking up her ears, repeated the gesture of strangulation at his own neck and struck himself meaningfully on the chest as if declaring that he would take it upon himself to get rid of Mumu.

'Oh, you won't really do it!' Gavrila responded with a wave of the hand.

Gerasim gave him a look, grinned scornfully at him, again struck himself on the chest and banged his door to behind him.

Everyone exchanged glances in silence.

'What's this mean?' Gavrila began asking. 'What's he locked his door for?'

'Leave him be, Gavrila Andreich,' said Stepan. 'If he's promised something, he'll do it. He's like that . . . If he's promised something, he'll keep his word. He's not like us in that way. The truth's the truth for him, that's for sure.'

'Yes,' they all repeated and nodded their heads, 'that's true, it certainly is.'

Uncle Ragtail opened his window and also said: 'It certainly is.'

'All right, we'll wait and see,' said Gavrila. 'But we'll keep a guard posted. Hey, you, Yeroshka!' he added, addressing a pale-faced chap in a yellow nankeen coat who was considered to be a gardener. 'Are you doing anything? Take a stick and sit here, and as soon as anything happens run along to me at once!'

Yeroshka took a stick and sat down on the bottom step of the stairs. The crowd dispersed with the exception of a few inquisitive ones and some small boys, and Gavrila meanwhile returned to his house and ordered Lyubov Lyubimova to tell the mistress that everything had been taken care of, but in any case for his own part he sent the postilion off to inform the local policeman. The lady of the house tied a knot in her handkerchief, poured some eau-de-cologne on it, sniffed it, rubbed her temples with it, drank some tea and, being still under the influence of the laurel water, fell asleep again.

About an hour after all this excitement the door of the room opened and Gerasim appeared. He was wearing his holiday caftan and he was leading Mumu on a string. Yeroshka stepped aside and let him pass. Gerasim went towards the gates. The little boys and all the rest of the people in the yard followed him with their eyes in silence. He did not even turn to look at them; he put on his cap only when he had reached the street. Gavrila sent Yeroshka after him as an observer. Yeroshka saw from a distance that he and his dog had gone into a tavern and started waiting for him to come out.

In the tavern they knew Gerasim and understood his sign language. He ordered cabbage soup and meat and sat down with his arms on the table. Mumu stood beside his chair, looking at him calmly with her intelligent eyes. Her coat literally shone: clearly she had only recently been combed. They brought Gerasim his cabbage soup. He broke some bread into it, cut up the meat into small pieces and set the bowl down on the floor. Mumu started eating with her customary delicacy, her muzzle hardly touching her food. Gerasim studied her for a long time; two heavy tears rolled suddenly out of his eyes: one fell on the dog's forehead, the other into the soup. He covered his face with his hand. Mumu ate half the bowl and walked away licking herself. Gerasim stood up, paid for the soup and left, accompanied by the rather puzzled gaze of the waiter. Yeroshka, seeing Gerasim, darted round a corner and, having let him pass by, again took to following him.

Gerasim walked without hurrying and did not let Mumu off the string. Reaching the corner of the street he stopped, as if in two minds, and suddenly set off with rapid strides straight towards the Crimean ford. On the way he went into the yard of a house to which a new wing was being added and picked up a couple of bricks, holding them under his arm. At the Crimean ford he turned along the bank of the river and came to a place where there were two rowing-boats with oars fastened to posts (he had noted them before) and he jumped into one of them along with Mumu. A lame old man came out from behind a hut perched in one corner of a kitchen garden and shouted at him. But Gerasim simply gave a shake of the head and set about rowing so strongly, even though it was against the flow of the river, that in an instant he had gone a hundred metres and more upstream. The old man went on standing there, scratched his back first with his left hand, then with his right, and turned away limping to the hut.

And Gerasim rowed and rowed. Moscow fell far behind. The banks stretching on either side were full of meadows: gardens, fields, copses and peasant huts came into view. It had a smell of the country. He cast aside the oars, bent his head down to Mumu who sat in front of him on a dry crosspiece – the bottom of the boat was full of water – and remained motionless with his powerful arms folded across her back while the boat was gently carried by the flow of the river towards the city.

MUMU

Finally Gerasim sat up straight, hurriedly, with a look of sickly bitterness on his face, tied the bricks together with string, made a noose, placed it round Mumu's neck, lifted her over the river, looked at her for the last time . . . Trustingly and without fear she looked at him and slightly wagged her tail. He turned away, grimaced and let go . . . Gerasim heard nothing, neither the quick whining of the falling Mumu, nor the heavy splash in the water; for him the noisiest day was still and soundless, as not even the quietest night can be soundless for us; and when he again opened his eyes the little waves were as ever hurrying along the river's surface, as if racing after each other, as ever they rippled against the sides of the boat, and only far behind one or two broad rings rippled towards the bank.

Yeroshka, as soon as Gerasim had gone from sight, returned home and reported what he had seen.

'Well, yes,' remarked Stepan, 'that means he'll drown her. There's no need to worry. If he's promised . . .'

In the course of the day no one saw Gerasim. He did not have dinner at home. Evening came; everyone gathered for supper except him.

'He's a wonder, is that Gerasim!' whined a fat laundrymaid. 'To get so soppy over a dog! I ask you!'

'Gerasim's been back,' exclaimed Stepan suddenly, spooning up his grits.

'What? When?'

'A couple of hours ago. You see, I met him in the gateway – he was going out again, going out of the yard. I wanted to ask him about the dog, but he didn't look like he was in the mood. He just gave me a shove, as if he just wanted me out of his way, as if he'd said, you know: "Don't get in my way!" but he gave me such a bash on the back oy-oy-oy it hurt!' And Stepan hunched himself up with an involuntary laugh and rubbed the nape of his neck. 'Yes,' he added, 'he's got one mighty big hand, he has!'

They all laughed at Stepan and after supper went off to sleep.

Meanwhile, at that very moment, there went striding away ceaselessly and diligently along the T— highroad a veritable giant of a man with a sack over his shoulder and a stick in his hand. This was Gerasim. He was hurrying along without a backward glance, hurrying home, to his own place in the village, to his native regions. After drowning poor Mumu he had rushed to his room, briskly stuffed some belongings into an old horse-cloth, tied it with a knot, flung it over his shoulder and set off. He had taken note of the road when they'd first brought him to Moscow; the village from which the lady of the house had taken him lay only about twenty miles off the highroad, which he now strode along with a kind of unconquerable valour, with a desperate and yet joyous resoluteness. He strode on and his chest expanded, his eyes directed hungrily and fixedly ahead. He hurried on his way, as though his old mother were awaiting him in his native land, as though she were calliming him back to her after long wanderings in foreign parts and among strangers . . . The summer night which had just fallen was calm and warm; on the one hand, where the sun had just set the edge of the sky still shone white and there was a faint blush as the last light of day ebbed – and on the other hand there rose up like a cloud a blue, greyish darkness. The night was coming from that direction. Quails in their hundreds pealed out their songs all around and corncrakes vied with each other in their calls . . . Gerasim could not hear them, could not even hear the delicate nocturnal rustlings of the trees past which his strong legs carried him, but he could smell the familiar scent of the ripening rye which wafted in from the dark fields, could feel how the wind flying to meet him – the wind from his homeland – softly played against his face and in his hair and beard; he saw before him the road shining white – the homeward road, straight as an arrow; he saw in the sky the countless stars lighting up his way and stepped out strong and bold as a lion, so that when the rising sun shed its moist red rays on the intrepid fellow who was just on the point of feeling exhausted, thirty miles already lay between him and Moscow.

In two days he was already home and in his small hut, to the great astonishment of the soldier's wife who had been installed in it. After praying before the icon, he at once set off to see the village headman. The headman was amazed at first; but the haymaking had just begun and so Gerasim, as an outstanding worker, was there and then given a scythe – and off he went scything away as in the old days, scything fit to make the peasants stare at his broad strokes and the piles of hay for raking.

But in Moscow, on the day after Gerasim's leaving, he was missed. They went into his room, turned it upside down and told Gavrila. He came and took a look, shrugged his shoulders and decided that the dumb man had either run away or drowned along with his stupid dog. The police were informed and so was the lady of the house. She flew into a temper, shed tears, ordered him to be found no matter what happened, avowed that she'd never ordered the dog to be destroyed and finally gave Gavrila such a dressing-down that he spent the whole day shaking his head and declaring 'Well I never!' until Uncle Ragtail made him see reason by telling him 'Well I never did, never did!' News eventually came from the village about Gerasim's arrival there. The lady of the house grew a little calmer; she started by giving an order that he should be brought back to Moscow without delay; afterwards, however, she announced that she had no need of such an ungrateful fellow. In any case, she died soon after that and her heirs weren't interested in Gerasim; and all the rest of the old woman's servants were dispersed on payment of quit-rent.

And to this day Gerasim lives by himself in his solitary hut, as healthy and strong as ever, and as ever he does the work of four men, and as ever he is solemn and staid. But the neighbours have noticed that since his return from Moscow he has given up women, doesn't even look at them, and he doesn't keep any kind of dog. 'Besides,' as the local peasants put it, 'it's not needing women keeps 'im so happy, and as for a dog – you wouldn't find a thief breaking into his place for love nor money!' Such is the dumb man's reputation for fabulous strength.

Asya

I was then about twenty-five (N. N. began) – as you can see, these matters belong to years long past. I had just broken free of my home and gone abroad – not in order to 'finish my education', as they put it in those days, but simply because I wanted to see what God's world looked like. I was healthy, young and happy, my money hadn't yet run out, worries hadn't yet succeeded in accumulating. I lived without a care and did just what I wanted – in a word, I flourished. In those days it never entered my head that a man is not a plant and can't flourish for long. Youth eats all the sugared fancy cakes and regards them as its daily bread. But there'll come a time when you'll start asking just for a crust. Still, that's not the point now.

I travelled without aim or plan. I stopped wherever I felt like it and set off again as soon as I felt the desire to see new faces. Only faces. People were my only interest. I loathed interesting monuments and note-worthy collections, one glimpse of a guide aroused in me a sensation of boredom and annoyance. I almost went out of my mind in the Dresden Grüne-Gewölbe.* Nature had an extraordinarily powerful effect on me, but I had no liking for its so-called beauties, such as remarkable mountains, crags and waterfalls. I didn't want it to solicit me and get in my way. But faces, living, human faces – the talk of people, their movements, their laughter – these things I couldn't do without. I was always particularly happy and at ease in a crowd. I was glad to follow others and shout when the others shouted, and at the same time I enjoyed watching the others shouting. I enjoyed observing people. Oh, it wasn't just that I observed them – I used to study them closely with a kind of rapt and insatiable curiosity. But again I'm digressing.

So, about twenty years ago, I was staying in the small German town of Z— on the left bank of the Rhine. I was seeking solitude. I had just had my heart broken by a young widow whom I'd met at a watering-place. She'd been very good-looking and intelligent, had flirted with everyone, me included, poor sinner, even encouraging me at first and afterwards wounding me cruelly when she threw me up for a red-cheeked Bavarian lieutenant. I have to confess that the wound to my heart was not very deep. But I considered it a duty to give myself over for some while to grief and loneliness – what doesn't youth enjoy doing! – and had settled in Z––.

This small town delighted me with its position at the foot of two tall hills, with its ancient walls and towers, its age-old lime-trees, its steep bridge over a sparkling river that ran down into the Rhine – but mainly I was delighted with its wine. Along its narrow streets each evening, just after sunset (it was June), there strolled extremely pretty fair-haired German girls and whenever they came across a foreigner they would say 'Guten Abend' in their pleasant soft voices – and some of them were still out strolling even when the moon had risen above the sharp-ended rooftops of the old houses and the smallest cobblestones of the streets were clearly outlined in its motionless beams. I loved wandering about the town at that time. The moon, it seemed, would stare down fixedly at it out of a clear sky, and the town would sense this gaze and keep still and peaceful, bathed in its light, that calm light which was at the same time so quietly exciting to the soul. The weather-cock on a high Gothic bell-tower gleamed the colour of pale gold. The wavelets on the lustrous blackness of the little river were criss-crossed with the same gold colour. Tiny candles (German economy!) burned modestly in the narrow windows beneath the slate roofs. Vines mysteriously poked out their curled tendrils from behind stone walls. Something darted in the shadow round the ancient well in the three-cornered square, the sleepy whistle of a night watchman resounded suddenly, a well-meaning dog growled, and the air literally caressed the face and the lime-trees smelt so sweet that one's lungs breathed deeper and deeper and the word 'Gretchen' came to one's lips, half cry, half question.

The town of Z–– is a couple of miles from the Rhine. I often went to take a look at the mighty river and, dreaming not without a certain effort about the treacherous widow, I would spend long hours on a stone seat under a solitary outspreading ash-tree. The small statue of a madonna with an almost childish face and a red heart on her bosom, pierced with swords, gazed sadly from among its branches. On the opposite bank

ASYA

was the town of L—, slightly larger than the one where I was staying.
One evening I was sitting on my favourite seat and gazing either at
the river or the sky or the vines. In front of me fair-haired boys were
clambering up the sides of a boat which had been dragged ashore and
upturned, its tarred bottom sticking upwards. Small boats floated quietly
by with limp sails and greenish waves slid past, barely swelling and
murmuring. Suddenly sounds of music came to me; I listened. In the
town of L— a waltz was being played. The double bass boomed out
sharply, the violin poured out indistinctly and the flute piped away
vigorously.

'What's that?' I asked an old man who approached me in a velveteen
waistcoat, blue stockings and shoes with buckles.

'That,' he answered, shifting the mouthpiece of his pipe from one
corner of his mouth to the other before speaking, 'that is students who've
come from B— for a Kommers.'

I'll take a look at this Kommers, I thought. In any case, I've never been
in L—. I sought out a ferryman and crossed to the other bank.

[2]

Perhaps not everyone knows what a Kommers (pron. *kommersh*) is. It
is a special kind of festival at which students of one region or brother-
hood (Landsmannschaft) gather together. Almost all participants in
a Kommers wear the long-established uniform of German students:
Hungarian jackets, large boots and small hats with cap-bands of certain
colours. The students usually gather for dinner under the chairmanship
of a senior, who is their president, and engage in revelry until morning,
drinking, singing songs such as Landesvater or Gaudeamus, smoking
and ridiculing all non-students. Sometimes they hire a band.

Precisely this kind of Kommers was taking place in the town of L— in
front of a small inn, under an overhanging sign of the sun, in a garden
overlooking the street. Flags fluttered above the inn and the garden
and the students were sitting at tables under lime-trees that had been
subjected to a special kind of topiary. An enormous bulldog lay under
one of the tables. To one side, in an ivy-covered arbour, were situated
the musicians and they played away zealously, fortifying themselves
from time to time with beer. A fairly large crowd had gathered on the
street, before the low garden wall: the good citizens of L— had no wish

to pass up the opportunity of having a good stare at their visiting guests. I also joined in the crowd of spectators and enjoyed watching the faces of the students. The way they embraced each other and called to each other, the innocent posturings of youth, the fiery glances, the involuntary laughter – the best laughter in the world – all this delighted ferment of life that was fresh and youthful, this burning desire to rush ahead – anywhere, so long as it was forward – all this well-meaning expansiveness touched and excited me. 'Should I join them?' I asked myself.

'Asya, have you seen enough?' a man's voice suddenly asked behind me in Russian.

'Let's stay a bit longer,' answered another, a woman's, voice in the same language.

I quickly turned round. My gaze fell upon a handsome young man in a cap and loosely fitting jacket. He was holding the arm of a girl of modest height wearing a straw hat which hid the upper half of her face.

'You're Russian?' broke from me.

The young man smiled and said:

'Yes, we're Russian.'

'I hadn't expected . . . in such a back of beyond,' I started saying.

'And we hadn't expected either,' he interrupted me. 'So much the better, eh? Let me do the introducing – I am Gagin and this is my . . .' he hesitated for one instant, 'my sister. And your name is?'

I gave my name and we started chatting. I learned that Gagin, travelling, as I was, for his own enjoyment, had reached L— a week ago – and had got stuck there. To tell the truth, I was unwilling to get to know Russians abroad. I would know them from a distance by their walk, the cut of their clothes and chiefly by the expression on their faces. Smug and disdainful, frequently supercilious, it was an expression that could change suddenly to one of caution and timidity, just as if the whole man had suddenly been put on his guard, the eyes darting to and fro ('My God, I've just made a complete fool of myself and they're all laughing at me!' this hurried look seemed to say). Then the instant would pass and the high and mighty look would return to the features, alternating with a look of blank incomprehension. Yes, I made a point of avoiding Russians, but I felt drawn to Gagin at once. There are in the world certain happy faces: one likes looking at them because it's just as if they warm you or soothe you. Gagin had a face like that – charming, kindly, with large soft eyes and soft curly hair. He spoke in such a way that, even if you couldn't see his face, you'd feel simply by the sound of his voice that he was smiling.

The girl whom he called his sister seemed to me from the first glance to be extremely attractive. There was something particularly her own in the shape of her dark-skinned round face, with its small delicate nose, almost child-like cheeks and black, shining eyes. She had a graceful figure, but she did not seem as yet fully grown. She in no way resembled her brother.

'Would you like to come to our place?' Gagin asked me. 'I think we've had enough of looking at Germans. Our students would have smashed all the glasses and broken all the chairs, you can be sure, but these are dreadfully modest! What do you think, Asya, shall we go home?'

The girl nodded her head affirmatively.

'We are living outside the town,' Gagin went on, 'in a vineyard, in a little cottage, high up. It's marvellous there, you'll see. Our landlady has promised to prepare some sour milk. It'll be dark soon now, and it'll be better for you to cross the Rhine in the moonlight.'

We set off. Through the low gates of the town (it was encircled on all sides by a cobblestone wall and even the embrasures had remained intact) we went out into open country and, after going about a hundred yards beside a stone wall, stopped before a narrow gate. Gagin opened it and led us up the hillside by a steep path. On both sides were vine-covered slopes. The sun had just set and its delicate crimson light rested on the green vines, on the tall stems, on the dry earth strewn with large and small stones and on the white wall of a small cottage with sloping black beams and four bright little windows which stood on the very top of the hill we were climbing.

'This is where we live!' cried Gagin as soon as we began to approach the cottage. 'And our landlady's bringing out the milk. Guten Abend, Madame! We'll eat at once, but first,' he added, 'take a look — isn't that a view?'

The view was magnificent. The Rhine lay at our feet all silver, between green banks. At one point it burned with the crimson gold of the sunset. The little town situated on its bank revealed all its houses and streets. On all sides stretched broad hills and fields. Down below it had been pleasant, but up here it was still better and I was particularly struck by the purity and depth of the sky, the glowing translucence of the air. Fresh and weightless, it softly quivered and fluttered in tremulous waves as if it literally felt more expansive at such a height.

'You've chosen a splendid place,' I said.

'It was Asya who found it,' answered Gagin. 'Well, Asya,' he continued, 'you must be mother. Get them to bring everything out here. We'll eat out in the open. Here we can hear the music better. Have you noticed', he added, turning to me, 'how waltz music sounds like nothing at all when heard close to – a lot of vulgar, coarse sounds – but at a distance how wonderful it sounds, it literally stirs up all one's romantic feelings!'

Asya (her real name was Anna, but Gagin always called her Asya and you must allow me to call her that too) – Asya went off into the cottage and soon returned with the landlady. The two of them were carrying a large tray with a jug of milk, plates, spoons, sugar, fruit and bread. We sat down and had supper. Asya took off her hat, and her black hair, which had been cut short and styled like a boy's, fell in large curls about her neck and ears. To start with, she was apprehensive of me, but Gagin said to her:

'Asya, stop bristling! He won't bite.'

She gave a smile and a little later struck up a conversation with me of her own accord. I had never seen anyone more full of movement. She never sat still for an instant, continuously jumping up, dashing into the cottage and running back again, singing some song under her breath and often laughing in a strange way, not at anything she'd heard but at different ideas that kept coming into her head. Her large eyes had a direct, bright, bold look, but sometimes when she half closed them her look would suddenly become deep and tender.

We chatted for a couple of hours. Daylight had long since gone and the evening, at first fiery, then lucid and crimson, then pale and darkling, had softly melted away and turned into night, but our conversation went on and on, as peaceful and docile as the air around us. Gagin ordered a bottle of Rhine wine and we sipped it slowly. The music as ever floated up to us, its sounds seeming sweeter and softer. Lights were lit in the town and over the river. Asya suddenly lowered her head, letting her curls fall over her eyes, fell silent and sighed, then told us she was sleepy and retired to the cottage. I saw, however, that, without lighting any candles, she spent a long time standing by the unopened window. At last the moon rose and its light twinkled in the waters of the Rhine.

Everything was illuminated and darkened and changed, and even the wine in our cut-glass goblets gleamed mysteriously. The breeze dropped, as if it had folded its wings, and died. The earth exuded a fragrant nocturnal warmth.

'Time to go!' I exclaimed. 'Otherwise I won't find a ferryman most likely.'

'Time to go,' repeated Gagin.

We went down the path. Suddenly there was a sound of falling stones behind us and Asya caught up with us.

'Shouldn't you be asleep?' asked her brother, but she, without saying a word to him, ran past.

The last dying lights which had been lighted by the students in the garden of the inn lit up the foliage of the trees from below, giving them a festive and fantastic appearance. We found Asya by the bank, talking to a ferryman. I jumped into the boat and said goodbye to my new friends. Gagin promised to call on me the following day. I squeezed him by the hand and stretched mine out to Asya, but she simply looked at me and shook her head. The boat cast off from the bank and was carried away by the fast river. The ferryman, a hale and hearty old fellow, thrust his oars against the dark water only with great effort.

'You've gone into a beam of moonlight, you've broken it!' Asya cried at me.

I lowered my eyes. All round the boat, shining black, the waves flickered.

'Goodbye!' her voice cried again.

'Till tomorrow!' Gagin called out in the wake of her cry.

The boat reached the other bank. I stepped out and looked back. There was no one to be seen on the opposite side. The beam of moonlight again stretched like a golden-bridge across the whole river. As if in farewell, the strains of the old-fashioned Lanner waltz* came rushing towards me. Gagin had been right. I felt all the strings of my heart quiver in response to its enticing melody. I set off home through the darkened fields, slowly breathing in the scented air, and arrived in my little room overwhelmed by a sweet tiredness made up of imprecise and endless expectations. I felt I was happy ... But why? I desired nothing, was not thinking of anything ... I was happy, that's all.

Almost laughing from an excess of pleasant and playful feelings, I plunged into my bed and had already closed my eyes when it suddenly occurred to me that not once in the course of the evening had I given a thought to my cruel and beautiful widow . . . 'What does it mean?' I asked myself. 'Can it be that I'm in love?' But having asked myself that, I at once fell asleep, it seemed, as soundly as a baby in a cradle.

[3]

The next morning (I was already awake but hadn't got up) I heard the noise of a stick tapping against my window and a voice, which I at once recognised as Gagin's, started singing:

> *Do you still sleep? With a guitar*
> *Will I arouse you . . .* *

I dashed to open the door for him.

'Hello,' Gagin said as he came in, 'I'm here on the early side, but just look what a morning it is! Freshness, dew, larks singing . . .' With his curly hair all gleaming, his open neck and rosy cheeks he was himself as fresh-looking as the morning.

I dressed and we went into the little garden, sat on a bench, ordered some coffee and started chatting. Gagin told me about his plans for the future. Being in possession of a respectable income and not dependent on anyone, he wanted to devote himself to painting and regretted only that he had been late in reaching this decision and had wasted so much time in doing nothing. I also mentioned what I had in mind and let him into the secret of my unhappy love affair. He gave me a sympathetic hearing but, so far as I could tell, I did not arouse in him any strong response to my passion. Following my example, having sighed once or twice out of politeness, Gagin proposed that I go to his place to have a look at his paintings. I agreed at once.

We didn't find Asya there. According to the landlady, she had gone off to the 'ruin'. A mile or so from the town of L— were the remains of a feudal castle. Gagin showed me his sketches. His paintings had a lot of vitality and truth, as well as a free and expansive manner, but not one of them was finished and the draughtsmanship seemed to me careless and inaccurate. I candidly gave him my opinion.

'Yes, yes,' he agreed with a sigh, 'you're right. It's all very poor and immature, there's no denying! I haven't studied as I should have, and that blasted Slavonic lack of discipline gets the better of me. So long as one's just dreaming about what to do, one can soar like an eagle and

ASYA

move mountains, it seems, but as soon as one starts doing it one gets worn out and tired.'

I tried to give him some encouragement, but he waved his hand and, gathering his sketches into a bundle, threw them on the divan.

'If I have the patience, I might make something of myself,' he muttered through his teeth. 'If I don't, I'll just remain a young aristocratic ignoramus.* Let's go and find Asya.'

We set off.

[4]

The road to the ruin twisted its way down a narrow wooded valley. At the bottom of the valley ran a stream that noisily babbled among the stones, as if hurrying to join the mighty river which glittered calmly beyond the dark edges of the sharp-toothed mountain tops. Gagin drew my attention to several happily sunlit places and if his words were not exactly those of a painter, he certainly spoke with artistic sense. Soon the ruin appeared. On the very summit of a bare cliff stood a square tower, all black and still strong, but literally chopped in two by a crack extending from top to bottom. Mossy walls adjoined the tower; here and there ivy grew; contorted bushes hung down from grey embrasure openings and tumbled arches. A stony path led to gates that were still intact. As we were approaching them we suddenly saw a female figure dart and rush hurriedly up a heap of fallen stones and come to a stop on an outjutting part of the wall directly above a precipice.

'That's Asya!' shouted Gagin. 'What a mad thing she is!'

We entered the gates and found ourselves in a small courtyard partly overgrown with nettles and wild apple-trees. It was in fact Asya who was on the outjutting piece of wall. She turned to us and laughed, but did not move from her position. Gagin wagged a finger at her and I loudly reproached her for not being careful.

'That's enough,' Gagin whispered to me. 'Don't tease her. You don't know her yet. She'll most likely climb right up the tower. You'd do better to admire the resourcefulness of the local inhabitants.'

I looked round. In one corner, hidden in a tiny wooden booth, an old woman was knitting a stocking and watching us over her glasses. She had on sale for tourists beer, cakes and seltzer water. We took our places on a bench and proceeded to drink some fairly cold beer out of heavy pewter tankards. Asya remained sitting motionless where she was, her legs drawn under her and her head tied about with a muslin scarf. The elegant outline of her figure stood out sharply and beautifully against the clear sky, but I kept on glancing up at her with a feeling of animosity. The previous day I had noticed something tense and not quite natural about her, and I thought to myself: 'She wants to surprise us. But why? Why all this childishness?' Just as if she had guessed what I was thinking, she suddenly threw me a quick and penetrating look, again gave a laugh, in two jumps sprang down from the wall and, going up to the old woman, asked her for a glass of water.

'You think I want to have a drink, don't you?' she said, turning to her brother. 'No, it's not that. There are flowers on the walls which need watering.'

Gagin said nothing to her, while she, glass in hand, started clambering up the ruin, stopping from time to time, bending down and with evident enjoyment dropping a few drops of water which shone brightly in the sunlight. Her movements were very attractive, but I was still feeling annoyed with her though I couldn't help admiring her skill and agility. At one dangerous point she deliberately gave a cry and then started laughing. I grew even more annoyed.

'Yes, she's as nimble as a goat,' the old woman mumbled to herself, tearing herself away from her knitting for a moment.

At last Asya had used up all the water in the glass and, playfully swaggering, she returned to us. A strange grin lightly played over her eyebrows, nostrils and lips, and half impudently, half happily she screwed up her dark eyes. 'You find my behaviour improper,' her face seemed to be saying. 'I don't care. I know you can't take your eyes off me.'

'Splendid, Asya, splendid,' murmured Gagin under his breath.

She at once appeared to feel ashamed, lowered her long eyelashes and modestly sat down beside us as if she were genuinely to blame for something. It was now for the first time that I had a good look at her face, the most lively face I'd ever seen. In a few moments it had become completely pale and acquired a concentrated, almost sorrowful expression. Its very features seemed to me larger, sterner and simpler. She had become completely calm. We walked round the entire ruin (Asya followed behind us) and admired the views. Meanwhile, lunchtime was approaching. While settling with the old lady, Gagin asked for another tankard of beer and, turning to me, exclaimed with a crafty grimace:

'Here's to your sweetheart!'

'Does he have one? Do you have a sweetheart?' Asya suddenly asked.

'Who doesn't?' answered Gagin.

Asya grew thoughtful for an instant. Her face again changed and there appeared on it a provocative, almost impudent grin.

On the way home she laughed and played the fool worse than ever. She broke off a long branch, placed it on her shoulder like a gun and wound her scarf round her head. I remember that we encountered a numerous family of fair-haired, stuffy English people who all of them, as if at a word of command, in chilly astonishment followed Asya with their glass-coloured eyes, while she, as if deliberately to provoke them, burst into loud song. On reaching home, she immediately went off to her room and appeared again only in time for the meal, dressed in her best dress, her hair carefully combed, her waist laced in and wearing gloves. At the table she was very correct, almost prissy, scarcely touching her food and drinking water from a wine glass. She evidently wanted to play a new role in front of me, that of a proper and well-educated young lady. Gagin didn't prevent her. It was clear that he was used to going along with her in everything. He simply glanced at me from time to time good-humouredly and slightly shrugged his shoulder, as if to say: 'She's a child; do be understanding.' As soon as the meal was over, Asya rose, curtsied and, putting on her hat, asked Gagin whether she could go to Frau Louise.

'Since when have you been asking whether you can?' he answered with his usual, on this occasion rather embarrassed, smile. 'Are you bored with us?'

'No, but I promised Frau Louise yesterday that I'd visit her. Besides, I think you two would be prefer to be alone. Mr N—' (she pointed to me) 'will be able to tell you something else about himself.'

She left.

'Frau Louise', began Gagin, trying to avoid my eyes, 'is the widow of a former local burgomaster, a kindly but empty-headed old woman. She's grown very fond of Asya. Asya has a passion for getting to know people of a lower class. I've noticed pride is always the cause of this. She's well and truly spoiled with me, as you can see,' he added after a pause, 'but what can I do? I could never be severe on anyone, least of all on her. I *have* to be lenient with her.'

I was silent. Gagin changed the subject. The more I got to know him, the stronger I felt drawn to him. I soon understood him. His was a straightforward Russian spirit, truthful, honourable and unaffected, but unfortunately rather feeble, without staying power and inner fire. His youthfulness did not so much bubble up in him as glow with a calm inner glow. He was extremely charming and clever, but I couldn't imagine what would become of him when he matured into real manhood. Be an artist ... Artists aren't made without bitter, unceasing labour, and hard work, I thought, looking at his soft features and listening to his unhurried way of talking – no, you'll never be able to work hard, you'll never know how to! But it was impossible not to be fond of him. One's heart was literally drawn to him. We spent about four hours together, either sitting on the divan or walking slowly backwards and forwards in front of the cottage, and in the course of those four hours we finally became friends.

The sun was setting and it was already time for me to go home. Asya still hadn't returned.

'She's such a law unto herself!' said Gagin. 'If you like I'll accompany you. We can call in on Frau Louise's on the way and I'll ask if she's there. It won't be far out of our way.'

We went down into the town and, turning into a narrow, crooked little street, stopped in front of a house of two windows' width and four storeys high. The second storey extended further over the street than the first and the third and fourth even further than the second. The whole house, with its ancient carving, its two fat columns at the base, its sharp tiled roof and its corner stretched out in the shape of a beak, looked like an enormous, crouched bird.

'Asya,' shouted Gagin, 'are you here?'

A small lighted window on the third floor creaked and opened and we saw Asya's dark head emerge. The toothless and myopic face of the old German woman peered out from behind her.

'I'm here,' said Asya, leaning her elbows affectedly on the sill, 'and I'm enjoying myself here. Catch, you down there,' she added, throwing Gagin a piece of a geranium. 'Imagine I'm your sweetheart!'

Frau Louise burst out laughing.

'N— is going,' said Gagin, 'and he wants to say goodbye to you.'

'Is that so?' said Asya. 'In that case, give him my piece of geranium and I'll come home at once.'

She banged shut the window and apparently kissed Frau Louise.

Gagin handed me the piece of geranium without a word. I silently put it in my pocket, walked down to the ferry and crossed to the other side.

I remember that I walked home without a thought in my head but with a strange weight on my heart, when I was suddenly struck by a strong, familiar but – in Germany – rare smell. I stopped and saw beside the road a small plantation of hemp. Its smell, so redolent of the steppes, instantly reminded me of my homeland and aroused in my soul a passionate longing for it. I wanted to breathe the air of Russia and walk on Russian soil. 'What am I doing here, why am I traipsing about in foreign parts, among strangers?' I cried out, and the dead weight which I had felt on my heart suddenly changed into a bitter and smarting excitement. I arrived home in a completely different mood from the previous day. I felt myself almost in a rage and took a long time to calm myself. A vexation, personally strange to me, was tearing me apart. Finally I sat down and, recalling my treacherous widow (an official recollection of this lady was my usual end to each day), I got out one of her notes. But I didn't even open it. My thoughts at once took another direction. I began to think . . . about Asya. I remembered that in the course of our conversation Gagin had hinted at certain difficulties in the way of his returning to Russia. 'Is she really his sister?' I asked out loud.

I undressed, lay down and tried to get to sleep, but an hour later I was sitting up in bed, leaning with one elbow on the pillow, and once more thinking about this 'capricious girl with the forced laughter . . .' 'She is just like the little Raphael Galatea in the Farnesino,' I whispered. 'Yes, I'm sure she's not his sister . . .'

And all the while the note from the widow lay quietly on the floor, shining white in the rays of the moon.

[5]

The next morning I again went into L—. I had convinced myself that I wanted to see Gagin, but secretly I wanted to see what Asya would do, whether she would 'show off' as she had done the previous day. I came across both of them in their sitting-room and – strange as it may seem, perhaps because I'd been thinking about Russia so much night and morning! – Asya seemed to me a completely Russian girl, yes, a simple girl, almost a maidservant. She was wearing an old dress, she had brushed her hair back behind her ears and was sitting motionless by the window sewing some embroidery, modestly and calmly, as if all her life she had never done anything else. She said scarcely a word, looking down quietly at her work, and her features had acquired such an insignificant, everyday look that I was reminded, come what may, of all our homegrown peasant girls, all our Katyas and Mashas. To complete the resemblance, she even started singing in a soft voice a peasant song 'Mother darling, dove of love'. I gazed at her yellowish, burnt-out little face, remembered my nostalgia of the previous night and felt a pang of regret. The weather was wonderful. Gagin announced that he was going to do a study from nature that day and I asked him whether I could accompany him – or perhaps I might get in his way?

'On the contrary,' he said, 'you can give me good advice.'

He put on a round hat à la Van Dyck and a blouse, put his painting things under his arm and set off. I drifted along in his wake. Asya remained in the cottage. As he left, Gagin asked her to see that the soup wasn't too thin and she promised to look after things in the kitchen. Gagin made his way to the valley, already familiar to me, sat down on a stone and began to draw an old hollow oak with outspread branches. I lay down on the grass and got out a book, but I didn't read more than a couple of pages and he did no more than mess up his sheet of paper. We devoted ourselves all the more to discussion, and so far as I can judge we had a fairly intelligent and detailed discussion about how to work, what to avoid and what to regard as essential and what precisely was the significance of an artist in our time. Gagin finally decided that 'he wasn't up to it today' and lay down beside me, and it was then that our youthful talk really flowed freely, talk that was often enthusiastic, or thoughtful, or excited, but almost always the vague kind of talk in which Russians indulge so easily. Having exhausted all we had to say and full to the brim with a feeling of satisfaction, as if we had actually achieved something, made a success of something, we returned home. I found Asya just as I had left her. No matter how closely I watched her, I couldn't detect a trace of coquettishness or deliberate play-acting in her. There was no reproaching her for artificiality on this occasion.

'Aha,' said Gagin, 'so it's sackcloth and ashes today!'

Towards evening she yawned several times quite unaffectedly and went off to her own room early on. I also soon said goodbye to Gagin and, returning home, had no time for dreams: it was a day that had passed in complete sobriety. I remember, though, that as I got into bed I exclaimed aloud: 'What a chameleon that girl is!' And after a moment's thought I added: 'No way is she his sister.'

[6]

Two weeks passed. Every day I went to the Gagins. Asya literally avoided me, but she never permitted herself any of the pranks which so surprised me in the first days of our acquaintance. She appeared to be secretly embittered or confused and laughed a great deal less. I watched her, fascinated.

She could speak French and German reasonably well, but it was obvious that from her childhood she had not been in female hands and had received a strange and unusual education which had nothing in common with Gagin's. Despite his hat à la Van Dyck and his blouse, he literally exuded all the softness and near-effeminacy of a true member of the Russian nobility, while she bore no resemblance to a young lady of quality. There was something restless in her every movement and it was as if she was only a recent graft to an old stock, as if the wine was still working in her. By nature shy and timid, she was annoyed at her own bashfulness and out of annoyance deliberately forced herself to appear carefree and bold, in which she was not always successful. I spoke to her several times about her life in Russia and her past. She answered my questions unwillingly, yet I learned that before coming abroad she had lived for a long time in the country. I once found her alone deep in a book. Leaning her head on her hands and burying her fingers deep in her hair, she was devouring the lines with her eyes.

'Bravo!' I said, as I went up to her. 'How busy you are!'

She raised her head and gave me a serious, severe look.

'You think I only know how to laugh,' she said and was on the point of going away. I glanced at the title of the book: it was some French novel.

'I can't congratulate you on your choice,' I said.

'What's the point of reading, then!' she exclaimed and, throwing the book on the table, added: 'So I'd better go and make a fool of myself!' and dashed off into the garden.

That evening I was reading to Gagin from *Hermann und Dorothea*. At first Asya did no more than dart to and fro past us, but then suddenly stopped, started listening, quietly sat down beside me and listened to the reading to the end. The next day I once again didn't recognise her until I realised that she'd suddenly taken it into her head to be housewifely and staid like Dorothea. In a word, she appeared to me to be a partial enigma. Touchy in the extreme, she attracted me even when I was angry with her. I became more and more convinced of one thing: she was not Gagin's sister. He did not treat her as a brother would, but was too tender, too solicitous and at the same time rather forced in his attentions.

A strange event seemed to confirm me in my suspicions.

One evening, as I was on my way to the vineyard where the Gagins lived, I found the gate locked. Without giving it much thought, I made my way to a place I'd already noticed where the wall had fallen down and jumped over it. Not much further on, just beside the path, was a small arbour of acacias. I drew level with it and had just passed by when I was astonished to hear Asya's voice tearfully and passionately pronouncing the following words:

'No, I don't want to love anyone but you, no, no, it's only you I want to love – for ever and ever.'

'That's enough, Asya, calm yourself,' said Gagin. 'You know I believe you.'

Their voices resounded in the arbour. I caught sight of both of them through the thin weave of branches. They hadn't noticed me.

'You, only you,' she kept on saying, throwing herself on his neck and in spasms of sobbing beginning to kiss him and press up against his chest.

'That's enough, enough,' he said, lightly stroking her hair with his hand.

I stood stock still a few moments. Then I roused myself. 'Should I join them? Never!' flashed through my mind. With rapid steps I returned to the vineyard wall, jumped over it on to the road and hurried home almost at a run. I was smiling and rubbing my hands in surprise at this lucky chance which had suddenly confirmed my guesses (I never doubted the truth of them for a moment), but at the same time my heart was filled with a very bitter feeling. 'However,' I thought, 'they certainly know how to hide their feelings! But why? Why should they want to fool me? I'd not expected such a thing from him . . . And why so touching a scene of explanation?'

I slept badly and rose early the next morning, fixed a knapsack to my back and, after telling my landlady that she needn't expect me back that night at all, set off on foot into the mountains, upstream along the river on which the small town of Z— stands. These mountains, outlying parts of the range known as the Dog's Back (Hundsrueck), are very interesting in a geological sense. They are particularly remarkable for the correctness and purity of their basalt strata; but I had no time for geological research. I could not account for what was happening within me, save that I was clear about one thing: an unwillingness to see the Gagins. I assured myself that the only reason for my sudden ill will towards them was annoyance at their deceitfulness. Who had made them pretend to be brother and sister? Anyhow, I tried not to think about them. I wandered unhurriedly up mountains and down valleys, spent much time sitting in country inns talking peaceably with the proprietors and patrons or lying on flat warm slabs of stone and watching the clouds float by in weather that remained astonishingly fine. In this way I spent three days, and not without enjoyment, although my heart was nipped by regret at moments. The tenor of my thinking seemed exactly suited to the tranquil nature of that region.

I gave myself up entirely to the calm play of chance and random impressions; unhurriedly succeeding one another, they flowed through my soul and left in it, finally, one general feeling, in which was concentrated everything I saw, felt and heard during those three days – literally everything: the delicate smell of resin in the forests, the singing and the tapping of woodpeckers, the inexhaustible babbling of glittering little streams with varicoloured trout on their sandy bottoms, the not too bold outlines of the mountains, frowning cliffs, neat little villages with venerable old churches and trees, storks standing in the meadows, cosy-looking watermills with busily churning wheels, the jovial faces of local people, their blue shirts and grey stockings, the slow, creaking wagons harnessed with plump horses, sometimes with cows, the long-haired young men wandering the clean by-ways planted with apple and pear trees . . .

Even now I find it pleasant to remember my impressions of that time. My greetings to you, humble corner of German soil, with your simple sufficiency of life, with your ubiquitous traces of busy hands and patient, if slow, labour . . . Greetings, and may peace be with you!

ASY A# ASYA

I got home at the very end of the third day. I have forgotten to say that out of annoyance with the Gagins I tried to resurrect in my mind the image of my hard-hearted widow, but all my attempts to do so were in vain. I remember that when I tried to think of her I saw before me a little peasant girl of about five years of age, with a round inquisitive little face and innocently wide-open eyes. She gazed at me with a look of such childish artlessness that I felt uneasy beneath her clear-eyed scrutiny and wanted to avoid telling any kind of lie in her presence and so said goodbye forever to the former object of my thoughts.

At home I found a note from Gagin. He expressed surprise at the suddenness of my decision, reproachfully wondered why I hadn't taken him with me and begged me to visit them as soon as I returned. I read this note without much enjoyment, but the next day I set off for L—.

[8]

Gagin gave me a friendly welcome and covered me with kindly reproaches, but Asya, quite deliberately, as soon as she saw me, burst out laughing for no reason and at once ran off somewhere, as was her custom. Gagin was embarrassed, called after her that she was mad and begged me not to hold it against her. I confess I was very annoyed with Asya. Even without all that I wasn't exactly feeling my real self, and now once again there was unnatural laughter and strange grimaces. However, I gave the impression that I hadn't noticed anything and began telling Gagin the details of my trip. He told me what he had been doing during my absence. But our conversation came to nothing, because Asya kept on coming into our room and running out again, and I eventually announced that I had some urgent work to do and had to return home. At first Gagin tried to detain me, but then, after scrutinising me closely, he volunteered to accompany me. In the hallway Asya suddenly came up to me and offered me her hand; I lightly pressed her fingers and gave her a partial bow. Gagin and I crossed the Rhine and, passing beside my favourite ash-tree and its little statue of the madonna, sat down on a bench to enjoy the view. Here a remarkable conversation took place between us.

We began by exchanging a few words and then fell silent, gazing at the glittering river.

'Tell me,' Gagin began suddenly with his habitual smile, 'what's your opinion of Asya? Isn't it true that she must seem to you rather strange?'

117

'Yes,' I answered, not without some confusion. I had not expected him to talk about her.

'One has to know her well in order to pass judgement on her,' he said. 'She has a very kind heart, but she's mischievous. It's difficult to get on with her. Yet you wouldn't blame her if you knew her background . . .'

'Her background?' I interrupted. 'Surely she's your . . .'

Gagin glanced at me.

'Are you already thinking she's not my sister? No,' he went on, paying no attention to my confusion, 'she is my sister, my father's daughter. Hear what I've got to tell you. I feel I can trust you and I'll tell you everything.

'My father was very kind, intelligent, educated – and unhappy. Fate treated him no worse than many others, but he couldn't even withstand its first blow. He married young, out of love. His wife, my mother, died very soon afterwards, leaving me a baby of six months. My father carried me off to the country and for a whole twelve years never went anywhere. He personally took care of my education and would never have parted with me if his brother, my uncle, hadn't visited us in the country. This uncle was a permanent resident of St Petersburg and occupied a fairly important post. He persuaded my father to let him take charge of me, since my father would on no account agree to leave the country. My uncle put it to him that it was bad for a boy of my age to live in complete isolation and that with such a perpetually depressed and taciturn mentor as my father I would most certainly fall behind my contemporaries and my whole character might easily be spoiled. My father resisted his brother's advice for a long time, but in the end he gave way. I cried on parting from my father. I loved him, though I'd never once seen a smile on his face . . . Yet once I was in St Petersburg I soon forgot our dark and unhappy ancestral nest. I entered a cadet school and after school I entered a Guards regiment. Every year I returned to the country for a few weeks and each year I found my father more and more melancholy, more buried in himself and pensive to the point of timidity. Every day he used to go to church and had almost forgotten how to speak. On one of my visits (I was already more than twenty years old) I saw for the first time in our house a frail, dark-eyed little girl of about ten—Asya. My father said she was an orphan who had been given succour – those were his words. I didn't pay any particular attention to her. She was as wild, agile and silent as a little animal, and as soon as I went into my father's favourite room – a large and sombre room where my mother had died and where even in the daytime candles were lit – she'd instantly hide behind a large armchair or a bookcase. It so happened that in the next two or three years my service duties prevented me from visiting the country. I received a short letter once a month from my father, but he would mention Asya only occasionally and then in passing. He was already more than fifty, but he still seemed a young man. Imagine my horror when I suddenly received, entirely unsuspecting, from the steward a letter in which he informed me of my father's fatal illness and begged me to come as soon as possible if I wanted to say goodbye to him. I galloped post-haste and found my father still alive, but already on the point of drawing his last breath. He was extremely delighted to see me, clasped me in his emaciated arms, looked me in the eyes for a long while with a gaze that was part scrutinising, part appealing, and, having made me promise that I would fulfil his last request, he ordered his old manservant to bring in Asya. The old man brought her in. She could scarcely stand upright and trembled all over.

' "So," my father said to me with an effort, "I bequeath to you my daughter, who is your sister. You will learn everything from Jacob," he added, indicating the old manservant.

'Asya burst into tears and fell face downwards on the bed . . . Half an hour later my father died.

'This is what I learned. Asya was my father's daughter by Tatyana, my mother's former maid. I remember this Tatyana well, her tall, shapely figure, her handsome, severe, intelligent face with its large dark eyes. She had a reputation as a proud and unapproachable girl. So far as I could ascertain from the respectful mumblings of Jacob, my father took up with her several years after my mother's death. Tatyana was not then living in the main house but in a peasant hut with her married sister, a cowherd. My father became strongly attached to her and after my departure from the country even wanted to marry her, but she refused to be his wife despite his requests.

' "The late Tatyana Vasilyevna", so Jacob declared to me, standing by the door with his hands behind his back, "were right sensible in everything and had no wish to hurt your father. What sort of a wife would I be to him? is what she says. What sort of a grand lady am I? Them were the words she used, them were the words she said to me, sir."

'Tatyana did not even want to move into our house and continued to live with her sister, together with Asya. In my childhood I used to see Tatyana only on the feast days, in church. Her head wrapped in a dark scarf, a yellow shawl round her shoulders, she would stand in the crowd beside a window (her severe silhouette would be sharply outlined against the transparent glass) and she would pray meekly and seriously, bowing low to the ground according to the old custom. When my uncle took me away, Asya was only two years old, and when she was nine she lost her mother.

'No sooner had Tatyana died than my father took Asya into the main house. He had previously expressed a desire to have her with him, but Tatyana had refused him. Imagine what it must have meant for Asya when she was taken to live with the master of the house. She still can't forget the moment when they dressed her in a silk dress for the first time and kissed her hand. While she was alive her mother had treated her very strictly; with her father she enjoyed complete freedom. He was her teacher. Besides him she saw no one. He did not spoil her, that's to say he didn't make a great fuss of her, but he loved her passionately and never forbade her anything because in his soul he regarded himself as guilty towards her. Asya soon learned that she was the chief person in the house and she knew that the master of the house was her father. But she also quickly understood her false position. Her selfishness became strongly developed, as did her mistrustfulness. She acquired deep-rooted bad habits and her simplicity vanished. She wanted (she herself once confessed this to me) to make *the whole world* forget her origins. She was both ashamed of her mother and ashamed of her shame – and yet she was proud of her too. You can see that she has known a great deal and still knows things she has no right to know at her age . . . But she can hardly be blamed for that, can she? The spirit of youth had awoken in her, her blood was on the boil, but there was no hand close by to guide her. She had complete independence in everything! Is it ever easy to have complete independence? She didn't wish to be any worse than other young ladies, so she turned to books. But what good was there to be gained from that? A life that had begun in the wrong way became mal-formed, but her heart remained unspoiled and her intelligence was unaffected.

'So there was I, a young man of twenty, with a thirteen-year-old girl on my hands! In the first days immediately after my father's death the very sound of my voice sent her into a fever, all my attempts at kindness made her miserable and it was only little by little, only by degrees, that she got used to me. True, later on, when she'd become convinced that I really did consider her to be my sister and really loved her like a sister, she became passionately attached to me, because she never feels anything by halves.

'I took her to St Petersburg. No matter how painful it was for me to part with her, I simply couldn't live in the same house with her. I placed her in one of the best boarding-schools. Asya understood the need for us to be apart, but she began by falling ill and almost dying. Later she grew accustomed to it and spent four years in the boarding-school, but against all my expectations she remained almost the same as she had been before. The headmistress frequently complained to me about her. "You can't punish her," she would say to me, "and she won't submit to kindness." Asya was extremely clever and excellent at her work, better than the others, but she never wanted to accept a common standard with the rest, she was stubborn and surly . . . I couldn't blame her overmuch. In her position she had the choice either to be obsequious or to be disobedient. Of all her schoolfriends she was on close terms only with one poor ugly and put-upon girl. The other young ladies with whom she was being educated, mostly from good families, took a dislike to her, taunted and needled her as much as they could. Asya never gave away to them one iota. Once in a divinity lesson the teacher started talking about vices. "The worst vices are flattery and cowardice," said Asya loudly. In short, she continued to go her own way. The only thing that improved was her manners, and I don't think she made great progress even in that respect.

'At last she turned seventeen and it wasn't possible to leave her at the boarding-school any longer. I found myself in a rather difficult position. Suddenly I had a good idea – I'd retire from the service, go abroad for a year or two and take Asya with me. No sooner said than done. So here we are on the banks of the Rhine where I'm trying to keep busy with painting while she . . . while she is up to her usual tricks and playing the fool as always. But I hope now that you won't judge her too severely. Though she pretends none of it matters to her, she treasures everyone's opinion, yours especially.'

And Gagin again smiled his calm smile. I firmly pressed his hand.

'So that's how it is,' he began again, 'but for me she's nothing but trouble. She's a real keg of gunpowder. So far she's not taken a liking to anyone, but what trouble there'll be if she really does fall in love with someone! Sometimes I don't know what to do with her. A few days ago she took it into her head to begin suddenly assuring me that I'd grown colder towards her than I was before and that she loved me alone and would love only me all her life . . . And then she burst into tears . . .'

'So that was . . .' I was on the point of saying, and bit my tongue.

'Tell me, then,' I asked Gagin, since it was now a time for confidences between us, 'has she never shown any signs of being fond of anyone? Surely in St Petersburg she must have seen some young men?'

'None of them appealed to her at all. No, what Asya needs is a hero, someone out of the ordinary – or a picturesque shepherd in a mountain glen. Look, I've been talking too much and holding you up,' he added, getting to his feet.

'Listen,' I began, 'let's go to your place, I don't want to go home.'

'What about your work?'

I said nothing in reply. Gagin smiled good-naturedly and we returned to L—. Catching sight of the familiar vineyard and the white cottage on the top of the hill, I felt a kind of sweetness – yes, a kind of sweetness – enter my heart, just as if someone had secretly poured honey into it. I felt light-headed after what Gagin had told me.

[9]

Asya met us in the doorway of the cottage. I again expected laughter from her, but she came out to meet us all pale and taciturn, with downcast eyes.

'Here he is again,' said Gagin. 'Mind you, it was he himself who wanted to come back here.'

Asya looked questioningly at me. I for my part stretched out a hand to her and on this occasion firmly clasped her cold little fingers. I began to feel very sorry for her. Now I understood a great deal about her that had previously puzzled me: her inner unease, her inability to behave properly, her desire to put on airs – it was all clear to me. I had a glimpse of this soul and saw the secret humiliation that constantly oppressed her, saw how the inexperience of her selfishness struggled in alarm and confusion, but I also saw how her whole being strove towards truth. I realised why this strange girl had so attracted me, not only by the half-wild charm that poured through every inch of her slender body, but also she attracted me because I liked her spirit.

ASYA

Gagin began rummaging about among his drawings and I asked Asya to come for a walk with me in the vineyard. She agreed at once with a cheerful and almost humble readiness. We went half way down the hillside and sat down on a broad slab of stone.

'Weren't you bored without us?' Asya began.

'And were you bored without me?' I asked.

Asya gave me a sideways glance. 'Yes,' she answered. 'Is it nice in the mountains?' she went on immediately. 'Are they high? Higher than the clouds? Tell me what you saw. You were telling my brother, but I didn't hear any of it.'

'It was you who decided to leave us,' I remarked.

'I left because . . . Well, I'm not leaving now,' she added in a voice full of trustful affection. 'You were angry today.'

'I was?'

'You were.'

'What on earth should make you . . .'

'I don't know, but you were angry and you went away angry. I was very annoyed that you went away like that and I'm very glad you've come back.'

'I'm also glad I came back,' I said.

Asya gave a little shrug of the shoulders, just like children do when they're happy.

'Oh, I know how to tell things like that!' she continued. 'I used to be able to tell simply through the way my father coughed in the next room whether he was pleased with me or not.'

Until that moment Asya had never spoken to me about her father. I was astonished by it now.

'Did you love your father?' I asked and suddenly, to my great annoyance, I felt that I was blushing.

She said nothing and also went red. We both fell silent. In the distance a steamer was plying the waters of the Rhine and sending up smoke. We started watching it.

'Why don't you tell me what you saw?' whispered Asya.

'Why did you burst out laughing today as soon as you saw me?' I asked.

'I don't know. Sometimes I want to cry and I find myself laughing. You mustn't judge me . . . by what I do. Oh, by the way, what's that story about the Lorelei? Isn't that *her* rock we can see? They say that she always used to drown everyone, but the moment she fell in love she threw herself in the water. I like that story. Frau Louise tells me all kinds of stories. Frau Louise has a black cat with yellow eyes . . .' Asya raised her head and shook her curls. 'Oh, I'm so happy,' she said.

At that moment broken, monotonous sounds rose up to us from below. Hundreds of voices raised in unison and with measured pauses were repeating the refrain of a prayer. It was a crowd of pilgrims trailing along the road with crosses and banners.

'Oh, I'd love to be with them!' said Asya, listening to the gradually diminishing explosions of voices.

'Are you as religious as all that?'

'I'd love to go somewhere far away to fulfil a prayer, to do something difficult and heroic,' she went on. 'But now the days are just going by, life is going by, and what have we actually done?'

'You're ambitious,' I remarked. 'You don't want to live your life in vain, you want to leave something behind you . . .'

'And is that impossible?'

'Impossible,' I almost repeated, but then I glanced into her bright eyes and simply said:

'You must try.'

'Tell me,' said Asya after a short silence, during which certain shadows ran across her face, already turned a little pale, 'were you very fond of that lady . . . Don't you remember that my brother drank her health at the ruin on the second day we knew you?'

I laughed.

'Your brother was joking – I was never fond of any lady. At least I'm not fond of her now.'

'And what do you like in women?' asked Asya, throwing back her head in innocent curiosity.

'What a strange question!' I exclaimed.

Asya was slightly confused.

'I shouldn't ask you such a question, should I? Forgive me. I'm so used to saying whatever comes into my head. That's why I'm frightened of speaking.'

'Speak, for God's sake, don't be frightened!' I insisted. 'I'm so glad you've finally stopped avoiding me.'

Asya lowered her eyes and gave a soft, carefree laugh. I'd never known her laugh like that before.

'Well, then, tell me about it,' she went on, smoothing out the hem of her dress and folding it over her legs as if she were preparing to sit a long while, 'either tell me or read me something, like when you read to us from *Onegin*, do you remember?'

She suddenly grew thoughtful . . .

> *'Where now the cross and leafy shade*
> *Lie o'er poor mother's simple grave!'**

she intoned in a soft voice.

'That wasn't quite what Pushkin wrote,' I remarked.

'And so I wanted to be Tatyana,' she continued in the same thoughtful way. 'Now tell me a story,' she demanded vivaciously.

But I was in no mood for telling stories. I gazed at her, all suffused by the clear sunlight, bathed in peace and quietness. Everything shone radiantly about us, above and below – the sky, the earth and the water. The air itself seemed to be permeated with brilliance.

'Look how beautiful it is!' I said, lowering my voice.

'Yes, it is beautiful!' she responded just as quietly, without looking at me. 'If the two of us were birds, how high we'd fly, how high we'd soar . . . We'd just drown ourselves in that blue sky! But we're not birds . . .'

'We could grow wings,' I objected.

'How?'

'You have to live and learn. There are feelings which can lift you above the earth. Don't worry, you'll grow wings.'

'Have you grown them?'

'How can I put it? So far, I think, I've not actually flown . . .'

Asya again grew thoughtful. I bent slightly towards her.

'Do you know how to waltz?' she suddenly asked me.

'I do,' I answered, rather taken aback.

'Come on, then, come on! I'll ask my brother to play us a waltz! We'll imagine we're flying, that we've grown wings!'

She dashed to the cottage. I ran after her – and in a few moments we were circling round the small room to the sweet strains of a Lanner waltz. Asya waltzed beautifully, with true enjoyment. Something soft and feminine suddenly emerged from behind her severe girlish appearance. For long afterwards my hand felt the touch of her soft waist, for long afterwards I heard her rapid, close breathing, for long afterwards I could recall the dark, motionless, almost closed eyes in the pale but lively face, playfully brushed by curls.

[10]

The whole of that day passed without a hitch. We were as happy as children. Asya was extremely charming and unaffected. Gagin was delighted, looking at her. It was late when I left. As we went out into the middle of the Rhine, I asked the ferryman to let the boat float down river with the current. The old man raised his oars and the majestic river carried us along. Looking about me, listening and recalling what the day had been like, I suddenly felt a secret unease in my heart and raised my eyes to the sky, but even in the sky there seemed to be no tranquillity. Dotted with stars, it constantly quivered and danced and shivered. I leaned down to the surface of the river, but even there, even in those dark, cold depths, the stars flickered and shimmered. A feeling of agitated life seemed to surround me and I felt a similar agitation rising within me. I leaned on the boat's edge . . . The whisper of the breeze in my ears, the soft murmuring of the water along the boat's stern irritated me, and the quick fresh breathing of the waves against the boat did not cool my feelings. A nightingale started singing on the bank and infected me with the sweet poison of its song. Tears gathered in my eyes, but they were not tears of abstract ecstasy. What I felt was not so much a vague, still recently experienced sensation of all-embracing desire, such as when the soul expands, resounds and seems to be aware that it understands everything and loves the whole world . . . No! It was a fierce yearning for personal happiness that had ignited within me. I still didn't dare give it a name, but it was happiness, happiness to saturation point, that I desired and longed for . . . And the boat was carried along by the current and the old ferryman sat and dozed, leaning on his oars.

[11]

Setting off the following day for the Gagins, I didn't ask myself whether I was in love with Asya, but I thought a great deal about her, her destiny preoccupied me and I was delighted by the unexpected closeness of our relationship. I felt that I had only really known her since yesterday, because previously she had always turned away from me. And now that she had finally revealed herself to me, how enchanting was the light shed by her, how new she was for me, what secret charms were shyly discernible within her!

I walked cheerfully along the familiar road, continuously glancing up at the whitewashed cottage in the distance. Not only was I not thinking about the future, I was not even thinking about the next day, so very happy did I feel.

Asya reddened when I walked into the room. I noticed that she had again dressed up in her best clothes, but the expression of her face did not suit her finery: it was one of sadness. And I had arrived feeling so happy! It even seemed to me that, as usual, she was on the point of dashing away, but she made an effort to overcome the impulse and stayed. Gagin was in that peculiar state of artistic fire and frenzy which, rather like a fit, suddenly seizes hold of dilettantes when they imagine they have succeeded, as they put it, in 'grabbing nature by the tail'. He stood there, all dishevelled and bespattered with paint, in front of the canvas and, making broad brush strokes over it, gave me an almost truculent nod of the head, turned away, screwed up his eyes and once more launched himself at his painting. I didn't disturb him and sat down next to Asya. Her dark eyes slowly turned towards me.

'Today you're not as you were yesterday,' I remarked after vain attempts to bring a smile to her lips.

'No, I'm not the same,' she admitted in a slow and lifeless voice. 'But it's nothing. I slept badly. I spent the whole night thinking.'

'What about?'

'Oh, many things. It's been a habit of mine since childhood, since the time when I lived with my mother . . .'

She uttered the word with an effort and then repeated it:

'When I lived with my mother . . . I was thinking: why is it nobody knows what's going to happen to him? And sometimes you can see what's going to go wrong and you can't save yourself. And why is it never possible to tell the whole truth? . . . And then I was thinking how little I know and how much I've got to learn. I've got to be retaught everything, I've been very badly educated. I don't know how to play the piano, I can't draw, I even sew badly. I haven't got any accomplishments and I must be very boring to be with.'

'You're not being fair to yourself,' I objected. 'You've read a lot, you're an educated person and with your intelligence . . .'

'I'm intelligent, am I?' she inquired with such naive wonder that I laughed despite myself. But she did not even smile. 'Brother, am I intelligent?' she asked Gagin.

He didn't answer her and went on working, ceaselessly changing brushes and raising his hand high.

'I sometimes don't know what's going on in my head,' Asya continued with the same thoughtful look. 'Heavens above, I'm sometimes quite frightened of myself! Oh, I'd like to . . . Is it true that women shouldn't read a lot?'

'Not a lot, but . . .'

'Tell me what I ought to read! Tell me what I ought to do! I'll do whatever you tell me,' she added, turning with innocent trustfulness towards me.

I couldn't find anything to say to her on the spur of the moment.

'You won't be bored by me, will you?'

'Of course not,' I began.

'Thank you!' replied Asya. 'And I thought you'd be bored.'

And her small hot hand squeezed mine firmly.

'N—!' Gagin called to me at that instant. 'Do you think the background's too dark?'

I went up to him. Asya rose and disappeared.

[12]

She returned an hour later, stopped in the doorway and summoned me with her hand.

'Listen,' she said, 'if I died, would you feel sorry for me?'

'What strange ideas you have today!' I exclaimed.

'I imagine I'll soon die. It sometimes seems to me that everything round me is saying goodbye. It's better to die than live like this . . . Oh, don't look at me like that! I'm not pretending, you know. Otherwise I'll start being frightened of you again.'

'Were you frightened of me?'

'If I behave strangely, I'm not really to blame, you know,' she objected. 'You see, I can't even laugh . . .'

She remained sad and worried until evening. Something was happening in her that I didn't understand. Her gaze frequently rested on me and my heart softly contracted under that enigmatic look. She seemed outwardly calm, while I, looking at her, wanted all the time to tell her not to get excited. I delighted in watching her and I found a touching charm in her pale features and her indecisive, slow movements, while she for some reason imagined I was in a bad mood.

'Listen,' she said to me shortly before saying goodbye, 'I'm tormented by the thought you consider me frivolous . . . In future you've got to believe everything I tell you, just as you've got to be honest with me. I'll always tell you the truth, I give you my word . . .'

This 'word' again made me laugh.

'Oh, don't laugh,' she cried animatedly, 'or I'll say to you today what you said to me yesterday: "Why are you laughing?" ' And after a short silence she added: 'Do you remember yesterday how you talked about wings? I've grown wings, but I've nowhere to fly.'

'Still,' I said, 'all paths are open to you . . .'

Asya looked me directly and intently in the eyes.

'You've got a poor opinion of me today,' she said, frowning.

'I? A poor opinion of you! . . .'

'Why are you out of your depths?' Gagin interrupted me. 'Would you like me to play you a waltz as I did yesterday?'

'No, no,' Asya objected, and clenched her fists. 'Not today, not at all!'

'I'm not forcing you, don't worry . . .'

'Not at all!' she repeated, going pale.

'Is she in love with me?' I wondered, as I went down to the Rhine, which hurriedly drove dark waves towards me.

[13]

'Is she in love with me?' I asked myself the next day as soon as I awoke. I had no wish to take a look inside myself. I felt that her image, the image of 'a girl with forced laughter', had entered into me and it would take me a long time to be rid of it. I went to L— and remained there the whole day, but I saw Asya only for an instant. She was unwell with a headache. She came downstairs, just for a minute, her forehead bandaged, looking pale and thin, with almost closed eyes, smiled weakly and said: 'It'll go, it's nothing, everything passes, doesn't it?' and then went away. I felt bored and somehow sad and empty. However, I was reluctant to leave and returned home late, not having seen her again.

The next morning passed in a kind of twilight sleep. I wanted to get down to work, but couldn't. I wanted to do nothing and not to think of anything – and didn't succeed. I wandered round the town, returned home and once again went out.

'Are you Mr N—?' a childish voice cried behind me. I looked round. A boy was standing there. 'It's for you from Fraulein Annette,' he added, handing me a note.

I opened it and recognised Asya's rapid and irregular handwriting. 'I have to see you,' she wrote. 'Come today at four o'clock to the stone chapel on the road by the ruin. I've done something very silly today . . . For God's sake come, you'll learn all about it. Tell the messenger: yes.'

'Will there be an answer?' the boy asked me.

'Say: yes,' I answered.

The boy ran off.

[14]

I returned to my own room, sat down and thought. My heart was beating strongly. I read through Asya's note several times. I looked at my watch: it wasn't twelve yet.

The door opened and in came Gagin.

His face was gloomy. He seized me by the hand and pressed it firmly. He seemed very upset.

'What's wrong?' I asked.

Gagin took a chair and sat down in front of me.

'Three days ago,' he began haltingly, with a forced smile, 'I astonished you with my story. Today I'll astonish you even more. With someone else I probably wouldn't have decided . . . so directly . . . But you're an honourable man, you're my friend, aren't you? Then listen to what I've got to say: my sister Asya is in love with you.'

I shuddered and was about to rise . . .

'Your sister, you say . . .'

'Yes, yes,' Gagin interrupted me. 'I tell you she's crazy and will drive me out of my mind. But, happily, she doesn't know how to lie – and she trusts me. Oh, what spirit that little girl has! But she'll ruin herself, that's for certain.'

'You must be mistaken,' I began.

'No, I'm not mistaken. Yesterday, as you know, she spent practically the whole day lying down, ate nothing, yet made no complaint. . . . She never complains. I wasn't worried, though towards evening she developed a slight fever. This morning, at two o'clock, our landlady woke me. "Come to your sister at once," she says. "She's not well." I dashed to Asya and found her still fully dressed, in a fever and in tears. Her brow was burning hot and her teeth were chattering. "What's wrong with you?" I asked. "Are you sick?" She flung herself on my neck and began begging me to take her away as soon as possible if I wanted her to remain alive ... I couldn't understand her, tried to calm her ... Her sobbing grew worse, and suddenly through these sobbings I heard ... Well, to put it briefly, I heard she was in love with you. I assure you, we're sensible people, you and I, and can have no idea how deeply she feels or with what unbelievable force these feelings express themselves in her. They come upon her as unexpectedly and irresistibly as a thunderstorm. You're a very nice chap,' Gagin went on, 'but why she should've fallen in love with you – that, I admit, I don't understand. She says that she was attracted to you at first sight. That was why she cried that time when she assured me she didn't want to love anyone apart from me. She imagines you despise her because you probably know who she is. She asked me whether I'd told you her story – and, of course, I said I hadn't. But her sensitivity to things is simply frightful. She only wants one thing – to go away, to go away at once. I sat with her until morning. She made me promise that we'd be gone by tomorrow – and only then did she go to sleep. I thought and thought – and then decided I ought to talk to you. In my opinion, Asya's right: the best thing would be for the two of us to leave. And I'd have taken her away today if I hadn't had a thought which stopped me. Perhaps, I thought, – how am I to know? – perhaps you're fond of my sister? If that's the case, what am I doing taking her away? So I decided, casting aside all modesty ... In any case, I thought I'd noticed something myself ... I decided to discover from you ...' Poor Gagin was covered in confusion. 'Please forgive me,' he added, 'I'm not used to such fuss and bother.'

I took him by the hand.

'You want to know', I said in a firm voice, 'whether or not I'm fond of your sister? Yes, I am fond of her.'

Gagin looked at me.

'But', he said haltingly, 'you're surely not thinking of marrying her?'

'How would you like me to answer such a question? Judge for yourself, can I now ...'

'I know, I know,' Gagin interrupted me, 'I've no right to demand an answer from you – and my question is the height of impropriety ... But what should I do? One can't play with fire. You don't know Asya.

She's in a state when she could collapse, run away, make a rendezvous with you ... Another girl would know how to hide everything and wait for things to happen, but not she! With her it's the first time, that's the trouble! If you'd seen how she sobbed at my feet this morning, you'd have understood my fears.'

I grew thoughtful. Gagin's words 'make a rendezvous with you' pierced me to the heart. It seemed to me shameful not to answer his candour with a similar frankness.

'Yes,' I said at last, 'you're right. An hour ago I received a note from your sister. Here it is.'

Gagin took the note, quickly read it and then dropped his hands to his knees. The expression of astonishment on his face was very entertaining, but I was not in the mood for laughter.

'You're an honourable man, I repeat,' he said, 'but what on earth do we do now? What do you think? She wants to leave, and here she is writing to you, and she reproaches herself for doing something very silly ... And when could she have found the time to write this? What's she want from you anyway?'

I calmed him down and we embarked on as cold-blooded a discussion of what we ought to do as was possible in the circumstances. We finally came to the conclusion that, to avoid trouble, I should go to the rendezvous and explain everything honestly to Asya. Gagin undertook to remain at home and give no indication that the note was known to him. We agreed we would meet again that evening.

'I place all my hopes in you,' said Gagin and squeezed my hand. 'Spare the two of us, her and me. And we'll be off tomorrow,' he added, rising, 'because you're not thinking of marrying Asya.'

'Give me until this evening,' I replied.

'Very well, but you won't be getting married.'

He left and I flung myself on the divan and closed my eyes. My head was going round from the excessive accumulation of impressions which had burst upon me. I was annoyed by Gagin's candour and I was annoyed by Asya. Her love both delighted me and embarrassed me. I couldn't understand what had made her tell her brother everything. The inevitability of a quick, almost instantaneous, decision was an absolute torture to me.

'Marry a seventeen-year-old girl with her temperament, that's impossible!' I said to myself, getting to my feet.

ASYA

15

At the appointed hour I crossed the Rhine and the first person who met me on the other bank was the same small boy who had visited me in the morning. He had evidently been waiting for me.

'From Fraulein Annette,' he said in a whisper and handed me another note.

It was from Asya telling me of a change of place for our meeting. In an hour and a half I should go not to the chapel but to Frau Louise's house, knock on the door downstairs and go up to the third floor.

'Is it again yes?' the boy asked me.

'Yes,' I repeated, and walked away along the bank of the Rhine.

There was no point in going home and I didn't want to wander about the streets. Beyond the town wall there was a little garden with a lean-to for skittles and tables for those who were fond of beer. I went there. A few elderly Germans were already playing skittles. The wooden balls bounced along with a clattering and there were occasional cries of approval. A pretty waitress with tear-stained eyes brought me a tankard of beer. I glanced in her face. She turned away quickly and went off.

'Yes, yes,' said a fat and red-cheeked local citizen who was sitting there, 'our Hannchen's very miserable today: her fiance's gone off to be a soldier.'

I looked at her. She was huddled in a corner and cupping her cheek in her hand. Tears ran one by one down her fingers. When someone ordered beer, she took him a tankard and again returned to her place. Her grief acted upon me and I started thinking about the meeting which awaited me, but all my thoughts were troubled and unhappy. It wasn't with a light heart that I was going to this meeting and I couldn't expect to be submitting to the joys of mutual love. I could only expect to have to keep my promise, to fulfil a difficult obligation. 'One can't play with fire' – Gagin's words, like arrows, buried themselves in my soul. And three days ago in that boat, borne along by the waves, wasn't it a fierce yearning for personal happiness that I'd longed for? It had become possible – and now I was wavering, I was rejecting it and I'd have to reject it once for all . . . Its unexpectedness disconcerted me. Asya herself, with her fiery headstrong ways, with her past and her education, this attractive, though strange, being – she frightened me, I confess. My feelings were engaged in a protracted struggle within me. The appointed time approached. 'I can't marry her,' I decided eventually, 'and she shan't learn that I've also fallen in love with her.'

I stood up and, placing a thaler in poor Hannchen's hand (she didn't even thank me), I set off for Frau Louise's house. Evening shadows were already pervading the air and the narrow strip of sky above the dark street was crimson with the light from the sunset. I knocked softly at the door and it was opened immediately. I entered and found myself in complete darkness.

'This way!' commanded an old woman's voice. 'You're expected.'

I took two steps, feeling my way, and then some bony hand seized hold of mine.

'Is it you, Frau Louise?' I asked.

'It is,' the same voice answered, 'it's me, my fine young man.'

The old woman led me upwards by a steep staircase and stopped on the third-floor landing. In the faint light filtering through a tiny window I saw the wrinkled face of the burgomaster's widow. A cloyingly crafty smile pulled at the edges of her sunken lips and crinkled her dull little eyes. She showed me to a small door. With a trembling hand I opened it and closed it to behind me.

[16]

It was fairly dark in the small room I entered and I didn't see Asya at first. Wrapped in a long shawl, she was sitting in a chair beside the window, her head turned away and almost hidden, like a frightened bird. She was breathing fast and quivering all over. I felt unutterably sorry for her. I went up to her. She turned her head still further from me . . .

'Anna Nikolaevna,' I said.

She suddenly straightened up, tried to look at me – and couldn't. I took her hand, which felt cold and lay in the palm of my own hand like a dead thing.

'I'd wanted,' Asya began, trying to smile, but her pale lips wouldn't move, 'I'd wanted . . . No, I can't,' she muttered and fell silent. Her voice faltered at every word.

I sat down beside her.

'Anna Nikolaevna,' I repeated, and I also couldn't add anything.

Silence reigned. I continued holding her hand and looking at her. She shrank away from me as before, breathing with difficulty and biting her lower lip to stop herself from crying, to hold back the accumulating tears . . . I gazed at her. There was something touchingly helpless about her timid immobility, just as if she had crawled to her chair out of exhaustion and literally collapsed into it. My heart melted.

'Asya,' I said hardly audibly.

She slowly lifted her eyes towards me . . . Oh, the look of a woman who is in love, who can describe it? They begged, those eyes, they trusted, they questioned, they surrendered . . . I couldn't resist their enchantment. A delicate fire ran through me like burning needles. I bent down and lightly pressed my lips to her hand . . .

There was a slight rustling sound, like a sigh cut short, and I felt on my hair the touch of a feeble hand quivering like a leaf. I raised my head and saw her face. How it had changed all of a sudden! The look of fear had gone, the eyes gazed far away and drew me with them, the lips were slightly parted, the forehead was pale as marble and the curls were flung back as though blown back by a wind. I forgot everything and drew her to me. Her hand submitted and her whole body was drawn behind her hand, the shawl fell from her shoulders and her head rested softly on my chest, lay under my burning lips . . .

'I'm yours,' she whispered almost soundlessly.

My hands were already slipping round her waist when suddenly the memory of Gagin struck me like a lightning flash.

'What are we doing!' I cried, and convulsively drew myself back. 'Your brother – he knows everything. He knows I'm seeing you.'

Asya dropped back into her chair.

'Yes,' I continued, standing up and walking to the far corner of the room, 'your brother knows everything . . . I had to tell him everything.'

'You had to?' she asked indistinctly. She evidently hadn't yet come to her senses and didn't understand what I was saying.

'Yes, yes,' I repeated with a kind of bitterness, 'and you're solely responsible, you alone. Why did you yourself give away your secret? Who made you tell your brother everything? He came to me today and told me of your talk with him.' I tried not to look at Asya and walked to and fro in the room taking large steps. 'Now everything's finished, everything, everything.'

Asya was on the point of rising from her chair.

'Stay,' I cried, 'stay, I beg you. You're dealing with an honourable man – yes, an honourable man. But, in God's name, what made you do it? Had you noticed any change in me? I wasn't able to hide anything from your brother when he came to me today.'

'What am I saying?' I thought to myself, and the thought that I was an immoral deceiver, that Gagin knew about our meeting, that everything had been perverted and exposed, literally rang like an alarm bell in my head.

'I didn't ask my brother to do it,' came Asya's frightened whisper. 'He came of his own accord.'

'Look at what you've done, then,' I went on. 'Now you want to leave . . .'

'Yes, I've got to leave,' she said in the same soft whisper. 'I asked you to come here just to say goodbye to you.'

'And you think it'll be easy', I objected, 'for me to say goodbye to you?'

'But then why did you tell my brother?' repeated Asya in confusion.

'I tell you — I couldn't behave otherwise. If you hadn't given yourself away . . .'

'I locked myself in my room,' she protested artlessly. 'I didn't know that my landlady had another key . . .'

This innocent excuse on her lips and at such a moment almost infuriated me then . . . but now I can't remember it without a feeling of tenderness. The poor, honest, sincere child!

'And now everything's over!' I began again. 'Everything! Now we've got to part from each other.' I glanced surreptitiously at Asya. Her face had quickly reddened. I sensed she had begun to feel ashamed as well as frightened. I was myself striding to and fro and talking as if in a high fever. 'You didn't allow a feeling to grow which had just begun to ripen. You yourself broke off our relationship, you didn't have any trust in me, you doubted me . . .'

While I was speaking Asya had been bending further and further forward — and then suddenly dropped on to her knees, let her head fall forward into her hands and burst into tears. I dashed to her and tried to help her to her feet, but she resisted me. I cannot stand a woman's tears. At the sight of them I am completely lost.

'Anna Nikolaevna, Asya,' I kept repeating, 'please, I beg you, for God's sake, do stop crying . . .' I once more took her by the hand.

But, to my greatest astonishment, she suddenly jumped up and with lightning swiftness dashed to the door and vanished from sight.

A few moments later, when Frau Louise came into the room, I was still standing in the middle of it, literally thunderstruck. I couldn't understand how the meeting could have had such a swift and stupid ending, how it could have ended when I hadn't said a hundredth part of what I'd wanted to say or should have said, when I still hadn't any idea how it could all be resolved . . .

'The fraulein has gone?' Frau Louise asked me, raising her yellow eyebrows right up to the edge of her false hair.

I looked at her like an idiot – and then left the room.

[17]

I made my way out of the town and straight into open country. Annoyance, wild annoyance, tore at my guts. I poured down reproaches on my head. How was it I couldn't have understood the reason that made Asya change the place of our meeting, why hadn't I appreciated what it must have cost her to go to that old woman, and why hadn't I kept her from leaving? Alone with her in that poorly lit, God-forsaken room I'd had the strength, I'd had the spirit, to thrust her from me, even to reproach her . . . But now her image pursued me and I begged its forgiveness. My memories of that pale face, of those moist and timid eyes, of the hair uncurled on her bent neck, of the light pressure of her head against my chest – these memories scorched me. 'I'm yours,' came her audible whisper. 'I acted out of conscience,' I insisted to myself. Nonsense! Was that really how I'd wanted it to end? Am I really ready to part with her? Can I really give her up? 'Idiot! Idiot!' I kept on telling myself bitterly.

In the meantime night had come on. With large strides I set off towards the cottage where Asya lived.

[18]

Gagin came out to meet me.

'Have you seen my sister?' he called to me from a distance.

'Isn't she at home?'

'No.'

'She hasn't come back yet?'

'No. It's my fault,' Gagin went on. 'I couldn't wait. In spite of what we'd agreed, I went off to the chapel. She wasn't there. Does that mean she didn't turn up?'

'She wasn't at the chapel.'

'So you haven't seen her?'

I had to admit that I'd seen her.

'Where?'

'At Frau Louise's. I said goodbye to her an hour ago,' I added. 'I was sure she'd returned home.'

'Let's wait for her,' said Gagin.

We entered the cottage and sat down side by side. We said nothing. Both of us felt extremely awkward. We continuously glanced round, looked at the door and listened. Finally Gagin stood up.

'This is beyond a joke!' he exclaimed. 'My heart's all over the place. She'll be the death of me, by God! Let's go and look for her.'

We went out. It was pitch dark out of doors.

'What did you say to her?' Gagin asked me, pulling his hat down over his eyes.

'I saw her for barely five minutes,' I answered. 'I told her what we'd agreed.'

'Do you know what?' he said. 'It would be better if we went different ways, that way we'll find her more quickly. In any case, come back here in an hour.'

[19]

I hurriedly descended through the vineyard and rushed towards the town. I quickly walked round all the streets and looked everywhere, even in Frau Louise's windows, then returned to the Rhine and ran along the bank. I came across the figures of women from time to time, but Asya was nowhere to be seen. It was no longer annoyance that tore at my guts, it was a secret panic fear, and it wasn't only fear I felt – no, I felt remorse, the most burning regret and love – yes, the tenderest love! I wrung my hands, called out Asya's name in the gathering nocturnal gloom, at first in a low voice, then louder and louder. Time after time I repeated that I loved her, that I vowed never to leave her. I would have given everything on earth once again to hold her cold hand, once again to hear her soft voice, once again to see her in front of me . . . She had been so close, she had come to me completely determined, in the complete innocence of her heart and feelings, she had brought me all her untrammelled youth . . . and I had not hugged her to me, I had deprived myself of the bliss of seeing how her dear face would break open with the joy and peace of pure delight . . . This thought was driving me out of my mind.

'Where could she have gone, what's she done with herself?' I cried out again and again in access of helpless desperation . . . A white blur appeared suddenly on the river bank. I knew the place. There, above the grave of a man who had drowned seventy years before, stood, half-overgrown, a stone cross with an antique inscription. My heart almost stopped. . . I ran towards the cross and the white figure vanished. I shouted: 'Asya!' My wild cry frightened even me – but no one answered.

I decided to go and find out whether Gagin had found her.

[20]

Quickly climbing up the path through the vineyard, I saw a light in Asya's room. This calmed me slightly.

I went up to the cottage. The door was closed and I knocked. A small unlighted window on the ground floor was cautiously opened and Gagin's head appeared.

'Have you found her?' I asked him.

'She's returned,' he answered me in a whisper. 'She's in her room and undressing. Everything's all right.'

'Thank God!' I exclaimed with an inexpressible burst of joy. 'Thank God! Now everything's splendid. But you know, we must have another discussion.'

'Another time,' he said, quietly drawing the window towards him. 'Another time, but now goodbye.'

'Till tomorrow,' I murmured. 'It'll all be decided tomorrow.'

'Goodbye,' Gagin repeated. The window was drawn shut.

I was on the point of tapping on the window. At that moment I wanted to tell Gagin that I would ask for his sister's hand. But it wasn't the time for matchmaking. 'Till tomorrow,' I thought. 'Tomorrow I'll be happy . . .'

Tomorrow I'll be happy! Happiness has no tomorrow. It has no yesterday. It does not remember the past, it does not think of the future. It only has a present time – and that's not a whole day, but only an instant.

I don't remember how I got back to Z—. It wasn't on foot and it wasn't by boat: it was broad, powerful wings that lifted me up. I went past the bush where the nightingale was singing and stopped and listened for a long while: it seemed that the bird was singing of my love and my happiness.

[21]

When, the next morning, I started to approach the familiar cottage, I was astonished by the fact that all the windows were open and the door was open. There was some paper lying about in front of the cottage. A maidservant with a broom appeared in the doorway.

I went up to her . . .

'They've left!' she screeched out before I had time to ask if the Gagins were at home.

'Left?' I repeated. 'How? Where?'

'They left this morning at six o'clock and didn't say where. Wait, though, you're Herr N—, aren't you?'

'I am Herr N—.'

'The landlady has a letter for you.' The maidservant went upstairs and came back with a letter. 'Here it is, sir.'

'But it can't be . . . How can it be?' I started saying . . .

The maidservant gave me a vacant look and started sweeping.

I opened the letter. Gagin had written it; there was not a line from Asya. He began by begging me not to be angry with him for their sudden departure. He was sure that after mature consideration I would approve his decision. He couldn't see any other way out of a situation which could become tiresome and dangerous. 'Yesterday evening,' he wrote, 'when we sat together in silence waiting for Asya, I finally became convinced of the necessity of separation. There are prejudices which I respect. I understand that you couldn't marry Asya. She has told me everything. For her own peace of mind I had to accede to her repeated and insistent demands.' At the end of the letter he declared his regret that our acquaintanceship had to end so quickly, wished me happiness, warmly shook me by the hand and implored me not to try and find them.

'What prejudices?' I cried out, as if he could hear me. 'What nonsense! Who gave him the right to steal her from me?' I seized myself by the head.

The maidservant began calling loudly for the landlady and her anxiety brought me to my senses. An idea had caught alight within me: I would go in search of them no matter what happened. To accept this blow, to be reconciled to such an outcome was out of the question. I learned from the landlady that at six o'clock they had caught the steamer and sailed away down the Rhine. I set off for the steamboat office and was told that they had taken tickets for Cologne. I went home with the aim of packing at once and following in their wake. On my way I had to go past Frau Louise's house. Suddenly I heard someone calling me. I raised my head and saw the burgomaster's widow in the window of the very room where I had met Asya the day before. She was smiling her unpleasant smile and calling to me. I turned away and was about to walk on, but she shouted after me that she had something for me. These words made me stop, and I went into her house. How can I express the feelings I had when I saw that little room once again . . .

'Truth to tell,' the old woman began, showing me a little note, 'I should've let you have this only if you'd come here of your own accord, but you're such a fine young man. Take it.'

I took the note.

On a tiny scrap of paper were the following words written hurriedly in pencil:

'Goodbye, we won't see each other any more. I'm not leaving out of pride. No, it's just that I couldn't do otherwise. Yesterday, when I cried in front of you, if you'd said one word to me, just one word, I'd have stayed. You didn't say it. So obviously it's better this way . . . Goodbye forever!'

One word . . . Oh, I'd been such an idiot! That word . . . I'd repeated it with tears the day before, I'd scattered it on the wind, rehearsed it over and over again to the empty fields . . . but I'd not said it to her, I'd not told her I loved her . . . No, I'd not been able to say that word then. When I'd met her in that fateful room, I'd not had any clear awareness of my love. It had not even awoken when I'd been sitting with her brother in that senseless and oppressive silence. It had burst alight with irresistible force only a few moments later when, alarmed by the possibility of misfortune, I'd started looking for her and calling her name . . . But then it was already too late. 'Oh, that's impossible!' I'll be told. I don't know whether it's impossible or not, I know it's the truth. Asya wouldn't have left if there'd been the slightest shadow of pretence about her and if her position hadn't been false. She wasn't able to tolerate what any other girl would. That was what I didn't understand. My unkind genius of ineptitude had stopped the confession on my very lips at my last meeting with Gagin before the darkened window, and the last thread which I could still have grasped had slipped out of my hands.

That very day I returned to L— with my trunk packed and I set sail for Cologne. I remember that the steamer had already cast off and I was mentally saying farewell to the streets and all the places I'd never be able to forget, when I caught sight of Hannchen. She was sitting on a bench at the riverside. Her face was pale, but not sorrowful. A handsome young man was standing next to her and laughing as he told her something. And on the other side of the Rhine my little madonna peered out as mournfully as ever from the dark foliage of the old ash-tree.

[22]

In Cologne I hit upon the Gagins' trail. I learned that they had gone to London. I set off after them, but in London all my enquiries were in vain. For a long time I didn't want to admit defeat, for a long time I held out some hope, but in the end I had to give up all hope of finding them.

And I never saw them again. I never saw Asya. Obscure rumours did reach me about him, but she vanished for me forever. I don't even know whether she's still alive. Once, a few years ago, when abroad, I caught sight of a woman in a railway carriage whose face reminded me of those unforgettable features... but I had probably been misled by an accidental resemblance. Asya remained in my memory as that very girl whom I'd known in the best period of my life, just as I'd seen her for the last time, leaning on the back of a low wooden chair.

Besides, I must confess that I didn't grieve over her excessively. I even found that fate had arranged things well in not uniting me with Asya. I comforted myself with the thought that I probably wouldn't have been happy with such a wife. I was young in those days – and the future, the brief, ephemeral future, seemed to me limitless. Surely the same thing could happen again, I thought, and perhaps be even better, even more beautiful? I have known many other women, but the feeling aroused in me by Asya – that burning, tender, profound feeling – has never been repeated. No, no eyes have ever replaced those which once looked at me with such love, to no heart pressed against my chest has my own heart responded with such a sweet and delighted aching! Condemned to the solitariness of a bachelor's homeless life, I am living out years of vacant boredom, but I treasure as sacred relics her notes and a dried geranium flower, the piece of geranium which she had thrown down to me out of the window on that occasion. It still has a faint fragrance, but the hand which gave it me, the hand which I only once had the chance to press to my lips, perhaps already lies rotting in some grave . . . And as for me, what's happened to me? What is left of me, of those blissful and exciting days, of those winged hopes and desires? So it is that the faint fragrance from an unimportant flower outlives all the joys and miseries of a man – and eventually outlives the man himself.

First Love

Dedicated to P. V. Annenkov

The guests had long since gone. The clock struck twelve-thirty. Only the host and Sergey Nikolaevich and Vladimir Petrovich remained in the room.

The host rang and ordered the remains of supper to be taken away.

'So we've decided,' said he, settling himself deeper into his armchair and lighting a cigar, 'each of us is obliged to tell the story of his first love. It's your turn to start, Sergey Nikolaevich.'

Sergey Nikolaevich, a well-rounded chap with a plumpish, whitish face, looked first at his host and then raised his eyes to the ceiling.

'I didn't have a first love,' he said eventually, 'but started straight off with my second.'

'How do you mean?'

'It's very simple. I was eighteen when I first started chasing after a very charming young lady, but I courted her just as if I wasn't new at the game at all – exactly, in fact, as I courted all the others later. Strictly speaking, I fell in love for the first and last time at the age of six – with my nurse. But that's a very long time ago. The details of our relations have been wiped from my memory, and even if I did remember them who could they possibly interest?'

'So what next?' began the host. 'In the case of my first love there was also not much of interest. I had never fallen in love with anyone before I met Anna Ivanovna, my present wife – and everything went without a hitch: our fathers arranged our match, we very quickly fell in love and got married without delay. My fairytale happiness is told in a couple of words. I confess, gentlemen, that in raising the question of first love I was relying on you, I won't say old, but no longer youthful bachelors. Haven't you got anything for us, Vladimir Petrovich?'

'My first love really does belong among the not exactly usual ones,' answered Vladimir Petrovich with a slight hesitancy. He was a man of forty, dark-haired, greying.

'Ah!' said the host and Sergey Nikolaevich simultaneously. 'So much the better . . . Go on, then, tell us.'

'If you like . . . or no, I won't start telling you, because I'm no good at telling things. They come out either too cut-and-dried or too long-winded and artificial. If you'll allow me, I'll write down everything I remember in an exercise book and then read it out to you.'

The friends wouldn't agree at first, but Vladimir Petrovich insisted. Two weeks later they gathered again and Vladimir Petrovich kept his promise.

This is what was written in his exercise book:

[1]

At the time I was sixteen. It all happened in the summer of 1833.

I was living in Moscow with my parents. They had taken a summer residence near the Kaluga Gate, opposite the Amusement Gardens. I was preparing to go to university, but was doing very little work and not hurrying.

Nobody restricted my freedom. I was able to do just what I wanted, especially after I'd said goodbye to my last French tutor who simply couldn't get used to the idea that he'd landed in Russia 'like a bomb' (*comme une bombe*) and used to spend whole days at a time lounging on his bed with a look of extreme distaste on his face. My father treated me in a fondly indifferent way and my mother hardly paid any attention to me, although she had no other children; she was consumed by other cares. My father, a man who was still young and very handsome, had married her for her money; she was ten years his senior. My mother led an unhappy life of continual worryings, jealousies and tempers – but never in my father's presence. She was afraid of him and he was always severe, cold, remote . . . I've never known a man more exquisitely composed, self-assured and authoritative.

I'll never forget the first weeks I spent there. It was wonderful weather. We moved out to the summer residence on 9 May, St Nicholas's Day. I used to go for walks, sometimes in the garden of our house, sometimes in the Amusement Gardens, sometimes beyond the Kaluga Gate. I used to take a book with me – a history book by Kaydanov, for instance – but opened it only rarely, and mostly I recited aloud verses, of which I knew a great many. I could feel a kind of effervescence in my blood and a sort of aching in my heart – it was all so delightful and silly. I was all the time expectant and shy and wonderfully receptive and prepared for anything. My imaginings played and darted continually about one and the same thing, like martins at twilight around a bell-tower. I would become thoughtful and sad and even cry, but through the tears and the sadness brought on by the melodiousness of a poem or the beauty of an evening there always emerged, like grass breaking through in spring, the joyous sense of young, bubbling life.

I had a little horse for riding, saddled it myself and would go out riding alone, and when going at a gallop would imagine I was a knight at a tournament – how the wind blew in my ears! – or, upturning my face towards the sky, would let the whole of its brilliant light and azure blue flow into my soul.

I remember at that time the image of a woman and the vision of a woman's love hardly ever arose in any definite way in my mind, but in everything I thought and felt there was a half-conscious, conscience-stricken anticipation of something new and inexpressibly sweet and feminine . . . This anticipation, this foreboding permeated every bit of me and I breathed it in with each breath, it was pumped through my veins in each drop of blood. It was soon destined to be more than a foreboding.

Our summer residence consisted of a main house, made of wood with columns at the front, and two wings on a lower level. The wing on the left was occupied by a small factory where rolls of cheap wallpaper were made. I often went to watch the dozen or so thin and dishevelled boys, in their long greasy coats and with their pinched faces, jumping up and down on the wooden levers that pressed out the square blocks and with the weight of their puny bodies thus stamp out the brightly coloured patterns of the wallpaper. The wing on the right was empty; it used to be rented out. One day three weeks or so after 9 May the shutters on the windows of this wing were opened and women's faces appeared in them – some family had taken up residence. I remember that after dinner on that very same day my mother inquired of the steward who our new neighbours were and, on hearing the name Princess Zasyekin, at first remarked not without a certain respect: 'Ah, a princess,' and then added: 'She obviously can't be well off.'

'They came in three carriages, ma'am,' said the steward, deferentially offering a dish. 'They have no carriage of their own, ma'am, and their furniture is very poor stuff.'

'I thought so,' remarked my mother. 'It's just as well.'

My father gave her a cold look and she fell silent.

In actual fact Princess Zasyekin could not have been a rich woman because the wing she had rented was so dilapidated, small and low-ceilinged that people even of modest means would not have agreed to reside there. However, at that time I didn't spare a thought for such matters. The title of 'Princess' had little effect because I had only just finished reading Schiller's *The Robbers*.*

[2]

It had become a habit of mine to wander about our garden each evening with a gun on the look-out for crows. I had long ago taken a dislike to these cautious, predatory and crafty birds. On the day with which this story is concerned I also went out into the garden and, having been up and down all the paths in vain (the crows knew me and simply cawed raucously from the distance), I accidentally came upon a low fence that separated *our* garden from the narrow strip belonging to the right-hand wing of the house. I was walking along with my head lowered. Suddenly I heard voices. I glanced over the fence and stood stock still. My eyes were greeted by a strange sight.

A few steps from me, on some open grass among green raspberry canes, there stood a tall, slender girl in a striped pink dress with a white scarf on her head. She was surrounded by four young men and she was tapping each in turn on the forehead with those small, pale-mauve flowers whose name I don't know but which are well known to children because they form small bags and burst open with a bang when you hit them against something hard. The young men offered their foreheads so willingly, and in the girl's movements (I saw her from one side) there was something so engaging, so commanding, so caressing, something so amusing and delightful that I nearly gave a cry of astonishment and pleasure and would have given anything in the world, I believe, if only those charming fingers had tapped me on the forehead as well. My gun slipped into the grass and I forgot everything. My eyes devoured the slender waist and small neck, the lovely arms and the slightly dishevelled fair hair under the white scarf, the intelligent half-closed eyes and the eyelashes and the soft skin of the cheek beneath them . . .

'Young man, young man,' suddenly said a voice close by me, 'do you think it's right and proper to look at strange young ladies like that?'

I shuddered all over, feeling stupefied. On the other side of the fence from me stood a young man with close-cropped black hair, looking at me ironically. At that very moment the girl turned towards me . . . I caught sight of large grey eyes in a lively, animated face – and suddenly the whole of this face began quivering with laughter, white teeth flashed, eyebrows lifted in amusement . . . I blushed, seized my gun from the ground and, pursued by loud but not malicious laughter, dashed back home to my room, flung myself on my bed and covered my face with my hands. My heart literally leapt inside me. I felt very ashamed and very happy. And I was incredibly excited.

When I'd got my breath back, I brushed my hair, cleaned up and went downstairs for tea. The image of the young girl still floated in front of me, but my heart had stopped leaping and simply felt pleasantly squeezed.

'What's happened to you?' my father suddenly asked. 'Have you killed a crow?'

I wanted to tell him all about it, but refrained and did no more than smile to myself. On going up to bed, I pirouetted round three times on one foot, I don't know why, greased my hair, lay down and spent the whole night dead to the world. Just before morning I awoke for an instant, raised my head, looked around me with excitement – and went back to sleep.

[3]

'How can I get to know them?' was my first thought as soon as I woke up the next morning. Before breakfast I went out into the garden, but I did not go too close to the fence and saw no one. After breakfast I strolled several times up and down the street in front of the house and glanced now and then at their windows . . . I once sensed that *her* face was behind the curtain and hurried away in fright. 'But I must get to know them,' I thought, aimlessly wandering about in the sandy area by the Amusement Gardens. 'Yet how? That is the question.' I called to mind the smallest details of the previous day's meeting. I remembered particularly clearly for some reason how she seemed to be laughing at me . . . But while I worked myself up and contrived various plans, fate was already taking me in hand.

In my absence my mother had received from her new neighbour a
letter on grey paper sealed with a brown wax of the kind used on notices
issued by the post office and on cheap wine-corks. In the letter, written
ungrammatically and in an untidy hand, the princess begged my mother
to use her good auspices on her behalf. In the words of the princess, my
mother was well aquainted with people of importance, upon whom her
own fate and that of her children depended, for she was involved in some
very significant lawsuits. 'I adress meself to yew', she wrote, 'as one
noblewoman to anuther, and it is a plesure to me to taike this oportunity.'
She concluded by begging my mother's permission to pay her a visit. I
found my mother in an unpleasant frame of mind, since my father was
not at home and she had no one to advise her. Not to answer such a
'noblewoman', a princess at that, would be out of the question, but my
mother was at a loss to know how. It seemed to her inappropriate to
write a note in French, but spelling in Russian was not her strong point,
as she knew only too well, and she did not want to be compromised.
She was overjoyed by my arrival and at once ordered me to go to the
princess and explain to her by word of mouth that she, my mother, was
always ready to be of service to her ladyship, in so far as she was able,
and begged her to call on her at about one o'clock. The unexpectedly
rapid fulfilment of my secret desires both delighted and frightened me.
However, I gave no sign of the embarrassment which had taken possession of me and took the precaution of going to my room beforehand in
order to change into a new tie and frock-coat, because at home I still
used to wear a short jacket and turned-down collars, although I was
thoroughly fed up with them.

[4]

In the narrow and untidy hallway of the wing occupied by the princess,
which I entered with a helpless trembling in every limb, there met me
an old and grey-haired manservant with a face the colour of darkened
bronze, pig-like, morose little eyes, and furrows on his forehead and
temples of such depth I'd never seen anything like them before in my
life. He was carrying a plate with a clean-picked herring bone on it and,
using his foot partly to close a door into another room, asked curtly:
'Whatya want?'
'Is Princess Zasyekin at home?' I asked.
'Boneyface!' a shrill female voice shouted from behind the door.

The manservant silently turned his back on me and in so doing revealed to me the badly worn back of his livery with one solitary rusty-looking crested button, and then, after placing the plate on the floor, he disappeared.

'Did you go to the police?' asked the same female voice again. The manservant murmured something. 'Eh? . . . Did you say someone'd come?' the voice could be heard saying. 'The young man from next door? Well, ask him to come in.'

'This way, sir, into the drawing-room,' said the manservant, once again reappearing in front of me and picking up the plate.

I straightened my clothes and entered the so-called 'drawing-room'.

I found myself in a small and not exactly tidy room filled with hastily arranged, poor quality furniture. By the window, sitting in an armchair with a broken arm, was a woman of about fifty, unattractive, with untended hair, in an ancient green dress and a somewhat motley worsted scarf wrapped round her neck. Her black little eyes quite literally drank me in. I approached her and bowed.

'Have I the honour of speaking to Princess Zasyekin?'

'I am Princess Zasyekin. And you are Mr V—'s son, are you?'

'Yes, ma'am. I have a message from my mother.'

'Do please sit down. Boneyface! Where are my keys? Have you seen them?'

I informed her of my mother's answer to her letter. She listened to me, tapping her fat red fingers on the window-sill, and when I'd finished she once more stared at me.

'Very good. I will be there without fail,' she said at last. 'How young you look! How old are you, may I ask?'

'Sixteen,' I answered with a stammer.

The princess extracted from her pocket some soiled-looking papers covered in writing, brought them right up to her nose and started sorting through them.

'A nice age,' she announced suddenly, twisting about and fidgeting in her chair. 'Please don't stand on ceremony with me. I'm a simple person.'

'Too simple,' I thought, surveying with considerable distaste the whole of her unprepossessing figure.

At that moment the other door of the drawing-room was flung open and there appeared in the doorway the girl I'd seen in the garden the previous evening.

'And this is my daughter,' said the princess, pointing her elbow at her. 'Zinochka, this is the son of our next-door neighbour, Mr V—. May I ask what your name is?'

'Vladimir,' I answered, rising to my feet and acquiring a slight lisp with the excitement.

'And your patronymic?'

'Petrovich.'

'Well I never! I once had a friend who was chief of police – he was also called Vladimir Petrovich. Boneyface! Stop looking for the keys, they're in my pocket!'

The girl went on looking at me with the same amused smile, slightly narrowing her eyes and leaning her head a little to one side.

'I have already met Monsieur Voldemar,' she began. (The silveriness of her voice ran over my skin like some delightful goose pimples.) 'Will you allow me to call you that?'

'Please do,' I stammered.

'Where was this?' asked the princess.

The daughter did not answer the mother's question.

'Are you busy now?' she asked, not taking her eyes off me.

'No, not at all.'

'Would you mind helping me wind some wool? Come this way, to my room.'

She nodded her head at me and went out of the drawing-room. I followed after her.

In the room which we entered the furniture was of a little better quality and it was arranged more tastefully. Mind you, at that moment I was almost incapable of noticing anything. I moved as in a dream and felt throughout my whole being a quite ridiculously intense happiness.

She sat down, produced a skein of red wool and, showing me to a chair opposite her, started painstakingly unwinding the skein and placing it on my hands. She did all this in silence, with a kind of amused deliberateness and the same bright, knowing smile on her slightly parted lips. She began winding the wool on to a piece of bent card and suddenly gave me such a swift and radiant look that I couldn't help myself and glanced away. When her eyes, which were half closed for the most part, opened to their full extent, her face changed completely, just as if some bright sunlight were pouring through it.

'What did you think of me yesterday, Monsieur Voldemar?' she asked after a short silence. 'You probably blamed me, didn't you?'

'I, er, princess . . . I didn't think anything . . . how could I?' I answered in confusion.

'Listen,' she responded. 'You don't know me properly yet. I'm the strangest kind of person: I always want people to tell me the truth. I heard you were sixteen. Well, I'm twenty-one, so you see I'm much older than you and you've always got to tell me the truth and do what I say. Look at me,' she added. 'Why aren't you looking at me?'

I grew even more confused, but I raised my eyes to hers. She gave me a smile, not her usual kind of smile but one of approval.

'Look at me,' she said, softly lowering her voice. 'I don't find it unpleasant. I like your face and I have a feeling we'll be friends. Do you like me?' she asked slyly.

'Princess . . .' I began.

'In the first place, you must call me Zinaida Alexandrovna, and in the second place, why this childish habit' (she corrected herself) 'this young man's habit of not saying exactly what you feel? You can leave that to grown-ups. Now, do you like me?'

Although it was very pleasant that she should be so open with me, I was also a little offended. I wanted to show her that she was not dealing with a boy and, adopting as far as possible a worldly-wise and serious look, announced:

'Of course, I like you very much, Zinaida Alexandrovna. I don't want to hide the fact.'

She slowly shook her head.

'Have you a tutor?' she suddenly asked.

'No, I haven't had a tutor for a long time.'

I was lying through my teeth, because it was scarcely a month since my Frenchman had left.

'Oh! Yes, I can see you're quite grown-up!' She lightly struck me across the fingers. 'Hold your hands out straight!' And she busied herself with winding the ball of wool.

I made use of the fact that she did not raise her eyes and started studying her, at first furtively and then more and more boldly. Her face seemed to me even more attractive than it had looked the previous day, so delicate

FIRST LOVE

were the features, so intelligent and charming. She was sitting with her back to the window which was screened by a white blind. The sunlight, pouring through this blind, suffused with its soft light her sumptuous golden hair, the pure nape of her neck, her sloping shoulders and her soft, placid bosom. I gazed at her and she became so dear and precious to me. I felt I'd known her for years and yet had known nothing and never lived till I'd seen her. She was wearing a dark-coloured, some-what worn dress with a pinafore and I would gladly have kissed every crease and seam in that dress and that pinafore. The ends of her shoes peeped out from beneath her dress an I would gladly have bowed down in adoration to those shoes . . . 'And here I am sitting in front of her,' I thought. 'I've got to know her – my God, what happiness!' I almost jumped up with delight, but in fact simply swung my legs a little like a child who's been given a sweet. I was as happy as a fish in water and could have spent the rest of my life in that room, could never have left that place.

She calmly raised her eyelids and once again her bright eyes flashed in my face like sunlight – and again she smiled softly.

'Why are you looking at me like that?' she asked slowly, and shook a finger.

I went red. 'She understands everything, she sees everything,' flashed through my mind. 'But then why shouldn't she understand and see everything?'

Suddenly there was a noise in the next room and the clinking of a sabre.

'Zina!' screamed the princess from the drawing-room. 'Belovzorov's brought you a kitten!'

'A kitten!' cried Zinaida and, jumping up from her chair, threw the ball of wool into my lap and dashed out.

I also stood up and, laying the skein of wool and the ball on the window-sill, walked into the drawing-room and stopped in amazement. In the middle of the room a tabby kitten was lying with its paws stretched out. Zinaida was kneeling in front of it and cautiously lifting its head. Beside the princess, and occupying practically the whole of the wall-space between the windows, was a blond, curly-haired young man, a hussar with a ruddy complexion and prominent eyes.

'Oh, what fun!' Zinaida kept on saying. 'And his eyes aren't grey, but green, and he's got such large ears! Thank you so much, Victor Yegorych! You're very kind.'

The hussar, in whom I recognised one of the young men I'd seen yesterday, smiled and gave a bow which set his spurs ringing and caused the chain-rings on his sabre to jingle.

'You were good enough to say yesterday that you would like a tabby cat with large ears – so I obtained one for you, ma'am. Your word is my command.' And again he gave a bow.

The kitten miaowed feebly and sniffed at the floor.

'Oh, he's hungry!' cried Zinaida. 'Boneyface! Sonya! Bring some milk!'

The maid, dressed in an old yellow dress, with a faded kerchief round her neck, came in with a saucer of milk and placed it in front of the kitten. The kitten quivered, puckered up its eyes and started drinking.

'Oh, what a lovely little pink tongue he has!' remarked Zinaida, bending her head down almost to floor level and looking at the kitten sideways. The kitten drank as much as it wanted and began purring, affectedly pawing at the floor. Zinaida stood up and, turning to the maid, said indifferently:

'Take him away.'

'For the kitten I ask your hand,' announced the hussar, smirking and giving a kind of squirm of his whole powerful body that fitted so tightly into his new uniform.

'Both of them!' replied Zinaida and stretched out her hands towards him. While he kissed them, she looked at me over her shoulder.

I stood stock-still on the one spot and had no idea whether I should laugh or say something or keep silent. Suddenly, through the open door into the hallway, I caught sight of the figure of our footman, Fyodor. He was making signs at me. Automatically I went out to him.

'What do you want?' I asked.

'Your mother has sent for you,' he said in a whisper. 'She is annoyed that you haven't come back with an answer.'

'Have I been here that long?'

'More than an hour.'

'More than an hour!' I repeated despite myself and, returning to the drawing-room, began bowing to the assembled company and scraping my heels.

'Where are you off to?' asked the young princess, glancing at me from behind the hussar.

'I have to go home, ma'am. So I'll say', I added, turning to her mother, 'that you will be coming to pay us a visit at one o'clock.'

'Yes, you say that, there's a good lad.' The princess hurriedly reached out for a snuff-box and took snuff so loudly that I even gave a jump. 'Yes, you say that,' she repeated, blinking with her eyes full of tears and wheezing.

I bowed once more, turned round and left the room with that feeling of awkwardness in my back which every young man feels when he knows he's being watched.

'Do come and see us again, Monsieur Voldemar,' called out Zinaida, and again burst out laughing.

'Why is she always laughing?' I asked myself as I went home with Fyodor, who said nothing but moved along behind me in a disapproving way. My mother scolded me and wondered what I could possibly be doing for so long at the princess's. I did not answer her and went to my room. I suddenly felt very sad and tried hard not to cry. I was envious of the hussar.

[5]

The princess, as promised, paid a visit to my mother and my mother didn't like her. I was not present at their meeting, but at dinner my mother told my father that the Princess Zasyekin seemed to her *une femme très vulgaire*, that she had been bored stiff by all her requests to put in a good word for her with Prince Sergey, that she had several lawsuits and monetary matters – *des vilaines affaires d'argent* – and that she was clearly a great one for spreading scandal. My mother added, however, that she had invited her and her daughter to dine the next day (on hearing the words 'and her daughter' I hid my face in my plate), because she was after all a neighbour and she had a title. In response my father announced to my mother that he now recalled who this lady was. In his youth he had known the late Prince Zasyekin, a man of outstanding education, but empty and worthless. In society he had been known as 'le Parisien' on account of his long residence in Paris. He had been very rich but had lost his entire fortune by gambling – and then for some unknown reason, scarcely for the money, since he could have made a better choice (added my father and smiled coldly), he married the daughter of some petty official and, having married, indulged in speculation and finally ruined himself completely.

'If only she doesn't start asking for loans,' my mother remarked.

'That's very likely,' my father said quietly. 'Does she speak French?'

'Very badly.'

'Hm. Well, no matter. I think you said you'd also invited her daughter. I've been told she's a very charming and educated young lady.'

'Oh! Then she doesn't take after her mother.'

'Nor after her father,' said my father. 'He was also educated, but a complete fool.'

My mother sighed and became thoughtful. My father kept silent. I had felt extremely embarrassed throughout the entire conversation.

After dinner I went into the garden, but without my gun this time. I had promised myself that I wouldn't go anywhere near the so-called Zasyekin 'garden', but some irresistible force drew me there – and not for nothing. I had hardly reached the fence when I saw Zinaida. She was alone. She had a book in her hands and she was walking slowly along a path. She did not notice me.

I was on the point of letting her pass by, but suddenly reconsidered and gave a cough. She turned her head but did not stop, drew aside a wide blue ribbon from her round straw hat, looked at me, smiled calmly and again directed her eyes into her book.

I took off my cap and after hesitating what to do for a short while walked away with a heavy heart. 'Que suis-je pour elle?' I thought (God knows why) in French. Familiar footsteps resounded behind me. I looked round and saw my father coming towards me with his light and rapid stride.

'Was that the princess?' he asked me.

'Yes.'

'Do you know her?'

'I saw her this morning at her mother's.'

My father stopped and, turning sharply on his heels, walked back. Drawing level with Zinaida, he politely bowed to her. She also bowed in his direction, not without a certain surprised look on her face, and lowered her book. I saw how she followed him with her eyes. My father always dressed very elegantly, simply and distinctively after his fashion, but his figure had never seemed to me more slender and his grey hat had never sat more handsomely on his scarcely age-thinned curls.

I was about to follow in Zinaida's direction, but she did not so much as glance at me, lifted up her book and walked off.

[6]

That whole evening and the following morning I spent in a kind of despairing numbness. I remember I tried to work and picked up Kaydanov. But the spaced-out lines and pages of the well-known history book flashed pointlessly in front of me. Ten times over I read the words: 'Julius Caesar excelled in military valour' and didn't understand a thing – and threw the book away. Before dinner I again put grease on my hair and again wore my frock-coat and tie.

'Why have you put them on?' asked my mother. 'You're not a student yet, and God alone knows if you'll pass the entrance exam. And your jacket wasn't made so long ago, was it? It can't be thrown away yet!'

'We're having guests,' I whispered, nearly desperate.

'What nonsense! Guests, indeed!'

I had to give in. I changed out of my frock-coat into my jacket, but I did not take off my tie. The princess and her daughter appeared half an hour before dinner. The old woman wore a yellow shawl over the green dress that was already known to me and had put on an old bonnet with ribbons of a bright, fiery red. She immediately started talking about her money problems and sighing and complaining of her poverty and 'carrying on' without any sense of propriety, taking her snuff just as loudly, and squirming and fidgeting in her chair just as freely as she would have done at home. It never seemed to occur to her that she was a princess. On the other hand Zinaida held herself very upright, almost haughtily, like a real princess. Her face acquired a look of cold immobility and seriousness – and I didn't recognise her, didn't recognise her swift glancing looks or her smile, though in this new character she struck me as being quite beautiful. She wore a light *barège* dress with a pale-blue pattern. Her hair fell round her cheeks in long curls in the English fashion. As a form of coiffure it went well with the cold expression of her face. My father sat next to her during dinner and with his customary elegant and calm courtesy engaged her in conversation. He would glance at her from time to time, and she would glance back, but rather oddly, almost with hostility. They conversed in French. I remember I was astonished by the purity of Zinaida's pronunciation. The princess behaved in her usual free-and-easy way while at table, eating a great deal and praising the food. My mother evidently found her a strain and answered her with a melancholy negligence; my father occasionally gave frowning looks. My mother also took a dislike to Zinaida.

'She's a stuck-up little thing,' was her opinion the next day. 'And what's she got to be so proud about *avec sa mine de grisette*?'

'Obviously you've not seen any *grisettes*,' my father remarked.

'Heaven forbid!'

'Exactly, heaven forbid! Only how can you judge about them in that case?'

Zinaida paid no attention to me at all. Soon after dinner the princess started saying goodbye.

'I will place all my hopes in what you can do for me, Marya Nikolaevna and Pyotr Vasilyevich,' she said in a sing-song plaint to my mother and father. 'It can't be helped – there were good times once and now they're gone! Now all I've got is my title,' she added with an unpleasant laugh, 'but it's no good being queen if your plate's licked clean.'

My father bowed to her very politely and accompanied her to the doorway of the hall. I stood there in my short jacket and stared at the floor, literally like a condemned criminal. Zinaida's treatment of me had finally done for me. Imagine my surprise, therefore, when, on passing by me, she said in a rapid whisper and with her former kindly expression of the eyes:

'Come and see us at eight o'clock without fail, do you hear . . .'

I simply spread my hands in amazement. But she'd already gone, covering her head with a white scarf.

[7]

Precisely at eight, in my frock-coat and with my hair brushed up in a quiff, I entered the hallway of the wing where the princess lived. The elderly manservant looked up gloomily at me and unwillingly rose from his bench. The drawing-room was full of happy voices. I opened the door and stepped back in astonishment. In the middle of the room was the young princess, standing on a chair and holding a man's hat in front of her. Five men were crowding round the chair. They were trying to put their hands into the hat, but she held it high up and was shaking it about violently. Seeing me, she cried:

'Stop! Stop! Here's a new arrival, we must give him a ticket,' and, jumping down lightly from the chair, she seized me by the cuff. 'Come on,' she said, 'what're you standing there for? Messieurs, allow me to introduce you. This is Monsieur Voldemar, our neighbour's son. And this', she added, turning to me and pointing to her guests one by one, 'is Count Malevsky, this is Dr Lushin, this is the poet Maidanov, this is the retired captain Nirmatsky and this is Belovzorov, the hussar, whom you've already met. I want you all to be friends.'

I was so overcome with embarrassment that I didn't bow to anyone. I recognised in Dr Lushin the man with the black hair who'd made such a cruel remark to me in the garden. The others were unknown to me.

'Count,' went on Zinaida, 'write out a ticket for Monsieur Voldemar.'

'That's not fair,' retorted the count with a slight Polish accent. He was a very good-looking and fashionably dressed man with brown hair, expressive deep-brown eyes, a small narrow nose and a thin moustache above a tiny mouth. 'This gentleman has not been playing forfeits with us.'

'It's not fair,' repeated Belovzorov and the man described as a retired captain, a man of about forty, with a complexion so pitted he was positively ugly, a negro's curly hair, round-shouldered and bow-legged and wearing a military tunic that was without epaulettes and unbuttoned.

'Write the ticket, I tell you,' the young princess repeated. 'Why all this rebelliousness? Monsieur Voldemar is with us for the first time and so the rules don't apply to him today. No more complaints. I just want you to write it out.'

The Count shrugged his shoulders, but humbly bowed his head, took the pen in his white, beringed hand, tore off a piece of paper and began to write on it.

'At least allow me to explain to Monsieur Voldemar what it's all about,' began Lushin in a sarcastic voice, 'or else he'll be completely lost. You see, young man, we're playing forfeits. The princess has to pay a forfeit and whoever picks out the winning ticket will have the right to kiss her hand. Have you understood what I've just told you?'

I simply looked at him and remained standing where I was in a daze while the young princess jumped back on the chair and started shaking the hat. Everyone crowded round her – and I was right at the back.

'Maidanov,' she said to a tall young man with a thin face, short-sighted little eyes and extremely long black hair, 'as a poet you should be mag-nanimous and surrender your ticket to Monsieur Voldemar, so that he'll then have two chances rather than one.'

But Maidanov shook his head in refusal, flourishing his long black

hair. I put my hand in the hat last of all, picked a ticket and opened it . . .
Good heavens, what a shock I got when I saw the word: Kiss!

'Kiss!' I cried out.

'Bravo, he's won!' exclaimed the little princess. 'I'm so pleased!' She
stepped down from the chair and looked at me directly in the eyes so
clearly and sweetly that my heart jumped. 'Are you pleased, too?' she
asked me.

'I?' I stammered.

'Sell me your ticket,' Belovzorov suddenly bellowed in my ear. 'I'll
give you a hundred roubles.'

I gave the hussar such a look of disapproval that Zinaida clapped her
hands and Lushin exclaimed: 'Splendid! But', he continued, 'as master
of ceremonies I have to see that the rules are kept. Monsieur Voldemar,
you must get down on one knee, that's the rule.'

Zinaida stood in front of me, bent her head a little to one side as if to
get a better view of me and with solemnity held out her hand to me. I
began to feel faint. I'd wanted to get down on one knee, but knelt on
both and touched my lips to Zinaida's fingers so ineptly that I slightly
scratched the end of my nose with one of her fingernails.

'Well done!' cried Lushin, and helped me to get up.

The game of forfeits continued. Zinaida sat me down beside her. She
invented all sorts of forfeits! Among others she had to pretend to be a
statue – and she chose as her pedestal the ugly Nirmatsky, ordered him
to lie prone and bury his chin in his chest. There was constant laughter.
For me, a boy brought up in a solitary, sober way in a staid home of the
upper classes, all this noise and din, all this informal, almost boisterous
gaiety, all these unheard-of goings-on with strange people literally went
to my head. I simply grew tipsy, as if I'd had too much wine. I started
laughing and chattering louder than the rest, so that even the princess
herself who'd been sitting in the next room with some minor official from
the law courts, summoned for a consultation, came in to take a look at
me. But I was so happy I didn't care who laughed at me or gave me looks.
Zinaida still showed me favours and always kept me by her. For one
forfeit I had to sit next to her, the two of us covered by a silk scarf, and
I was ordered to tell her *my secret*. I remember how close our two heads
were in the stuffy, semi-transparent, perfumed shade, how closely and
softly her eyes shone in this shade and how hot the breath was from her
open lips and how I could see her teeth and felt the burning, tickling

touch of the ends of her hair. I didn't say a word. She smiled mysteriously and slyly and at last whispered: 'Come on, why don't you?' and I simply went red and laughed and turned away and hardly dared breathe. When forfeits grew boring, we started playing a game with some string. My God, what delight I felt when she gave me a strong, sharp rap over the hands for not paying attention and I then deliberately pretended not to pay attention and she teased me by not touching my hands when I held them out!

All the things we got up to that evening! We played the piano and sang and danced and pretended to be gypsies. Nirmatsky was dressed up as a bear and made to drink salt and water. Count Malevsky showed us card tricks and ended by shuffling himself a whist hand full of trumps, on which feat Lushin 'had the honour to congratulate him'. Maidanov declaimed excerpts from his poem 'The Murderer' (what I am relating occurred at the height of Romanticism), which he planned to publish in a black cover with the headings printed in blood-red ink. The minor official from the law courts had his hat snatched from his knees and was forced by way of ransom to dance a Cossack dance. Old Boneyface was decked out in a bonnet and the young princess put on a man's hat ... There was no end to all our fun! Only Belovzorov remained by himself in one corner, frowning and angry. From time to time his eyes would grow bloodshot, he would turn red and it seemed he would fling himself at us and scatter us on all sides like wood-chips, but the young princess would look at him, wag her finger and he'd again go back to his corner.

At last we were exhausted. The princess was ready for anything, as she put it – not even the loudest shrieks upset her – and yet even she felt tired and was ready for a rest. At midnight supper was served, consisting of some old, dry cheese and cold pies filled with chopped ham, which seemed to me tastier than any pâté. There was only one bottle of wine and rather odd at that, made of dark glass and with a very wide neck; the wine itself had a pinkish colour – in any case, no one drank it. Worn-out and happy to the point of collapse, I left the wing where they lived; in parting Zinaida squeezed my hand firmly and again smiled enigmatically.

The night air breathed oppressively and rawly on my heated face. It seemed that a thunderstorm was brewing. Black clouds had arisen and were creeping across the sky, visibly altering their smoky shapes. A breeze restlessly made the dark trees quiver and somewhere far beyond the horizon the thunder grumbled angrily and dully, literally as if to itself.

I reached my room by the back stairs. My manservant was asleep on the floor and I was obliged to step over him. He woke up, saw me and announced that my mother was again angry with me and had wanted to send for me, but my father had dissuaded her. (The fact was that I never went to bed without first saying goodnight to my mother and receiving her blessing.) Well, I couldn't do a thing about that now! I told my manservant I'd undress myself and go to bed – and put out the candle. But I didn't undress and I didn't go to bed.

I sat down in a chair and remained seated there for a long time as if under a spell. All my sensations were so new and so sweet . . . I sat there, hardly looking round me and not stirring, slowly breathing and only occasionally laughing quietly when I remembered, or feeling an inward shivering whenever I had the thought that I was in love, that this was it, this was love. Zinaida's face calmly floated in front of me in the darkness – floated into view and would not float away. Her lips had the same enigmatic smile, her eyes looked at me slightly sideways, questioningly, thoughtfully and softly, just as they'd looked when I said goodbye to her. Eventually I stood up, went on tip-toe to my bed and carefully, without undressing, laid my head down on the pillow, as if apprehensive that a sharp movement might spill the feeling with which I was full to the brim . . .

I lay down but did not even close my eyes. I soon noticed that faint flashes were constantly lighting up the room. I raised myself and looked out of the window. The frame was clearly outlined against the mysteriously and vaguely white brilliance of the glass panes. 'A thunderstorm,' I thought, and indeed it was a thunderstorm, but so far off that the thunder was inaudible. It was simply that the sky was ceaselessly filled with dull flashes and long, forking streaks of lightning. They did not flash so much as tremble and quiver like the wing of a dying bird. I got up, went to the window and stood there till morning. The flashes of lightning never ceased for an instant. It was a summer night 'full of sparrows', as the peasants call it. I gazed at the silent sandy area, the dark mass of the Amusement Gardens, the yellowish façades of far buildings, which also seemed to shudder at every pale flash. I gazed and couldn't tear myself away: these noiseless flashes of lightning and sedate gleams seemed like answers to the dumb and secret longings which were also emitting flashes inside me. Morning began and the dawn broke with crimson stipplings. As the sun arose the lightning flashes grew paler and less frequent. Their tremulous light became rarer and rarer and finally vanished altogether, drowned in the sobering and certain illumination of approaching day.

And my lightning flashes within me also ceased. I had a feeling of great tiredness and quietness. But the image of Zinaida continued to dwell in triumph in my heart. Save that in itself this image seemed now at peace, like a swan risen into the air above the marsh grasses, it stood out from the other graceless figures surrounding it an in falling asleep I cast myself before it for the last time in trustful and valedictory adoration.

Oh the docile feelings, the soft sounds, the goodness and tranquillity of a soul moved by love, the melting joy of love's first raptures – where are you, where have you gone?

[8]

The next morning, when I went down to breakfast, my mother scolded me – less, however, than I'd expected – and forced me to give an account of what I'd done the previous evening. I answered her in a few words, leaving out a great many details and trying to give the whole thing the most innocent appearance.

'Nevertheless they are not *comme il faut*,' my mother remarked, 'and you really mustn't go wasting your time with them instead of working and preparing for your exams.'

Since I knew that my mother's concern for my work would be limited to those few words, I didn't think it necessary to react, but after breakfast my father took me by the arm and, setting off with me into the garden, made me tell him everything I'd seen at the Zasyekins'.

My father had a strange influence over me and our relationship was unusual. He almost never concerned himself with my education, but he never hurt my feelings. He respected my independence and, if I can put it this way, he even treated me with polite deference. Except that he always kept his distance. I loved and admired him; he seemed to me to be an ideal example of a man – and, my God, how passionately I'd have adored him if only I'd not been constantly aware of his restraining hand! Yet when he wished he knew how to arouse in me unlimited devotion to him almost in a flash, by some word or other or by a special movement. Then my heart was laid bare to him and I chattered away with him as if I were with some intelligent friend or understanding counsellor. Then he would just as suddenly turn from me – and his hand would again restrain me, tenderly and gently, but it would restrain me.

Sometimes he would be in high spirits and then he'd join in fun and games with me like a small boy (he enjoyed every kind of strong physical movement). Once – just once – he was so gentle with me that I almost cried. But both his high spirits and his gentleness had a way of vanishing without trace, and what took place between us gave me no hopes for the future, no more than if I'd dreamt it. I used to study his intelligent, handsome and unclouded face, and my heart would start thumping and my whole being would strive to please him, and he'd literally sense what was happening inside me and casually pat me on the cheek – then instantly he'd be off, or busying himself with something, or he'd suddenly freeze as he alone knew how to, and I'd coil up inside at once and also grow cold. The rare outbursts of kindness towards me they never caused by my silent but understandable eagerness for them; were always occurred unexpectedly. In considering my father's character later on, I came to the conclusion that he had no liking for me or for family life. He loved something different and enjoyed it to the full. 'Take what you can and don't hand yourself over to anyone; belong only to yourself – that's what life's all about,' he said to me once. On another occasion, in the capacity of a young democrat, I started discussing freedom in his presence (he was being 'kind' that day, as I called it, and so I could talk to him about whatever I liked).

'Freedom,' he repeated, 'do you know what can give a man freedom?'

'What?'

'The will, your own will, and the power it can give, which is better than freedom. Learn how to express your will – and you'll be free, and you'll be in command.'

Above and beyond anything else my father wanted the will to live – and he lived . . . Perhaps he had a premonition that he didn't have long to enjoy 'what life's all about': he died when he was forty-two.

I gave my father a detailed account of my visit to the Zasyekins. He listened half-attentively, half-distractedly, sitting on a bench and drawing in the sand with the tip of his riding-crop. He occasionally gave a laugh, glanced at me brightly and humorously and egged me on with little questions and rejoinders. I'd started by deciding not to mention Zinaida by name, but then changed my mind and began referring to her.

My father still went on giving short laughs. Then he became thoughtful, stretched himself and stood up.

I remembered that, on leaving the house, he'd ordered his horse to be saddled. He was an excellent horseman and knew how to break in the wildest horses long before M. Rarey.

'Shall I come with you, father?' I asked him.

'No,' he answered, and his face acquired its usual indifferently fond expression. 'Go alone if you like, but tell the coachman that I won't be riding today.'

He turned his back on me and went off in a hurry. I followed him with my eyes as he disappeared through the gates and I saw his hat moving along above the fence: he was on his way to the Zasyekins. He remained there no more than an hour, but then at once set off for the town and returned home only towards evening.

After dinner I myself went to the Zasyekins. In the drawing-room I found the old princess sitting by herself. On seeing me, she engaged in scratching her head under her bonnet with a knitting needle and then suddenly asked me if I could copy out a petition for her.

'With pleasure,' I said, and sat down on the edge of a chair.

'Only see that you write in big letters,' muttered the princess, handing me a soiled sheet of paper. 'Could you do it today, young man?'

'I could do it today, ma'am.'

The door to the next room opened slightly and in the opening I could see Zinaida's face – pale and thoughtful, with her hair thrown carelessly back. She looked at me with large cold eyes and quietly closed the door.

'Zina, Zina dear!' called the old woman.

Zinaida did not respond. I took away the old woman's petition and spent the whole evening over it.

[9]

From that day my 'passion' began. I remember that then I felt something similar to what a man must feel who has just taken his first job: I ceased to be simply a little boy; I was in love. I said that from that day my passion began. I could add that my sufferings also began that day. In Zinaida's absence I felt utterly depressed: I had no ideas, I was clumsy, for days on end I thought intensely about her . . . I was depressed by that, but in her presence I wasn't any better. I felt jealous, I felt insignificant, I was stupidly touchy and stupidly servile, and yet an invincible force still drew me to her and each time I entered her room I trembled with happiness. Zinaida guessed at once that I had fallen in love with her and I didn't dream of hiding the fact. She found my passion for her amusing, teased me, spoiled me and tormented me. To be the sole cause, the arbitrary and unanswerable source of the greatest joys and the deepest sorrow for someone else is a very nice thing to be – and in Zinaida's hands I was like soft wax. Besides, I wasn't the only one in love with her. All the men who visited her house were out of their minds about her and she held all of them on leads, at her feet. She enjoyed arousing in them either hopes or fears and turning them this way and that as she wished (she called it: 'knocking people against each other'). They never thought of opposing her wishes and gladly submitted to her. Her entire being, so vital and beautiful, contained a particularly charming blend of cunning and carelessness, artificiality and simplicity, peacefulness and playfulness. In everything she did and said, in her every movement, there was an easy, delicate attractiveness, uniquely graced by the special playfulness within her. And the expression of her face was always changing, always playful. Simultaneously, or almost simultaneously, it could be full of mockery or thoughtfulness or passion. The most varied feelings, light and swift as cloud shadows on a sunny, windy day, would constantly be playing about her eyes and lips.

Each of her admirers was needed by her. Belovzorov, whom she sometimes called 'my beast' or sometimes simply 'mine', would gladly have flung himself into the flames for her. Placing no hopes on his intellectual resources and other attributes, he was always making her proposals of marriage, hinting that the others were so many talkers. Maidanov appealed to the poetic strings of her spirit: a man of fairly cold temperament, like almost all writers, he strove to assure her – and perhaps himself as well – that he adored her, wrote endless verses in her honour and declaimed them to her with a kind of unnatural and yet sincere enthusiasm. She both sympathised with him and tended to make fun of him because she didn't entirely trust him and, after listening to his outpourings, made him read some Pushkin 'in order to clear the air', as she put it. Lushin, the mocking, cynical doctor, knew her better than them all and loved her more than all the others, though he scolded her to her eyes and behind her back. She respected him but did not let him off scot-free and occasionally took a particularly malicious pleasure in making him feel that he was in her hands. 'I'm a coquette, I'm heartless, I'm an actress by nature,' she once said to him in my presence. 'All right, then! Give me your hand and I'll stick a needle in it, you'll feel ashamed in front of this young man, you'll feel pain, but still, Mister Truth-teller, you'll laugh!' Lushin went red, turned away, bit his lip, but ended by offering his hand. She stuck in a needle and he did start laughing . . . and she laughed too, forcing in the needle fairly deeply and looking him in the eyes, which darted about in helpless agony.

I least understood the relationship which existed between Zinaida and Count Malevsky. He was good-looking, capable and clever, but something dubious, something false was apparent in him even to me, a sixteen-year-old boy, and I was amazed that Zinaida didn't notice it. Or perhaps she did notice this falseness and wasn't put off by it. Inadequate education, strange company and odd habits, the constant presence of her mother, poverty and disorder at home, everything, beginning with the very freedom the young girl enjoyed and her awareness of being superior to those around her, contrived to nurture in her a certain half-disdainful callousness and lack of choosiness. Whatever happened, whether Boneyface came to announce there was no more sugar, or some rubbishy piece of gossip came to light, or guests started quarrelling, she'd simply give her curls a shake and cry: 'What nonsense!' – and that would be that.

For my own part, my blood would boil whenever Malevsky went up to her, slinking towards her like some sly fox, leaned elegantly on the back of her chair and began whispering in her ear with a self-satisfied and ingratiating little smile; and she would fold her arms across her bosom, look up attentively at him, smile and nod her head.

'Why do you want to have Mr Malevsky about the place?' I asked her once.

'He's got such beautiful little moustaches,' she answered. 'Anyhow, it's none of your business.'

'You don't think I'm in love with him, do you?' she asked me on another occasion. 'I'm not. I can't love people I've got to look down on. I need someone who would break me in two – and I'll never come across anyone like that, God willing! I'll never fall into anyone's clutches, never, never!'

'You mean you'll never love anyone?'

'What about you? Do you think I don't love you?' she asked, and struck me on the nose with her glove.

Yes, Zinaida had a lot of fun at my expense! For three whole weeks I saw her every day – and what she used to get up to with me! She rarely came to our house and I didn't regret it. In our house she turned herself into a young lady, into a young princess, and I felt shy of her. I was frightened of giving myself away in front of my mother. She was extremely ill-disposed towards Zinaida and observed the two of us together with displeasure. I didn't fear my father in the same way because he literally didn't notice me and spoke to Zinaida only a little, but what he said was particularly clever and significant. I gave up working and reading. I even gave up going for walks or rides on horseback. Like a beetle tied by one leg, I constantly circled round the adored wing where they lived and I think I would have stayed there forever . . . But that was impossible because my mother grumbled and Zinaida herself sometimes drove me away. Then I would lock myself away in my room or go down to the very end of the garden and climb up on to the ruined wall of a tall stone conservatory and sit for hours at a time, staring and staring and seeing nothing, my legs hanging over the edge of the wall which faced on to the road. Beside me, in the dusty nettles, white butterflies flitted lethargically about; a chirpy sparrow would alight not far away on a half-broken red brick and twitter away annoyingly, endlessly twisting and turning its body and spreading out its tail; crows, still mistrustful, would caw occasionally, perched high, high up on the very top of a birch tree; the sun and wind would play calmly in its sparse branches; the sound of bells from the Don Monastery would filter to me sadly and peacefully from time to time – and I would sit and stare and listen and be filled with some nameless sensation which contained everything: sadness and joy and premonitions of the future and desire and the fear of life. But at that time I didn't understand any of this and wouldn't have known how to describe what was fermenting inside me, or would have given it just the one name – the name of Zinaida.

And Zinaida went on playing with me like a cat with a mouse. Either she flirted with me and I grew excited and melted, or she would suddenly push me away from her and I wouldn't dare approach her or dare even look at her.

I remember that for several days on end she was extremely cool with me. I was completely overwhelmed and, on my cowardly visits to them in their wing of our house, I would try to keep close to the old princess despite the fact that she was very fractious and loud at that time because her financial arrangements were going badly and she'd already had two encounters with the local policeman.

On one occasion I was walking beside the notorious fence in our garden and I caught sight of Zinaida. Leaning back on both arms, she was sitting in the grass and keeping quite still. I wanted to creep quietly away, but she suddenly raised her head and signalled to me peremptorily. I stopped still on the spot, not understanding her at first. She repeated her signal. Immediately I jumped over the fence and dashed happily towards her, but one glance from her stopped me and indicated the path a couple of paces from her. In confusion, not knowing what to do, I knelt down at the edge of the path. She was so pale and such bitter sorrow, such profound exhaustion showed in every feature of her face that my heart sank and I muttered:

'What's wrong?'

Zinaida stretched out a hand, tore off a blade of grass, bit it and threw it away.

'You love me very much, don't you?' she asked at last. 'Don't you?'

I didn't answer. I didn't see why I should.

'Don't you?' she repeated, looking at me as she used to. 'Yes. The very same eyes,' she added, becoming thoughtful and covering her face with her hands. 'Everything's horrible,' she whispered. 'I want to go away to the end of the world, I can't stand it, I can't get it right ... How awful it's going to be! I feel so miserable ... My God, I feel miserable!'

'Why?' I asked timidly.

Zinaida didn't answer and simply shrugged her shoulders. I remained kneeling and looked at her with deep despondency. Every word she spoke literally inscribed itself in my heart. At that instant, I think, I would gladly have given up my life simply to make sure she stopped feeling so sad. I gazed at her, and though I didn't understand why she was so miserable I vividly imagined to myself how she had suddenly, in a fit of overwhelming grief, gone into the garden and fallen to the ground as though scythed down. It was bright and green all around; a breeze rustled among the leaves and now and then shook a long raspberry cane above Zinaida's head. Somewhere doves cooed and bees buzzed, flying to and fro low down among the scarce blades of grass. The sky shone a warm blue above – and yet I felt so sad ...

'Read me some poetry,' said Zinaida softly, and leaned on one elbow. 'I like it when you read poetry. You have a way of singing it, but it doesn't matter, it's because you're young. Read me "The Hills of Georgia."* But first of all you must sit down.'

I sat down and read 'The Hills of Georgia'.*

' "For not to love my heart's unable," ' repeated Zinaida. 'That's why poetry's so wonderful: it speaks to us of what doesn't exist and of what's not only better than what doesn't exist but even more like the truth ... "For not to love my heart's unable" – yes, it would want not to but it can't!' She once more fell silent and then suddenly trembled and stood up. 'Let's go. Maidanov's with Mama. He brought me his new poem and I left him there. He's also very upset now, but it can't be helped! You'll learn all about it one day ... only you mustn't be angry with me!'

Zinaida squeezed my hand hurriedly and ran off ahead of me. We returned to the wing where they lived. Maidanov started reading his recently printed poem *The Murderer* but I didn't listen to it. He shrieked out in a sing-song his four-foot iambic lines, the rhymes alternated and tinkled like sleigh-bells, fatuously and stridently, but I gazed all the time at Zinaida and tried to understand what her last words had meant.

> *'Maybe some secret rival has*
> *By chance o'erwhelmed you once for all?'*

Maidanov suddenly declaimed nasally – and at that moment my eyes met Zinaida's. She dropped her eyes and blushed slightly. I saw her blush and went cold with fright. I had already been jealous of her, but it was only at that instant that the idea she might be in love flashed through my mind:

'My God,' I thought, 'she's in love!'

[10]

My real torments began at that moment. I racked my brains, thinking about it over and over again and constantly, although as secretly as possible, keeping watch on Zinaida. It was clear that a change had taken place in her. She would go out for walks by herself and spend a long time on such strolls. Sometimes, when there were guests, she didn't appear and spent hours at a time sitting in her room. She had never done this before. I suddenly became – or I thought I did – extraordinarily perceptive. 'Is it he, or perhaps it isn't?' I asked myself, agitatedly running through her suitors in my mind. Count Malevsky (although I was ashamed of Zinaida in admitting such a thing to myself) seemed to me secretly to be more dangerous than the others.

My powers of observation didn't allow me to look beyond my nose and my secretiveness probably didn't fool anyone. At least Dr Lushin soon found me out. In any case, he had changed recently: he had grown thinner, laughed just as often but his laughter had become hollower, wickeder and shorter. A conscious nervous irritability had replaced his former easy irony and pretended cynicism.

'What are you always coming over here for, young man?' he asked me once when the two of us were alone in the Zasyekins' drawing-room. (The young princess had not yet come back from her walk and the screeching voice of the old princess could be heard upstairs as she scolded her maidservant.) 'You should be studying, working, while you're still young – so what are you doing here?'

'You have no way of knowing whether or not I work at home,' I replied not without a certain haughtiness, but also not without a certain confusion.

'You can't claim you work! That's not what's on your mind. Still, I don't deny that, er, at your age it's as it should be. But your choice is terribly unfortunate. Can't you see what sort of a house this is?'

'I don't understand you,' I remarked.

'You don't understand me? So much the worse for you. I consider it my duty to warn you. People of my sort, old bachelor that I am, may come here: what can happen to us? We're a hard-skinned lot and won't be affected by anything. But your skin's still soft and the atmosphere of this place isn't healthy for you. Believe me, you could catch an infection.'

'How do you mean?'

'I mean what I say. Do you think you're healthy now? Do you think your condition's normal? Do you think what you're feeling is of use to you, is good for you?'

'What am I feeling exactly?' I asked, but in the depths of my heart I knew the doctor was right.

'Oh, young man, young man,' the doctor continued, wearing the sort of expression which suggested that those two words contained something very insulting for me, 'don't try and pretend. Good God, what's in your heart is written all over your face! But what's the point of talking about it? I wouldn't come here myself if only' (the doctor clenched his teeth) 'if only I weren't so crazy. The only thing that surprises me is how you, with your intelligence, can't see what's going on around you.'

'And what exactly is going on?' said I, bristling all over.

The doctor looked at me with a kind of mocking pity. 'A lot of good I am,' he muttered to himself, it seemed, 'and a lot of good it'll do to tell him. In one word,' he added, raising his voice, 'I tell you again – the atmosphere of this place is not right for you. You may like it here, but so what? A hothouse can also smell very pleasant, but you can't live in it. Just you listen to me: go back to Kaydanov!'

The old princess came in and began complaining of toothache to the doctor. Then Zinaida appeared.

'Now,' added the old princess, 'Mr Doctor, sir, you must tick her off. She drinks iced water all day. Do you think that's good for her with her weak chest?'

'Why do you do it?' asked Lushin.

'What can happen if I do?'

'What can happen? You can catch a chill and die.'

'Really? Is that so? Well, then, that's the way for me!'

'So that's it!' cried the doctor gruffly.

The old princess went out.

'So that's it,' Zinaida repeated. 'Is life all that marvellous? Look around you – does it look all that good? Or do you think I don't understand it, don't feel it? I enjoy drinking iced water. Can you seriously assure me that this sort of life's not worth risking for a moment's enjoyment? I'm not talking about happiness.'

'Well, yes,' remarked Lushin, 'capriciousness and independence – those two words sum you up. Your entire nature's in those two words.'

Zinaida gave a nervous laugh. 'You've missed the post, my dear doctor. You've not been keeping your eyes open, you've got behindhand. You must put on your glasses. I'm not one for playing games now, making fun of you, making fun of myself – no such fun now! And as for independence . . . Monsieur Voldemar,' Zinaida added suddenly and stamped her foot, 'you mustn't make such a dreadfully sad face! I can't stand it when people pity me.' She dashed out of the room.

'The atmosphere here is harmful, harmful, young man,' Lushin said to me once again.

FIRST LOVE

On the evening of that day the usual guests gathered at the Zasyekins' and I was one of them. The talk turned to Maidanov's poem. Zinaida praised it wholeheartedly.

'But do you know something,' she said to him, 'if I were a poet, I'd choose other subjects. Perhaps it's all nonsense, but strange ideas sometimes come into my head, especially when I can't sleep, just before morning, when the sky begins to grow both rosy and grey. For instance, I'd . . . You won't laugh at me?'

'No! No!' we all cried with one voice.

'I would imagine', she continued, folding her arms on her bosom and looking intently to one side, 'a whole crowd of young girls at night, in a large boat, on a calm river. The moon is shining and they're all dressed in white and they have wreaths of white flowers on their heads and they're singing, you know, a sort of hymn.'

'I understand, I understand, go on,' said Maidanov in a voice full of dreamy meaning.

'Suddenly there's a lot of noise, laughter, torches, tambourines on the bank . . . a crowd of Bacchanalian revellers is running along, singing and shouting. It's your job to paint the picture, Mr Poet, only I'd like the torches to be red and very smoky and the eyes of the revellers must glitter under the wreaths and the wreaths have got to be dark. Also, you mustn't forget the tiger skins and the goblets and the gold, lots of gold.'

'Where's the gold got to be?' asked Maidanov, throwing back his flatly hanging hair and spreading his nostrils.

'Where? On their shoulders, on their arms, on their legs, everywhere. They say that in olden times women used to wear golden bracelets on their ankles. The revellers call the girls in the boat to them. The girls have stopped singing their hymn – they couldn't go on with it – but they make no move, because the river is carrying them towards the bank. And then suddenly one of them stands up . . . You must give a good description of how she calmly stands up in the moonlight and how frightened the other girls are . . . She steps over the edge of the boat, the revellers surround her and rush away into the night, into the darknesss . . . Imagine now clouds of smoke and everything mixed up. Only their shrieks are heard, and her wreath left lying on the bank.'

Zinaida stopped. ('Yes, she's in love!' I thought again.)

'And that's all?' asked Maidanov.

'That's all,' she answered.

'That can't be the subject for an entire poem,' he remarked solemnly, 'but I'll use your idea for a lyric.'

'In the Romantic manner?' asked Malevsky.

'Of course, in the Romantic, Byronic manner.'

'In my opinion, Hugo's better than Byron,' the young count remarked casually. 'More interesting.'

'Hugo is a first-class writer,' responded Maidanov, 'and my friend Softneck in his Spanish novel *El Trovador* . . .'

'Is that the book with the question-marks upside down?' Zinaida interrupted.

'Yes. It's the Spanish custom. I wanted to say that Softneck . . .'

'Oh, you'll start arguing again about Romanticism and Classicism,' Zinaida interrupted for the second time. 'Let's play a game . . .'

'Of forfeits?' chimed in Lushin.

'No, forfeits are boring. Let's play comparisons.' (Zinaida had invented this game herself: some object was named, everyone tried to compare it with something else and the one who made the best comparison won a prize.)

She went over to the window. The sun had only just set and long red clouds drifted high up in the sky.

'What do those clouds look like?' Zinaida asked and, without waiting for one of us to answer, said: 'I think they look like those purple sails on Cleopatra's golden ship when she sailed out to meet Antony. Do you remember, Maidanov, you recently told me about that?'

We all agreed, like Polonius in *Hamlet*, that the clouds reminded us of those very sails and that not one of us would be able to find a better comparison.

'How old was Antony then?' asked Zinaida.

'He was probably a young man,' Malevsky remarked.

'Yes, he was young,' Maidanov confidently confirmed.

'Excuse me,' exclaimed Lushin, 'but he was over forty.'

'Over forty,' repeated Zinaida, shooting a quick glance at him.

I soon went home. 'She's in love,' my lips whispered despite themselves, 'but with whom?'

[12]

Days went by. Zinaida became yet stranger and more incomprehensible. On one occasion I entered her room and saw her sitting in a chair with a straw seat, her head pressed down to the sharp edge of the table. She straightened up . . . . Her entire face was covered in tears.

'Oh, it's you!' she said with a cruel smile. 'Come over here!'

I went up to her. She put her hand on my head and, suddenly seizing me by the hair, began twisting it.

'That hurts,' I said eventually.

'Oh, so it hurts! Don't you think it hurts me too? Don't you?' she repeated.

'Hey!' she cried suddenly, seeing that she'd torn out a small lock of my hair. 'Look what I've done? Poor Monsieur Voldemar!'

She carefully smoothed out the torn-out hairs, wound them round her finger and twisted them into a little ring.

'I'll put your hairs in a locket and wear it,' she said, but there were tears glistening in her eyes. 'Perhaps that'll make it up to you a little. And now goodbye.'

I returned home and found an unpleasant atmosphere. My mother had been having it out with my father. She was reproaching him for something, while he, in his usual way, was maintaining a cold, polite silence – and then he soon left. I couldn't hear what my mother had been saying and I wasn't interested. I only remember that at the end of the exchange she ordered me to come to her own room and there expressed herself in a very disapproving manner about my frequent visits to the princess who, in her words, was *une femme capable de tout*. I kissed her hand (which was what I always did when I wanted to end a conversation) and went to my room. Zinaida's tears had completely astounded me. I hadn't the faintest idea what to make of them and was on the point of tears myself: I was still a child, despite being sixteen. I didn't have any thoughts any more about Malevsky, although Belovzorov became daily more and more threatening and would glare at the sly count like a wolf about to devour a sheep. I didn't think about anything or anyone. I was lost in conjectures and had a mind only for solitary places. I was particularly fond of the ruined conservatory. I would climb up on the high wall, sit down and remain seated there, such a picture of unhappy, lonely and melancholy youth that I'd even begin feeling pity for myself – and these sensations of misery were such a delight to me, I revelled in them so!

One time I was sitting on the wall, gazing into the distance and listening to the sound of bells, when suddenly I felt something passing over me, not so much a light breeze or a trembling of the air, as the softest of puffs, the slightest of intimations of someone's presence. I lowered my eyes. Below me, along the road, in a grey summer dress with a pink parasol on her shoulder, Zinaida came hurrying. She noticed me, stopped and, turning back the brim of her straw hat, looked up at me with her velvet eyes.

'What are you doing there, so high up?' she asked me with a strange kind of smile. 'Look,' she went on, 'you're always claiming you love me. Jump down into the road if you really love me.'

Zinaida had hardly had time to say the words before I dropped down through the air, just as if someone'd pushed me from behind. The wall was about fourteen feet high. I landed on my feet, but the jolt was so strong that I couldn't keep my balance, I collapsed and lost consciousness for an instant. When I came to, without opening my eyes I could feel Zinaida close to me.

'My darling boy,' she said, bending over me, and her voice was full of tenderness and alarm, 'how could you do such a thing, how could you obey me! You know I love you . . . Get up now.'

Her bosom rose and fell close to me, her hands touched my head, and suddenly – what I must have felt at that moment! – her soft fresh lips began covering my face with kisses . . . they touched my own . . . But then Zinaida guessed, no doubt, from the expression on my face that I'd recovered consciousness, although I still hadn't opened my eyes, and, briskly getting up, she said:

'Up on your feet now, you naughty boy, you silly thing! What are you lying in the dust for?'

I stood up.

'Give me my parasol,' said Zinaida. 'Just look where I threw it! And don't go on looking at me like that – it's so idiotic! You haven't hurt yourself, have you? Did you get stung by the nettles? I've told you, don't go on looking at me like that . . . Oh, he doesn't understand anything, he doesn't answer,' she added, seemingly talking to herself. 'Go home, Monsieur Voldemar, get cleaned up, and don't you dare follow me or I'll be angry and I'll never again . . .'

She didn't complete what she was saying and hurriedly went on her way, while I sat down on the road, my legs having given way beneath me. The nettles had stung my hands, my back ached and my head was going round, but the feeling of sheer bliss which I experienced at that moment has never once been repeated in my whole life. It was like a sweet ache in all my limbs and finally resolved itself in excited leaps and shouts. True, I was still a child!

[13]

All that day I was so happy and proud, I retained so vividly on my face the feel of Zinaida's kisses, I remembered her every word with such a shudder of excitement, I so cherished my unexpected happiness that I even began to feel frightened and didn't even want to see her, the cause of these new sensations. I thought that nothing more could be asked of fate, that it was now time to 'take a breath, breathe one's last and die.' Yet the next day, on going to the wing where they lived, I felt great confusion, which I tried in vain to hide beneath an appearance of modest familiarity appropriate for someone who wished to make it known that he could keep a secret. Zinaida received me very simply, without any fuss, and did no more than wag her finger at me and ask whether I had any bruises. All my modest familiarity and capacity for keeping secrets vanished instantly, as did my confusion along with them. Of course, I had not been expecting anything in particular, but Zinaida's composure was like being doused by a bucket of cold water. I realised I was no more than a child in her eyes – and I really couldn't bear that! Zinaida spent the time walking up and down the room, giving quick smiles whenever she glanced at me, but her thoughts were far away, I saw that clearly. 'Should I say something about what happened yesterday?' I wondered. 'Or perhaps ask her where she was hurrying so as to learn finally . . .?' but I did no more than dismissively wave my hand and take a seat in a corner.

Belovzorov entered and I was glad of his arrival.

'I haven't found you a horse to go riding, a quiet one,' he announced in a harsh voice. 'Freitag swears by one of them, but I'm not sure. I have my doubts.'

'You have your doubts about what, may I ask?' inquired Zinaida.

'My doubts? Well, you don't know how to ride. God forbid that anything should go wrong! And why has this fantastic idea come into your head suddenly?'

'It's my affair, my dear Monsieur Beast. In that case I'll ask Pyotr Vasilyevich...' (My father was called Pyotr Vasilyevich. I was astonished that she should make such a free-and-easy mention of his name, as if she were sure of his readiness to be of service to her.)

'I see,' said Belovzorov. 'You want to go riding with him?'

'With him or someone else, it's no concern of yours. Only not with you.'

'Not with me,' repeated Belovzorov. 'As you wish. Very well, then, I'll get you a horse.'

'Only see that it's not an old cow! I warn you that I want to gallop.'

'Gallop, then ... With whom will you be riding? With Malevsky perhaps?'

'And why shouldn't it be with him, Mr Soldier? Well, take it easy,' she added, 'and don't flash your eyes at me! I'll take you as well. You know that for me Malevsky's now – nothing at all!' And she gave a toss of her head.

'You're saying that just to please me,' grumbled Belovzorov.

Zinaida frowned. 'That pleases you, does it? O . . . O . . . O Mr Soldier!' she said at last, as though she couldn't find another word for him. 'And you, Monsieur Voldemar, would you come riding with us?'

'I don't like to be . . among a lot of people,' I muttered without raising my eyes.

'You prefer a *tête-à-tête*? Well, one man's meat is another man's poison,' she said with a sigh. 'Off with you, Belovzorov, and get busy with it! I need a horse for tomorrow.'

'And where's the money going to come from?' broke in the old princess.

Zinaida knitted her brows. 'I won't be asking you for it. Belovzorov will trust me.'

'He'll trust you, he'll trust you,' grumbled the old princess, and then she suddenly shrieked out at the top of her voice: 'Dunyashka!'

'Maman, I gave you a little bell,' Zinaida remarked.

'Dunyashka!' the old woman shrieked again.

Belovzorov bowed his way out and I went with him. Zinaida did not try to stop me.

[14]

The next morning I got up early, cut myself a stick and set off for a walk outside the town limits. I'll walk, I thought, and forget my sorrows. It was a beautiful day, bright and not too hot; a joyful, fresh breeze danced over the earth and duly rustled and played, making everything quiver and causing no alarm. I wandered for a long time among the hills and woods. I didn't feel happy and had left home with the intention of giving in to despair, but youth, the beautiful weather, the fresh air, the delight of a brisk walk and the luxury of lying in solitary splendour in the thick grass had got the better of me and the recollection of her unforgettable words and her kisses crowded into my heart once again. I found it pleasant to think that Zinaida couldn't, after all, fail to do justice to my determination and my heroism . . . 'Others are better for her than I am,' I thought. 'So be it! But the others only talk about what they'll do, whereas I do it! And what more I could do for her!' My imagination came into play. I began to imagine how I would save her from the hands of her enemies, how, covered from head to foot in blood, I would seize her from some dark prison, how I would die at her feet. I remembered a picture hanging in our drawing-room: Malek-Adel carrying off Matilda . . .* and was then entirely preoccupied by the appearance of a large and colourful woodpecker which busily climbed up the slender trunk of a birch tree and looked anxiously from behind it to right and left like a musician looking out from behind the neck of his double-bass.

After that I started singing *Not the white snows* and then drifted into the popular song of that time *I wait for you when zephyrs playful*; and after that I began a loud recitation of Yermak's address to the stars in Khomyakov's tragedy.* I made an effort to compose something in the sentimental manner and even thought of the line which would conclude the poem: 'O, Zinaida! Zinaida!' but nothing came of it. Meanwhile, dinner-time arrived. I descended into the valley by a narrow sandy path which wound along it and led to the town. I was going along this path when the hollow clatter of horses' hooves resounded behind me. I looked round, stopped and took off my cap: it was my father and Zinaida. They were riding side by side. My father was saying something to her, bending towards her from the waist and leaning one hand on the neck of his horse. He was smiling. Zinaida was listening to him in silence, her eyes severely lowered and her lips pressed together. To start with I saw only them and it was only after some moments that, from behind a turn in the valley, Belovzorov appeared in a hussar's uniform with a fur-lined cloak riding a foaming black horse. The fine animal shook its head, snorted and pranced as its rider simultaneously reined it in and spurred it on. I stepped out of their way. My father took up his reins, turned aside from Zinaida and she slowly raised her eyes to his. Then they both galloped off. Belovzorov rushed after them, his sabre rattling. 'He's red as a lobster,' I thought, 'but she's . . . Why is she so pale? She's been riding all morning – and she's pale?'

I redoubled my pace and succeeded in reaching home just before dinner. My father was already changed, washed and refreshed, sitting beside my mother's chair and reading to her a feuilleton from the *Journal des Débats* in his even, resonant voice, but my mother was listening to him without paying attention and, on seeing me, asked where I had been all day and added that she didn't like it when people went traipsing off God knows where and with God knows whom. I was about to answer that I was by myself all the time, but I glanced at my father and for some reason said nothing.

[15]

In the course of the next five or six days I hardly saw Zinaida at all. She was said to be unwell, but this didn't prevent the usual visitors to the wing where they lived performing their devotions, as they put it – all, that is, except Maidanov, who always lost interest and became bored when he had no opportunity of being *exalté*. Belovzorov sat gloomily in a corner, all buttoned-up and red-faced. A malicious smile persistently dwelt on Count Malevsky's delicate features. He had really fallen out of favour with Zinaida and was making particular efforts to ingratiate himself with the old princess by accompanying her on her visit by hired carriage to see the Governor-General. However, that visit turned out to be unsuccessful and even proved to be unpleasant for Malevsky himself: he was reminded of an affair involving some communications officers and in his explanation he had to plead inexperience. Lushin would drive up once or twice a day but would not stay for long. I was a little frightened of him after our last encounter and at the same time I felt sincerely drawn to him. On one occasion he came with me for a walk in the Amusement Gardens, was extremely amiable and pleasant, told me the names and characteristics of different herbs and flowers and suddenly

– right out of the blue, as it were – he struck himself on the forehead and exclaimed:

'And I, idiot that I am, thought she was a coquette! But evidently some people enjoy sacrificing themselves.'

'What do you mean by that?' I asked.

'To you I don't mean anything,' Lushin replied sharply.

Zinaida avoided me. My presence – I could hardly fail to notice – produced an unpleasant impression on her. She would automatically turn away from me – yes, *automatically*, that's what I found so bitter, so damning! But there was nothing to be done about it – I tried to keep out of her sight and simply kept watch on her from a distance, in which I wasn't always successful. Something strange was happening to her, as had occurred before. Her face had changed and she became an entirely different person. I was particularly struck by the change that had occurred in her one calm warm evening. I was sitting on a low little bench under a widely overhanging elder bush. It was a place I loved because it gave me a view of the window of Zinaida's room. I was sitting there and above my head in the darkened foliage a small bird was busily fussing about. A grey cat crept cautiously and with outstretched back into the garden and the first cockchafers were making a strong whirring sound in air that was still translucent, if no longer bright. I sat there and looked at the window and waited, wondering if it would open. Then it did open and Zinaida appeared. She was wearing a white dress and she herself, her face, her shoulders, her arms, appeared pale to the point of seeming white. She stayed there motionless for a long while and for a long while she stared straight ahead of her from beneath puckered brows. I had never known her to have that look before. Then she pressed her hands together very tightly and raised them to her lips and forehead – and suddenly, opening her fingers wide, pushed back her hair from her ears, shook it and, throwing her head backwards with evident determination, slammed shut the window.

Some three days later she and I met in the garden. I wanted to turn aside, but she herself stopped me.

'Give me your hand,' she said with her former gentleness. 'You and I haven't had a chat for a long time.'

I looked at her and saw her eyes were shining calmly and her face was smiling as if through a mist.

'Are you still unwell?' I asked her.

FIRST LOVE

'No, it's all over now,' she answered, and plucked a small red rose. 'I'm a bit tired, but that'll pass.'

'And then you'll be as you were before?' I asked.

Zinaida raised the rose to her face and it seemed to me that the gleam from the bright petals shone in her cheeks.

'Have I changed?' she asked me.

'Yes, you have,' I answered in a low voice.

'I know I've been cold to you,' Zinaida began, 'but you shouldn't have paid any attention to that . . . I couldn't have been anything else . . . Well, there's no point in talking about it!'

'You don't want me to love you, that's what!' I burst out gloomily.

'No, you must love me, but not as you did before.'

'How, then?'

'Let's be friends, that's how!' Zinaida gave me the rose to smell. 'Look, I'm much older than you, I could be your auntie – well, no, not your auntie, but your elder sister. While you . . .'

'In your eyes I'm just a child,' I interrupted her.

'Well, yes, you are a child, but a nice, good, clever child, whom I love very much. Do you know what? From this very day I'm going to make you into a pageboy. And you mustn't forget that pageboys must never be separated from their mistresses. Let this be a sign to you of your new position,' she added, sticking the rose in the buttonhole of my jacket, 'a sign of my favour towards you.'

'In the past I used to receive other favours from you,' I said.

'Ah!' cried Zinaida, and gave me a sideways glance. 'What a memory he's got! All right, I'm ready now as well . . .'

And, leaning towards me, she pressed on my forehead a clean, calm kiss.

I did no more than look at her and she turned away with the words: 'Follow behind me, pageboy!' and set off for the wing of the house. I followed behind her and was in a quandary. 'Is this mild, sensible girl the same Zinaida I used to know?' And the way she walked seemed to me calmer, her whole figure seemed nobler and more elegant.

And, my God, how my love blazed within me with renewed force!

[16]

After dinner guests again assembled in the wing where they lived, and the young princess came out to receive them. The entire company was present to a man, as on that – for me – first unforgettable evening. Nirmatsky was even in attendance; Maidanov had been the first to arrive this time: he had brought his new verses. Forfeits were again played, but without the former strange escapades, without the horseplay and noise. The gypsy element was lacking. Zinaida gave a new mood to our gathering. I sat beside her in my role as pageboy. Among other things she proposed that whoever had to pay a forfeit should tell us his dreams. But this was not a success. The dreams turned out either to be uninteresting (Belovzorov dreamed that he'd been feeding carp to his horse and his horse had had a wooden head) or to be unnatural and made-up. Maidanov regaled us with a long yarn containing burial chambers and angels with lyres and talking flowers and sounds carried from afar. Zinaida didn't allow him to finish.

'If it's become a matter of making up stories,' she said, 'then let's each tell something really made-up.'

It fell to Belovzorov to speak first. The young hussar was covered in confusion. 'I can't think of anything!' he exclaimed.

'What nonsense!' retorted Zinaida. 'Imagine, for instance, that you're married and tell us how you'd get on with your wife. Would you lock her up?'

'I'd lock her up.'

'And you yourself would go and sit with her?'

'And I'd certainly go and sit with her.'

'Splendid. And what if she got bored by this and was disloyal to you?'

'I'd kill her.'

'And if she ran away?'

'I'd run after her and still kill her.'

'I see. Well, what if I was your wife, what would you have done then?'

Belovzorov was silent for a moment.

'I'd have killed myself . . .'

Zinaida burst out laughing.

'I see your song's soon sung!'

The second forfeit was Zinaida's. She raised her eyes to the ceiling and became thoughtful.

'Well, now, listen,' she began at last, 'this is what I've thought of . . . imagine a magnificent ballroom, a summer night and an astonishing ball. It is being given by a young queen. Everywhere there is gold, marble, crystal, silk, torches, diamonds, flowers, incense, all the delights of luxury.'

'Are you very fond of luxury?' Lushin interrupted her.

'Luxury is beautiful,' she replied, 'and I like everything beautiful.'

'More than beauty itself?' he asked.

'That's too clever for me, I don't understand it. Stop interrupting me. So, it's a magnificent ball. There are many, many guests, all young men, handsome and brave and all madly in love with the queen.'

'Are there no ladies among the guests?' asked Malevsky.

'No – or wait a moment, yes, there are.'

'They're all ugly, are they?'

'They're all lovely. But the men are all in love with the queen. She is tall and elegant and she wears a small gold diadem on her black hair.'

I looked at Zinaida and at that moment she seemed to me so far above all of us, her white forehead and straight eyebrows seemed redolent with such lucidity of thought and such authority that I thought: 'She is the queen herself.'

'They all crowd round her,' Zinaida continued, 'and they all make the most extravagantly flattering speeches to her.'

'Does she enjoy flattery?' asked Lushin.

'How insufferable he is, always interrupting! . . . Who doesn't enjoy flattery?'

'Just one final question,' remarked Malevsky. 'Has the queen got a husband?'

'I hadn't thought of that. No, why should she?'

'Of course,' responded Malevsky, 'why should she?'

'*Silence!*' cried Maidanov, who was in fact not good at French.

'*Merci,*' Zinaida said to him. 'So the queen listens to their speeches and listens to the music, but she does not look at a single one of her guests. Six windows have been opened from top to bottom, from floor to ceiling, and beyond them can be seen a dark sky with enormous stars and a dark garden with enormous trees. The queen gazes into the garden. There, near the trees, is a fountain, and it shines whitely in the dusk, tall as tall can be, like an apparition. Through the talk and music the queen hears the quiet splashing of the water. She looks and thinks: you are all, gentlemen, noble, clever and rich, you have placed your-selves round me, you treasure every word I say, you're all ready to lay down your lives at my feet, I rule over you . . . But there, by the fountain, by that splashing water, stands and waits the one I love, the one who rules over me. He has no rich clothing, no precious jewels, no one knows him, but he is waiting for me and he is sure I will come – and I will come, there is no force in the world that could stop me when I decide to go to him and stay with him and lose myself with him there, in the darkness of the garden, under the rustling of the trees and the splashing of the fountain . . .'

Zinaida fell silent.

'Is this really made up?' asked Malevsky knowingly.

Zinaida did not even glance at him.

'What would we have done, gentlemen,' Lushin suddenly said, 'if we'd been among those guests and known about this fortunate one by the fountain?'

'Stop, stop!' broke in Zinaida. 'I'll tell you what each of you would have done. You, Belovzorov, you'd have challenged him to a duel. You, Maidanov, you'd have written an epigram . . . Or no, you don't know how to write epigrams, you'd have written a long iambic poem in the manner of Barbier and published it in the *Telegraph*.* You, Nirmatsky, you'd have borrowed from him . . . no, you'd have loaned him money at high interest. You, doctor . . .' She stopped. 'I don't know what you'd have done.'

'In my capacity as physician in ordinary,' said Lushin, 'I'd have advised the queen not to give balls when she's got no time for guests . . .'

'Probably you'd be right. As for you, count . . .'

'As for me?' asked Malevsky with his wicked smile.

'You'd have offered him a poisoned sweet.'

Malevsky's face went slightly awry and acquired for one moment a Jewish look, but he at once started laughing.

'As for you, Voldemar,' Zinaida went on, 'no, that's enough, let's play something else.'

'Monsieur Voldemar, in his capacity as the queen's pageboy, would have held up her train as she ran into the garden,' remarked Malevsky venomously.

I was incensed, but Zinaida quickly placed a hand on my shoulder and, standing up, declared in a slightly unsteady voice:

'I've never given Your Excellency the right to be rude and I therefore ask you to leave.' She showed him the door.

'For pity's sake, princess,' muttered Malevsky and went completely white.

'The princess is right,' exclaimed Belovzorov and also stood up.

'For heaven's sake, I hadn't expected anything like this,' continued Malevsky. 'There was nothing in what I said, I think . . . It didn't enter my head to insult you . . . Forgive me.'

Zinaida encompassed him with a chill glance and chilly smiled.

'Stay if you wish,' she said with a careless gesture of the hand. 'Monsieur Voldemar and I have no occasion to be annoyed. You enjoy stinging people, then do so to your heart's content.'

'Forgive me,' said Malevsky again, and I, remembering Zinaida's gesture, thought once more that a real queen could not have shown an impudent fellow the door with greater adroitness than she did.

The game of forfeits was not continued for long after this brief scene. Everyone felt a little embarrassed, not so much by the scene itself as by another, ill-defined but oppressive feeling. No one mentioned it, but each one sensed it in himself and in his neighbour. Maidanov read us his verses, and Malevsky praised them highly with exaggerated enthusiasm. 'Just look how kind he's trying to be now!' Lushin whispered to me. We soon went our separate ways. Zinaida had suddenly fallen into a pensive mood and the old princess sent word that she had a headache. Nirmatsky began to plead his rheumatism . . .

I was unable to fall asleep for a long time. Zinaida's story had amazed me. 'Did it contain some hint?' I asked myself. 'And who was she hinting at? And if something was definitely being hinted at, how can I be sure what it was? No, no, it couldn't be . . .' I whispered, turning from one burning cheek to the other. But I remembered the expression on Zinaida's face during her story, and I remembered the exclamation which had been torn from Lushin in the Amusement Gardens, the sudden changes in her attitude towards me – and I became lost in speculations. 'Who is he?' These words literally stood before my very eyes, inscribed on the darkness. It was literally as if there was an ominous low cloud hanging over me and I could feel its weight upon me and waited for it all of a sudden to disperse. I had grown used to many things in the recent past and witnessed many things at the Zasyekins': their disorderliness, the greasy stubs of candles, the broken knives and forks, the sombre Boneyface, the disreputable maidservants, the old princess's manners – all this strange life no longer caused me to feel surprise. But I couldn't get used to what now troubled me in Zinaida. 'Adventuress', my mother had once called her. An adventuress – she, my idol, my goddess! This name scorched me, I tried to hide from it by hiding myself in my pillow, I fretted at it – and at the same time what I wouldn't have agreed to, what I wouldn't have given just to be that fortunate man standing by the fountain!

My blood was on fire and boiling over. 'The garden . . . the fountain,' I thought. 'I'll go into the garden.' I hurriedly dressed and slipped out of the house. The night was dark and the trees scarcely whispered. A calm chill air fell from the sky; the scent of dill was wafted from the kitchen garden. I traversed all the paths and the light sound of my footsteps both alarmed and encouraged me. From time to time I would stop and wait and listen to my heart-beats, so loud and rapid. At last I approached the fence and leaned on the thin cross-piece. Suddenly – or was I imagining it? – I glimpsed a female figure only a few steps from me. I forced my eyes to scour the darkness and held my breath. What was that? Was I hearing footsteps? Or was it again the noise of my heart? 'Who's there?' I murmured barely audibly. What was that? A suppressed laugh? A rustling in the leaves? Or a human sigh close to my ear? I grew frightened. 'Who's there?' I repeated still more quietly.

The surrounding air was filled with movement for an instant. A streak of fiery light flashed in the sky: it was a falling star. 'Zinaida?' I was about to ask, but the sound died on my lips. And suddenly everything around me fell profoundly silent, as often happens in the middle of the night. Even the grasshoppers stopped their chirring in the trees. The only sound was of a window slamming shut somewhere. I stood there and stood there and then returned to my room and my bed, which had grown cold. I felt a strange excitement, as if I had set out for a rendezvous – and had remained alone and walked past someone else's happiness.

[17]

The next day I saw Zinaida only for an instant. She was off somewhere by cab with her mother. On the other hand, I saw Lushin, who hardly deigned to greet me, and Malevsky. The young count grinned and struck up a friendly conversation with me. Of all the visitors to the wing of the house he was the only one who had known how to bluff himself into our house and make himself very agreeable to my mother. My father had no time for him and treated him with a politeness bordering on the insulting.

'Ah, *monsieur le page*!' began Malevsky. 'I'm very pleased to meet you What is your beautiful queen doing?'

His fresh, handsome face was so abhorrent to me at that moment and he looked at me in such a playfully mocking way that I didn't answer.

'Are you still angry with me?' he went on. 'There's no need. It wasn't I who named you pageboy, but pageboys are mostly in attendance on queens. But allow me to remark that you're not doing your job very well.'

'What do you mean?'

'Pageboys must be inseparable from their mistresses. They must know everything they do. They must keep watch on them', he added, lowering his voice, 'day and night.'

'Why do you say that?'

'Why do I say that? I think I make myself clear. Day – and night. By day it's neither here nor there, everything's bright and there are people about. But at night – that's when you've got to be careful! I advise you not to sleep at night and keep watch as hard as you can. Remember, it's in the garden, at night, by the fountain – that's where you've got to keep watch. You'll live to thank me.'

Malevsky gave a laugh and turned his back on me. Probably he didn't attribute much significance to what he said to me, for he had a reputation as an outstanding hoaxer and he was famed for his ability to fool people at masked balls, which was greatly aided by the almost unconscious mendacity that pervaded his whole being. He'd wanted to do no more than tease me, but his every word flowed like a poison in my veins. I was enraged. 'So that's it!' I said to myself. 'Very well, then! It turns out that my forebodings of yesterday were right! It turns out I wasn't drawn into the garden for no reason at all! So I must put a stop to this!' I exclaimed loudly and struck my fist against my chest, though I'd no idea really what had to be stopped. 'If Malevsky himself appears in the garden,' I thought (he might have blurted out too much; he would have the cheek for it), 'or someone else' (our garden fence was very low and no one would have difficulty climbing over it), 'it'll be a bad lookout for whoever gets in my way! I don't advise anyone to tangle with me! I'll show the whole world and her, the treacherous creature' (I actually called her a treacherous creature), 'that I know how to take my revenge!'

I returned to my room, got out of my desk a recently purchased

English penknife, felt the sharpness of its blade and, knitting my brows, placed it in my pocket with cold and concentrated determination, precisely as if I were to the manner born for such matters. My heart had risen up angrily in me and turned to stone. Till nightfall my brows remained knitted and my lips pressed tight shut, and I continuously strode backwards and forwards, my hand squeezing the penknife that had grown warm in my pocket and mentally preparing myself for some frightful deed. These new and unprecedented sensations so occupied and even delighted me that I thought very little about Zinaida. My thoughts were filled with visions of Aleko, the young gypsy.* 'Where are you going, my handsome fellow? Lie there . . .' and then: 'All smeared in blood are you! O, what have you done?' 'Nothing!' The cruelty in my smile as I repeated that word: 'Nothing!'

My father was not at home, but my mother, who for some time past had been in a state of almost continuous speechless irritation, paid attention to my fatalistic look and said to me over supper: 'What's got into you? Has the cat got your tongue?' I simply smirked condescendingly in answer to her and thought: 'If only they knew!'

The clock struck eleven. I went to my room, but I did not undress and waited for midnight. At last that struck as well. 'Now's the time!' I muttered to myself through my teeth and, buttoning up my jacket to my neck and rolling up my sleeves, I set out for the garden.

I had already chosen the place where I would keep watch. At the end of the garden, where the fence separating our part from the Zasyekins' joined the common wall, there was a solitary fir growing. Stationed beneath its low thick branches, I could have a good view, so far as the night-time dark permitted, of what was happening around me. Winding close by was the path which had always seemed to me mysterious: it crept like a snake along the fence, which showed signs at that point of the feet that had clambered over it, and led to a round bower of thick acacias. I reached the fir, leaned against its trunk and began to keep watch.

The night was just as calm as it had been last time, but there were fewer clouds in the sky and the outlines of bushes, even of tall flowers, were more clearly visible. The first moments of waiting were agonising, almost frightening. I had decided to stop at nothing. My only consideration was: how to do it? Should I cry out thunderously: 'Who goes there? Halt! Be recognised or die!' or simply take them by surprise?

Every sound, every rustle and murmur seemed to me significant and unusual . . . I kept myself in readiness . . . I leaned forward . . . But half an hour passed, then an hour; my blood grew calmer and colder; I began to be invaded by a sense that I was doing all this for nothing, that I was even being rather stupid and that Malevsky had been making fun of me. I abandoned my hiding place and walked round the whole garden. As if by design, there was not the slightest sound anywhere; everything was sound asleep; even our dog was fast asleep, curled up by the gate. I climbed up on the wall of the ruined conservatory, saw the far fields laid out before me, remembered the encounter with Zinaida and began thinking to myself . . .

I suddenly shuddered . . . It seemed to me I heard the squeak of a door being opened and then the light snapping of a twig. In a couple of leaps I was down from the conservatory and frozen to the spot. Rapid, light, but cautious steps could clearly be heard coming through the garden. They were approaching me. 'It's him! It's him at last!' raced through my heart and, trembling, I drew the penknife out of my pocket and with trembling fingers opened it . . . Red sparks whirled before my eyes, my hair stood up on end in fright and anger . . . The footsteps were coming directly towards me. I bent down and was ready to spring up at him . . . a man came into view . . . My God, it was my father!

I recognised him at once, although he was wrapped about in a dark cloak and had pulled his hat down over his face. He came by on tip-toe. He did not see me, though there was nothing to hide me, but I had crouched so low and was so huddled up that I was practically level with the ground. The jealous Othello who had been ready to commit murder was suddenly turned into a schoolboy . . . I was so frightened by the unexpected appearance of my father that at first I didn't even notice where he had come from or where he had gone. Only afterwards did I straighten up and ask myself: 'Why is father walking about in the garden at night?' – and then once again everything fell silent around me. From fear I dropped my penknife in the grass, but I didn't even start looking for it: I was very ashamed. I had come to my senses in a flash. On my way home, however, I went up to the little low bench under the elder bush and glanced at the little window of Zinaida's bedroom. The small, slightly curved panes of the window shone faintly blue in the feeble light falling from the night sky. Suddenly their colour began to change. Behind them – I saw this quite clearly – the whitish blind was being lowered quietly and carefully. It was drawn right down to the window sill – and that's where it stayed.

'What's it all mean?' I asked aloud almost despite myself when I had got back to my room. 'Is it all a dream, an accident or . . .?' The ideas which suddenly entered my head were so new and strange that I didn't even dare yield to them.

[18]

I got up in the morning with a heartache. The previous day's sense of excitement had vanished. It had been replaced by an oppressively confused sense and a hitherto unfamiliar feeling of deep grief, just as if something within me had died.

'Why've you got the look of a rabbit with half its brain removed?' asked Lushin when he met me.

At lunch I covertly glanced at my father and mother: he, as usual, was calm and collected, while she was, as usual, secretly annoyed. I waited, wondering whether my father would make some friendly remark to me, as he sometimes did, but he didn't even treat me in his normally cold, affectionate way. 'Should I tell Zinaida everything?' I asked myself. 'It makes no difference now. Everything's ended between us.' I set off to see her, but not only did I tell her nothing, I didn't even succeed in talking to her as I would have liked. The princess's son, a twelve-year-old cadet, had come from St Petersburg for his holidays. Zinaida at once entrusted me with looking after her brother.

'Here,' she said, 'my dear Volodya' (this was the first time she had called me by this name) 'is a friend for you. He's also called Volodya. Please, be nice to him. He's a bit shy and untamed, but he's got a kind heart. Show him the Amusement Gardens, take him for walks, look after him. You'll do that, won't you? You're such a kind boy!'

She fondly placed her two hands on my shoulders and I was completely lost. The arrival of this schoolboy turned me into a schoolboy as well. I gazed in silence at the cadet, who stared back at me just as silently. Zinaida burst out laughing and pushed us towards each other.

'Go on, children, kiss!'

We kissed.

'Would you like to come into the garden?' I asked the cadet.

'If you like, sir,' he answered in a hoarse, straightforwardly cadetish voice.

Zinaida again burst out laughing. I managed to notice that her face had never before had such a charming colouring. The cadet and I left. We had an old swing in our garden. I put him on the little seat and began to give him a swing. He sat there motionless in his new uniform of thick cloth with its broad bands of gold braid and held on tightly to the cords.

'You could undo your collar,' I said to him.

'It doesn't matter, sir, we're quite used to it,' he said, and gave a short cough.

He resembled his sister, particularly in his eyes. I enjoyed looking after him and yet at the same time there was an aching grief gnawing at my heart. 'Now I'm no more than a child,' I thought, 'whereas yesterday...' I remembered that I'd dropped my penknife yesterday and went looking for it. The cadet begged it from me, pulled off a thick stem of cow-parsley, cut a little flute from it and started tooting on it. Othello tooted as well.

But that evening how he cried, that very same Othello, in Zinaida's arms, when, having found him in a corner of the garden, she had asked him why he was so sad! My tears flowed in such a torrent that she was frightened by them.

'What's the matter with you? What's wrong with you, Volodya?' she kept on asking and, seeing that I didn't answer her and didn't stop crying, she tried to kiss my wet cheek. But I turned away and muttered through my sobs:

'I know everything. Why have you been playing with me? What... what do you need my love for?'

'I'm to blame, Volodya,' said Zinaida. 'Oh, I'm very much to blame in your eyes!' she added, and pressed her hands together. 'How much bad and dark and sinful there is in me!... But I'm not playing with you now, I do love you – you don't even have any idea why or how... Still, what do you know?'

What could I say to her? She was standing in front of me and looking at me – and I belonged to her then completely, from head to foot, so long as she looked at me... A quarter of an hour later I was already running about with the cadet and Zinaida, playing catch-as-catch-can, and I wasn't crying, I was laughing, though my eyes swollen with laughter were shedding tears; and round my neck, in place of my tie, was tied one of Zinaida's ribbons, and I shouted with joy when I succeeded in catching her by the waist. She was doing with me whatever she wished.

I would be in great difficulty if I were forced to describe in detail what happened to me in the course of the week following my unsuccessful nocturnal expedition. It was a strange, feverish time, a kind of chaos, in which the most contradictory feelings, thoughts, suspicions, hopes, joys and sufferings were all whirled about together. I was terrified of glimpsing what was going on inside me, if indeed a sixteen-year-old boy can look inside himself at all. I was terrified of being aware of anything. I simply wanted to live each day in a rush – until evening, and then at night I'd sleep . . . boyish lightheartedness came to my aid. I didn't want to know whether I was loved and didn't want to admit to myself that no one loved me. I kept out of my father's way, but I couldn't keep out of Zinaida's. Her presence scorched me like a fire, but I didn't bother to find out what this fire was on which I burned and melted: it was a blessed sweetness just to burn and melt. I gave myself up completely to my impressions and fooled myself into not remembering anything and shutting my eyes to what might happen. This unthinking, dreamy state of things probably couldn't have gone on for long. A thunderclap put an end to it at one stroke and set me going in another direction.

Returning on one occasion for dinner after a fairly long walk, I learned with surprise that I'd be having dinner by myself, that my father had left and my mother was unwell, didn't want to eat and had locked herself in her bedroom. From the looks on the servants' faces I guessed that something strange had happened. I didn't dare ask them, but I had a young friend among the waiters, Philip, who was passionately fond of songs and playing the guitar, and I turned to him. I learned from him that there had been a terrible scene between my mother and father (every word of which had been heard in the maids' quarters; much had been said in French, but Masha the chambermaid had spent five years living with a seamstress in Paris and understood everything), that my mother had accused my father of being unfaithful and having an affair with the young lady next door, that my father had defended himself to start with but had then flared up and said something cruel 'about the age of certain people', at which my mother had burst into tears; and that my mother had mentioned a loan allegedly made to the old princess and had said very bad things both about her and the young lady, and that my father had then uttered a threat.

'An' this all came about', Philip went on, 'through an anonymous letter. Nobody knows who wrote it. If it weren't for that, there'd be no reason for these things to be known at all.'

'But was there anything in it?' I asked with difficulty, while my arms and legs went cold and something deep down in my breast began to quiver.

Philip winked meaningfully. 'There were something. You can't hide things like that. No matter how careful your father were this time, he'd still to order a carriage or something like that . . . an' you can't get away without the servants knowing as well.'

I sent Philip away and flung myself down on my bed. I didn't cry and I didn't give in to despair. I didn't ask myself when and how it had all happened. I didn't feel surprised at not having guessed the truth for so long and I didn't even blame my father. What I had learned was too much for me. The unexpected revelation had crushed me. It was all finished now. All the flowers of my dreams had been torn up in one instant and lay around me, scattered and trampled on.

[20]

The next day my mother announced that she was returning to the town. In the morning my father went to her bedroom and was alone with her for a long time. Nobody heard what he said to her, but my mother stopped crying. She grew calm and ordered food brought to her, but she did not leave her room and did not alter her decision to leave. I remember that I spent the whole day wandering about, but did not go into the garden and never once glanced at the Zasyekins' wing. That evening I was witness to an astonishing occurrence. My father led Count Malevsky by the arm through the drawing-room, into the hall and, in the presence of a footman, coldly said to him:

'Several days ago Your Excellency was shown the door in a certain home. I will not enter into explanations with you on this occasion, but I have the honour to inform you that if you visit me again I will throw you out of the window. Your handwriting displeases me!'

The count bowed, gritted his teeth, humbled himself and vanished.

Preparations were begun for the return to town, to the Arbat, where we had a house. My father probably had no wish to stay any longer in our holiday home, but he evidently also succeeded in persuading my mother not to start spreading stories. Everything was done quietly and without haste. My mother even ordered compliments to be sent to the old princess and a declaration of her regret that, owing to ill health, she could not see her before leaving. I wandered about as if I were deranged and longing only that everything should be over as soon as possible. One thought persisted in my head: how could she, a young girl, and a princess as well, decide on such a step, knowing that my father was not free and having the opportunity to marry Belovzorov, for instance? What had she been hoping for? Hadn't she been frightened of ruining all her future prospects? Yes, I thought, that's what love is, that's what passion is, that's what devotion is . . . And I was reminded of Lushin's words: 'Some people enjoy sacrificing themselves.' I once chanced to catch sight of a pale blur in one of the windows of the wing .'Can it be Zinaida's face?' I thought. Yes, it was. I couldn't resist any longer. I couldn't leave her without saying a final goodbye. I waited for a suitable moment and then went to the wing where they lived.

In the drawing-room the old princess welcomed me in her usual untidy and uncaring way. 'Well, young man, why are your people in such a hurry to be off?' she asked, pushing snuff up both nostrils.

I looked at her and my heart felt easier. The word 'loan', which had been used by Philip, had bothered me. She didn't suspect anything – or at least that's how it seemed to me at that time. Zinaida appeared from the next room, in a black dress, looking pale, with her hair let down. Without a word she took me by the hand and led me to her room.

'I heard your voice,' she began, 'and came out to see you at once. Do you find it so easy to leave us, you bad boy?'

'I came to say goodbye, princess,' I answered, 'probably forever. You've heard, perhaps, that we're going?'

Zinaida looked intently at me. 'Yes, I've heard. Thank you for coming. I'd already thought I wouldn't see you. Don't think badly of me. I've sometimes done nasty things to you. Still, I'm not what you imagine me to be.'

She turned and leaned against the window.

'No, really I'm not. I know you have a poor opinion of me.'

'I have?'

'Yes, you . . . you.'

'I have?' I repeated bitterly, and my heart began beating hard as usual under the influence of her irresistible, inexpressible fascination. 'I have? Believe me, Zinaida Alexandrovna, no matter what you did, no matter what nasty things, I will love you and worship you to the end of my days.'

She quickly turned round to me and, opening wide her arms, seized my head in an embrace and kissed me strongly and passionately. God knows who it was this prolonged farewell kiss sought to find, but I greedily savoured all its sweetness. I knew it would never be repeated.

'Goodbye, goodbye,' I kept on saying ...

She tore herself away from me and went out. And I left as well. I'm incapable of describing the feeling with which I left. I wouldn't want it ever to be repeated, but I would have considered myself unfortunate if I'd never experienced it.

We returned to town. I didn't quickly throw off the past and I didn't quickly start my studying again. My wound was slow to heal. But I harboured no bad feelings towards my father. On the contrary, he seemed to grow in my eyes. Let psychologists explain this contradiction as best they can.

One day I was walking along a boulevard and, to my indescribable pleasure, I bumped into Lushin. I was fond of him for his direct and unhypocritical manner, and in any case he was dear to me on account of the memories which he aroused in me. I dashed towards him.

'Aha!' he cried, and frowned. 'So it's you, young man! Let's have a look at you. You're still looking sallow, but there's not the rubbishy look there used to be in your eyes. You look like a man not a puppy dog. That's a good thing. Well, how are you? Are you working hard?'

I gave a sigh. I didn't want to tell lies, but I was ashamed to tell the truth.

'Well, it doesn't matter,' Lushin went on, 'don't be afraid. The main thing is to live normally and not give way to temptations. What good are they? Wherever the wave is likely to carry you will be bad. A man's got to stand on firm ground, on his own two feet. Oh, here I am coughing away ... Have you heard about Belovzorov?'

'What about him? No.'

'Lost without trace. They say he went off to the Caucasus. Let it be a lesson to you, young man. It's all because people don't know how to give up in time, how to escape from the net in time. You, I think, got away all right. See you don't get caught again. Goodbye.'

'I won't get caught again,' I thought, 'because I'll never see her again.' But I was destined to see Zinaida one more time.

[21]

Every day my father would go out riding. He had a splendid English chestnut roan with a long slender neck and long legs. The mare was restless and vicious. Her name was Electric. No one could ride her save my father. One day he approached me in good spirits, which had not been the case for a long time. He was preparing to go out riding and had already put on his spurs. I started asking him to take me with him.

'You'd be better off playing leap-frog,' my father answered me, 'because you'd never keep up with me on your clapped-out animal.'

'I'll keep up. I'll put on spurs as well.'

'Well, all right.'

We set off. I had a black, shaggy little horse, strong on his legs and fairly frisky. True, he had to gallop furiously to keep up with Electric when she was going at a trot, but I didn't fall behind. I have never seen a rider like my father. He rode so beautifully and casually but so skilfully that it seemed the very horse beneath him sensed this and delighted in it. We rode along all the boulevards, visited Devichy field, jumped over several fences (I was frightened to jump at first, but my father despised all timid people and I stopped being frightened), crossed the Moscow River twice, and I'd already thought we were on our way home, particularly since my father had noticed my horse was tired, when he suddenly turned from me in the direction of the Crimean ford and galloped along the bank. I hurried after him. Drawing level with a tall pile of old timber, he swiftly jumped off Electric, ordered me to get down and, handing me the reins of his horse, told me to wait there by the timber and himself turned into a little alleyway and vanished. I started walking backwards and forwards along the bank, leading the horses and cursing Electric, who kept on pulling with her head, shaking herself, snorting and whinnying. Whenever I stopped she would paw the ground with both hooves in a ploughing motion and, neighing, bite my horse in the neck. In short, she behaved like a spoilt thoroughbred. My father did not return. An unpleasant rawness rose from the river. A light shower began and speckled the stupid, boring, grey logs I was parading in front of with tiny dark spots. I began to feel miserable and still my father did not return. Some local officer of the law, a Finn, to judge by his looks, also grey all over, with an enormous ancient military helmet in the shape of a vase on his head and carrying a halberd (what on earth, I thought, was such a man doing on the banks of the Moscow River!) came up to me and, turning towards me his wrinkled, hag-like face, said:

'What are you doing with them horses, young man? Give 'em to me, I'll hold 'em.'

I didn't answer him. He begged some tobacco from me. In order to be rid of him – impatience was also tormenting me – I took several steps in the direction my father had gone. Then I went right down the alleyway to the end, turned the corner and stopped. In the street, about forty paces from me, in front of the open window of a wooden house, stood my father with his back to me. He was leaning his chest against the window-sill and in the house, half screened by a curtain, a woman in a black dress was sitting and talking to him. This woman was Zinaida.

I froze. I confess I'd never expected this. My first impulse was to run away. 'My father'll look round,' I thought, 'and I'll be lost . . .' But a strange feeling, a feeling stronger than curiosity, stronger even than envy and stronger than fear stopped me. I began watching and I tried hard to hear what they were saying. It seemed that my father was insisting on something. Zinaida was not agreeing. As if it were this very moment I can see her face – sad, serious and beautiful and with an indescribable look of devotion, grief and love – and a kind of deep despair (I can find no other word to describe it). She was saying words of only one syllable, without raising her eyes and simply smiling – smiling submissively and stubbornly. Just in that smile I recognised my former Zinaida. My father shrugged his shoulders and straightened his hat on his head, which was always a sign with him that he was losing patience. Then I heard the words:

'*Vous devez vous séparer de cette* . . .'

Zinaida had straightened up and stretched out her hand. Suddenly something unbelievable happened right before my eyes: my father suddenly raised his riding-crop, which he had been using to flick the dust off the folds of his coat, and I heard the sharp blow as it struck the arm bared to the elbow. I only just stopped myself from shouting out loud, but Zinaida gave a shudder, looked in silence at my father and, slowly raising her arm to her lips, kissed the scarlet weal which had appeared on it. My father flung the riding-crop aside and, hurriedly running up the porch steps, dashed into the house. Zinaida turned round – and, stretching out her arms and tossing back her head, also moved away from the window.

With the ending of my fright and with a kind of confused horror in my heart, I hurled myself backwards and, running the length of the alleyway, almost letting go of Electric, I returned to the bank of the river. I couldn't collect my thoughts. I knew that my cold and reserved father sometimes had fits of rage, and yet I couldn't make any sense of what I'd seen. But at that moment I felt that, no matter how long I lived, it would be forever impossible for me to forget Zinaida's movement, her look, her smile, that this vision of her, this new vision so suddenly exposed to me, would be imprinted forever in my memory. I stared senselessly at the river and didn't notice that there were tears pouring down my cheeks. 'They're whipping her,' I thought, 'whipping her . . . whipping her . . .'

'Well, there you are! Give me my horse!' my father's voice commanded behind me.

Mechanically I handed him the reins. He jumped on to Electric. The horse, which had become frozen stiff, reared up on her hind legs and leapt forward a couple of yards, but my father soon had control of her. He drove his spurs into her sides and struck her on the neck with his fist.

'Ah, I haven't got my riding-crop!' he muttered. I remembered the recent whistling blow delivered by this very crop and shuddered.

'What have you done with it?' I asked my father after a while.

My father didn't reply and galloped ahead of me. I caught up with him. I absolutely had to have a glimpse of his face.

'Were you bored without me?' he asked through his teeth.

'A bit. Where did you drop your riding-crop?' I asked him again.

My father glanced swiftly at me. 'I didn't drop it,' he said, 'I threw it away.'

He became thoughtful and lowered his head. And it was then, for the first and almost the last time, I saw how much gentleness and compassion his severe features could express.

He again galloped off and this time I couldn't catch up with him. I got home a quarter of an hour after him.

'That's what love is,' I told myself again, sitting at night in front of my desk on which books and notebooks had begun to appear. 'That's real passion! Not to object, to bear a blow of any kind, even from someone you love very much – is that possible? It's possible, it seems, if you're in love ... But I'd – I'd imagined ...'

In the last month I'd grown very much older – and my love, with all its ecstasies and sufferings, had begun to seem to me something so insignificant and childish and miserable by comparison with that other, unknown something, at which I could scarcely guess and which terrified me like an unfamiliar, beautiful but ominous face which one tries in vain to make oneself see in the twilight ...

That very night I dreamed a strange and awful dream. I dreamed that I went into a dark low-ceilinged room. My father was standing there with a whip in his hand and stamping his feet. Zinaida was crouching in a corner and there was a bright red weal not on her arm but on her forehead. And behind both there rose the figure of Belovzorov all covered in blood, and he opened his pale lips and angrily threatened my father.

Two months later I entered the university and six months after that my father died (from a stroke) in St Petersburg where he had recently moved with my mother and me. A few days before his death he received a letter from Moscow which was extremely upsetting to him. He went to beg something from my mother and they say that he even cried – he, my father! On the very morning of the day on which he had his stroke he began a letter to me in French: 'My son,' he wrote to me, 'beware a woman's love, beware that happiness, that poison ...' After his death my mother sent a large sum of money to Moscow.

[22]

Four years passed. I had only just left university and as yet had no clear idea what I ought to start on, which door to tap on, and was passing the time doing nothing. One fine evening I met Maidanov at the theatre. He had married and entered government service, but I could see no change in him. He was just as needlessly *exalté* as ever and just as suddenly depressed.

'You know,' he said to me, 'by the way, that Mrs Dolsky is here.'

'What Mrs Dolsky?'

'You haven't forgotten, have you? The former Princess Zasyekin with whom we were all in love, you as well. Don't you remember – the holiday place, by the Amusement Gardens?'

'She's married to Dolsky?'

'Yes.'

'And she's here, in the theatre?'

'No, in St Petersburg. She arrived a few days ago. She's preparing to go abroad.'

'What sort of a man is her husband?' I asked.

'A splendid fellow, with money of his own. One of my colleagues in Moscow. You understand – after what happened – You must know all about that' (Maidanov smiled meaningfully)' – she didn't find it easy to arrange a suitable marriage. There were consequences, you know. But with her kind of cleverness everything's possible. Do go and see her: she'll be very pleased. She's more beautiful than ever.'

Maidanov gave me Zinaida's address. She was staying in Hotel Demuth. Old memories were awakened in me. I gave myself a promise that next day I would call on my former 'passion'. But other matters intervened and a week passed, then another, and when I finally went to Demuth's and asked for Mrs Dolsky I was told that she had died four days before, quite suddenly, in childbirth.

It was as if my heart had been pierced. The thought that I could have seen her and hadn't seen her and would never see her again – this bitter thought entered my heart with all the force of an irresistible reproach. 'She has died!' I repeated, staring vacantly at the hall-porter, and quietly made my way back on to the street and wandered off, not knowing where. All the past flashed for an instant in front of me. So that's how it's all worked out! It's to this that that young, ardent, brilliant life has come after all its haste and excitement! In thinking this I imagined to myself those features so dear to me, those eyes, those curls all locked away in a narrow box in their damp underground darkness – here, not far from me who was still alive, perhaps only a short distance from my father. I had all these thoughts and all these strong imaginings, and yet the words:

From lips indifferent heard I news of death,
*And with indifference heeded I the message**

resounded in my soul.

O youth! youth! you have no concerns, you possess, as it were, all the treasures of the universe, even grief is a comfort to you, even sadness suits your looks, you are self-assured and bold, you say: 'Look, I'm the only one alive!' while the very days of your life run away and vanish without trace and without number and everything in you disappears like wax, like snow in the heat of the sun . . . And perhaps the entire secret of your charm consists not in the possibility of doing everything, but in the possibility of thinking you can do everything, perhaps it consists precisely in the fact that you wantonly scatter on the wind energies that you wouldn't know how to use for anything else, perhaps it consists in the fact that each one of us seriously regards himself as a spendthrift and seriously considers that he has the right to say: 'Oh, the things I could have done if only I hadn't wasted my time!'

As for me ... what did I hope for, what did I expect, what rich future did I look forward to when – with no more than a sigh, a nagging sense of loss – I said goodbye to the fugitive and momentary ghost of my first love?

And what has come of all that I hoped for? And now, when the shadows of evening are already beginning to stretch over my life, has anything remained fresher or dearer to me than the memory of that brief thunderstorm of feelings in the springtime morning of my days?

But I am not being fair to myself. Even then, in that light-minded time of youth, I was not deaf to the sad voice that called to me, to the solemn sounds that rose to me from beyond the grave. I recall that a few days after I'd learned about Zinaida's death I was myself present, as if drawn irresistibly to be so, at the death of a poor old woman who lived with us in the same house. Covered in rags, laid on hard boards, with a sack placed under her head, she was dying painfully and with difficulty. Her whole life had been one of bitter struggle with day-to-day needs. She had seen no joy in her life, had never tasted the honey of happiness – why, then, I thought, shouldn't she be glad of death, of its freedom and its peace? And yet so long as her frail body still struggled, so long as her chest rose and fell agonisingly beneath the ice-cold hand resting on it, so long as her final strength remained the old woman went on crossing herself and whispering: 'Dear God, forgive me my sins,' and it was only with the last spark of consciousness that there vanished from her eyes the look of fear and horror at her approaching end. And I remember that as I stood there, beside the death-bed of that poor old woman, I began to feel terrified for Zinaida and I felt I wanted to pray for her, for my father – and for myself.

King Lear of the Steppes

There were six of us gathered one evening in winter at the house of an old university friend. The conversation turned to Shakespeare and his types and how they were taken profoundly and truly from the very depths of human nature. We marvelled particularly at their truth to life and their everyday normality; each of us could name Hamlets, Othellos and Falstaffs, even Richard IIIs and Macbeths (these last, true, only in potential) whom we'd come across.

'But I, gentlemen,' exclaimed our host, a man already elderly, 'I've known a King Lear!'

'How so?' we asked him.

'Yes, just so. Would you like me to tell you?'

'Please.'

And our friend immediately set about telling his story.

[I]

All my childhood — he began — and my first youth up to the age of fifteen I spent in the country, on the estate of my mother who owned much property in — province. Practically the sharpest recollection from that now distant time remains in my memory associated with the figure of our closest neighbour, a certain Martin Petrovich Harlov. And it would be hard to erase that impression, for I've never met anyone similar to Harlov in my life since. Imagine to yourself a man of truly gigantic build! A fantastically large head set slightly askew, without any trace of neck, on an enormous body. A whole sheaf of dishevelled yellow-grey hair sticking out of the head, starting practically at the bushy eyebrows. Sticking out of the broad area of the face, looking blue-grey like a peeled egg, was a fir-cone of a nose, tiny bright blue eyes stuck out haughtily and then there was the opening of his mouth, also tiny, but crooked and chapped, and the same colour as the rest of the face. Although the voice that came out of this mouth was hoarse, it was extraordinarily strong and stentorian. The sound of it reminded one of the rasping of iron bars carried in a cart over a poor road, and when Harlov spoke it was as if he were shouting at someone in a strong wind across a broad ravine. It was hard to say what exactly Harlov's face expressed, it was so expansive. You certainly couldn't take it in at a glance! But it wasn't unpleasant – there was even a certain grandeur in it, save that it was of a very remarkable and unusual kind. And the hands he had – the size of pillows! And what fingers, what feet! I remember that I couldn't look at Martin Petrovich's back, that was two yards long, or at his shoulders, the size of mill-stones, without a certain respectful horror. But it was his ears that particularly struck me. Complete cottage loaves, with all the twists and funny bits! His cheeks literally held them up from both sides. Summer and winter Martin Petrovich used to wear a long coat of green material, tied with a Cherkess belt, and greased boots. I never saw him wear a tie – and what indeed could he tie a tie round? His breathing was long-drawn and heavy, the way an ox breathes, but he could walk about soundlessly. One might think that, on entering a room, he would be in constant fear of overturning and breaking everything and therefore he moved about the place cautiously, usually in a sideways motion, as if by stealth. He possessed literally Herculean strength and as a consequence enjoyed great respect in the area, since our peasantry still revere the great heroes of legend. Legends were even made up about him. They used to tell how he'd once come across a bear in a forest and all but done for him, or how he'd found a strange peasant thieving among his bees and taken him along with his horse and cart and thrown them over the fence, and so on. Harlov himself never boasted of his strength. 'If my right hand is blessed with strength,' he used to say, 'then that's the will of God!' He was proud; only he didn't take pride in his strength, but in his name, his background and his native intelligence.

'Our family's from Shweden' (that's how he pronounced Sweden), 'from the Shwede Harlus it comes,' he assured me, 'who in the reign of Ivan Vasilyevich the Dark (way back when!) came to Russia. And that Shwede Harlus didn't want to be any Finnish count, but he wanted to be your real Russian nobleman and have his name noted in the Golden Book.* That's where we Harlovs have come from! And that's the reason why all of us Harlovs have been born with fair hair and blue eyes and clean complexions! We're all snow-people!'

'Yes, Martin Petrovich,' I would try to object, 'but there wasn't any Ivan Vasilyevich the Dark, or Blind as he was called, but there was an Ivan Vasilyevich the Terrible. It was Grand Prince Vasily Vasilyevich who was called the Blind.'

'Tell me another!' Harlov answered me calmly. 'If I say it's true, then it's true!'

On one occasion my mother thought to praise him to his face for his truly remarkable indifference to his personal interests.

'Ah, Natalya Nikolaevna,' he declared almost with annoyance, 'there you've hit the nail on the head! For us, the lords and masters, it can't be any other way, so that no serf or peasant or the like should dare think badly of us! I, Harlov, have a family line coming from way up there . . .' (and he pointed his finger at somewhere very high up above himself on the ceiling) 'and so how could I not be a man of honour? It's impossible'!

On another occasion it occurred to some visiting official who was staying with my mother to have some fun at Martin Petrovich's expense. The latter again trotted out the Shwede Harlus, who had come to Russia . . .

'In the time of King Nebuchadnezzar, you mean?' the official interrupted.

'No, not in the time of King Nebuchadnezzar, but in the reign of Grand Prince Ivan Vasilyevich who was called the Blind.'

'Yet I would surmise', the official went on, 'that your family line's a great deal more ancient and goes back even to times before the Flood when there were mastodons and megatheres about . . .'

These scientific terms were completely unknown to Martin Petrovich, but he realised that the official was making fun of him.

'Perhaps,' he barked out, 'our family line is indeed very ancient. The story goes that at the time my ancestor arrived in Moscow there was a fool living there who was no worse than Your Excellency, and fools like that are only born once every thousand years.'

The official took umbrage, while Harlov simply shook his head back, stuck out his chin, snorted – and that was that. Two days later he turned up again. My mother began to reproach him. 'It was a lesson for him, dear lady,' Harlov interposed, 'not to jump blind, before asking himself who he's dealing with. He's still wet behind the ears and he needs to be taught a lesson.' The official was almost the same age as Harlov, but this giant was accustomed to regard everyone else as only partly developed. He had great faith in himself and feared no man. 'What can they do to me? Where is there a man on this earth who can?' he used to ask and suddenly burst out laughing with a short but deafening guffaw.

[2]

My dear mother was very selective in her acquaintances, but she would receive Harlov with particular warmth and was always ready to make allowances for him because, twenty-five years before, he had saved her life by holding back her carriage on the edge of a deep ravine into which the horses had already fallen. The traces and breech-bands of the harnesses had already snapped, but Martin Petrovich did not let go the wheel he had seized even though the blood spurted out from beneath his nails. My mother also found him a wife. She married him to a seventeen-year-old orphan who had been brought up in her house. He was then past forty. Martin Petrovich's wife was a frail little thing and it was said that he carried her to his own house in the palm of his hand, and she lived only a short while; yet she bore him two daughters. Even after her death, my mother continued to extend her patronage to Martin Petrovich. She found a place for his elder daughter in a government boarding-school and later found her a husband – and had another in mind for the second daughter. Harlov was a good boss – he had just over eight hundred acres – and was slowly building a place for himself, and his peasants were obedient, there was never the least doubt of that! Due to his size Harlov hardly went anywhere on foot: the ground wouldn't bear his weight. He travelled everywhere in a low racing droshky and drove the horse himself, a broken-down thirty-year-old mare with a scar on her shoulder from a wound she had received at the battle of Borodino where she had been ridden by a cavalry sergeant-major. This horse seemed constantly lame in all four legs at once. She couldn't go at a walk, but used to make a kind of running jump attempt to go at a trot. She used to eat wormwood of various kinds along the roadside, which I'd never seen any other horse do. I remember I was always amazed how this half-dead creature could pull such a frightful weight. I don't dare repeat how much our neighbour weighed. Behind

Martin Petrovich's back on the racing droshky there used to be his swarthy servant boy Maximka. His whole body and face pressed up against his master and his bare feet resting on the rear axle of the droshky, he looked like a small leaf or a worm that had accidentally stuck to the giant torso in front of him. This same servant boy gave Martin Petrovich a shave once a week. To perform this operation they say he used to stand on a table. Some jokers insisted that he had to make his way round his master's chin at a run. Harlov was not fond of staying at home, and therefore he could frequently be seen travelling round in his invariable transport, with the reins in one hand (the other, with elbow turned out, rested on his knee) and a tiny ancient cap perched on the very top of his head. He would good-humouredly survey all around him with his small bruinish eyes and thunder out greetings to peasants and tradesmen and merchants met on the way. To priests, of whom he was not very fond, he would give strongly-worded promises of devotion and once, having drawn level with me (I was out for a walk with my gun), he set up such a view-halloo over a hare lying beside the road that the noise and din of it went on ringing in my ears until evening.

[3]

My dear mother, as I've said, used to give a warm welcome to Martin Petrovich. She knew how greatly he respected her. 'Dear lady! Madame! Light of my life!' is how he referred to her. He praised her as his benefactress, while she regarded him as a devoted giant who wouldn't hesitate to come to her aid single-handed against a whole horde of peasants; and although she did not foresee the likelihood of such a confrontation, still, in my mother's view, in the absence of a husband (she was widowed early) it was wrong to neglect such a defender as Martin Petrovich. Besides, as a man he was completely straight, sought no one's favour, was not in debt and did not drink – and he was no fool, though he'd received no education. My mother trusted Martin Petrovich. When the time came for her to draw up her will she demanded that he be one of the witnesses, and he deliberately went home to fetch his iron-framed round spectacles without which he couldn't write. And with his spectacles perched on his nose he just managed, puffing and grunting, in the course of fifteen minutes to write out his rank, first name, patronymic and surname, using enormous capital letters, with twirls and embellishments, and having completed the task he declared he was worn out and that writing for him was as hard as catching fleas. Yes, my mother respected him . . . but she never let him beyond the dining-room in our house. He emitted an extremely strong odour – something earthy, of the forest depths, redolent of bogs. 'A veritable leprechaun, if ever there was one!' my old nurse used to say. At dinner Martin Petrovich was given a separate table in a corner and he was not offended by this – he knew that others preferred not to sit next to him and it left him freer to eat; and he used to eat, I think, as no one has ever eaten since the time of Polyphemus. At the very beginning of the meal he would be given, as a form of precaution, six pounds of oatmeal in a bowl. 'Otherwise you'll eat me out of house and home,' my mother would say.' 'That's what I'll do in any case, dear lady,' Martin Petrovich'd answer, grinning.

My mother was fond of hearing his opinions about the running of the estate, but she couldn't put up with his voice for long.

'My dear good man,' she'd exclaim, 'you really ought to be treated for it! You've deafened me! What a trumpet of a voice!'

'Natalya Nikolaevna! My benefactress!' Martin Petrovich would invariably answer. 'I've no control over my vocal chords. And what medicine would be any good to me, may I ask! I'd better be quiet a little while.'

In fact, I don't think any medicine would have done any good to Martin Petrovich. Anyhow, he was never ill.

He was no story-teller and didn't want to be. 'Long speeches make you out of breath,' he'd remark reproachfully. Only when he was drawn to talk about the year 1812 (he served in the militia and received a bronze medal, which he wore at festivals on his Vladimir ribbon), when he was asked questions about the French, he would recount one or two anecdotes, although he persistently asserted that there'd never been any Frenchmen, not real ones, in Russia, and it'd only been a lot of marauding rag-tag and bob-tail who'd been driven into the country by hunger and he'd given that lot a real thrashing in the forests.

[4]

Yet even this uncrushable and self-assured giant had moments of melancholy and reflection. Without any apparent cause he would suddenly begin to sulk. He would lock himself in his room and set up a humming noise, literally like a whole swarm of bees. Or he'd summon

Maximka and order him either to read aloud from the only book that had found its way into the house, a random volume of Novikov's *The Idle Labourer*, or to sing. And Maximka, who by some fluke of circumstance could read haltingly, would start shrieking out phrases, with words usually pronounced disjointedly and accents misplaced, such as:

' "But pass-ion-ate hum-áns extract from the said Empti-ness, which they do find in all Cre-at-ures, utt-er-ly oppos-ed Conclu-sions. No Cre-at-ure of itself, they say, is strong in do-ing me a Happ-in-ess!" ' and so on – or he intoned in his high-pitched thin voice a melancholy song in which all that could be made out was: 'Ee . . . ee . . . eh . . . ee . . . eh . . . ee . . . Aaa . . . ska! . . . O . . . oo . . . oo . . . bee . . . ee . . . ee . . . ee . . . la!'

And all the while Martin Petrovich would shake his head, comment on the transitoriness of all things, how everything comes to dust, how everything fades like the grass of the field, how everything goes and will never return! He happened to have a picture of a burning candle surrounded on all four sides by the winds of heaven with puff-filled cheeks; underneath it was the inscription: 'Such is human life!' He was very fond of this picture and had hung it in his study, but at normal times, when he was not melancholic, he had turned it to face the wall so as not to be disturbed by it. Harlov, this colossus, was frightened of death! However, during attacks of melancholia he rarely turned to the aid of religion or to prayer. He preferred to put his hope in his own native intelligence. He was not particularly devout and was not often seen in church; true, he used to say that he didn't go to church for the simple reason that he feared the size of his body would squeeze everybody else out. His attacks of melancholy usually ended with Martin Petrovich starting to whistle – and suddenly in a thunderous voice he would order the droshky harnessed and drive off somewhere in the neighbourhood, brandishing his free hand above the peak of his cap as much as to say: 'Everything's okay now!' He was as Russian as Russian could be.

[5]

Strong, silent men like Martin Petrovich are for the most part phlegmatic by temperament. He, by contrast, was fairly easily annoyed. He was particularly impatient with the brother of his late wife who had been given a roof over his head in our house in the capacity of domestic jester and hanger-on, a certain Bychkov who had been nicknamed Souvenir at an early age and had remained Souvenir to everyone, even to the servants, who graced him with the grander title of Souvenir Timofeich. He himself, it seems, didn't know his real name. He was a wretched fellow, despised by everyone – a sponger, in short. He had lost all the teeth from one side of his mouth, which made his small, wrinkled face look lopsided. He was eternally fussing and fidgeting about, either in the maids' quarters or the estate office, either making a nuisance of himself where the priests lived or in the hut of the peasant elder. They'd drive him away from everywhere and all he'd do would be to cringe and screw up his squinting little eyes and give his rubbishy, weak little laugh that sounded like a bottle being rinsed out. It always seemed to me that if Souvenir'd had money he'd have been the beastliest kind of man – immoral, evil, even cruel. Poverty of necessity 'curbed' him. He was allowed to drink only on holidays. He was dressed decently, on my mother's orders, because in the evenings he had to play picquet or boston with her. Souvenir used to make a habit of saying: 'I, er, permit me, ach-once, ach-once.' 'What's this *ach-once*?' my mother would ask in annoyance when he pronounced 'at once' in this way. He'd instantly draw back his arms, get cold feet and babble: 'As you say, ma'am!' Listening at doors, spreading gossip and, above all, 'needling' people were his only occupations, and he would 'needle' as if he felt he had a right to, as if he were having his revenge for something or other. He called Martin Petrovich 'my dear brother' and loathed his guts. 'Why did you kill off my little sister Margarita Timofeyevna, eh?' he'd say to him, squirming and tittering in front of him. One time Martin Petrovich was sitting in the billiard-room, a cool room where no one ever saw a fly and which our neighbour, who hated heat and sunshine, was therefore very fond of. He was sitting between the wall and the billiard-table. Souvenir snaked his way past his belly, teased him, cavorted ... Martin Petrovich wanted to thrust him away and moved both hands forward. To Souvenir's good fortune he managed to get out of the way in the nick of time – the palms of his 'dear brother's' hands came up against the edge of the billiard-table and the heavy wooden structure instantly flew off its six retaining screws ... How wafer-thin Souvenir would have been if he'd fallen victim to those powerful hands.

[6]

I'd long been interested to see what sort of a place Martin Petrovich had built for himself, what his home was like. Once I offered to ride with him to Yeskovo, as his estate was called. 'Is that so? You want to see what my domain looks like?' said Martin Petrovich. 'With pleasure! I'll show you my garden and my house and my barn – everything. I've got a whole heap of things!' We set off. From our village to Yeskovo was about a couple of miles. 'There it is, that's my domain!' roared Martin Petrovich suddenly, making an effort to turn his immobile head and stretching his hands out to left and right. 'It's all mine!' Harlov's house was at the top of a low-lying hill. Below it a few wretched peasant huts were dotted round a small pond. By the pond itself, on a raft, an old peasant woman in a checked woollen skirt was paddling a heap of washing.

'Axinya!' barked Martin Petrovich, and so loudly that the rooks rose in flocks from a nearby field of oats. 'Are you washing your husband's pants?'

The old woman turned round at once and bowed low to the waist.

'Yes, his pants, master,' came her faint reply.

'Good, good! Now look at that,' Martin Petrovich went on, trotting beside a half-rotten fence, 'that's my hemp – and over there, that's the peasants'. Do you see the difference? And this is my garden. I planted the apple trees myself, and the willows, too. But for that there wouldn't be any trees here at all. That's a lesson for you.'

We turned into a yard surrounded by paling. Directly opposite the gates rose a small and extremely ancient building with a straw roof and a little porch on thin supports. To one side stood another, a bit newer, which boasted a minute upper floor, but it also stood on thin little legs. 'And here's another lesson for you,' said Harlov. 'You can see what hovels our fathers lived in, but now I've built myself a real palace!' This palace resembled nothing so much as a house of cards. Half-a-dozen dogs, each more shaggy and ugly than the next, greeted us with barking. 'Shepherds!' remarked Martin Petrovich. 'Real Crimean shepherd dogs! Shut up, you brutes! I'll take you and I'll hang the lot of you!' On the steps of the newer of the houses appeared a young man in a long nankeen coat, the husband of Martin Petrovich's elder daughter. Springing briskly up to the droshky, he respectfully supported his father-in-law's elbow as the latter alighted – and with one hand even made it seem he would take hold of the giant leg which the other, as he leaned his body forward, swung over the seat. He then helped me to get down from my horse.

'Anna!' shouted Harlov. 'Natalya Nikolaevna's son is paying us a visit and we must be hospitable! Where's Yevlampiushka?' (Anna was his elder daughter, Yevlampiya his younger.)

'She's not at home. She's gone to pick cornflowers,' Anna answered, appearing in a little window beside the door.

'Have we any cottage cheese?' asked Harlov.

'Yes.'

'Any cream?'

'Yes.'

'Well, lay it ready, and meanwhile I'll show him my study. This way, this way, if you please,' he added, turning to me and summoning me with his finger. He didn't use a familiar form of address to me in his own home: a host has to be polite. He led me along a corridor. 'This is where I spend my time,' he said, stepping through a wide doorway, 'and here's my study. Please come in.'

The study turned out to be a large room, unplastered and almost empty. On the walls, on unevenly placed nails, hung two whips, a rust-coloured tricorn hat, a single-barrelled gun, a sabre, an unusual horse-collar with brasses and the picture of the burning candle surrounded by the four winds of heaven. In one corner stood a wooden sofa covered with a colourful rug. Hundreds of flies buzzed lustily on the ceiling; yet the room was cool, except that it smelt very strongly of that special woody smell which accompanied Martin Petrovich everywhere.

'A nice study, don't you think?' Harlov asked me.

'Very nice.'

'See, dear boy, that's my Dutch horse-collar hanging on the wall,' Harlov continued, dropping into the familiar form again. 'A magnificent horse-collar! Did a swop with a Jew. Just you look at that, dear boy!'

'It's a nice horse-collar.'

'First-class for working with! Just take a sniff of it – first-class leather!'

I sniffed the horse-collar. It gave off a smell of mouldy blubber and nothing else.

'Well, sit yourself down, young man – on that little chair, be my guest,' said Harlov, but he lowered himself on to the divan and literally started dozing, closing his eyes and even snoring slightly. I gazed at him in silence and could scarcely marvel enough at the mountainous size of the man. Suddenly he woke up.

'Anna!' he shouted, and at the same instant his enormous stomach rose and fell like a wave of the sea. 'What's up with you? Get a move on! Or didn't you hear what I said?'

'It's all ready, father, come along,' his daughter's voice called.

I inwardly marvelled at the speed with which Martin Petrovich's orders had been carried out and followed him into the sitting-room where on a table covered with a red cloth decorated with a white design there was laid ready a meal of cottage cheese, cream, white bread and even castor sugar and ginger. As I set about the cottage cheese, Martin Petrovich, having mumbled kindly: 'Eat, dear boy, eat, my dear fellow, don't scorn our simple country fare,' again found a seat in a corner and again literally started dozing. In front of me, motionless and with lowered eyes, stood Anna Martinovna, and through the window I could see her husband walking my horse about the yard and wiping the snaffle bit with his own hands.

[7]

My mother had little time for Harlov's elder daughter; she called her stuck-up. Anna Martinovna hardly ever paid us a visit and in my mother's presence was always cool and on her dignity, although it was through my mother's kindness that she had been educated at boarding-school and had been married and had received a thousand roubles in notes from her as well as a yellow Turkish shawl, which was slightly worn, true. She was a woman of medium height, on the thin side, very lively and brisk in her movements, with thick auburn hair and a hand-some, swarthy face in which the narrow, pale-blue eyes stood out rather strangely but pleasantly. She had a straight and delicate nose, delicate lips and a pointed chin. Someone at a first glance would probably have thought: 'Well, she's clever all right and I bet she's got a temper!' And all this notwithstanding there was something attractive about her. Even the dark birth-marks scattered like buckwheat all over her face suited her and reinforced the feeling which she aroused. Slipping her hands under her kerchief, she surreptitiously looked down at me (I was sitting, she was standing) and an unkind glimmer of a smile flitted over her lips and her cheeks and in the shadow of her long eyelashes. 'Oh, what a spoilt little aristocratic brat you are!' this smile seemed to say. Every time she breathed her nostrils enlarged slightly – and this was also rather strange; and yet I nevertheless felt that if Anna Martinovna were to be fond of me and even wanted to kiss me with her thin hard lips I'd have jumped as high as the ceiling in my excitement! I knew that she was very severe and demanding and the girls and old women feared her like the plague, but – the hell with it! – Anna Martinovna secretly fired my imagination . . . However, I was then only fifteen, and at that age . . .

Martin Petrovich again woke up.

'Anna!' he cried out. 'Play us something on the piano! Young men love that.'

I looked round: the room did contain a pitiful imitation of a piano.

'All right, father,' Anna Martinovna answered. 'Only what'll I play him? It'll not be interesting for him.'

'What did they teach you in your *bear*ding-school?'

'I've forgotten everything . . . Anyhow the strings are broken.'

Anna Martinovna had a very pleasant little voice, resonant and a bit plaintive, rather like that of a predatory bird.

'Well, then,' said Martin Petrovich and thought about it. 'Well, then,' he began again, 'you might like to take a look at the barn? Volodka can take you. Hey, Volodka!' he shouted at his son-in-law who was still walking my horse about the yard. 'Take the young gentleman to the barn . . . and generally show him round. But I've got to have a nap. That's right! Happy to have had you here!'

He went out and I followed after him. Anna Martinovna immediately started clearing the table, briskly and rather petulantly. In the doorway I turned and bowed to her, but she literally didn't notice my bow and simply smiled once more, this time more wickedly than ever.

I took my horse from Harlov's son-in-law and led it by the bridle. The two of us went to the barn, but because there wasn't anything specially interesting there and he couldn't suppose that I, a young boy, was outstandingly fond of estate management, we returned through the garden to the road.

I knew Harlov's son-in-law well. He was called Vladimir Vasilyevich
Slyotkin; he was an orphan, the son of a minor official who had been
entrusted with my mother's business, and she had brought him up.
He'd been sent to the county school to start with, then he'd entered the
patrimonial registry, after that he'd been sent to work in official government shops and finally he'd been married off to Martin Petrovich's
daughter. My mother described him as a Jew-boy, and with his curly
hair and dark eyes, always as moist as prunes, his hawk-shaped nose and
broad red mouth he did really resemble the European type, save that
the colour of his skin was white and he was in general far from bad-
looking. He was of a subservient temperament so long as his own personal interests were not involved. As soon as they were he'd be overwhelmed with greed, even to the point of tears. Over some bit of rag
he'd spend a whole day pestering, he'd remind one of a promise given
a hundred times over and he'd take offence and whine if the promise
weren't fulfilled at once. He liked to traipse around the field with a gun
and whenever he happened to bag a hare or a duck he'd stow it away
with special care, saying: 'Well, it doesn't matter now what you do,
you won't be going anywhere! Now you're going to sing for *my* supper!'

'A good little horse you've got there,' he said in his wheedling voice
as he helped me into the saddle. 'If only I had a horse like that! Likely
I'd get one! It's not my luck. Though if you asked your mother, gave
her a reminder . . .'

'Did she promise you one?'

'If only she had! No. But I assumed that out of her great beneficence . . .'

'You should ask Martin Petrovich.'

'Martin Petrovich!' Slyotkin cried in protracted repetition of the
name. 'For him I'm no more than some insignificant servant-boy like
that Maximka. He ill-treats the lot of us, and there's never any reward
from him for all the work we do.'

'Is that really so?'

'Yes, it is, by God! When he says: "My word is sacred!" that's an end
to it, just like he'd cut off your head with an axe. Ask or don't ask it's all
the same thing. Yes, and Anna Martinovna, my wife, doesn't have the
advantage over him that Yevlampiya Martinovna has . . . Oh, my God,
my godfathers!' he suddenly interrupted himself and spread his arms in

despair. 'Just look – what on earth's that? Someone's cut a whole quarter acre of our oats, our own oats! Would you credit it? Oh, the life around these parts! Thieves, a lot of thieves! It's absolutely true what they say: Never trust Yeskovo, Beskovo, Yerin and Belin!' (These were four local villages.) 'Ah, ah, dammit! One and a half roubles, say, or two roubles dead loss!'

There were signs of sobbing in Slyotkin's voice. I kicked my horse's flanks and rode away from him.

Slyotkin's exclamations were still not out of earshot when suddenly, at a turn in the road, I came across Harlov's second daughter Yevlampiya who, according to Anna Martinovna, had gone out to pick cornflowers. A dense garland of these flowers was wound round her head. We exchanged bows in silence. Yevlampiya was also very handsome, no less than her sister, but in another way. She was of tall build like her parent. Everything about her was large: her head and her legs and her arms and her teeth white as snow, and particularly her eyes, which were protuberant and languishingly dark-blue like beads. Everything about her was even monumental (she was not Martin Petrovich's daughter for nothing), but beautiful. She evidently had no idea what to do with the plaited mass of thick fair hair and had wound it three times round the top of her head. Her mouth was charming and fresh as a rose and raspberry-red, and when she spoke the middle of her upper lip rose very cutely. But the look in her large eyes had something wild and almost ferocious about it. 'She's wilful, she's got Cossack blood,' Martin Petrovich used to say of her. I was frightened of her . . . This stately beauty reminded me of her father.

I rode on a little further and heard her begin singing in an even, strong, somewhat sharp, peasant's voice, and then she suddenly stopped. I turned round and from the top of a hill saw her standing next to Harlov's son-in-law in front of the cut quarter acre of oats. The latter was waving and pointing, but she remained unmoved. The sun lit up her tall figure and the garland of cornflowers shone bright blue on her head.

[9]

I think I've already told you, gentlemen, that my mother had arranged a bridegroom for this second of Harlov's daughters. It was a poor neighbour of ours, a retired army major, Gavrila Fedulych Zhitkov, a man no longer young and, as he liked to put it, not without a certain self-satisfaction, in any case as a kind of self-recommendation, 'beaten and broken'. He was barely literate and very stupid, but he entertained the secret hope of becoming one of my mother's managers, since he felt himself to be a 'guv'nor'. 'Whatever else, ma'am, getting my teeth into them peasants, that I've got a fine understandin' of,' he used to say, practically grinding his own teeth, ''cos I got used to it,' he would explain, 'in my former, you know, position.' Had Zhitkov been less stupid, he'd have realised that he had no chance whatever of becoming a manager for my mother, since a present manager would have had to be removed, a certain Kvitsinsky, a business-like Pole who was full of character and whom my mother completely trusted. Zhitkov had a long, horsy face. It was entirely overgrown with dusty fair hair, including even the cheeks below the eyes, and in the severest of frosts it would be covered in plenteous sweat resembling dew-drops. At the sight of my mother he immediately drew himself up ramrod straight, his head would begin to quiver with the strain, his enormous hands would lightly flap against his thighs and his whole figure would literally seem to proclaim aloud: 'Command! I will obey!' My mother had no misconceptions about his capabilities, but this did not prevent her from concerning herself with his marriage to Yevlampiya.

'Do you think you'll get on with her, my good man?' she asked him once.

Zhitkov gave a complacent smile.

'Of course, Natalya Nikolaevna! I kept a whole company of men in order, kept them all in line, so what would this be, ma'am? Easy as spittin'.'

'That was a company of men, my good man, but this is a well-brought-up girl, your wife,' my mother remarked with displeasure.

'Of course, ma'am, Natalya Nikolaevna!' Zhitkov again exclaimed. 'I can understand that very well. Briefly, it's a young lady, someone needing tenderness!'

'Well,' my mother finally decided, 'Yevlampiya will be able to stick up for herself.'

[10]

On one occasion – it was in June and evening was approaching – a footman announced the arrival of Martin Petrovich. My mother was surprised because, although we hadn't seen him for more than a week, he

never used to visit us as late as this. 'Something must have happened!'
she exclaimed under her breath. Martin Petrovich's face, when he
lumbered into the room and instantly sank down into a chair beside the
door, had such an unusual expression, was so pensive and even pale, that
my mother repeated her exclamation aloud and despite herself. Martin
Petrovich fixed his eyes on her, fell silent, gave a heavy sigh, fell silent
again and at last announced that he had come on a certain matter . . .
which . . . was of such a kind that by reason of . . . Having mumbled
these disjointed words, he suddenly rose and left.

My mother rang and ordered the footman who entered to run after
Martin Petrovich and bring him back, but the latter had already managed
to get into his droshky and drive away.

The next morning my mother, who had been astonished and even
disconcerted both by Martin Petrovich's unusual facial expression and
by his strange behaviour, was on the point of sending someone to him
when he once again put in an appearance. On this occasion he appeared
calmer.

'Tell me, my dear man, tell me,' my mother exclaimed as soon as she
saw him, 'what's up? Yesterday I thought, my God, has our old friend
gone soft in the head?'

'No, dear lady, I've not gone soft in the head,' answered Martin
Petrovich. 'I'm not that sort of a man. But I need your advice.'

'About what?'

'Except I doubt whether you'll like it . . .'

'Speak, speak, man, and make it simple. Don't excite me! What is
this *it*? Speak simply. Or have you had another attack of melancholia?'

Harlov frowned.

'No, it's not melancholia, that only happens to me when it's a new
moon. But let me ask you, dear lady, what do you think of death?'

My mother gave a start.

'Of what?'

'Of death. Can death spare anyone on this earth, do you think?'

'What'll you be thinking of next, my dear man? Which of us is
immortal? You've been born the giant you are, but you'll die as well.'

'Oh, I will! I will!' Harlov agreed, and lowered his eyes. 'It happened
I've had a dream . . .' he brought out eventually.

'What are you saying?' my mother interrupted.

'I've had a dream,' he repeated. 'I see things in dreams!'

'You do?'

'I do! Didn't you know?' Harlov sighed. 'Well, it's like this, I lay down for a rest a week ago, dear lady, just about the time of the beginning of St Peter's fast. I lay down after dinner to have a little rest and I fell asleep. I dreamed that a black foal ran into my room. And this foal started frisking about, baring its teeth. It was a foal as black as a beetle.'

Harlov stopped.

'Well?' my mother asked.

'And this blessed foal suddenly turns and kicks me in the left elbow, right on the elbow! I woke up and my arm and my left leg wouldn't move. Well, I thought, I'm paralysed, but I loosened it up a bit and I could make movements, except that I had pins and needles in my joints and still have them. As soon as I unclench my fist they start up.'

'You've been lying on your arm too long, Martin Petrovich.'

'No, dear lady, you oughtn't to say that! No, it's a warning to me . . . about my death, that's to say.'

'Oh, what next!' my mother began protesting.

'It's a warning! Be prepared, O mortal man! That's what it means. And so, dear lady, this is what I want to lay before you without delay. In no way wishing', cried out Harlov suddenly, 'that death itself should take me unawares, servant of God that I am, I have decided in my own mind to divide my estate, in my lifetime, between my two daughters, Anna and Yevlampiya, as the Lord God directs me!' Martin Petrovich stopped, gave a sigh and then added: 'Without delay.'

'What of it? That's a good idea,' my mother remarked. 'Only I don't see why you need to be in such a hurry.'

'And because I in fact wish', continued Harlov, raising his voice even higher, 'to observe the proper order and legality in this matter, so I humbly ask your son, Dmitry Semyonovich, – I do not dare to trouble you, dear lady, – I humbly ask your son, Dmitry Semyonovich, and I lay it to the duty of my relative, Bychkov, to be present at the completion of the formal act and transference into the possession of my two daughters, Anna, a married woman, and Yevlampiya, a spinster; which act will be brought into effect the day after tomorrow, at twelve o'clock midday, in my estate of Yeskovo, known also as Kozyulkino, with the participation of the duly appointed authorities and officials, who are thereto invited.'

Martin Petrovich was scarcely able to finish this set speech which had clearly been learned by heart and was interrupted by frequent sighs. It was as if he simply did not have sufficient breath in his lungs. Then his pale face once again acquired its pink colouring and he wiped away the sweat several times.

'And, my dear man, have you already drawn up the act dividing the property?' my mother asked. 'When did you have time to do it?'

'Oh, I've managed it! Day and night not eating, not drinking . . .'

'Did you write it yourself?'

'Oh, Volodka helped!'

'And you've applied for permission?'

'I've applied, and the Palace of Justice has confirmed it, and the County Court has authorised it, and the temporary division of the land tribunal . . . oh! . . . it's been deputed to appear.'

My mother laughed.

'I can see, Martin Petrovich, you've arranged everything as it should be – and how quickly! You haven't spared any expense, have you?'

'No, I haven't, dear lady.'

'Good, good! But you say you want to have my advice. Well, Mitenka can go, and I'll let Souvenir go with him, and I'll speak to Kvitsinsky . . . Have you invited Gavrila Fedulych?'

'Gavrila Fedulych . . . Mr Zhitkov . . . has also been . . . informed by me. As a future son-in-law he has to be!'

Martin Petrovich had evidently exhausted all his reserves of eloquence. Besides, it had always seemed to me that he had never been well disposed to the son-in-law my mother had sought out for him. Perhaps he had been expecting something more advantageous for his Yevlampiya. He rose from his chair and clicked his heels.

'My thanks for your agreement!'

'Where are you off to?' my mother asked. 'Stay a bit. I'll order you a bite to eat.'

'Many thanks,' answered Harlov, 'but I can't stay . . . I've got to be off home!'

He had stepped back and was just on the point of going sideways through the door, as was his habit, when my mother went on:

'Stop, stop . . . Surely you're not giving everything to your daughters without keeping something for yourself?'

'Without a thing.'

'Well, you yourself – where will you live?'

Harlov even waved his hands.

'How do you mean – where? In my own house, as I've lived *the livelong day till now*. That's how it'll be from now on, too. What sort of change can there be?'

'And you're quite certain about your daughters and your son-in-law?'

'You're referring to Volodka, are you? To that bit o' rag? Yes, I'll push him this way and that, whichever way I want . . . What sort of authority has he got? But they, my daughters, I mean, it's their first duty to feed me and see I've enough to drink, enough clothes, enough to wear on my feet – for pity's sake! I won't be around to plague them for long. Death's not over the hill, you know, but standing right beside me.'

'In death it is God who disposes,' my mother remarked, 'but it is their duty, that's true. Only you've got to forgive me, Martin Petrovich, if I say your elder daughter, Anna, is as proud as proud, and your other daughter, well, she tends to look at you the way a wolf would . . .'

'Natalya Nikolaevna!' interrupted Harlov. 'What're you saying? That they . . . my daughters . . . or that I . . . That they should forget what they owe me? They wouldn't even dream . . . They go against? Against whom? Their own father? They'd dare? Think how long they'd be cursed for, eh? They've spent their lives in fear and submission – and now suddenly? Good Lord?'

Harlov started coughing and wheezing.

'Well, all right, all right,' my mother hurried to calm him down, 'except I don't see why you're making the division *now*? They'll get everything after you've gone. I think your melancholia's at the bottom of it all.'

'Oh, my dear good woman,' retorted Harlov, not without annoyance, 'you will go on about my melancholia! Here there's most likely some higher power at work, and all you can think of is melancholia! At the bottom of it, dear lady, is my thought that I, personally, while still among the living, in my own way would decide who should own what and who is to be rewarded with what, what person is to be the possessor and be grateful and do what should be done, and what their father and benefactor has decided, then for his great kindness . . .'

Harlov's voice broke once again.

'Well, enough of that, enough, my good man,' broke in my mother, 'or that black foal will appear.'

'Oh, Natalya Nikolaevna, don't talk about it!' groaned Harlov. 'It's my death coming for me! I must ask forgiveness. And as for you, young sir, I have the honour to expect you the day after tomorrow!'

Martin Petrovich went out. My mother followed him with her eyes and gave a significant shake of the head.

'No good'll come of it,' she whispered, 'no good at all. You've noticed', she addressed herself to me, 'how when he speaks he seems to be screwing up his eyes the whole time as if the sun were too bright. That's a bad sign. It's a sign he has a weight on his heart and unhappiness is in the offing. The day after tomorrow, then, you'll go off with Vikenty Osipych and Souvenir.'

[11]

On the appointed day our large four-seat family carriage drawn by six dark-bay horses, with the chief coachman, the grey-bearded and thickset Alekseyich, in the driving seat, rolled smoothly up to the front door of our house. The importance of the action which Harlov was intending to take and the solemnity with which he had invited us had had their effect on my mother. She had herself given the order for this extraordinary vehicle to be used and had instructed Souvenir and myself to be dressed in our best, evidently wishing to be respectful to her protégé. Kvitsinsky was, in any case, always in the habit of wearing white tie and tails. The entire journey Souvenir chattered away like a magpie, giggled and wondered whether his dear brother would offer him something, at one and the same moment idolising him and disparaging him. Kvitsinsky, who was gloomy and peevish in general, finally had enough of it. 'Haven't you had enough', he said in his precise Polish accent, 'of talking such nonsense? Is it impossible for you to sit quietly without all this "absolutely unnecessary"' (his favourite expression) 'rubbish being talked?' 'Very well, ach-once,' said Souvenir with displeasure, and squinted fixedly out of the little window. In scarcely more than a quarter of an hour, by which time the even-stepping horses had barely worked up a sweat beneath the thin straps of the new harness, the Harlov residence came into view. Our carriage rolled into the forecourt through the wide-open gates. The diminutive postilion, whose legs reached less than half way down the horses' sides, bobbed up and down in the soft saddle with a boyish shout for the last time, Alekseyich's elbows simultaneously spread out and lifted up, and with an easy cry of 'Whoa!' we came to a stop. No dogs greeted us with their barking, nor did small boys with their shirts open to reveal large stomachs: they'd vanished somewhere. Harlov's son-in-law was waiting for us by the front door. I remember that I was particularly struck by the branches of birch which had been fixed on both sides of the steps, making it look like Trinity Sunday. 'Pomposity of pomposities!' sang out Souvenir nasally, alighting first from the carriage. And it was true that pomposity was everywhere observable. Harlov's son-in-law wore a velveteen tie and a satin bow and an unusually narrow black frock-coat, while the hair of Maximka, who had bobbed up behind his back, was so plastered down with kvass that it even dribbled down from it. We entered the sitting-room and saw Martin Petrovich looming motionless – literally looming – in the centre of the room. I don't know what Souvenir and Kvitsinsky felt at the sight of his colossal figure, but I experienced something akin to worshipful awe. Martin Petrovich was resplendent in a grey coat – it must have been a military coat, of 1812 vintage – with a black, stand-up collar, a bronze medal visible on his chest and a sabre hanging at his side; his left hand was resting on the handle of the sabre, his right hand on a table covered in red cloth. Two sheets of paper covered in handwriting lay on his table. Harlov was motionless, he was not even breathing heavily; and what pomp and circumstance informed his pose, what confidence in himself and in his limitless and undoubted authority! He greeted us with scarcely more than a nod of the head and, saying hoarsely: 'Please!' he pointed with the index finger of his left hand in the direction of a row of chairs. By the right-hand wall of the sitting-room stood both Harlov's daughters arrayed in their Sunday best: Anna in a green and lilac two-tone dress with a yellow silk belt. Yevlampiya in a rose-coloured dress with pink ribbons. Beside them was Zhitkov in a new uniform, with his usual expression of blunt and greedy expectation in his eyes and an even greater than usual abundance of sweat on his hairy face. By the left-hand wall sat the priest in a worn cassock the colour of tobacco, an old man with rough brown hair. This hair and his dull, despondent eyes and large gnarled hands which seemed literally to weigh him down and lay in heaps on his knees, and the greased boots peeping out from beneath his cassock – all bore witness to a joyless and hard-working life, for his parish was extremely poor. Next to him was the local superintendent, a stoutish, rather pale, untidy little gentleman, with short, puffy little hands and feet, dark eyes, clipped black moustache and a permanent, happy, but pointless little smile on his face. He was reputed to be a great bribe-taker and even a tyrant, as it was called in those days, but it was not only the landowners – even the peasants had grown used to him and were fond of him. He was glancing around him very uninhibitedly and somewhat scornfully, evidently enjoying the whole 'procedure'. In fact, what really interested him was the anticipated vodka and refreshments. On the other hand, the attorney sitting beside him, a lean man with a long face and narrow side-whiskers stretching from ear to nose as they were worn at the time of Alexander the First, entered heart and soul into Martin Petrovich's arrangements and did not once take his large serious eyes off him. Out of very strained attention and consideration his lips were continuously working; however, he did not open them. Souvenir sat down in the place beside him and started whispering to him, having announced to me previously that he was the principal freemason in the province. A temporary division of a land tribunal consists, as is well known, of a local superintendent, an attorney and a constable, but the constable either wasn't there, or if he was he kept himself so much to himself that I didn't notice him. Besides, he was known in the county by the nickname 'non-existent' just as forgetful people of a certain type are known as 'non-rememberers'. I sat down beside Souvenir and Kvitsinsky sat beside me. The face of the practical Pole showed annoyance at this 'absolutely unnecessary' journey and the pointless waste of time written all over it . . . 'My dear lady! What a lot of aristocratic Russian fuss and nonsense!' he seemed to be exclaiming to himself. 'These Russians'll be the death of me!'

[12]

When we had all seated ourselves, Martin Petrovich raised his shoulders, cleared his throat, surveyed us all with his small bruinish eyes, and after a loud sigh, began to say the following:

'Ladies and gentlemen, I've asked you to come here for the following reason. I am growing old, ladies and gentlemen, and my powers are failing . . . I've already had one warning that the hour of death, like a thief in the night, is coming nigh . . . Isn't that so, your reverence?' And he turned to the priest.

The reverend gentleman gave a start.

'It is, it is,' he mumbled, shaking his beard.

'And so,' Martin Petrovich went on, suddenly raising his voice, 'not wishing that death itself should catch me unawares, I have decided in my own mind . . .' And Martin Petrovich repeated word for word what he had told my mother two days before. 'On the strength of this, my decision,' he shouted still more loudly, 'this act' (he brought his hand down sharply on the papers lying on the table) 'has been drawn up by me, and the duly appointed authorities have been invited as witnesses, and in what my will consists the stipulations that follow make clear. I have had my time as king, now there's an end of me!'

Martin Petrovich fixed on his nose his round iron-framed spectacles, took one of the papers off the table and began:

'The Partitional Act of the Estate of the artillery lieutenant and hereditary nobleman Martin Harlov, executed by his own hand in full possession of his faculties and through his own personal consideration, in which it is clearly set forth which of his lands and appendages is apportioned to his daughters, Anna and Yevlampiya' ('Please bow!' – they bowed) 'and in what manner his servants and other goods and livestock are to be divided between the said daughters! By my own hand!'

'This paper of his', whispered the superintendent to Kvitsinsky with his incessant little smile, 'is his own work, and he wants to read it out for the beauty of the style, but the legal act itself has been drawn up in the proper way without all these flourishes.'

Souvenir started to giggle . . .

'In accordance with my will!' put in Harlov, the superintendent's words having not escaped his notice.

'That's true of all the stipulations,' the latter answered hurriedly and gaily, 'except the form, you know, Martin Petrovich, must be observed. And the unnecessary details have been removed. Because the law simply can't go into all the stuff about skewbald cows and turkey-fowl.'

'Come here, you!' barked Harlov, at his son-in-law, who had entered the room behind us and had stopped in the doorway, looking obsequious. He at once hurried towards his father-in-law. 'Take this and read it out! I find it difficult. Only don't gabble it! Everyone here must be able to get the meaning of it.'

Slyotkin took the sheet of paper in both hands and began tremulously, but audibly, as well as with taste and feeling, to read out the Partitional Act. It delineated with the greatest accuracy what was to go to Anna and what to Yevlampiya and how it was to be divided between them. From time to time Harlov would interrupt the reading with such remarks as: 'Listen, that's for you, Anna, for all your efforts!' – or:

'That's for you, my dear Yevlampiya, as a gift!' – and both sisters would bow, Anna down to the waist, Yevlampiya with a nod of the head. With gloomy pomposity Harlov would gaze at them. The 'main house' (the new one) was bestowed upon Yevlampiya 'as the younger daughter, according to ancient custom'. The reader's voice rang out with a quivering sound as it pronounced these unpleasant words; and Zhitkov licked his lips. Yevlampiya glanced sideways at him. If I had been in Zhitkov's place I wouldn't have liked that look. The condescending expression habitual to Yevlampiya, as to every true Russian beauty, had a particular nuance to it. Martin Petrovich gave himself the right to live in the rooms he occupied and allocated to himself, as 'special resident', full lodging and board 'with natural provisions' and ten paper roubles a month for clothes and footwear. The last section of the Partitional Act Harlov read out loud himself:

'And this my parental will,' it read, 'it is beholden upon my daughters to fulfil and observe as sacredly and inviolably as a commandment; for after God I am their father and head of the family, and I am not bounden to give account to anyone and have not so given; and if they fulfil my will, then my fatherly blessing will go with them, but if they do not fulfil my will, from which God protect us, they will call down upon themselves my fatherly inexhaustible curse, from this time and for ever more, amen!'

Harlov raised the sheet of paper high above his head and Anna at once sank quickly to her knees and lowered her forehead to the floor. Her husband also followed suit. 'Well, what about you?' Harlov asked Yevlampiya. The latter crimsoned and also bent down to the ground. Zhitkov bent his whole body forward.

'Sign!' exclaimed Harlov, pointing to the bottom of the paper. 'Here: I thank you and I accept, Anna! I thank you and I accept, Yevlampiya!'

Both daughters rose to their feet and signed one after the other. Slyotkin also stood up and was on the point of reaching for the pen, but Harlov thrust him aside, sticking his middle finger into his tie so that he swallowed hard. There followed a moment's silence. Suddenly Martin Petrovich literally sobbed and, saying: 'Well, it's all yours now!', turned away. The daughters and son-in-law exchanged glances, went up to him and started kissing him just above the elbow. He was too tall for them to reach his shoulder.

The superintendent read out the real, formal act, the endowment deed drawn up by Martin Petrovich. Afterwards, together with the attorney, he went out on to the steps and announced the significance of the event to the neighbours, the witnesses, Harlov's peasants and a few of the house servants who had gathered by the gates. The formal admission of the two new mistresses of the estate now began. They also appeared on the steps and were pointed at by the superintendent when he, slightly puckering one eyebrow and momentarily lending his usually carefree face a threatening look, gave a warning to the peasants about 'obedience'. He could have dispensed with these warnings, for humbler faces than those belonging to Harlov's peasants I don't suppose exist anywhere in nature. Arrayed in threadbare coats and torn sheepskins, but tied in very tightly at the waist, as is the custom on solemn occasions, they stood stock-still, and as soon as the superintendent let fly such interjections as 'Listen, you devils! Get that clear, you bastards!', they would bow low all at once, as if on command. Each of these 'devils' and 'bastards' held his cap firmly in both hands and did not take his eyes off the window in which the figure of Martin Petrovich could be seen. The witnesses themselves were hardly less submissive.

'Do you know of any just impediments?' the superintendent shouted at them, 'why these sole and lawful heiresses and daughters of Martin Petrovich Harlov should not be admitted to possession of the estate?'

All those called as witnesses at once shrank back.

'Do you know of any just impediments?' the superintendent shouted again. 'Eh, you devils?'

'No, your honour, we know of none,' was the stout answer given by a pock-marked old chap with a trimmed beard and whiskers, a former soldier.

'Well, he's a right bold chap is Yeremeich!' the witnesses said of him as they dispersed.

Despite the requests made by the superintendent, Harlov refused to come out on to the steps with his daughters. 'My subjects will be obedient to my will without that!' he answered. On the completion of the Partitional Act he had been seized by something akin to grief. His face had again gone white. This new and unfamiliar look of grief was so inappropriate to the plump and expansive features of Martin Petrovich that I simply didn't know what to think. Perhaps he was suffering from one of his attacks of melancholia again? As for the peasants, they were evidently perplexed. And for good reason: 'Our master's still alive – that's him standing there, and what a man he is: Martin Petrovich! And suddenly he doesn't own us any more . . . Wonders'll never cease!' I don't know whether Harlov sensed the thoughts running through the heads of his 'subjects', or whether he wanted for one last time to raise his spirits, except that he suddenly opened the small window known as a *fortochka*, placed his head by the opening and shouted in his thunderous voice: 'Do what you're told!' Then he slammed the *fortochka* shut. The perplexity of the peasants was not of course allayed by this, nor was it lessened. They had been quite turned to stone and didn't even dare look up. A group of household servants (among them were two buxom young women in short calico dresses and with calves of a kind only to be seen in Michelangelo's 'Last Judgement', and an extremely ancient – so ancient, indeed, that he was white all over – half-blind man in a rough woollen overcoat, who was rumoured to have played the bass horn in a band during Potyomkin's time;* Harlov had reserved the servant boy Maximka for himself) – this group showed more vivacity than the peasants; at least, it shifted its weight from one foot to the other. The new mistresses behaved very solemnly, especially Anna. Pursing together her dry lips, she gazed stubbornly at the ground. Her stern figure held out little promise of anything good for the servants. Yevlampiya also did not raise her eyes, save that on one occasion she turned and, literally with surprise, directed her slow gaze towards her intended, Zhitkov, who had followed Slyotkin in also considering it necessary to appear on the steps. 'Who said you could be here?' those fine, prominent eyes seemed to be asking. Slyotkin changed more than all the others. His entire being evinced a brisk jauntiness, as if he felt the stirrings of his appetite. The movements of his head and feet remained as obsequious as ever, but how cheerfully he waved his hands about and how busily he wiggled his shoulder-blades, as if to say: 'Finally I've made it!' Having completed the 'procedure' of admission to ownership, the superintendent, whose cheeks were even beginning to fill with saliva in anticipation of the refreshments, rubbed his hands together in that special manner which usually precedes what is called 'the imbibing of the first glass'. But it turned out that Martin Petrovich wanted first to have a service with holy water. The priest put on a chasuble that was almost completely in tatters; a deacon, scarcely able to keep body and soul together, emerged from the kitchen blowing with great difficulty at incense in an ancient brass censer. The service began. Harlov sighed the whole time. Due to his size he couldn't make obeisances to the ground, but, crossing himself with his right hand and bowing his head, he would direct a finger of his left hand at the floor. Slyotkin literally glowed and even shed a few tears. Zhitkov, in a dignified, military way, made slight finger movements between the third and fourth buttons of his tunic. As a Catholic Kvitsinsky remained in another room. By contrast, the attorney was so zealous in his prayers, accompanied Martin Petrovich's sighs with such commiserating sounds, whispered the prayers and chewed his lips so assiduously, giving such heavenward looks of devotion, that I felt touched and began fiercely praying myself. At the conclusion of the service and the blessing of the water, at which all present, even the blind Potyomkin horn-player and Kvitsinsky, moistened their eyes with the holy water, Anna and Yevlampiya once again, at Martin Petrovich's command, thanked him by bowing down to the ground. Then, at last, the moment for the refreshments arrived. There was a great deal to eat and it was all delicious: we all overate terribly. The inevitable bottle of Don wine appeared. The superintendent, as the person among us who was most familiar with the customs of high society – and, of course, as the representative of the lawful authority – was the first to pronounce a toast to the health of the 'beautiful mistresses of the estate'. Then he proposed that we drink to the health of the most respected and most magnanimous Martin Petrovich. At the sound of the word 'most magnanimous' Slyotkin gave a yelp and rushed to kiss his benefactor. 'Well, good, good, but there's no need,' murmured Harlov in apparent annoyance, elbowing him away . . . But at that moment there occurred a rather unpleasant episode, as one might say.

[14]

It was this: Souvenir, who had been drinking ceaselessly since the serving of refreshments, suddenly stood up from his chair, red as a beetroot, and, pointing at Martin Petrovich, burst into feeble good-for-nothing laughter.

'Magnanimous! Magnanimous!' he rattled off. 'We'll see how much he likes this magnanimity when they drive him out, him, the servant of God, bare-backed – and into the snow!'

'What're you going on about? Bloody fool!' declared Harlov scornfully.

'Bloody fool, bloody fool!' repeated Souvenir. 'Only the Lord God above knows which of us is the real fool. But you, dear brother o' mine, you killed off my little sister, your wife – and now you've done for yourself as well . . . ha-ha-ha!'

'How can you dare insult our respected benefactor?' piped up Slyotkin and, tearing himself from Martin Petrovich's shoulder, round which he had placed his arm, he dashed at Souvenir. 'Don't you know that if our benefactor wishes we can put an end to the act of partition this minute?'

'But you'll still drive him out bare-backed – and into the snow,' retorted Souvenir, taking refuge behind Kvitsinsky.

'Be quiet!' roared Harlov. 'I'll give you such a slap, there'll be nothing left of you but a wet spot! And you be quiet, too, you puppy-dog!' he cried, turning to Slyotkin. 'Don't poke your nose in where it's not wanted! If I, Martin Petrovich, have decided to draw up an act of partition, then who's going to put an end to it? Who's going to go against my will? There's no authority on earth would dare . . .'

'Martin Petrovich!' began the attorney suddenly in a deep, juicy voice. He had also had a good deal to drink, but this had merely increased his pomposity. 'Well, it could be the gentleman has deigned to speak the truth! You have done a great deed, but actually, God preserve us, it may be . . . instead of the proper gratitude, it'll end in some kind of affront?'

I glanced surreptitiously at both Martin Petrovich's daughters. Anna's eyes were fixed venomously on the speaker, and I'd never seen a more malicious and snake-like and yet – in its very malace – a more beautiful face! Yevlampiya had turned away and folded her arms. More than ever now a scornful smile twisted her full red lips.

Harlov rose from his chair, opened his mouth, but evidently his tongue turned traitor. He suddenly struck the table with his fist, so that everything in the room jumped and tinkled.

'Father dear,' Anna said hastily, 'they don't know us and so they don't understand us, saying the things they do. But you mustn't fret yourself. There's no need for you to lose your temper. Look at your poor face, all twisted up!'

Harlov looked at Yevlampiya. She did not move, though Zhitkov, sitting beside her, gave her a nudge.

'Thank you, Anna, my daughter,' said Harlov in a hollow voice, 'you're a sensible woman. I put my trust in you and in your husband.' Slyotkin again gave a yelp. Zhitkov stuck out his chest and tapped his foot, but Harlov did not notice his efforts to attract attention. 'This good-for-nothing', he went on, directing his chin at Souvenir, 'is pleased to make fun of me, but it is not for you, my good sir,' he turned to the attorney, 'it is not for you to pass judgement on Martin Harlov, you've not yet reached years of discretion. And you're an official, what's more, so you talk the purest nonsense. Anyhow, the matter's over, there won't be any change in my decision . . . Well, I'm glad to have seen you! I'm going. I'm not the master here any more, I'm just a guest. Anna, you know what you've got to do. But I'm going off to my room. Enough is enough!'

Martin Petrovich turned his back on us and, without another word, went slowly out of the room.

The sudden departure of the host could hardly fail to upset the party, the more so because the two hostesses also quickly disappeared. Slyotkin tried in vain to detain us. The superintendent did not overlook the chance of reproaching the attorney for his inappropriate candour.

'Couldn't do otherwise!' the latter responded. 'My conscience dictated it!'

'You can see he's a freemason,' Souvenir whispered to me.

'Your conscience!' the superintendent retorted. 'We know your conscience! It resides in your pocket, as it does with the rest of us!'

Meanwhile, the priest, already standing up, but anticipating a quick end to the refreshments, was despatching mouthful after mouthful of food.

'I see you've got a strong appetite,' Slyotkin remarked to him sharply.

'Reserve supplies,' answered the priest with a humble grimace. Long-standing hunger resounded loudly through his answer.

The carriages rolled up and we went our separate ways.

On the return journey no one prevented Souvenir from holding forth and chattering, since Kvitsinsky had announced that he was bored stiff by all these 'absolutely unnecessary' displays of bad taste and had set off home on foot before us. Zhitkov took his place in the carriage. The retired major had an exceedingly dissatisfied look and continually twitched his whiskers about like a cockroach.

'Eh, your high-and-mightiness,' babbled Souvenir, 'has subordination been, you know, undermined? Just you wait and see! They'll give you the boot, too! Oh, you bride-bait, you poor old bride-bait!'

Souvenir was literally in his element, while poor Zhitkov could do nothing but twitch his whiskers.

On reaching home I recounted everything I'd seen to my mother. She heard me out and shook her head several times.

'No good'll come of it,' she muttered. 'I don't like all these new-fangled things!'

[15]

The next day Martin Petrovich came to dinner. My mother congratulated him on the satisfactory completion of his undertaking.

'You're a free man now,' she said, 'and you must feel a lot easier.'

'Easier, yes, dear lady,' answered Martin Petrovich, not indicating in the very least, however, by the expression on his face that he felt a lot easier. 'I can now give thought to my soul and prepare myself properly for the hour of my death.'

'Do you still get pins and needles?' my mother asked.

Harlov opened and closed his left hand a couple of times.

'Yes, dear lady, I do. And I'll tell you something else. As soon as I fall asleep I hear someone shouting in my head: "Watch out! Watch out!"'

'It's . . . just nerves,' remarked my mother and started talking about the previous day, referring to certain circumstances accompanying the completion of the act of partition.

'Well, yes, yes,' Harlov interrupted her, 'there was something . . . unimportant. Only this is what I'll tell you,' he added, dwelling on each word. 'I wasn't put out by the stupid things Souvenir said. Even the attorney, though he's a man of some weight – no, I wasn't put out by him. I was put out by . . .' At this point Harlov hesitated.

'By whom?' asked my mother.

Harlov glanced at her.

'Yevlampiya!'

'Yevlampiya? Your daughter? In what way?'

'Permit me, dear lady, – she's absolutely made of stone! A stone statue! Doesn't she have any feelings at all? Her sister Anna – well, she's all right. She's got delicacy! But Yevlampiya, well, I've shown her – I can't help it! – much preference! But doesn't she have any feelings for me at all? It means things are going badly for me, it means I feel I've not got long to live on this earth, if I hand over everything to them, but she's just made of stone! She wouldn't even speak! She bows, yes, but she shows no gratitude.'

'Just pause a moment,' remarked my mother. 'We'll get her married to Gavrila Fedulych. She'll soften when she's married to him.'

Martin Petrovich again glanced at my mother from beneath his brows.

'Really, that Gavrila Fedulych! You put your trust in him, do you, dear lady?'

'I do.'

'I see, ma'am. Well, you ought to know. But I'll tell you this: Yevlampiya's like me, we've got the same character. Cossack blood and a heart fiery as a burning coal!'

'Have you really got a heart like that, my dear chap?'

Harlov didn't answer. There was a short silence.

'Tell me, Martin Petrovich,' my mother began, 'in what way do you intend to save your soul? Will you be going to Mitrofan or to Kiev? Or perhaps you'll go to the Optina Pustyn, since it's close by?* They say a holy monk has appeared there – he's called Makarius and no one can remember anyone like him! He can see right through all your sins!'

'If she really does turn out to be an ungrateful daughter,' said Harlov in a hoarse voice, 'then I think it'd be better if I killed her with my own hands!'

'What on earth! What're you saying! Heaven help you! Just think!' cried my mother. 'What *are* you saying? What a business! You should've listened to me when you came to me for advice. And now see what you'll be torturing yourself with – instead of thinking about the good of your soul! You'll be torturing yourself – and it won't be a case of biting your own elbow! Oh, yes! Now you're starting to pity yourself, you're losing your nerve . . .'

This reproach, it seemed, pierced Harlov to the heart. All his former pride of spirit came rushing back. He shook himself and thrust out his chin.

'I'm not that sort of a man, my dear Natalya Nikolaevna, I'm not the kind to pity myself or lose my nerve,' he said gloomily. 'I had simply wanted to inform you, as my benefactress and a person whom I much respect, of my feelings. But the Lord God knows' – here he raised his hand above his head – 'that the world itself will sooner fly to pieces than will I renounce my own words or . . .' at which point he even gave a snort ' . . . or lose my nerve or repent of what I've done! I have my reasons! And my daughters will not be disobedient, from this time forth and for ever more, amen!'

My mother covered her ears.

'What trumpeting, my dear good man! If you're so sure of your kith and kin, then God be with you! But you've quite deafened me!'

Martin Petrovich apologised, sighed once or twice and then fell silent. My mother again mentioned Kiev, the Optina Pustyn and Father Makarius, to which Harlov expressed agreement and said: 'I need to, I need to . . . I will . . . for my soul . . .' and no more. He was in low spirits right up to his departure. From time to time he opened and closed his fist, looked at the palm of his hand and said that what he feared most of all was to die without repentance, of a stroke, and that he had vowed to himself not to lose his temper, because from bad feeling the blood goes bad and rushes to the head . . . In any case, he had now cast off all responsibilities, so why should he have cause to be angry? Let others labour and make their blood go bad!

In saying goodbye to my mother he looked at her in a strange way, thoughtfully and questioningly, and suddenly, rapidly extracting from his pocket a volume of *The Idle Labourer,* thrust it into her hand.

'What's this?' she asked.

'Read it . . . there,' he muttered hurriedly, 'where the corner's turned down, about death. In my view, it's terribly well said, but I can't understand it. Couldn't you interpret it for me, my benefactress? When I come again, then you can interpret it for me.'

With these words Martin Petrovich left.

'It's all wrong! Oh, it's all wrong!' my mother remarked as soon as he had disappeared through the door, and then she opened *The Idle Labourer.*

On the page which Harlov had indicated were the following words:

'Death is a Mighty and Important work of Nature. It is none other than this, that It is a Spirit more gentle, more light, more graceful and much more penetrating than those Elements to which It is subject, even the Very Force of Electricity, thus being purified by Chemical means It strives till such time as It feels a Spiritual Place equal to It . . .' and so on.

My mother read this passage twice, exclaimed: 'Phew!' and cast the book aside.

About three days later she received news that her sister's husband had died and, taking me with her, she set off for her place in the country. My mother had anticipated spending a month with her, but she remained there until late autumn – and it was the end of September by the time we returned to our estate.

The first news which greeted me from my manservant Prokofy (he was regarded as our official huntsman) was that there'd never been so many woodcock about and they were particularly plentiful in the birch woods by Yeskovo (Harlov's estate). There were still three hours before dinner and I at once seized my gun and game-bag and dashed together with Prokofy and a setter to the Yeskovo woods. We did in fact find many woodcock there and with about thirty shots killed about five. Hurrying home with my bag, I saw a peasant ploughing beside the road. His horse had stopped, and he, swearing tearfully and horribly, was mercilessly tugging at the horse's bent head with a piece of rope. I took a look at the wretched creature, whose ribs were almost breaking through the skin and whose sweating sides rose and fell fitfully and unevenly like a feeble blacksmith's bellows, and immediately recognised the frail old mare with the scar on her shoulder that had served Martin Petrovich for so many years.

'Is Mr Harlov still alive?' I asked Prokofy. The woodcock had so pre-occupied us that we hadn't spoken of anything else until that moment.

'Yes, sir. Why do you ask, sir?'

'That's his horse, isn't it? Has he sold her?'

'That sure is his horse, sir. But it's not he that's sold it. They done taken it from 'im and given it away to that peasant.'

'What d'you mean – they done taken it? Did he agree to it?'

'They didn't rightly ask 'im, sir. Since you been away things've changed,' said Prokofy with a faint grin in response to my look of surprise. ''Tis bad? My God, it is! Now it's Mr Slyotkin who's in charge over there.'

'And Martin Petrovich?'

'And Martin Petrovich's become the last person as ever is. Dry victuals for 'im, what else? They've done for 'im. Soon they'll drive 'im out for good an' all.'

The idea that such a giant could be *driven out* seemed hardly credible.

'And what's Zhitkov doing about it?' I asked eventually. 'He's married to the younger daughter, isn't he?'

'Married?' repeated Prokofy, and this time smiled with the whole of his mouth. 'They don't even let him into the house! We don't need you, they say; turn round and go back. It's what I said: Slyotkin's in charge.'

'And what about his bride-to-be?'

'You mean Yevlampiya Martinovna? Oh, master, I'd tell you . . . only you're young, that's what. Things've come to such a pass that ee . . . ee . . . ee! Oh, look, there's Diana settin' to!'

In fact, my setter had stopped dead before a large oak that stood at the end of a narrow defile coming out on to the road. Prokofy and I ran towards the dog. A woodcock rose from a bush. We both fired at it and missed. The bird settled elsewhere and we went after it.

Soup was already on the table when I returned. My mother scolded me. 'What's this?' she said with displeasure. 'The first day back and I'm forced to wait for dinner.' I brought her the woodcock we'd killed, but she didn't even look at them. Besides her, Souvenir, Kvitsinsky and Zhitkov were also present. The retired major was standing in one corner, the very picture of a guilty schoolboy. The expression on his face was a mixture of confusion and vexation. His eyes were red, and one might even have thought that he'd been in tears a short while before. My mother continued to be in a bad mood. It didn't cost me much effort to guess that my late arrival had nothing to do with it. During dinner she hardly spoke. The major occasionally raised sorrowful eyes towards her, but he ate exceptionally well. Souvenir was trembling all over. Kvitsinsky maintained his usual pose of self-assurance.

'Vikenty Osipych,' my mother said to him, 'I want you to send a carriage for Martin Petrovich tomorrow, since I've been informed that he's no longer got one of his own. And he must be told to come here at once, that I want to see him.'

Kvitsinsky was on the point of making some remark, but desisted.

'And let Slyotkin know', my mother continued, 'that I am ordering him to come and see me . . . Do you hear? I am or-der-ing!'

'That's exactly what . . . that good-for-nothing needs,' Zhitkov started saying under his breath, but my mother looked at him so scornfully that he at once turned away and fell silent.

'Do you hear? I am ordering!' my mother repeated.

'Yes, ma'am,' said Kvitsinsky, obediently but with dignity.

'Martin Petrovich won't come!' Souvenir whispered to me, accompanying me out of the dining-room after dinner. 'Just you wait and see what's happened to him! It goes against reason! I suggest whatever you say to him he won't understand. Oh, yes! They've speared the snake good and proper this time!'

And Souvenir burst into his flabby little laugh.

[17]

Souvenir's forecast turned out to be correct. Martin Petrovich did not want to visit my mother. She wasn't satisfied with this and sent him a letter; he sent her back a quarter-sheet of paper on which the following words were written in large letters: 'Oh dear, oh dear, I cannot. Too ashamed. Let me die as I am. Thank you. Don't torment me. Marty Harlov.' Slyotkin came, but not on the day my mother had 'ordered' him to come, so much as a whole twenty-four hours later. My mother ordered him to be brought to her room. God knows what their conversation was about, but it lasted only a short time – about a quarter of an hour, no more. Slyotkin left my mother with his face all red and with such a poisonously wicked and impertinent expression that, meeting him in the drawing-room, I was simply flabbergasted, and Souvenir who had been loitering there didn't even finish the laugh he'd just begun. My mother came out of her room also red in the face and observed to all and sundry that Mr Slyotkin was not to be allowed in her house again on any pretext. And if Martin Petrovich's daughters should decide to come – for they might indeed have the impudence – they were to be refused admission as well. At dinner she suddenly exclaimed: 'What a miserable little Jew-boy! I pulled him out of the mire by the ears, I made him respectable, he owes everything, everything to me – and he dares to tell me that I'm meddling in their affairs! That Martin Petrovich has become eccentric and mustn't be indulged! Indulged! What's that mean? Oh, he's an ungrateful little pup! Beastly Jew-boy!' Major Zhitkov, who was also among the diners, imagined that this was the moment when God had ordained he should take the opportunity and put in his word . . . but my mother at once cut him short: 'Well, a fat lot of good you are, my man!' she said. 'You couldn't make it up with a girl and you an officer! You commanded a company! I can just imagine how it obeyed you! You wanted to be a manager! A splendid manager you'd make!'

Kvitsinsky, sitting at the end of the table, smiled to himself not without a certain malicious pleasure, while the poor Zhitkov could do no more than twitch his whiskers and raise his eyebrows and bury his hairy face in his napkin.

After dinner he went out on to the porch to smoke his pipe as usual – and he seemed to me so pitiful and lonely that, though I wasn't fond of him, I felt I had to join him.

'How did it come about, Gavrila Fedulcyh,' I began without further ado, 'that things went wrong between you and Yevlampiya Martinovna? I'd supposed you'd be married long ago.'

The retired major looked gloomily at me.

'That snake in the grass', he began, striving miserably to enunciate each letter in each word, 'stung me and turned all my hopes in life to dust! And I'd tell you all his dirty tricks, Dmitry Semyonovich, but I'm afraid of making your mother angry!' ('Only you're young, that's what . . .' Profoky's words flashed through my mind.) 'So that's how it is . . .'

Zhitkov wheezed.

'Patience . . . patience . . . That's all there is left!' (He struck his fist against his chest.) 'Be patient, old veteran, be patient! I served the Tsar in faith and truth . . . without blemish, yes indeed! I didn't spare my blood and sweat, and now look what I've come to! If I were in the regiment and things depended on me,' he went on after a short pause, sucking convulsively at his cherrywood pipe, 'I'd have . . . I'd have ordered him to be beaten on the back with the flat of the bayonet by the whole regiment – three times . . . until he couldn't take any more . . .'

Zhitkov took his pipe out of his mouth and directed his gaze into the distance, as if inwardly delighting in the picture he had conjured up.

Souvenir ran up and began teasing the major. I went off to one side and decided that I had to see Martin Petrovich with my own eyes at whatever cost . . . My child's curiosity had been strongly aroused.

[18]

The next day I again set off with my gun and my dog, but without Prokofy, to go to the Yeskovo woods. The day turned out to be wonderful. I think that nowhere save in Russia are there such days in September. Such silence dwelt everywhere that at a hundred paces one could hear a squirrel bounding through the dry leaves or catch the sound of a broken twig as it caught in other branches and fell at last into the soft grass – falling forever, for it would never move again until it had rotted away. An air that was neither warm nor fresh, but simply fragrant and literally sour-tasting, very faintly and pleasantly nipped at my eyes and cheeks. Fine as a silk thread, with a white fluffiness at the centre, a long spider's web floated smoothly on the air and, attaching itself to the barrel of my gun, stretched out in a straight line – a sure sign of settled warm weather! The sun was shining, but with so little heat it could have been the moon. I came across woodcock fairly frequently, but I paid no particular attention to them. I knew that the woods stretched almost right up to Harlov's house and right up to his very garden fence, and so I made my way along that side although I had no idea how I would reach the house itself and even doubted whether I ought to try to, since my mother had become so angry with the new owners.

The sound of human voices came from not far off. I started listening. Someone was coming through the wood . . . directly towards me.

'That's what you should've said,' a woman's voice remarked.

'Be sensible!' another voice, a man's voice, interrupted her. 'D'you think it can be done all at once?'

The voices were familiar to me. A woman's pale-blue dress could be glimpsed through the few nut-trees and beside it a dark caftan. A moment passed and there right out into the open, only five paces from me, came Slyotkin and Yevlampiya.

They were immediately disconcerted. Yevlampiya retreated at once back into the nut-trees. Slyotkin thought a moment – and approached me. His face bore not a trace of that obsequious humility with which, some four months previously, walking to and fro across the courtyard of Harlov's house, he had wiped the snaffle bit of my horse. But I also couldn't discern in it any of that impudently challenging look which had so struck me the day before, outside my mother's room. It was as ever pale and handsome, but it seemed broader and more solid.

'What? Have you bagged many woodcock?' he asked me, raising his cap, smirking and running his hand through his black hair. 'You're hunting in our wood . . . Be our guests! We don't object . . . On the contrary!'

'I've not killed anything today,' I answered, replying to his first question, 'and I'll leave your wood at once.'

Slyotkin hurriedly replaced his cap.

'Oh, but why? We're not driving you away – and we're even very pleased. Yevlampiya Martinovna'll say the same thing. Yevlampiya Martinovna, come here! Where've you gone to?'

Yevlampiya's head appeared among the bushes, but she didn't approach us. She had grown even better looking recently and had literally grown taller and plumper.

'I've got to confess', Slyotkin went on, 'that it's even very pleasant for me to have "bumped" into you here. You're still young, but you've got real brains. Yesterday your mother lost her temper with me and didn't want to hear any of my reasons, but as before God, so before you now, I declare I'm not guilty of anything. It's impossible to treat Martin Petrovich any other way: he's completely fallen into his second child-hood. I mean, we can't do all the eccentric things he wants. But we still show him all the proper respect! Ask Yevlampiya Martinovna!'

Yevlampiya did not stir, but the usual scornful smile wandered about her lips and her beautiful eyes had an unfriendly look.

'But why then, Vladimir Vasilyevich, did you sell Martin Petrovich's horse?' (I'd been particularly upset at finding his horse in the possession of a peasant.)

'Why, sir, did we sell his horse? Yes, well, what good was it? It was simply eating hay for nothing. For a peasant it can at least do some ploughing. And Martin Petrovich, if he's a mind to ride out somewhere, has only got to ask us. We won't refuse him a carriage! He can have one with pleasure on the days when there's no work.'

'Vladimir Vasilyevich!' cried Yevlampiya in a hollow voice, as if summoning him, and yet still remaining where she was. She was twisting several flower stalks round her fingers and knocking off their heads by striking them together.

'And as for the servant-boy Maximka,' Slyotkin went on, 'Martin Petrovich complains we've taken him away from him and sent him away for schooling. But judge for yourself: what would he have done if he'd stayed with Martin Petrovich? Twiddle his thumbs, nothing else. He couldn't be a proper servant, by reason of him being so stupid and so young. But now we've given him for schooling to a harness-maker. He'll become a master of his craft and do himself some good, and then he'll pay us quit-rent. And on our little farm that's an important matter, sir! On our little farm we mustn't waste a thing!'

And this is the man Martin Petrovich called 'a bit o' rag'! I thought. 'But who now reads to Martin Petrovich?' I asked.

'What's there to read? There was a book, but it got mislaid somewhere . . . And reading's not for him at his age!'

'And who shaves him?' I asked, putting the next question.

Slyotkin laughed appreciatively, as if in response to an amusing joke.

'No one. At first he tried singeing his beard off with a candle – but now he's just let it grow. And it looks marvellous!'

'Vladimir Vasilyevich!' Yevlampiya repeated insistently. 'Vladimir Vasilyevich!'

Slyotkin waved his hand at her.

'Martin Petrovich has clothes and shoes and he eats what we eat – what more should he want? He himself has said that he wants nothing else in this world save to care for the needs of his soul. If only he'd get it into his head that everything's this way and that – but it's ours. He also says we don't give him any money, but we ourselves don't always have any money. And what's he need it for when everything's provided? But we treat him as a parent should be treated, I say that sincerely. For instance, the rooms in which he lives, how badly we need them! Without them there's simply nowhere to turn, but still – it doesn't matter! – we put up with it. We even wonder what pastimes to offer him. For St Peter's Day I bought him some excellent fish-hooks – real English ones, expensive ones! So he could go fishing. There's carp in the pond. He could sit and fish! After an hour or so he'd have enough for a nice fish-soup. For an old man that'd be a most appropriate occupation!'

'Vladimir Vasilyevich!' cried Yevlampiya demandingly for a third time, and threw far away from her the flower stalks which she had been winding round her fingers. 'I'm going!' Her eyes met mine. 'I'm going, Vladimir Vasilyevich!' she repeated and disappeared behind a bush.

'In a moment, Yevlampiya Martinovna, in a moment!' shouted Slyotkin. 'Martin Petrovich himself now approves of us,' he continued, turning to me again, 'though to start with he was offended, yes, and even complained before, you know, he saw the point of it. He used to be – you can probably remember – hot-tempered and sharp. It was awful! Well, he's become quite quiet now. Because he can see the point of it all. Your mother – Oh, my God! – she came down on me like a ton of

bricks! It's obvious why: she's as keen on exercising her authority as
Martin Petrovich used to be. Well, you come and see for yourself – and
put in a word for us when you can. I am very conscious of all the good
things Natalya Nikolaevna's done for me, but we've got to live our own
lives as well.'

'But why was Zhitkov refused?' I asked.

'Fedulych? That sponger?' Slyotkin gave a shrug of the shoulders.
'What would he have been good for? He's spent all his life soldiering and
now he thinks of taking up farming. "I can deal with the peasants," he
says. "'Cos I'm used to bashing them in the face." No, sir, he's no good
for anything. And you've got to know how to bash them in the face. But
Yevlampiya Martinovna herself refused him. A quite unsuitable man.
Our whole farm'd have collapsed!'

'Hey!' came the resonant sound of Yevlampiya's voice.

'In a moment! In a moment!' Slyotkin called back. He stretched out
his hand to me and, though unwillingly, I shook it.

'We beg your pardon, Dmitry Semyonovich,' said Slyotkin, displaying his line of white teeth. 'Shoot as many woodcock as you like.
It's a bird of flight, it doesn't belong to anyone. If you should come
across a hare, then don't kill it – that's for us to bag. Oh, and another
thing! Would there perhaps be a puppy from your bitch? We'd be very
grateful!'

'Hey!' came Yevlampiya's voice once again.

'Hey, there! Hey, there!' Slyotkin cried back and dashed into the
bushes.

[19]

I remember, when I was left alone, that I was preoccupied by the
thought: why hadn't Harlov given Slyotkin such a slap 'that there'd be
nothing left of him but a wet spot', and why hadn't Slyotkin been
frightened of such a fate? Evidently Martin Petrovich had become
'quiet', I thought, and I wanted more strongly than ever to penetrate
Yeskovo and to catch no more than a glimpse of that colossus whom I
simply couldn't imagine harried and submissive. I had reached the edge
of the wood when suddenly, right from beneath my feet and with a
strong beating of wings, a large woodcock jumped up and rushed into
the depths of the copse. I took aim but my gun misfired. I was extremely
annoyed. It was a very fine bird and I decided to see if I could start it

again. I followed the path of its flight and, after about two hundred yards, I saw in a small glade, beneath an outspreading willow, not the woodcock but the very same Mr Slyotkin. He was lying on his back with his arms folded behind his head and, smiling contentedly, he was gazing upwards at the sky, slightly rocking his left leg which was crossed over his right knee. He did not notice my approach. A few steps from him Yevlampiya was wandering slowly about the glade with lowered eyes. It seemed that she was looking for something in the grass – mushrooms, perhaps – and from time to time she leaned forward, stretched out her hand and sang softly. I stopped instantly and began listening. I couldn't make out at first what she was singing, but then I recognised only too well the following well-known verses of the old ditty:

> Look for it, look for it, thundercloud threatening,
> Kill, O kill father-in-law, father-in-law,
> Destroy, O destroy mother-in-law, mother-in-law,
> While the young wife 'tis I who'll be killing!

Yevlampiya's singing grew louder and louder, and she drew out the final words of each line particularly strongly. Slyotkin remained lying on his back, laughing to himself, and she seemed to be circling round him.

'What next!' he exclaimed at last. 'The things that get into people's heads!'

'What?' asked Yevlampiya.

Slyotkin slightly raised his head.

'What? What's it you've just been saying?'

'It's a song, Volodka, you know yourself you can't leave words out of a song,' answered Yevlampiya. She turned round and saw me. We both cried out at once and both ran off in different directions.

I hurried out of the copse and, crossing a narrow strip of open land, found myself in front of Harlov's garden.

[20]

I'd no time and no reason to think over what I'd just seen. I was simply reminded of the word 'enchantment' which I'd learned recently and whose meaning I had marvelled at a great deal. I walked along beside the garden fence and, after a few moments, from behind silvery poplars (they had not yet lost a single leaf and were luxuriously broad and glistening) I saw the courtyard and Martin Petrovich's houses. The buildings seemed to me to have been tidied up and cleaned. Everywhere were signs of strict and constant supervision. Anna Martinovna appeared on the porch steps and, screwing up her pale-blue eyes, gazed for a long time in the direction of the copse.

'Have you seen the master?' she asked a peasant who was crossing the yard.

'Vladimir Vasilyevich?' the man asked, taking his cap off his head. 'He'll be gone to the wood, ma'am.'

'I know he's gone to the wood. Has he returned? Have you seen him?'

'I've not ... not 'ereabouts.'

The peasant went on standing capless in front of Anna Martinovna.

'Well, be off with you,' she said. 'Or no ... wait a moment ... Where's Martin Petrovich? Do you know?'

'Er, Martin, the, er, Petrovich,' answered the peasant in a sing-song voice, raising first his right, then his left, hand, as if he were pointing to something, 'is sittin' yonder by the pond with 'is rod. He's sittin' in them reeds with 'is rod. Likely he's fishin', though God knows what he's doin'.'

'All right ... Be off with you,' repeated Anna Martinovna. 'And pick up that wheel there, it shouldn't be lying about.'

The peasant ran to do what he was told, while she stood a few moments more on the porch, still looking towards the wood. Then she gently made a threatening gesture with one hand and slowly went back into the house.

'Axyutka!' resounded her commanding voice beyond the door.

Anna Martinovna had had a bothered look and she had particularly firmly pursed up her lips, which were thin enough in any case. She had been dressed carelessly and a strand from her plaited hair had fallen loosely on her shoulder. But despite the carelessness of her dress and her bothered look, she seemed to me as attractive as ever, and it would have been with great pleasure that I would have kissed the narrow, albeit bad-tempered, hand with which she twice, in vexation, threw back the loose strand of hair.

[21]

'Has Martin Petrovich really taken up fishing?' I asked myself as I set off for the pond which was situated on the other side of the garden. I climbed up on the dam and looked this way and that, but Martin Petrovich was nowhere to be seen. I went along one side of the pond – and eventually, almost at the head of it, by a small inlet, among the flat and broken stalks of rust-coloured reeds, I came across an enormous greyish lump... On looking more closely I saw it was Harlov. Without a cap, all dishevelled, in a coarse canvas caftan which had split at the seams and with his legs tucked up under him, he sat motionless on the bare earth. He was sitting so still that at my approach a sandpiper tore away from some dried mud a couple of paces from him and flew with twitching wing-beats and whistlings over the smooth surface of the water. No doubt it was a long time since anyone had moved in its vicinity and frightened it. Harlov's whole figure was so unusual that as soon as she saw him my dog drew up sharply, tucked in her tail and began to growl. He made a very slight movement of his head and stared at me and my dog with demented eyes. A great change had been made in him by his beard which, though short, was thick and curly, in white whorls, like astrakhan. In his right hand one end of his fishing rod was resting, the other end dipped feebly in the water. My heart gave an involuntary jump. Still, I gathered my spirits together, went up to him and greeted him. He blinked slowly, as though half asleep.

'What are you doing, Martin Petrovich?' I began. 'Are you fishing?'

'Yes... fishing,' he answered in a hoarse voice, and lifted up the rod at the end of which there dangled a thread about a yard long and no hook.

'Your line's broken,' I remarked, and then I noticed that Martin Petrovich had no can beside him and no worms... And anyhow what sort of fishing can you do in September?

'Broken, is it?' he said, and ran his hand across his face. 'It's no matter!'

He again cast his line.

'Aren't you Natalya Nikolaevna's boy?' he asked me after a couple of minutes, during which I'd been studying him not without secret astonishment. Although he had lost weight, he still looked like a giant, but what tatters he was wearing and how neglected he looked!

'Yes, I am,' I answered, 'I'm the son of Natalya Nikolaevna B—.'

'Is your mother well?'

'My mother is well. She was very distressed by your refusal,' I added, 'because she hadn't expected you wouldn't want to visit her.'

Martin Petrovich hung his head.

'Have you been . . . over there?' he asked, nodding his head to one side.

'Where?'

'There . . . at the house. You haven't? Then pay 'em a visit. What's there for you to do here? Pay 'em a visit. It's no good talking to me – I don't like it.'

He was silent a moment.

'A lot of good it'll do you, messing about with a gun! When I was young, I used to do the same thing. Except my father . . . and I respected him, he was a right one! Not like they are nowadays. My father gave me a thrashing with his whip – and that was that! That was the end of messing about! I respected him for that . . . O-o-oh, yes!'

Harlov again fell silent.

'Don't you hang about here,' he went on again. 'Pay 'em a visit at the house. The farm's in tip-top shape over there now. Volodka . . .' At this he hesitated for a moment. 'Volodka's got his finger in everything. Sharp, that's what he is! And he's a real terror, too, you know!'

I didn't know what to say. Martin Petrovich spoke very calmly.

'And take a look at my daughters. You probably remember I had daughters. They're also in charge . . . and clever with it. But I've grown old, my lad. I've been pushed to one side. For a rest, you know . . .'

Some rest! I thought, looking round. 'Martin Petrovich,' I said aloud, 'you must definitely come and visit us!'

Harlov glanced at me.

'Be off, lad, be off.'

'Don't distress my mother, pay us a visit.'

'Be off, lad, be off,' Harlov repeated. 'Why should you talk to the likes of me?'

'If you haven't got a carriage, my mother will send you ours.'

'Be off!'

'Really and truly, Martin Petrovich!'

Harlov again became crestfallen and it seemed to me that his darkened cheeks, which looked as if they had been plastered with earth, blushed very slightly.

'Really, come and visit us,' I went on. 'Why should you sit here? Why get depressed?'

'How do you mean: depressed?' he asked with pauses between the words.

'I mean why get depressed,' I repeated.

Harlov said nothing and seemed to be deep in thought.

Encouraged by this silence, I decided to be frank and come straight to the point. (It mustn't be forgotten that I was only fifteen.)

'Martin Petrovich,' I began, sitting down beside him, 'I think I know everything, absolutely everything! I know how your son-in-law treats you – of course, with your daughters' consent. And now you're in this position ... But why give in to it?'

Harlov did not say a word and only let his fishing-rod drop, while I – how clever, what a philosopher I felt I was!

'Of course,' I started saying again, 'you took a risk when you handed everything over to your daughters. It was very magnanimous on your part, and I'm not going to reproach you. In our time that is far too rare a quality! But if your daughters are so ungrateful, you ought to show your scorn of them ... precisely your scorn ... and not become depressed ...'

'Stop it!' muttered Harlov suddenly, grinding his teeth, and his eyes, which were fixed on the pond, flashed angrily. 'Go away!'

'But, Martin Petrovich ...'

'Go away, I tell you! – or I'll kill you!'

I had moved quite close to him, but at this I jumped to my feet.

'What are you saying, Martin Petrovich?'

'I'll kill you, I tell you! Go away!' His voice was torn from his throat with a wild, groaning roar, but Harlov did not turn his head and continued to stare angrily straight ahead of him. 'I'll pick you up and throw you along with all your silly advice in the water! That'll teach you not to upset old people, you puppy-dog!'

'He's gone out of his mind!' was the thought that occurred to me in a flash. I glanced down at him more closely and was utterly stunned: Martin Petrovich was crying!! Tear-drop after tear-drop was running down his cheeks from beneath his eyelashes and his face had acquired a completely frenzied look.

'Go away!' he cried out again. 'Or I'll kill you, by God I will, so it'll be a lesson to others!'

He thrust his whole body to one side and bared his teeth like a wild boar. I picked up my gun and dashed away at a run. My dog ran barking after me. She was frightened, too!

On reaching home, I didn't mention a word of what I'd seen to my mother, but on coming across Souvenir – the devil knows why; – I told him everything. This disagreeable man was so overjoyed at my story, laughed so shrilly and even pranced about, that I almost hit him.

'Oh, I'd love to have seen it,' he went on and on, gasping with laughter, 'that idiot, that silly Shwede Harlus, getting stuck in the mud and sitting in it!'

'Go and see him by the pond if you think it's so interesting.'

'All right. But he'll kill me, won't he?'

Souvenir bored me stiff and I was full of regret for my unseemly talkativeness, but Zhitkov, to whom he told my story, looked on the matter rather differently.

'It's a matter for the police,' he decided, 'and perhaps a body of troops ought to be sent for.'

His forebodings about sending for a body of troops came to nothing; but something out of the ordinary did really happen.

[22]

In the middle of October, about three weeks after my meeting with Martin Petrovich, I was standing by the window of my room on the first floor of our house and, thinking about nothing at all, I gazed out despondently at our courtyard and the road beyond it. This was the fifth day running that we had had atrocious weather and any idea of going hunting was out of the question. Every living thing had taken cover. Even the sparrows had stopped chattering and the rooks had long been gone. The wind either made a hollow wailing sound or it whistled piercingly. A sky of low, unbroken clouds had changed from an unpleasant white colour to one that was leaden and even more ominous, and the rain which had poured and poured down noisily and incessantly suddenly became still heavier and more slanting and lashed the window-panes in violent gusts. The trees had become completely dishevelled and began to look antiquely grey. It seemed that everything possible had been taken from them, but the wind wouldn't desist and would once again start pestering them. Everywhere stood puddles full of dead leaves. Huge bubbles, continually bursting and reappearing, jumped and slid about on them. The mud on the roads was impassably thick. The cold penetrated into the rooms, under one's clothes and to one's very bones. Spasms of shivering ran through one's body – and how sick one felt in one's soul! Sick, not sad. It seemed the earth would never see sunlight again or brilliance or colour, and there would always be this mire and slime, this grey universal dampness and raw sour air – and the wind would go on wailing and moaning for ever! So there I was standing deep in thought by the window – and I remember that it suddenly grew very dark with a midnight blue darkness, although the clock showed it was no more than twelve o'clock midday. Suddenly I imagined that there, running across our courtyard, from the gates to the porch, was a bear! True, it wasn't on all fours but as they look when they're depicted standing on their hind legs. I couldn't believe my eyes. If it wasn't a bear I saw, then in any case it was something large, black and shaggy . . . I hadn't had time to think out what it might have been when a furious knocking resounded down below. Something quite unexpected and dreadful seemed to be forcing its way into our house. There was a commotion and much rushing to and fro . . .

I quickly ran downstairs and dashed into the dining-room . . .

In the drawing-room doorway, face to face with me, stood my mother in rooted amazement. Behind her could be glimpsed several frightened female faces, while the butler and a couple of footmen and a servant-boy, all with mouths gaping in astonishment, were crowding in the hall doorway. But in the middle of the dining-room, kneeling on the floor, swaying heavily this way and that and apparently on the point of collapse, covered in filth, all dishevelled, tattered and damp (so damp that steam was rising and water was pouring in trickles on to the floor), was that very monster which had just run across the courtyard before my very eyes! And who was this monster? None other than Harlov! I approached him sideways and could see not his face, but his head, which he had seized in his hands by his mudstained hair. He was breathing heavily and convulsively. There was even a kind of gurgling sound coming from his chest, and in all this bespattered, dark mass the only features that could be clearly made out were the tiny, wildly darting whites of his eyes. He was terrible to look at! I was reminded of the visiting official whom he'd once torn to shreds for comparing him with a mastodon. In actual fact, it was just such a look that an antediluvian animal would have possessed if it had just escaped from another and stronger animal which had attacked it in the age-old silt of primeval swamps.

'Martin Petrovich!' exclaimed my mother at last, and threw up her arms. 'Is it you? My God! Dear, merciful God!'

'It's me . . . me . . .' came his breaking voice, uttering each sound with painful effort. 'Oh, it's me!'

'My God, what's happened to you?'

'Natalya Nikolae . . . vna . . . I've come to you . . . straight from home . . . run . . . ning on foot . . .'

'And through such mud! You don't even look like a human being! Stand up and sit down at least . . . And you,' she said, turning to the servants, 'get towels straightaway! Haven't we some dry clothing?' she asked the butler.

The butler gestured, as much as to say where'll we find clothes to fit his size?

'I could bring a blanket,' he suggested, 'or there's that new horse-cloth.'

'Do stand up, Martin Petrovich, do stand up and have a seat,' my mother repeated.

'They drove me out, dear lady!' Harlov suddenly groaned, throwing his head back and stretching out his arms in front of him. 'They drove me out, Natalya Nikolaevna! My own daughters drove me out of my own hearth and home . . .'

My mother gave a cry.

'What're you saying – they drove you out! Oh, how sinful! How sinful!' She crossed herself. 'Only do get up, Martin Petrovich, there's a good chap!'

Two maids came in with towels and stopped in front of Harlov. It was obvious they couldn't make up their minds how to set about clearing up such a mass of mud.

'They drove me out, dear lady, they drove me out!' Harlov went on insisting; and in the meantime the butler returned with a large woollen blanket and also stopped in bewilderment, while Souvenir's head appeared round the door and then vanished.

'Martin Petrovich, stand up, have a seat and tell me everything from start to finish!' my mother commanded in a decisive tone of voice.

Harlov rose. The butler tried to help him, but simply got his hands dirty and retreated to the door, wiping the dirt off his fingers. Swaying from side to side and stumbling, Harlov managed to get to a chair and sit down. The maids approached him once more with their towels, but he waved them aside and refused to accept the blanket. Anyhow, my mother did not start insisting, since it was obvious that there would be no possibility of making Harlov get dry. All that could be done was to quickly wipe away the marks he left behind on the floor.

[23]

'How did they drive you out?' my mother asked Harlov as soon as he had had time to get his breath back.

'Dear lady, Natalya Nikolaevna!' he began in a tense voice – and I was again struck by the ceaseless darting to and fro of the whites of his eyes. 'I will tell the truth: I am more to blame than anyone else.'

'Exactly what I said but you didn't want to listen to me then,' said my mother, settling into a chair and lightly waving a scented handkerchief in front of her nose, since Harlov was extremely smelly. Not even a forest marsh smelt quite as strongly.

'Oh, I'm not blaming myself for that, dear lady, but for my pride. My pride's been the ruin of me, no worse than it was King Nebuchad-nezzar's. I'd always thought the Lord God had not begrudged me a mind and intellect. So if I decided something, that's how it was going to be . . . And then along came the fear of death and I go right out of my mind! I told myself I'd show at last my real power and authority! I'll endow them, and then they'll feel it right up to the grave . . .' (Harlov suddenly grew excited.) 'Now they've driven me out of my house like a mangy dog! That's their gratitude for you!'

'But how?' my mother again asked.

'They took my servant-boy Maximka away from me,' Harlov interrupted her (his eyes continued to dart about and he kept both his hands by his chin, the fingers intertwined), 'they took away my carriage, they cut off my monthly allowance, they didn't pay the money that'd been agreed – they cut down everything all round, and I didn't say a word, I put up with it all! And I put up with it on account of . . . Oh, on account of my pride! I didn't want my enemies saying: "Look, the silly old fool's regretting it now." And you, dear lady, you warned me about biting my elbow, didn't you? So I put up with it . . . Except that today I come into my own room and I find it's already occupied and my bed's been put up in the attic! "You can go and sleep there," they say; "we'll let you do that; but your room's needed for running the farm." And who's this saying all this to me? It's Volodka Slyotkin, that serf, that turd . . .'

Harlov's voice broke.

'But your daughters? What about them?' my mother asked.

'I put up with everything,' Harlov went on with his story, 'and things were bitter for me and I was *so* ashamed . . . I couldn't so much as face God's world! That's why I didn't want to visit you, my dear – out of shame, out of the disgrace of it! You see, my dear, I tried everything – kindness, threats, appeals to their conscience and – just think of it! – bowing to them, like this' (Harlov showed us how he used to bow to them). 'And all to no avail! And I put up with everything! To start with, at the beginning, I didn't think like that, but I said I'd take them all and give 'em such a shaking and thrashing they'd not have any seeds left inside 'em . . . That'll learn 'em! Well, afterwards, I gave in! It's my cross, I thought, and I've got to prepare myself for death, that's to say. And suddenly today I'm thrown out like a dog! And who did it? That bloody Volodka! You were asking about my daughters, whether or not they had a will of their own, weren't you? They're just Volodka's slaves! That's what they are!'

My mother was astonished.

'I could understand that of Anna. She's his wife. But what about your second one . . .'

'Yevlampiya, you mean? She's worse than Anna! She's given herself into Volodka's arms completely. That's the reason she refused your soldier. On his orders, on Volodka's orders. It's obvious Anna should've taken offence, the more so since she can't stand her sister – but she submits to it! He's enchanted her, the devil! And, mind you, Anna doesn't mind telling herself, well, there you are, Yevlampiya, such a haughty one you used to be, and now look what's become of you! . . . Oh, oh, oh, my God, my God!'

My mother gave me an anxious glance. I retreated a little to one side as a precaution, lest I should be sent away altogether . . .

'I am very sorry, Martin Petrovich,' she began saying, 'that my former protégé has caused you such grief and turned out to be such a bad man, but then I was mistaken in him as well . . . Who could have expected this of him?'

'My dear lady,' howled Harlov, and struck himself on the chest, 'it's the ingratitude of my daughters I can't bear! I can't, I can't! I gave them everything I had, everything! And on top of it all my conscience's been torturing me. Many – oh, so many times! – over and over I've thought about it as I sat there by the pond! "If only you'd done someone some good in your life!" I'd be thinking to myself. "If only you'd given to the poor, or set your peasants free as a reward for having oppressed them all their lives! You're responsible for them before God, aren't you? Take it upon your conscience now when their little tears are poured out one by one!" And what's their fate to be now? I'd made their lives a deep enough pit, there's no denying, but now there's no bottom to it at all! I took all these sins on my soul and sacrificed my conscience for my children – and they don't care a damn! They throw me out of the house like a dog!'

'There's no point in thinking about it, Martin Petrovich,' my mother remarked.

'And when he said to me, your Volodka, I mean,' Harlov went on with renewed force, 'when he told me I wasn't to live in my own room any longer, in that very study every timber of which I'd laid with my own hands – and when he told me that, God alone knows what happened to me! Everything went black, it was like a knife in my heart . . . Well, it was either a case of killing him or of getting out of the house! So I've come running to you, my benefactress, Natalya Nikolaevna . . . Where else could I turn! But then the rain, the mud . . . I must've fallen down twenty times! And now here I am . . . in this dreadful state . . .'

Harlov glanced at himself and fidgeted, as if he was on the point of standing up.

'Don't worry, Martin Petrovich, don't worry,' my mother hastened to say. 'What's that matter? That you've left some mud on the floor? It doesn't matter at all. Now I want to make a suggestion. Listen a moment! We'll give you a special room now and a clean bed. You undress, wash, lie down and have a sleep . . .'

'My dear Natalya Nikolaevna, I wouldn't be able to sleep!' Harlov cried despondently. 'I've got hammers beating in my brain! Like some animal they didn't need, they just threw me . . .'

'Lie down, have a sleep,' my mother insisted. 'Afterwards we'll have some tea and we'll talk it over. Don't let it get you down, my dear old friend! Even if they've driven you out of *your* house, you'll always find a haven in mine. I've never forgotten that you once saved my life.'

'Benefactress!' groaned Harlov, and covered his face with his hands. 'Now *you* must save my life!'

This plea touched my mother almost to tears.

'I'll gladly help you, Martin Petrovich, in any way I can. But you must promise me you'll obey me in future and put all evil thoughts out of your head.'

Harlov took his hands away from his face.

'If necessary,' he said, 'I can even forgive them!'

My mother nodded her head approvingly.

'I'm very pleased to see you in such a truly Christian state of mind, Martin Petrovich, but we can talk about that later. First of all you must put yourself to rights – and most of all you must have a sleep. Take Martin Petrovich to the green room, the one that belonged to the master,' said my mother to the butler, 'and whatever he wants, see that he gets it at once! Have his clothes dried and cleaned, and whatever linen may be needed, ask the chambermaid – do you hear?'

'Yes, ma'am,' answered the butler.

'And when he wakes up, have the tailor take his measurements. And his beard'll have to be shaved. Not now, but afterwards.'

'Yes, ma'am,' repeated the butler. 'This way, if you please, Martin Petrovich.'

Harlov rose, looked at my mother, made a move towards her but stopped, bowed to waist height, crossed himself three times in the direction of the icon and followed the butler out of the room. I also slid out behind him.

[24]

The butler took Harlov to the green room and immediately ran off in search of the maid since it turned out that there was no linen on the bed. Souvenir, who had encountered us in the hallway and slipped into the room along with us, at once, with much affectation and laughter, started cavorting round Harlov who, with arms and legs slightly spread, had stopped deep in thought in the middle of the room. Water still continued to pour off him.

'The Shwede, the Shwede Harlus!' squeaked Souvenir, bent double and holding himself by his sides. 'The great founder of the famous line of Harlovs, look now upon your descendant! What's he look like now? Can you recognise him? Ha, ha, ha! Your Excellency, offer me your hand! What are you wearing black gloves for?'

I wanted to restrain Souvenir, to shame him into silence . . . but nothing doing!

'Oh, you used to call me a hanger-on, a sponger! "You've got no home of your own!" you used to say. And now you've become just as much of a hanger-on as I am, sinful man that I am! Martin Harlov and

that rascal Souvenir are both in the same boat now! You'll be fed on
hand-outs now as well! You'll be glad to snatch up the crust that the
dog's sniffed at and left behind . . . "Here, this is for you!" they'll say.
Ha, ha, ha!'

Harlov remained standing motionless, his head thrust in his chest and
his legs and arms spread.

'Martin Harlov, hereditary nobleman!' Souvenir went on squeaking.
'Oh, the way you used to put on airs! How high and mighty you were!
"Don't come close," you'd say, "or I'll do you an injury!" And when
out of your great intelligence you started giving way and dividing up
your estate – what a to-do there was then! "Gratitude!" you go shouting about the place: "Gratitude!" And why did you pick on me? Why
didn't you give me anything? I'd probably have shown more gratitude!
And I told the truth, you know, when I said they'd drive you out
bare-backed . . .'

'Souvenir!' I shouted, but Souvenir was not going to be stopped.
Harlov had not moved at all and it seemed that he had only just begun to
feel how damp his clothes were and was waiting until they could be taken
off him. But the butler did not return.

'And what a war veteran you were!' Souvenir began again. 'Oh, in
1812 you saved the whole country and displayed such valour! But what
really happened was, you went around pulling the trousers off a few
frozen-stiff marauding troops, and as soon as a girl so much as stamped
her foot at you your spirits'd sink right down to your own trousers . . .'

'Souvenir!' I shouted a second time.

Harlov gave Souvenir a sideways glance. Until that moment he'd
literally not seemed to notice his presence and it was only my shout that
aroused his attention.

'Watch out, mate,' he mumbled indistinctly, 'or you'll be out of the
frying pan right into the fire!'

Souvenir literally gave vent to a peal of laughter.

'Oh, how you frighten me, most respected brother-in-law! Oh, you
really strike terror, you do! At least you ought to put a comb through
your hair, otherwise when it dries, God preserve us, you'll never be
able to get it clean and you'll have to mow it with a scythe!' Then
Souvenir suddenly let himself go. 'Just you go on being the big bully!
Not a rag to your back, but you go on being the bully-boy! Where's
your house and home now, what you were always boasting about so

much? You tell me that! "At least I've got a house and home," you used to say, "but you've got none! My ancestral house and home!" you'd say.' (Souvenir had developed a fixation for the expression 'house and home'.)

'Mr Bychkov!' I cried. 'What're you doing? Take care!'

But he went on chattering away and jumping up and down and skipping about in front of Harlov. And still the butler did not return with the maid!

I began to feel alarmed. I started noticing that Harlov, who in the course of talking to my mother had gradually grown calmer and towards the end had even seemed to become reconciled to his fate, was again growing annoyed. His breathing grew quicker, his cheeks beneath his whiskers seemed literally to become puffed up, his fingers started working and his eyes began their darting to and fro in the dark mask of his mud-spattered face.

'Souvenir! Souvenir!' I screamed. 'Stop it, I'll tell mother!'

But it was as if Souvenir had become possessed by a devil.

'Yes, oh, yes, my most respected brother-in-law!' he rattled on again. 'You and I now find ourselves in the most subtle of circumstances! There are your daughters, with your son-in-law, Vladimir Vasilyevich, making as much fun of you as they like in your very own *house and home*! And you should've put your curse on them, as you promised! And you didn't even have enough guts to do that! Anyhow, you weren't any match for Vladmir Vasilyevich. You used to call him Volodka! What sort of Volodka is he to you? He's Vladimir Vasilyevich, Mr Slyotkin Esquire, a landowner, a nobleman – and what are you?'

A wild roar blotted out Souvenir's words. Harlov had exploded. His fists were clenched and raised, his face had turned blue, foam appeared on his cracked lips and he shook with fury.

'House and home, you say!' he roared in his clangorous iron voice. 'My curse, you say! No, I won't put my curse on them – it'll mean nothing to 'em! But the house and home ... I'll destroy their house and home, they won't have any any more, just as I haven't! Then they'll know who Martin Harlov is! I've still got my strength! They'll learn what it means to make fun of me! They shan't have any house and home!'

I was stunned. I'd never before in my life witnessed such uncontrolled fury. It wasn't a man but a wild beast that roared its head off in front of me. I was stunned – and Souvenir had scrambled under the table in fright.

'They shan't!' roared Harlov for the last time and, practically knocking the butler and maid (who had just come in) off their feet, he dashed out of the house and as fast as a spinning top traversed the courtyard and vanished beyond the gates.

[25]

My mother was frightfully angry when the shamefaced butler brought her the news of Martin Petrovich's new and unexpected departure. He did not dare hide the cause of the departure and I was obliged to confirm what he said.

'So it's you!' my mother shouted at Souvenir who had come haring forward and even tried to kiss her hand. 'Your beastly tongue's to blame!'

'Allow me, I'll explain ach-once, ach-once,' babbled Souvenir, stammering and thrusting his elbows behind his back.

'Ach once . . . ach once – I know your "ach once"!' my mother repeated reproachfully, and sent him about his business. Then she rang, ordered Kvitsinsky to be brought to her and ordered him at once to take the carriage to Yeskovo and at all costs find Martin Petrovich and bring him back. 'Don't return without him!' she concluded. The gloomy Pole gave a silent nod of the head and left.

I returned to my room, again seated myself by the window and spent a long time, I remember, cogitating on what had happened before my very eyes. I found myself in a quandary. I simply couldn't understand why Harlov, who had borne the insults inflicted on him by those at home almost without protest, couldn't keep his self-possession and put up with the mockery and needling of such an insignificant creature as Souvenir. I didn't know at that time what intolerable anguish could be contained in an empty taunt, even when it came from despised lips . . . The hateful name of Slyotkin, when uttered by Souvenir, had fallen like a spark into dry tinder. The sore spot hadn't been able to stand this last needle-thrust.

About an hour went by. Our carriage drove into the courtyard, but only our manager was sitting in it. And my mother had given him strict instructions not to return without him! Kvitsinsky jumped briskly out of the carriage and ran up the porch steps. His face showed how upset he was, something which almost never occurred in his case. I rushed downstairs and entered the drawing-room on his heels.

'Well? Have you brought him?' my mother asked.

'I haven't,' answered Kvitsinsky, 'and I couldn't.'

'Why is that? Did you see him?'

'Yes.'

'What had happened to him? A stroke?'

'Certainly not. Nothing had happened to him.'

'Then why didn't you bring him?'

'He was destroying his home.'

'What?'

'He was standing on the roof of his house – and tearing it down. Some forty planks or more had already come off and five or so laths.' (I remembered Harlov's words: 'They shan't have any house and home!')

My mother stared at Kvitsinsky.

'By himself . . . he's standing on his roof and tearing it down by himself?'

'Precisely, ma'am. He's going backwards and forwards along the roof-planking and smashing it to right and left. His strength, you will be pleased to know, is simply superhuman! Still, truth to tell, the roof's a poor thing. It's done on the criss-cross, with thin overlays and ordinary plank nails.'*

My mother looked at me as if trying to be sure she'd not misheard.

'Criss-cross thin overlays,' she repeated, obviously not understanding the meaning of any of these words. 'Well, what're you going to do?'

'I've come for instructions. I can't do anything without some men to help. The peasants over there have all gone into hiding.'

'But his daughters – what about them?'

'His daughters're useless. They're running about and shouting . . . What's the good of that?'

'And Slyotkin's there?'

'He's there as well. He's making more noise than all the rest, but eh can't do anything about it.'

'And Martin Petrovich is standing on the roof, is he?'

---

* A roof is made 'at random' or 'criss-cross' when between every two planks an empty space is left covered over by another plank; such a roof is cheaper to build but less durable. An overlay is used to describe the thinnest board, about ¾″ thick; a plank is normally 1″ thick. (Author's note.)

'On the roof . . . That's to say, he's standing in the roof space and tearing the roof to pieces.'

'Yes, yes,' my mother said, 'the criss-crosses . . .'

It was clear we were faced by something quite out of the ordinary. What should we do? Send to the town for the police? Gather the peasants together? My mother had no idea.

Zhitkov, who had come to dinner, also had no idea. True, he mentioned something once again about a body of troops, but he had no advice to proffer and he did no more than look subservient and devoted. Kvitsinsky, seeing that he was not likely to receive any instructions, informed my mother – with his customary scornful deference – that if she would give him permission to take a few grooms, gardeners and other menservants, he would endeavour to . . .

'Yes, yes,' my mother interrupted him, 'you try that, my dear Vikenty Osipych! Only as quickly as possible, if you please, and I'll take the responsibility for it!'

Kvitsinsky smiled coldly.

'I must make one thing clear beforehand, ma'am: it's impossible to vouch for the result, because Mr Harlov's strength is great and also his desperation. He regards himself as very deeply insulted!'

'Yes, yes,' my mother agreed, 'and that beastly Souvenir's the one to blame for it all! I'll never forgive him for this! Be off with you, take the men and go over there, Vikenty Osipych!'

'Make sure, Mr Manager, that you take plenty of ropes and fire-hooks,' declared Zhitkov in a deep bass voice, 'and if there's a net to be had, it'd be no bad thing to take that along as well. I remember once in the regiment . . .'

'Be good enough not to tell me what to do, my dear sir,' Kvitsinsky broke in with annoyance. 'I know what has to be done without you telling me.'

Zhitkov took offence and announced that since he supposed he would be summoned as well . . .

'No, no!' inserted my mother. 'You'd much better stay here! Let Vikenty Osipych do it by himself . . . Off with you, Vikenty Osipych!'

Zhitkov took even graver offence, while Kvitsinsky bowed and went out.

I dashed to the stables, quickly saddled my horse by myself and galloped off along the road to Yeskovo.

[26]

It had stopped raining, but the wind blew with renewed force – right into my face. About half-way along the road my saddle almost slipped off because the saddle-girth had loosened. I dismounted and started tightening the straps with my teeth when all of a sudden I heard someone calling me by name. It was Souvenir running towards me across a field.

'What, my boy,' he shouted to me from some distance, 'has curiosity got the better of you? Yes, it must be that. Look, I'm off there myself, as straight as a die following the route Harlov took . . . I'd sooner die than not get a sight of this!'

'You want to admire the work of your own hands; that's all,' I muttered with indignation, jumped on my horse and was again away at a gallop. But the insufferable Souvenir kept up with me and even while running kept on laughing and pulling faces. At last Yeskovo came in sight – there was the dam, there the long fence and the willows planted round the houses . . . I rode up to the gates, dismounted, tethered my horse and stopped in astonishment.

Of the front third of the roof on the new house and the mezzanine there remained nothing but the bare framework. Shingles and planks lay on the ground in untidy heaps on both sides of the house. Granted that the roof was a poor thing, as Kvitsinsky had put it, it was still incredible to see what had been done! In the roof-space, raising clouds of dust and dirt, with an awkward briskness there moved a blackish-grey mass, either shaking the remaining brick-built chimney (the other had already fallen down), or tearing up a plank and throwing it down, or seizing at the very rafters. This was Harlov. At that moment he looked to me completely bear-like: his head and back and shoulders looked like those of a bear, and the way he placed his legs wide apart without flexing the soles of his feet was also bear-like. The sharp wind blew at him from all sides, ruffling up his matted hair. It was awful to see how his naked body showed red through the rents in his clothing and to hear his fierce, hoarse muttering. The courtyard was full of people. Old women, little boys and servant-girls crowded together along the fence. A few peasants huddled together a little further off in a separate group. The elderly priest, whom I knew, was standing hatless on the porch steps of the other house and, a bronze cross held in both hands, from time to time silently and hopelessly raised and seemed to show it to

Harlov. Yevlampiya was standing beside the priest and, leaning back against the wall, gazed motionlessly at her father. Anna was continually thrusting her head out of the little window, then disappearing, then jumping out into the courtyard, then going back into the house, while Slyotkin, pale in the face and yellow-looking, in an old dressing-gown and skull-cap, holding a single-barrelled gun in his hands, scurried about from place to place. He had gone completely Jewish, as they say. He continually gasped for breath, shook his fist, unsteadily took aim at Harlov, then slung his gun over his shoulder, then again took aim, shouted and shed tears . . . Seeing Souvenir and myself, he literally flung himself at us.

'Look, just look what's going on!' he whined. 'Look! He's gone mad, he's round the bend – look what he's doing! I've already sent for the police, but no one's come! No one's come! If I shoot at him, the law can't do anything to me surely, because everyone's got a right to defend his own property, hasn't he? And I will shoot! By God, I will shoot!'

He ran towards the house.

'Martin Petrovich, take care! If you don't come down, I'll shoot!'

'Shoot!' resounded the hoarse voice from the roof. 'Shoot! And here's something for you to be going on with!'

A long piece of board flew down and, turning over a couple of times in the air, landed with a crash at Slyotkin's feet. The latter literally jumped in the air and Harlov roared with laughter.

'Dear Lord Jesus!' someone babbled behind me. I looked round and saw it was Souvenir. 'Ah,' I thought, 'he's not laughing any more now!'

Slyotkin seized a nearby peasant by the scruff of the neck.

'Go on, get up there, get up there, you children of Satan,' he screamed, shaking him with all his might, 'save my property!'

The peasant took a couple of steps, threw back his head, waved his arms and shouted: 'Hey, you, sir! Hey, sir!'

Then he did a little shuffling dance on the spot and turned back.

'A ladder! Fetch a ladder!' said Slyotkin to the other peasants.

'Where do we get one?' was the response.

'And even if there were a ladder,' said someone unhurriedly, 'who'd want to go climbing up there? We're no bloody fools! He'd snap your neck in a flash!'

'He'd do you in double-quick!' said one fair-haired youth with a stupid face.

'Wouldn't he just, eh?' the others agreed. It seemed to me that, even if there hadn't been any obvious danger, the peasants would have still been unwilling to do what their new master told them. They were almost approving of Harlov, despite the astonishment he caused them.

'Oh, you're a lot of bandits!' groaned Slyotkin. 'Just let me get you all . . .'

But at this moment the last chimney collapsed with a thunderously heavy crash and amidst the instantly rising cloud of yellow dust Harlov, emitting an ear-splitting cry and raising his blood-stained hands aloft, turned to face us. Slyotkin again took aim at him.

Yevlampiya pulled him by the elbow.

'Don't do that!' he shouted at her furiously.

'And don't you dare!' she cried, and her blue eyes flashed threateningly beneath her knitted brows. 'Father is destroying his own house. It's his.'

'Rubbish – it's ours!'

'You say it's ours, I say it's his.'

Slyotkin began hissing angrily, while Yevlampiya literally bored into him with her eyes.

'Oh, very good, very good, my dear daughter!' Harlov roared from above. 'Very good, Yevlampiya Martinovna! How are you making out with your boy-friend? Do you like kissing, do you like having fun?'

'Father!' came the cry of Yevlampiya's resonant voice.

'What, daughter?' answered Harlov and came to the very edge of the wall. So far as I could make out, his face wore a strange smile – bright and happy and precisely for that reason particularly terrible and malicious . . . Many years later I saw exactly the same smile on the face of a man who had been condemned to death.

'Stop, father, come down.' (Yevlampiya used no endearment in addressing him.) 'We're to blame. We'll return everything to you. Come down.'

'What're you giving away all our property for?' broke in Slyotkin. Yevlampiya simply knitted her brows all the more.

'I'll give back my own part, I'll give back everything. Stop, father, come down! Forgive us. Forgive me.'

Harlov continued to smile.

'It's too late, my darling,' he said, and every word he spoke rang out brassily. 'Your stony heart's been stirred too late! Everything's tumbled down, there's no stopping it now! And don't look at me now! I'm done for! You'd much better look at your Volodka – see what a handsome chap you've found! Yes, and look at your ugly sister – see her poking her foxy nose out of the window, see how she's been egging on her husband! No, ladies and gentlemen, you wanted to deprive me of my house and home, so I'm not going to leave you one beam standing on another! I put them there with my own hands and I'll destroy them with my own hands – with these very hands! Look, I haven't even used an axe!'

He blew on both his palms and again set about the rafters.

'Enough, father,' said Yevlampiya, and her voice became somehow wonderfully caressing, 'forget the past. Well, you can trust me. You always did trust me. Come down now. Come lie down in my loft, on my soft bed. I'll dry you and see you're warm. I'll bind your wounds – look how you've hurt your hands! You'll be able to live with me as in Christ's very bosom, have plenty of good things to eat and sleep that's even sweeter. We were to blame, we really were! We got too big for ourselves, we sinned! Now forgive us!'

Harlov shook his head.

'A lot of fine words! I trust you – I wish I could! You've killed my trust! You've killed everything! I used to be an eagle, but for you I became nothing but a worm – are you going to stamp your foot on that worm now? Stop it! I loved you, you yourself know that – only now you're not a daughter to me and I'm not a father to you . . . I'm a man who's done for! Don't get in the way now! As for you, you coward, you pretend hero, you, just you shoot your gun!' Harlov suddenly barked at Slyotkin. 'What're you aiming at me the whole time for? Or do you mind what the law says: if the one who received a gift should perchance have designs on the life of the giver,' said Harlov, pausing between the words, 'then the giver is empowered to take back all that he has given? Ha-ha, don't be frightened, my legal friend! I won't demand it back, I'll put an end to it myself . . . Now here we go!'

'Father!' Yevlampiya pleaded for the last time.

'Shut up!'

'Martin Petrovich, dear brother, forgive me – out of the goodness of your heart!' babbled Souvenir.

'Father, dear father!'

'Shut up, you bitch!' shouted Harlov. He did not even look at Souvenir, but simply spat in his direction.

[27]

At that moment Kvitsinsky appeared at the gates with his band of men in three carts. The tired horses snorted and the men jumped down one after another into the mud.

'Aha!' cried Harlov at the top of his voice. 'An army, just look at it! They've sent a whole army against me! All right, then! But I warn you, whoever tries to climb up here onto the roof, I'll send that man head over heels down again! I'm a stern master and I don't like uninvited guests! Not at all!'

He seized with both hands the foremost pair of rafters, the so-called 'feet' for the pediment, and began shaking them strongly. Leaning out from the edge of the flooring, he literally hauled at them, regularly chanting like a Volga boatman: 'Heave-ho! And again! Heave-ho!'

Slyotkin dashed to Kvitsinsky and started complaining and whining. The latter told him not to interfere and set about putting into effect his plan of action. He took up a position right in front of the house and began by way of diversion to explain to Harlov that he was not behaving as a member of the Russian nobility should . . .

'Heave-ho, heave-ho!' chanted Harlov.

. . . and that Natalya Nikolaevna was very dissatisfied by his behaviour and had not expected it of him . . .

'Heave-ho! And again! Heave-ho!' Harlov went on chanting.

In the meantime Kvitsinsky had despatched four of the healthiest and boldest grooms to the opposite end of the house, so that they should climb on to the roof from the back. This plan of attack, however, did not escape Harlov's notice. He suddenly abandoned the rafters and ran briskly to the rear section of the mezzanine floor. His appearance was so frightening that two grooms who had managed to climb up into the roof space at once shinned down to ground level again by way of a drainpipe, to the intense delight and laughter of the small servant-boys. Harlov shook his fist at them and, returning to the front part of the house, once again seized hold of the rafters and started rocking them, again chanting like a Volga boatman.

Then he suddenly stopped and stared . . .

'Maximka, little Maximka, my dear boy, my friend!' he exclaimed. 'Is it you?'

I looked round and saw that the servant-boy Maximka had in fact separated himself from the crowd of peasants and come forward, grinning and showing his teeth. His master, the saddler, had probably let him go home on leave from his apprenticeship.

'Climb up here to me, little Maximka, my good and faithful servant,' Harlov went on. 'Together the two of us'll fight off these vile Tartars and thieving Lithuanians!'

Maximka, still grinning, started climbing up slowly, but he was seized and pulled back – God knows why – perhaps as an example to others, for he would not have been of much help to Martin Petrovich.

'All right, then! So be it!' cried Harlov in a threatening voice and once more seized the rafters.

'Vikenty Osipych, allow me to shoot!' Slyotkin said, turning to Kvitsinsky. 'I'll only do it to scare him. My gun's only loaded with small shot.'

But before Kvitsinsky could answer him the foremost pair of rafters, which had been furiously shaken by Harlov's iron hands, keeled forward, cracked and crashed down into the courtyard – and along with them, with nothing to hold on to, came Harlov, thudding down heavily on to the ground. Everyone shuddered and a great cry went up . . . Harlov lay motionless face-downwards on his chest and his back was weighed down by the upper longitudinal beam of the roof, the ridging piece, which had plunged down along with the pediment.

[28]

People dashed to Harlov, pulled the beam off him and turned him face upwards. His face was lifeless, blood appeared at his mouth and he wasn't breathing. 'He's had all the breath knocked out of him,' muttered peasants who approached him. They ran to the well for water, fetched a whole bucketful and tipped it over Harlov's head. The mud and dust were washed from his face, but the lifeless look remained. They brought up a bench, placed it by the house and after lifting Martin Petrovich's enormous body with difficulty they set it down on the bench with the head resting against the wall. The servant-boy Maximka came up, knelt down on one knee and with the other leg stretched out far behind him somewhat theatrically took hold of his former master's hand. Yevlampiya, pale as death, stood directly in front of her father, fixing upon him her large round eyes. Anna and Slyotkin did not come close. Everyone fell silent, awaiting something. Finally there came broken, gulping sounds from Harlov's throat, as if he were choking . . . Then he feebly moved one hand – his right hand (Maximka was holding the other), opened one eye – the right eye – and slowly looking about him, as if he were a drunkard on some terrible binge, groaned and said with blurred, drunken speech: 'I'm bush-ted, busted . . .' And then, after a moment's thought, he added: 'There it is, the bla-a-ack foal!' And blood suddenly gushed thickly out of his mouth and his whole body shuddered . . .

'The end!' I thought. But Harlov still kept his right eye open (his left eyelid was shut tight as a corpse's) and, fixing it on Yevlampiya, he uttered barely audibly: 'Well, daughter . . . It's you I won't for . . .'

With a sharp hand movement Kvitsinsky summoned the priest who was still standing on the porch steps. The old man came up, his frail knees getting tangled up in the tight cassock. But suddenly Harlov's legs and stomach started working hideously, and irregular convulsions passed upwards over his face – and Yevlampiya's face shuddered and became similarly distorted. Maximka began crossing himself . . . It was too much for me, I ran to the gates and pressed myself to them, not daring to look back. A minute later some quiet sound rose from all the lips behind me and I realised Harlov was dead.

He had fractured the back of his head and his chest had been crushed, as was revealed by the autopsy.

[29]

'What did he want to say to her as he died?' I asked myself the whole way back home on my horse: ' "It's you I won't for-get . . ." or "It's you I won't for-give . . ."?' The rain had begun again, but I rode at a walking pace. I wanted to be alone as long as possible, I wanted to give myself over completely to my own reflections. Souvenir had set off in one of the carts which had arrived with Kvitsinsky. No matter how young and frivolous I may have been at that time, the sudden universal change of mood (not limited to individuals) which is always aroused in all hearts by the unexpected or expected (it's all the same!) appearance of death, its solemnity, seriousness and total honesty, couldn't fail to startle me. I was indeed startled . . . But at the same time my confused boyish eyes took in a great deal: Slyotkin hastily and self-consciously throwing away his gun as if it were something he'd stolen, he and his wife instantly becoming objects of silent, but universal, abhorrence and a space forming round them . . . This abhorrence did not extend to Yevlampiya, although she was probably no less to blame than her sister. She even aroused a certain pity when she fell at the feet of her dead father. But that she was guilty as well – this was sensed by everyone. 'You did wrong by the old man,' said one grey-haired, important-looking peasant, leaning, like some judge from antiquity, with both his hands and his beard on a long stick, 'you have a sin on your soul! You did wrong by him!' This 'doing wrong by him' was immediately accepted by everyone as a sentence of finality. The people's judgement had been made, I understood that at once. I also noticed that Slyotkin didn't so much as *dare* to give any orders to start with. It was without him that they lifted up the body and carried it into the house. Without asking him, the priest went off to the church for the things he needed and the elder ran into the village to arrange for a horse and cart to go into the town. Anna Martinovna herself did not use her usual bossy tone when saying that the samovar should be put on 'so there'd be hot water to wash the corpse.' Her order sounded more like a timid request and it received a rude rebuff . . .

I was still exercised by the question of what he'd meant when he'd spoken to his daughter. Had he wanted to forgive her or forget her by putting his curse on her? I decided in the end that he'd wanted to forgive.

Three days later Martin Petrovich's funeral took place, paid for by my mother who had been very grieved by his death and gave orders that no expense should be spared. She did not go to the church herself because she did not want to see those two awful women, as she put it, and that beastly little Jew. But she sent Kvitsinsky, myself and Zhitkov, whom from that moment she had taken to describing as 'you old woman!' Souvenir she did not even allow within sight and long afterwards she remained angry at him, calling him the murderer of her friend. He took this disgrace very much to heart. He would constantly walk on tip-toe round the room next to hers, consumed by some apprehensive and grovelling melancholy, quivering and whispering: 'Ach-once, ach-once!'

In church and during the procession Slyotkin seemed to me to be once again in his element. He gave orders and fussed about in his customary way and greedily ensured that not a single unnecessary copeck was spent, although it wasn't his pocket that was being affected. Maximka, in a new coat also donated by my mother, emitted such tenor notes from the choir that no one could be in the least doubt about the sincerity of his devotion to the deceased! Both the daughters were in their mourning clothes, as was proper, but they seemed upset rather than grief-stricken, particularly Yevlampiya. Anna adopted a contrite look suited to one who was fasting, but made no effort to shed tears and did no more than smooth her dry-skinned, beautiful hand over her hair and cheeks. Yevlampiya looked thoughtful throughout. That universal, inexorable abhorrence – the abhorrence which I had noticed on the day of Harlov's death – seemed to me to be present on the faces of all the people in the church, in all their movements, in all their glances, but now more affectedly, less personally. It seemed that all these people knew that the sin into which the Harlov family had fallen, that great sin had now passed into the keeping of the one true Judge of all men and that, consequently, they no longer had any need to worry and complain. They prayed earnestly for the soul of the deceased, whom in life they had not particularly loved and had even feared. His death had been a great surprise, after all.

'If only 'e'd been a man for the drink, mate,' said one peasant to another in the porch.

'You can't get drunk if you don't drink,' the other said. 'It's the way things turn out.'

'They done 'im wrong,' the first peasant said, reiterating their final opinion on the matter.

'They done 'im wrong,' others said behind him.

'But he was your oppressor, wasn't he?' I asked one of the men whom I recognised as a Harlov peasant.

'He was our master, that's for sure,' he answered. 'But still, they done 'im wrong!'

'They done 'im wrong!' echoed through the crowd.

Yevlampiya stood by the graveside like someone lost to the world. She was consumed by her thoughts, her weighty thoughts. I noticed that she treated Slyotkin, who made several attempts to speak to her, in the way she had treated Zhitkov, only worse.

A few days later the rumour spread throughout our area that Yevlampiya Martinovna Harlov had left home for good, having left to her sister and brother-in-law her part of the estate and taking with her only a few hundred roubles . . .

'She's bought her off, that Anna has!' my mother remarked. 'It's just that you and I', she added, turning to Zhitkov, with whom she was playing picquet (he had taken Souvenir's place), 'have got hands that are good for nothing!'

Zhitkov looked gloomily at his powerful fists. 'Yes, they're good for nothing!' was what he seemed to be thinking.

Soon after that my mother and I moved away to Moscow – and many years were to pass before I saw Martin Petrovich's two daughters again.

[30]

But I did see them. I met Anna Martinovna in the most ordinary way. On visiting our estate after my mother's death, which I hadn't visited for more than fifteen years, I received an invitation from the arbitrator (in those days throughout Russia the rearrangement of land boundaries* proceeded with a slowness not forgotten to the present time) – an invitation to attend for a meeting, along with other landowners of the district, on the estate of the widow Anna Slyotkin. The news of the end of the earthly existence of my mother's 'Jew-boy' with the prune-coloured eyes had not, I confess, saddened me in the least, but I was interested to take a look at his widow. She had a reputation as an excellent mistress of her estate. And it was true: her estate, the buildings and the house itself (I couldn't help looking at the roof, which was of metal sheeting), everything appeared to be in tip-top order, everything was properly arranged, cleaned and swept, and the repainting had been done where necessary, just as if she were a German housewife. Anna Martinovna had of course grown older, but that special, dry and, as it were, wicked charm which had once so excited me had not completely left her. She was dressed in country style, but elegantly. She received us without warmth – that word did not describe her – but politely, and on seeing me, the witness of that fearful happening, she did not so much as raise an eyebrow. She let not a single word drop about my mother, or her father, or her sister, or her husband, as if she'd filled her mouth with water and daren't open it.

She had two daughters, both extremely pretty and slender, with charming little faces and expressions of happiness and tenderness in their dark eyes; and she also had a son, who took a little after his father, but was also a broth of a boy! During the discussions among the landowners Anna Martinovna behaved calmly and with dignity, displaying neither marked stubbornness, nor especial greed. But no one was better than her at appreciating what was to their advantage and knowing how to make a convincing show of defending their rights. All the 'appropriate' laws, even ministerial circulars, were familiar to her. She spoke little and in a quiet voice, but every word was to the point. It ended with our agreeing to all her demands and making such concessions that we could do little else save express astonishment. On the return journey some of the landowning gentlemen even swore at themselves; and all of us clucked about it and shook our heads.

'She's got a head on her shoulders!' one exclaimed.

'A right bitch, she is!' exclaimed another, a somewhat less delicate landowner. 'She looks soft and cosy, but she's really hard as nails!'

'And tight-fisted!' exclaimed a third. 'A glass of vodka and a spot of caviare for a bloke – what's wrong with that?'

'What can you expect from her?' exclaimed suddenly one of them who had so far said nothing at all. 'We all know she poisoned her husband, didn't she?'

To my astonishment none of them considered it necessary to dispute such an appalling and no doubt quite baseless accusation. This astonished me all the more since, notwithstanding the abuse I have just quoted, we all felt genuine respect for Anna Martinovna, the indelicate landowner included. The arbitrator even waxed emotional.

'Put her on the throne', he cried, 'and she'd be another Semiramis or Catherine the Great! The control exercised over her peasants is exemplary, the education given to her children is exemplary! What a head for business, what brains!'

Leaving aside Semiramis and Catherine the Great, there was no doubt that Anna Martinovna led a very happy life. A satisfaction both inward and external and a pleasant tranquillity of spiritual and corporeal health were conspicuous in her, in her family and in her entire way of life. The extent to which she deserved this happiness is another matter. However, youth is the only time for putting such questions. Everything on earth – both the good things and the bad things – is not given to a man according to his just deserts, but as a result of certain as yet unknown, yet logical, laws which I won't even undertake to suggest to you, although it sometimes seems to me that I feel them as through a glass darkly.

[31]

I inquired of the arbitrator about Yevlampiya Martinovna and learned that she had no sooner left home than all trace of her had been lost – 'and no doubt she's given up the ghost long ago.'

That was how our arbitrator put it . . . but I'm sure I've actually *seen* Yevlampiya, that I've met her. This is how it happened.

About four years after my meeting with Anna Martinovna I took a place for the summer in Murino, a little village outside St Petersburg, well known to summer residents of average means. The opportunities for hunting round Murino were not bad at that time and I went out with my gun almost every day. I had a companion, a certain Vikulov, of bourgeois background, a kindhearted chap and by no means a fool, but, as he used to say of himself, of completely 'unaccountable' behaviour. The places this fellow had been and the things he'd done! Nothing was capable of surprising him, he knew it all – but the only things he was fond of were hunting and drinking. On one occasion he and I were returning to Murino and we had to go past a solitary house standing at a cross-roads and surrounded by a tall, thick fence. It wasn't the first time I'd seen the house and each time it had aroused my curiosity. There was something mysterious, enclosed and gloomily uncommunicative about it, something that reminded one of a prison or a hospital. All that could be seen from the road was its steeply pitched roof painted some dark colour. There was only one set of gates in the surrounding fence and they appeared to be tight shut; never a sound could be heard beyond them. Despite this, one couldn't help feeling that someone was living in the house, since it did not have the look of a place that was empty. On the contrary, everything about it looked so strong and solid and sturdy it could easily have withstood a siege!

'What is this fortress?' I asked my companion. 'Do you know?'

Vikulov puckered his eyes slyly.

'An odd structure, isn't it? The local constable gets quite an income from it!'

'How do you mean?'

'I mean just that. You've heard of the religious sect known as the flagellants, haven't you, the ones who don't have any priests?'

'Yes.'

'Well, their chief mother-figure lives there.'

'A woman?'

'Yes, their mother-figure, their madonna.'

'You don't mean it!'

'I'm telling you. They say she's very stern, an absolute harridan! She's worth thousands of roubles! I'd take all these madonnas and . . . Oh, there's no point in talking about it!'

He called to his Pegashka, a wonderful dog with an excellent sense of smell but no idea at all of how to stand still. Vikulov had to bind up one of its back legs in order to stop it from running about so wildly.

His words lodged in my memory. I used to make a point of going out of my way in order to walk past that mysterious house. On one occasion I was just passing it when – O wonder of wonders! – the bolt suddenly rattled in the gates, a key squeaked in the lock and then the gates themselves quietly opened wide. A large horse's head appeared with its fringe of mane plaited beneath a colourfully painted yoke and slowly there came out on to the road a small cart of the kind used by horse-dealers and travelling salesmen. On my side, sitting on the leather seat, was a man of about thirty, of strikingly handsome and distinguished appearance, in a smart peasant-style topcoat of black and a black cap pulled down low on the forehead. He was making a stately show of driving a well-fed horse that was as broad in the beam as a stove. Next to him, on the other side, sat a tall woman, as straight as an arrow. Her head was covered in an expensive black shawl and she was wearing a short olive-coloured velvet jacket and a dark-blue merino skirt. Her white hands supported each other in forming a decorous cross on her bosom. The little cart turned left along the road and the woman came within a couple of yards of me. She moved her head slightly and I recognised Yevlampiya Harlov. I recognised her at once and never doubted it for an instant, nor could I have, for I had never seen anyone else with such eyes as she had and those particular lips, simultaneously so haughty and so sensual. Her face had grown longer and coarser, her complexion had darkened and there were wrinkles in places, but what had particularly changed was the expression of her face. It is difficult to convey in mere words the self-assurance, severity and haughtiness of that expression! Every feature exuded not merely the calm assurance of power, but a surfeit of authority. In the casual glance which she directed at me there could be discerned a long-standing, habitual expectation of nothing but devoted, unquestioning obedience. This woman obviously lived surrounded not by admirers but by slaves. She had obviously long since forgotten the time when her every command and wish weren't instantly fulfilled!

I loudly called out her name and patronymic. She started slightly, gave me a second glance – not of fear but of angry contempt, as if to say: 'How do you dare do that?' – and, hardly opening her lips, issued an order. The man sitting beside her sprang into action, struck the reins on the horse's back and it dashed away at a smart and powerful trot – and the cart went out of sight.

I never came across Yevlampiya again. How Martin Petrovich's daughter became a madonna of the flagellants' sect, I simply can't imagine. But who knows, perhaps she has founded a branch which will be named after her, or is already so named – Yevlampianism? All things are possible.

And that's all I have to tell you about my King Lear of the steppes, his family and his doings . . .

The speaker fell silent, we chatted for a while and then went our separate ways.

The Song of Triumphant Love

Dedicated to the memory of Gustave Flaubert
'Wage Du zu irren und zu traümen!'
[Dare to err and dream] Schiller

The following is what I read in an ancient Italian manuscript:

[1]

Near the middle of the sixteenth century in Ferrara – it flourished at that time under the sceptre of its magnificent ducal rulers, patrons of the arts and poetry – there lived two young men, Fabio and Muzzio by name. Of similar age and closely related, they were almost inseparable; a friendship of the heart had bound them together from early childhood . . . the similarity of their fates had made fast this bond. Both belonged to ancient families; both were rich, independent and unmarried, their tastes and interests were similar. Muzzio was interested in music, Fabio in painting. The whole of Ferrara took pride in them as the finest adornment of the court, society and town. In appearance, however, they were dissimilar, although both were outstanding for their shapely, youthful beauty; Favio was taller, pale of face and fair-haired, and his eyes were blue: Muzzio, by contrast, had a swarthy face and black hair, and his dark-brown eyes did not contain the happy gleam, his lips did not have the welcoming smile that were Fabio's; his thick eyebrows extended over narrow eyelids, while the golden eyebrows of Fabio rose in delicate semi-circles on his pure, smooth brow. In his conversation Muzzio was also less lively; despite this, both friends were equally attractive to the ladies, for both were models of chivalrous courtesy and generosity.

At one and the same time there lived in Ferrara a girl by the name of Valeria. She was considered one of the first beauties of the town, although she could only be seen very rarely since she led a secluded life and left her house only to go to church – and at festival time to some fête or other. She lived with her mother, a noble but impoverished widow who had no other children. To all who met her, Valeria suggested a feeling of involuntary surprise and – just as involuntary – a feeling of tender respect, so modest was her bearing, so little, it seemed, did she realise the full extent of her charms. Some people, it is true, found her appearance a little pale; the look in her eyes, which were almost always lowered, expressed a certain shyness and even timidity; there was seldom a smile on her lips – and then only a faint one; her voice was scarcely audible. But there was a rumour that she had a beautiful voice and that, locked by herself in her room in the early morning, when the rest of the town was still asleep, she liked to sing old songs to the sound of the lute, on which she herself played. Despite the pallor of her face, Valeria was blooming with health; and even old folk, looking at her, could not but think: 'Oh, how happy will be the young man for whom this untouched and virginal flower, still folded within its petals, will eventually open!'

[2]

Fabio and Muzzio saw Valeria for the first time at a sumptuous public reception arranged on the orders of the Duke of Ferrara, Ercol, son of the famous Lucrezia Borgia, in honour of certain eminent gentlemen who had come from Paris on the invitation of the Duchess, daughter of the French king Louis XII. Together with her mother Valeria sat in the middle of an elegant tribune erected after a design by Palladio in the main square of Ferrara and intended for the most respected ladies of the town. Both of them – both Fabio and Muzzio – fell passionately in love with her that very day; and since they hid nothing from each other, each quickly knew what had happened in his friend's heart. They reached an agreement between them: both of them would strive to become acquainted with Valeria – and if she deigned to choose one of them, then the other should uncomplainingly abide by her decision. Several weeks later, thanks to the good name which they justly deserved, they succeeded in penetrating the widow's inaccessible house; she allowed them to pay her a visit. After that they were able almost each day to see Valeria and talk to her – and with each day that passed the fire ignited in both young men's hearts flared up stronger and stronger; however, Valeria showed no preference for either of them, although their presence evidently pleased her. With Muzzio she played music; but with Fabio she talked more; she was less shy with him. Finally they decided to learn what their fate was to be – and they sent Valeria a letter in which they asked her to make her intentions clear and say to whom she was prepared to give her hand. Valeria showed the letter to her mother and announced she was prepared to remain a spinster; but if her mother considered it was time for her to marry, she would marry whichever it was her mother chose. The respectable widow shed some tears at the thought of being separated from her beloved child; but there was no reason for rejecting the suitors: she considered them both equally worthy of her daughter's hand. Still, secretly preferring Fabio and suspecting that Valeria favoured him more as well, she chose him. The next day Fabio learned of his good fortune; while Muzzio was left to keep his word – and abide by Valeria's decision.

That is what he did; but to be a witness of his friend's, his rival's, triumph was beyond his powers. He at once sold the greater part of his possessions and, having gathered together several thousand ducats, he set off on a far journey to the East. In saying goodbye to Fabio he told him that he would not return until he felt that the last traces of passion had vanished within him. It was hard for Fabio to part with his friend of childhood and youth . . . but the joyous expectation of bliss close at hand swallowed up all other feelings and he gave himself up entirely to the raptures of a love crowned by mutual joy.

Soon he was wedded to Valeria – and it was only then he learned the full value of the treasure which it had fallen to his lot to own. He had a beautiful villa surrounded by a shady garden a short distance from Ferrara; he moved there together with his wife and her mother. A time of unclouded joy began for them. Married life showed in a new and enchanting light all Valeria's virtues; Fabio became a remarkable painter – no longer a simple amateur, but a master. Valeria's mother was delighted and gave thanks to God as she observed the happy pair. Four years passed unnoticed like a blissful dream. The young couple lacked only one thing; they had only one cause for sorrow: there were no children . . . but they never abandoned hope. At the end of the fourth year they were visited by a great and, on this occasion, quite real grief: Valeria's mother died after a few days' illness.

Valeria shed many tears; for a long while she could not accustom herself to her loss. But another year passed, life again reasserted its rights and flowed on along its former course. And then one fine summer evening, without warning, Muzzio returned to Ferrara.

During the entire five years which had passed since his departure no one had heard anything from him; all rumours concerning him had ceased, just as if he had vanished from the face of the earth. When Fabio met his friend on one of the streets of Ferrara, he almost cried out, at first from fright, then from joy – and instantly invited him to his villa. He had there in his garden a commodious pavilion standing by itself; he suggested to his friend that he should stay in this pavilion. Muzzio gladly agreed and the very same day he moved there with his servant, a dumb Malay – dumb, but not deaf, and even, judging by the vivacity of his eyes, a man of quick intelligence . . . His tongue had been cut out. Muzzio brought with him dozens of chests filled with a great variety of different valuables which he had collected in the course of his prolonged travels. Valeria was delighted by Muzzio's return; and he offered her a friendly greeting that was happy but calm: it was clear from all he did that he had kept his promise to Fabio. It took a day for him to settle into his pavilion; he unpacked, with the help of the Malay, the many rare things he had brought with him: carpets, silks, velvet and brocade apparel, weapons, drinking vessels, dishes and bowls decorated with enamel, gold and silver objects inlaid with pearl and turquoise, carved boxes of jasper and ivory, cut-glass bottles, spices, tobaccos, animal skins, the feathers of unknown birds and a multitude of other things whose very use seemed mysterious and incomprehensible. Among all these treasures there was a rich pearl necklace which Muzzio had received from the Shah of Persia in gratitude for some great and secret service; he sought Valeria's consent to place this necklace round her neck with his own hands; it seemed to her heavy and endowed with some strange warmth which made it literally cling to her skin. Towards evening, after dinner, sitting on the terrace of the villa, in the shade of oleanders and laurels, Muzzio began to speak of his travels. He spoke of the far countries he had seen, of mountains rising above the clouds, of waterless deserts, of rivers like seas; he spoke of enormous buildings and temples, of thousand-year-old trees, of flowers and birds arrayed in all the colours of the rainbow; he named the cities he had visited and the peoples – names out of fairy tales. The whole of the East was familiar to Muzzio: he had travelled across Persia and Arabia, where the horses are nobler and more beautiful than all other living creatures, he had penetrated into the very depths of India, where human beings resemble the grandest of nature's growths, he had reached the limits of China and Tibet, where the living God, called the Dalai-Lama, dwells on the earth in the shape of a silent man with narrow eyes. His tales were only to be marvelled at! As though spellbound Fabio and Valeria listened to him. In his person the features of Muzzio's face had changed little; swarthy since childhood, his face had darkened a little, becoming tanned by the rays of a brighter sun, and the eyes seemed more deepset than before – and that was all; but the expression of the face was different: concentrated and serious, it betrayed no vivacity even when he mentioned dangers which beset him at night, in the forests, surrounded by the roaring tigers, or by day, on empty roads, where thugs lie in wait for travellers and strike them down in honour of the iron goddess which demands human sacrifices. And Muzzio's voice had become deeper and steadier; the movements of his hands and body had lost the flamboyancy characteristic of Italians. With the aid of his servant, the obsequiously nimble Malay, he demonstrated to his hosts some of the tricks he had been taught by Indian Brahmins. Thus, for example, having first concealed himself behind a curtain, he appeared suddenly sitting in the air with legs tucked up under him, the tips of his fingers resting lightly on an upright bamboo stick, a feat which greatly astonished Fabio and even alarmed Valeria . . . 'Perhaps he deals in black magic?' was her thought. When he began, by playing on a little flute, to summon out of a closed basket some tame snakes, and when, with flicking tongues, their dark flat heads appeared from beneath a brightly coloured cloth, Valeria was horrified and begged Muzzio to cover up the beastly creatures at once. At supper Muzzio regaled his friends with Shiraz wine from a round bottle with a long neck; it had pronounced bouquet and body, being of a golden colour shot with greenish tints, and it shone curiously when poured out in small jasper glasses. It tasted unlike any European wines; it was very sweet and spicy and, drunk slowly, in small sips, it aroused in every limb a sensation of pleasant drowsiness. Muzzio made both Fabio and Valeria drink a small glass of it and drank some himself. Over his own glass, bending forward, he whispered something, moving his fingers. Valeria noticed this; but because in general in Muzzio's manners and his whole behaviour there was something alien and unusual, she simply thought to herself: 'Hasn't he, perhaps, adopted some new religion in India, or some of their customs?' Later, after a short silence, she asked him whether he had continued his interest in music on his travels. In reply Muzzio ordered the Malay to bring him his Indian violin. It resembled present-day ones, except that instead of four strings it had three, the top of it was covered in bluish snakeskin and the delicate reed bow had a semi-circular appearance, and on the end of it glittered a pointed diamond.

First of all Muzzio played several melancholy – as he called them – folk songs, strange and even savage to Italian ears; the sound of the metallic strings was mournful and feeble. But when Muzzio began the final song, this very sound suddenly grew stronger and quivered resonantly and powerfully; a passionate melody poured out from beneath the broad sweeps of the bow, poured out in beautiful sinuous coils like that very snake whose skin covered the top of the violin; and the melody burned with such fire, was radiant with such triumphant joy, that both Fabio and Valeria were pierced to their very hearts and tears came into their eyes; and Muzzio, with his head bent forward, pressed over the violin, his cheeks grown pale and his brows drawn together in one straight line, seemed even more concentrated and solemn – and the diamond on the end of the violin bow shed sparkling rays as it moved, as if it had also been ignited by the fire of the wondrous song. When Muzzio finished and, though still holding the violin firmly between his chin and shoulder, dropped the hand which held the bow, Fabio cried out: 'What is it? What have you just played us?' Valeria did not say a word, but it seemed that all her being repeated her husband's question. Muzzio placed the violin down on the table and, slightly shaking his hair, said with a polite smile: 'What is it? It's a melody ... a song I heard once on the island of Ceylon. The song is considered by the people there to be a song of happy and satisfied love.' 'Play it again,' whispered Fabio. 'No, it mustn't be repeated,' answered Muzzio, 'and it's already late. Signora Valeria should be going to bed; and it's time for me as well. I'm tired.' Throughout the day Muzzio had treated Valeria with respectful simplicity, as a long-time friend; but on saying goodbye, he pressed her hand ever so firmly, pushing his fingers into her palm and looking her so insistently in the face that she, though she did not raise her eyes, nonetheless felt the look on her suddenly burning cheeks. She said nothing to Muzzio, but withdrew her hand quickly, and when he had gone she looked at the door through which he had left. She remembered how in former years she had been frightened of him ... and now she was overcome by confusion. Muzzio returned to his pavilion; the married couple retired to their bedroom.

Valeria did not fall asleep at once; her blood had been softly and languidly stirred, and in her head there was a slight ringing – from the unfamiliar wine is what she supposed, but perhaps also from Muzzio's stories and his playing on the violin. Towards morning she did eventually fall asleep and she dreamed an unusual dream.

She dreamed that she entered a spacious room with a low vaulted ceiling. She had never seen such a room in her life. The walls were all embellished with tiny blue tiles and gold tracery; delicate carved pillars of alabaster supported the vault of the marble ceiling; the ceiling itself and the pillars seemed semi-transparent and a pale, rosy light everywhere penetrated the room, illumining all the objects mysteriously and uniformly; brocaded cushions lay on a narrow strip of carpet placed in the middle of the smooth, mirror-like floor. In the corners, scarcely noticeable, stood tall smoking censers in the form of fantastic animals; there were no windows; the door, hung with a velvet curtain, stared silent and black out of a recess in the wall. And suddenly the velvet curtain softly slides across, is moved back . . . and Muzzio enters. He bows, opens his arms to embrace her, laughs . . . His rough hands go round Valeria's waist; his dry lips have set fire to her entire body . . . She falls on her back, on the cushions . . .

Moaning in horror, after prolonged struggles, Valeria awoke. Still unable to understand where she was and what had happened to her, she sat up in bed and looked round her . . . She was trembling in every limb . . . Fabio was lying beside her. He was asleep; but his face, in the light of a bright, round moon gazing in through the window, was pale like a dead man's and more sorrowful than a dead face. Valeria woke her husband – and as soon as he looked at her he said: 'What's happened to you?' 'I've had a dream . . . a frightful dream,' she whispered, still trembling all over.

But at that moment from the direction of the pavilion there came strong strains of music, and both of them – both Fabio and Valeria – recognised them as the melody which Muzzio had played them, calling it the song of requited, triumphant love. Fabio looked with perplexity at Valeria . . . she closed her eyes and turned away – and both of them listened to the song with bated breath. When the last sound died away,

the moon went behind a cloud and the room was suddenly darkened . . .
Both let their heads drop on their pillows without another word – and
not one of them noticed when the other fell asleep.

[5]

The next morning Muzzio came to breakfast; he seemed full of himself –
and greeted Valeria cheerfully. She reacted to him with embarrassment,
glancing at him briefly, and she was terrified by the self-satisfied,
cheerful face, by the penetrating and inquisitive eyes. Muzzio was about
to embark on another of his stories, but Fabio cut him short at the
start.

'Perhaps you couldn't get to sleep in your new surroundings? My
wife and I heard you playing the song you played yesterday.'

'Really? You heard me playing it, did you?' said Muzzio. 'I did play
it, but I slept first and even had an astonishing dream.'

Valeria was on tenterhooks.

'What was your dream?' asked Fabio.

'I dreamed,' answered Muzzio, not taking his eyes off Valeria, 'that I
entered a spacious room with a ceiling decorated in an Eastern style.
Carved pillars supported the ceiling, the walls were covered in tiles, and
although there were neither windows nor lights the whole room was
filled with a rosy light just as if it had all been made out of translucent
stone. In the corners stood Chinese censers, on the floor there was a
narrow carpet laid with brocaded cushions. I entered through a door
hung with a curtain, and in another door immediately opposite there
appeared a woman whom I had once loved. And she seemed to me so
beautiful I was inflamed through and through with my former love . . .'

Muzzio stopped significantly. Valeria sat motionless and slowly went
pale . . . and her breathing grew deeper.

'Then', Muzzio went on, 'I awoke and played that song.'

'But who was this woman?' asked Fabio.

'Who was she? The wife of an Indian gentleman. I met her in Delhi . . .
She is no longer alive, she died.'

'And the husband?' asked Fabio, not knowing himself why he put
this question.

'I gather the husband is also dead. I soon lost touch with both of
them.'

'Extraordinary!' remarked Fabio. 'My wife also had a strange dream last night.' Muzzio glanced piercingly at Valeria. 'Which she didn't tell me about,' added Fabio.

But that moment Valeria rose and left the room. Immediately after breakfast Muzzio also left, announcing that he had to be in Ferrara on business and would not be returning before evening.

[6]

Some weeks before Muzzio's return Fabio had begun a portrait of his wife, depicting her with the attributes of St Cecilia. He had made significant progress as a painter; the celebrated Luini, a pupil of Leonardo da Vinci, visited him in Ferrara and, while helping him with his own advice, also conveyed the injunctions of his great teacher. The portrait was almost complete; it remained only to complete the face with a few strokes and Fabio could justly take pride in what he had done. Having seen off Muzzio to Ferrara, he went to his studio where Valeria was usually waiting for him; but he did not find her there; he called to her but she did not reply. Fabio was overcome by a secret anxiety; he set off to find her. She was not to be found in the house; Fabio ran into the garden – and there, on one of the most remote paths, he caught sight of her. With her head sunk on her bosom, her hands crossed on her knees, she was sitting on a bench – and behind her, standing out from the dark green of a cypress, a marble satyr, his face distorted by a malicious grin, was placing his pointed lips to a pipe. Valeria was evidently pleased by the appearance of her husband and answered his anxious questioning by saying that she had a slight headache; but that it meant nothing and she was ready to go for the sitting. Fabio led her to the studio, sat her down, took up his brush; but to his great annoyance he could not finish her face as he had wished. And it was not because she was a little pale and seemed tired ... no; it was that pure, holy expression which he had liked so much and which had given him the idea of portraying Valeria as St Cecilia – that was what he could not find today. He finally threw his brush away, told his wife he was not in the mood and did not want to prevent her having a rest, since in appearance she seemed a little unwell – and placed the easel with the portrait facing the wall. Valeria agreed with him she ought to have a rest and, repeating her complaint about a headache, retired to her bedroom.

Fabio remained in the studio. He felt a strange confusion which was incomprehensible to him. Muzzio's arrival in his house on a visit which he, Fabio, had himself requested embarrassed him. And it wasn't a matter of jealousy – it wasn't possible to be jealous of Valeria! – but simply that in his friend he did not recognise his former comrade. Everything alien, unknown and novel that Muzzio had brought with him from those far lands and had become, it seemed, part of his flesh and blood – all these magic tricks, songs, strange wines, the dumb Malay, even the very spicy fragrance which came from Muzzio's clothes and hair and breath – it all contrived to arouse in Fabio a feeling akin to mistrust, perhaps even one of apprehension. And why did the Malay, when serving at table, look with such unpleasant attention at him, Fabio? True, some might think that he could understand Italian. Muzzio had said of him that, having paid with his tongue, the Malay had made a great sacrifice and therefore now possessed a great strength. What strength was it? And how could he acquire it at the price of his tongue? All this was very strange, very hard to understand! Fabio went to his wife in her bedroom; she was lying on her bed, dressed – but not asleep. On hearing his steps she shuddered, and then again was evidently pleased at seeing him as she had been in the garden. Fabio sat down beside her bed, took Valeria by the hand and, after a short silence, asked her what the unusual dream was which had so frightened her during the night. Was it similar to the dream which Muzzio had described? Valeria blushed and hurriedly said: 'Oh, no, no! I dreamed of some fantastic creature which wanted to tear me apart.' 'A fantastic creature? In the shape of a man?' asked Fabio. 'No, in the shape of a beast . . . a beast!' And Valeria turned away and hid her crimson face in the pillow. Fabio went on holding his wife's hand for a while; then he silently raised it to his lips – and went out.

Both of them passed that day unhappily. It seemed that something sinister was hanging over their heads . . . but what it was they were unable to say. They wanted to be together, just as if some danger were threatening; but what they could say to each other – of that they had no idea. Fabio tried once again to work on his portrait or to read Ariosto, whose poem,* which had recently appeared in Ferrara, had achieved fame throughout Italy; but he was unsuccessful . . . Late in the evening, about suppertime, Muzzio returned.

He seemed calm and self-satisfied, but had little to tell; instead, he asked Fabio about former common acquaintances, about the expedition to Germany, about the Emperor Charles; and he spoke of his desire to visit Rome to see the new pope. Again he offered Valeria some Shiraz wine – and in response to her refusal muttered as if to himself: 'Well, it's not needed now.' Returning with his wife to their bedroom, Fabio quickly fell asleep . . . and on waking an hour later felt sure no one shared his bed with him: Valeria had gone. He swiftly sat up – and at that very instant he saw his wife in her nightdress entering the room from the garden. The moon was shining brightly, although shortly before there had been a brief shower. With closed eyes and an expression of secret horror on her immobile features, Valeria approached the bed and, feeling her way with outstretched hands, rapidly and silently lay down. Fabio turned to her with a question, but she didn't answer; she seemed to be asleep. He touched her and felt raindrops on her nightdress and her hair, and on the soles of her bare feet there were grains of sand. At that he jumped up and ran into the garden through the half-open door. Moonlight, of a harsh brightness, bathed everything. Fabio looked round and saw on the sand of the pathway traces of two pairs of feet – one of them was bare; and these footprints led to an arbour of jasmines between the pavilion and the house. He stopped in bewilderment – and then suddenly there resounded the strains of the song which he had heard the previous night! Fabio shuddered and dashed to the pavilion. Muzzio was standing in the middle of the room and playing on his violin. Fabio flung himself towards him.

'You were in the garden, weren't you, you went out, your clothes are wet from the rain, aren't they?'

'No . . . I don't know . . . it seems . . . I haven't been out,' Muzzio answered haltingly, literally taken by surprise by Fabio's arrival and his excitement.

Fabio seized him by the hand.

'And why are you again playing that melody? Surely you haven't had the same dream again?'

Muzzio looked at Fabio with the same air of astonishment and said nothing.

'Answer me!'

> '*The moon is risen like a round shield.*
> *Just like a snake the river gleams . . .*
> *My friend's awake, my enemy dreams –*
> *The hawk's claws have seized, it seems,*
> *The chicken's neck . . . Help! Help!*'

muttered Muzzio in a kind of sing-song, as if in a trance.

Fabio took a couple of steps backward, stared at Muzzio, thought for a moment and then returned to the house and to the bedroom.

With her head leaning on her shoulder and her arms spread out helplessly, Valeria was fast asleep. He did not succeed in awakening her immediately, but as soon as she saw him she threw herself on his shoulder and embraced him convulsively; her whole body was trembling.

'What's wrong with you, my dear? What's wrong with you?' Fabio asked repeatedly, trying to calm her. But she continued to cling to him.

'Oh, what terrible dreams I'm having!' she whispered, pressing her face against him. Fabio would have liked to ask what she meant, but she simply shuddered . . .

The glass in the windows was beginning to glow crimson with the light of early morning when she finally fell asleep in his arms.

[8]

The next day Muzzio was absent since morning and Valeria announced to her husband that she intended to visit the local monastery, the home of her spiritual father, an old and conservative monk to whom she felt limitless devotion. In answer to Fabio's questions she replied that she wanted to relieve her soul by confession, a soul weighed down by the extraordinary impressions of the last few days. Looking at Valeria's drawn face and hearing her exhausted voice, Fabio approved her intention, believing that the respected Father Lorenzo could offer her useful advice and disperse her doubts . . . Under the protection of four attendants Valeria set off for the monastery, while Fabio remained at home and, until his wife's return, wandered about the garden trying to understand what had happened to her and feeling perpetual fear and anger and the ache of undefined suspicions . . . More than once he looked into the pavilion; but Muzzio had not returned and the Malay gazed at Fabio like a statue, with obsequiously lowered head and – so at least it seemed to Fabio – a faintly, very faintly mysterious smile on his bronze face. Meanwhile, at her confession, Valeria had told everything to her spiritual father, not so much in shame as in horror. He listened to her attentively, gave her his blessing and absolved her of her unwitting sin – while to himself he thought: 'Sorcery and devilish spells . . . Things cannot be left like this,' and joined Valeria in returning to her villa as if finally to calm and comfort her. At the sight of the spiritual father Fabio grew extremely alarmed; but the very experienced old monk had already thought out the way he should behave. On finding himself alone with Fabio he did not, of course, reveal any of the confidences of the confessional, but he advised him, given the opportunity, to rid his house of the invited guest who, by his stories, songs and general conduct, had brought such derangement to Valeria's imagination. In any case, in the old man's opinion Muzzio had formerly, he recalled, not been entirely assured in his beliefs and, having spent such a long time in countries that were not illumined by the light of Christianity, could have brought back from there the infection of false doctrines and might even have dabbled in the mysteries of magic and although long-standing friendship had exerted its rights, sensible caution pointed to the need for separation! Fabio entirely agreed with the worthy monk and Valeria even brightened up completely when her husband informed her of the old man's advice – and, accompanied by their heartfelt good wishes and laden with expensive presents for the monastery and the poor, Father Lorenzo returned home.

Fabio made up his mind to speak to Muzzio immediately after supper; but his strange guest did not return for supper. Fabio decided to postpone his talk with Muzzio till the following day, and he and his wife then retired for the night.

[9]

Valeria soon fell fast asleep; but Fabio was unable to. In the silence of the night he was able to imagine to himself even more vividly everything he had seen and felt; and he was even more insistent in asking himself the questions to which he had not formerly been able to give any answers. Had Muzzio in fact become a practitioner of the black arts? Had he already poisoned Valeria? She was ill . . . but what was her illness? While he, his head in his hand and his burning breath coming in short gasps, gave himself up to his burdensome thoughts, the moon again rose into a cloudless sky; and along with its rays, through the semi-transparent panes of the window, from the direction of the pavilion – or was this all Fabio's imagining? – there began to pour a very faint breath of air, similar to a light whiff of perfume . . . and he heard an insidious, passionate whispering . . . and at the same moment noticed that Valeria began to stir weakly. He was instantly awake and saw that she was getting up, lowering first one foot, then the other from the bed – and like a lunatic, lifelessly staring ahead of her with dull eyes, her hands outstretched, she moved towards the door into the garden! In a flash Fabio had darted through the other door of the bedroom and, dashing at great speed round the corner of the house, slammed shut the door leading into the garden . . . Scarcely had he managed to seize the bolt than he felt someone was trying to open the door from the inside, was pressing against it, pushing again and again . . . Then there were tremulous, quivering moanings . . .

'But surely Muzzio can't have come back from the town?' was the thought that darted through Fabio's head, and he dashed towards the pavilion.

What sight met his eyes?

Coming towards him along the pathway, brightly lit by the gleaming rays of the moon, coming towards him, also like a lunatic, also with arms outstretched and lifelessly open eyes, was Muzzio . . . Fabio ran up to him, but the latter went on walking without noticing him, regularly taking one step after another, and his immobile features were drawn into a kind of grinning laugh in the moonlight, like the expression on the Malay's face. Fabio was about to shout out his name, but at that moment he heard the noise of a window opening in the house behind him . . . He looked round.

The bedroom window had in fact been opened from top to bottom and, with one foot already across the sill, there was Valeria in the window opening . . . and her hands seemed to be seeking Muzzio . . . she was straining towards him.

Indescribable rage poured through Fabio's heart in a fierce torrent. 'The damned wizard!' he screamed wildly and, seizing Muzzio with one hand round the throat, he felt with the other for the dagger in his belt and drove the blade into his side right up to the hilt.

Muzzio let out a piercing scream and, pressing the palm of his hand to the wound, ran stumbling back into the pavilion . . . But at the very same instant that Fabio had stabbed Muzzio, Valeria screamed just as piercingly and fell to the ground as if cut down by a scythe.

Fabio rushed to her, picked her up, carried her to the bed, talked to her . . .

For a long while she lay without moving; but eventually she opened her eyes, sighed deeply, with a shudder of happiness, like someone who had just been saved from certain death, caught sight of her husband and, winding her arms round his neck, pressed herself to his chest. 'It's you, you, you,' she muttered. Little by little her arms relaxed their grip, she threw back her head and, whispering with a blissful smile: 'Thank God, everything's over . . . But how tired I am!' she fell into a sound but not an oppressive sleep.

[10]

Fabio sank down beside her and, without taking his eyes from her pale face which, though thin, already had a contented look, began thinking about what had happened . . . and also about what he ought to do now. What should he do? If he had killed Muzzio – and remembering how deeply the blade of the dagger had gone in, he could not doubt that he had – if he had killed Muzzio, then it couldn't be hidden! He would have to inform the duke and the judges . . . but how on earth could he explain or give an account of such an incomprehensible happening? He, Fabio, had killed in his own house one of his own kin and his best friend? People would ask: Why? For what reason? But what if Muzzio hadn't been killed? Fabio simply couldn't remain any longer in ignorance, and after making sure that Valeria was still asleep he cautiously rose, left the house and went in the direction of the pavilion. All was quiet within; in one window only could a light be seen. With a sinking heart he opened the outer door (there were traces of blood-stained fingers on it and drops of blood dotted the sand of the pathway), crossed the first room, which was dark, and stopped at the next doorway in total amazement.

In the centre of the room, on a Persian carpet, with a brocaded cushion under his head and covered in a wide red shawl with a black pattern, lay Muzzio, every limb stretched out straight. His face, yellow as wax, with closed eyes and the lids tinged blue, was turned towards the ceiling; there was no sign of breathing: he appeared to be a corpse. At his feet, also arrayed in a red shawl, knelt the Malay. He was holding in his left hand a branch of some unknown plant resembling a fern and, bending slightly forward, was looking steadily at his master. A small torch which had been stuck in the ground burned with a greenish light and was the sole illumination in the room. Its flame did not flicker or smoke. The Malay did not stir at Fabio's entrance, simply gave him one glance and again fixed his eyes on Muzzio. From time to time he raised and lowered the branch and waved it in the air and his speechless lips slowly opened and moved as if pronouncing soundless words. Between the Malay and Muzzio there lay on the floor the dagger with which Fabio had struck his friend; the Malay brought the branch down once on the blood-stained blade. One minute passed . . . then another. Fabio approached the Malay and, bending down to him, whispered the question: 'Is he dead?' The Malay lowered his head and, freeing his right hand from beneath the shawl, pointed commandingly at the door. Fabio tried to repeat his question, but the commanding hand repeated its gesture and Fabio went out, indignantly and in amazement, but still obediently.

He found Valeria asleep as he had left her, with her face wearing an even more contented look. He did not undress, but sat down by the window, leant on his arm and again fell into deep thought. The risen sun found him in the same place. Valeria was still asleep.

[11]

Fabio had wanted to wait for her to wake up and then go to Ferrara, when suddenly someone tapped lightly at the bedroom door. Fabio went out and saw standing before him his old steward Antonio.

'Signor,' began the old man, 'the Malay has just announced to us that Signor Muzzio is unwell and wishes to remove himself with all his belongings into the town; and he therefore begs you to send him servants to help with the packing and at dinner-time pack-horses and riding horses and a few attendants. Do you permit this?'

'The Malay announced this to you, did he?' asked Fabio. 'How? Surely he's dumb.'

'Here, Signor, is the piece of paper on which he wrote everything in our language – and very correctly.'

'And Muzzio is ill, you say?'

'Yes, very ill – and it's impossible to see him.'

'Hasn't a doctor been sent for?'

'No. The Malay hasn't allowed it.'

'And the Malay wrote this for you?'

'Yes, he did.'

Fabio was silent a moment.

'Well, then, see to the arrangements,' he said at last.

Antonio withdrew.

Fabio gazed after his servant in bewilderment. 'So he's not been killed?' was what he asked himself, and he did not know whether to be happy or regretful. Was he really ill? But it was only a few hours ago that he had seen a corpse!

Fabio returned to Valeria. She had woken up and raised her head. Husband and wife exchanged a long and significant look. 'Is he still here?' Valeria suddenly asked. Fabio shuddered. 'How . . . still here? You don't mean . . .' 'Has he left?' she continued. A weight fell from Fabio's heart. 'Not yet, but he is leaving today.' 'And I'll never, never see him again?' 'Never.' 'And I won't have any more of those dreams?' 'No.' Valeria again gave a happy sigh; a blissful smile appeared on her lips. She held out both hands to her husband. 'And we'll never talk about him, never, do you hear, my dear? And I won't go out of the room until he has left. And you must now send me in my maidservants . . . But wait: take this thing!' She indicated the pearl necklace lying on a bedside table, the necklace given her by Muzzio. 'Take it and throw it at once into our deepest well! Embrace me – I am your Valeria – and don't come to me again until he's gone.' Fabio took the necklace – the pearls seemed to him to have faded – and fulfilled his wife's command. Then he began wandering about the garden, glancing from time to time at the pavilion round which the commotion of packing had already begun. Servants were carrying out trunks and loading up the horses, but the Malay was not among them. An irresistible feeling drew Fabio to take another look at what was happening inside the pavilion. He remembered that in the rear of it there was a secret door through which it was possible to gain entrance to the room where Muzzio had been lying that morning. He crept up to the door, found it unlocked and, parting the folds of a heavy curtain, glanced in tentatively.

Muzzio was no longer lying on the carpet. Dressed in a travelling cloak, he was sitting in an armchair, but he looked like a corpse, just as he had seemed at Fabio's first visit. His seemingly petrified head was leaning against the back of the chair and his outstretched hands placed flat on his knees were yellow and motionless. His chest did not rise and fall. Around the chair, on the ground strewn with dried herbs, stood several shallow cups filled with a dark liquid which exuded a strong, almost suffocating, odour, the odour of musk. Around each cup there wound, its golden eyes occasionally flashing, a small bronze-coloured snake; and directly in front of Muzzio, only two steps from him, rose the tall figure of the Malay decked out in a long, richly coloured, brocaded garment tied at the waist with a tiger's tail and wearing a high head-dress in the form of a horned tiara on his head. But he was not motionless; he constantly bowed reverently and literally seemed to pray, or straightened himself out to his full height and even stood on tip-toe; he constantly spread out his arms wide in a rhythmical way or moved them persistently in Muzzio's direction and seemed to threaten or command him, knitted his brows and stamped his foot. All these movements evidently cost him great effort and even caused him pain, for he was breathing heavily and sweat was pouring down his face. Suddenly he stopped and, filling his lungs with air, his brows knitted in a frown, he pressed his hands together in a great effort and drew them towards him exactly as if he were holding reins . . . and then, to Fabio's indescribable horror, Muzzio's head slowly lifted itself from the back of the chair and followed the movements of the Malay's hands . . . The Malay let his hands drop and Muzzio's head again fell back heavily; the Malay repeated his movements and the obedient head followed them. The dark liquid in the cups began to boil; the cups themselves began to make a delicate ringing sound and the little bronze snakes started coiling in wave-like motions round each of them. Then the Malay took a step forward and, raising his brows high and enlarging his eyes until they were enormous, he shook his head at Muzzio . . . and the eyelids of the corpse began to quiver, opened unevenly and from beneath them appeared eyeballs dull as lead. The Malay's face glowed with triumphant pride and joy, a joy that was almost malicious; he opened wide his lips and from the very depths of his throat there burst with an effort a protracted howl . . . Muzzio's lips also parted and a feeble moan quivered on them in response to the inhuman sound ...

But Fabio couldn't stand it any longer. He felt he was witnessing some devilish spells! He also cried out and dashed away homewards without a glance behind, muttering prayers and crossing himself.

[13]

Three hours later Antonio came with the information that everything was ready, all the things had been packed, and Signor Muzzio was preparing to leave. Without saying a word to his servant, Fabio went out on to the terrace where he had a view of the pavilion. Several pack-horses stood idly in front of it; at the very entrance stood a powerful black stallion with a wide saddle designed for two riders. Also standing there were servants with bared heads and armed attendants. The door of the pavilion opened and Muzzio appeared, supported by the Malay who was now wearing his usual clothes. Muzzio's face was deathly and his arms hung down like a dead man's, but he was moving his feet – yes, he was moving his feet! – and when seated on the horse he held himself upright and felt for the reins with his hands. The Malay placed his feet in the stirrups, jumped up into the saddle beside him, placed an arm round his waist and then the whole caravan moved off. The horses went at a walking pace, and when they were turning in front of the house it seemed to Fabio that two white dots flashed for an instant in Muzzio's dark face ... Could it be that he had turned his eyes towards him? The Malay alone bowed to him – mockingly as ever.

Did Valeria see all this? The blinds of her windows were closed, but perhaps she had been standing behind them.

[14]

At dinner-time she came to the dining-room and was very quiet and pleasant; however, she still complained of tiredness. But there was not a trace of anxiety in her, nor any of the former constant amazement and secret alarm; and when, the day after Muzzio's departure, Fabio again started on her portrait, he found in her features that pure expression, the momentary eclipsing of which had so confused him, and his brush ran over the canvas easily and truly.

The young couple renewed their former life. Muzzio vanished for them, as if he had never existed at all. And Fabio and Valeria, both were in absolute agreement in not saying a word about him and not enquiring about his subsequent fate. In any case, that remained a mystery to everyone. Muzzio literally vanished, just as if the earth had swallowed him up. There was one occasion when Fabio felt that he ought to tell Valeria what had happened on that fateful night, but she most likely guessed his intention and held her breath, narrowing her eyes as though in anticipation of a blow ... And Fabio understood her: he did not deliver the blow.

One beautiful autumn day Fabio was completing his picture of St Cecilia; Valeria was seated before the organ and her fingers were running over the keys ... Suddenly, against her own will, there arose from beneath her hands the sound of that song of triumphant love which Muzzio had once played – and at that moment, for the first time since her marriage, she felt within her the first trembling signs of a new life about to be born ... Valeria gave a shudder and stopped her playing.

What did it mean? Could it be ...

At this point the manuscript came to an end.

NOTES

THE DIARY OF A SUPERFLUOUS MAN

First published in 1850; this translation has been based on the text in I. S. Turgenev, *Polnoye sobraniye sochineniy i pisem* (hereafter referred to as *Sochineniya*), vol. V, Moskva-Leningrad, 1963, pp. 178–232. The ensuing notes have been drawn largely from this edition, the fullest edition of Turgenev's works published to date, and they are intended principally to explain Russian references which may be unfamiliar to English readers.

40 *The Prisoner of the Caucasus.* This is presumably a reference to the famous poem of 1822 by A. S. Pushkin (1799–1837). The two-part poem, the most obviously Byronic of Pushkin's 'southern poems' (those written during his exile in Southern Russia, 1820–4), tells how a nameless Russian officer taken prisoner by Circassians in the Caucasus is befriended by a Circassian girl who drowns herself after helping him to escape.

43 *old hurts.* A reference to a line in the 1840 poetic dialogue between a journalist, reader and writer ('Zhurnalist, chitatel' i pisatel'') by M. Yu. Lermontov (1814–41).

62 Poprishchin, hero of *The Diary of a Madman* by N. V. Gogol (1809–52), jotted down in his diary entry for 4 October that: 'At home I lay most of the time on my bed.'

72 *made the hair of his flesh stand up.* The reference is to the Book of Job 4: 15.

72 The final lines of Pushkin's poem of 1829 'Whenever I wander along noisy streets . . .', a poetic reverie on death and the brevity of life.

MUMU

First published in 1854; this translation has been based on the text in *Sochineniya*, vol. V, pp. 264–92.

80 *the Minin and Pozharsky hand.* The hand referred to is that belonging to Minin in the statue erected on Red Square in Moscow in 1826. Minin was a butcher from Nizhny Novgorod (now Gorky) who organized an army under the command of Prince Pozharsky

NOTES

which finally ejected the Poles from Moscow in 1612 and led to the
establishment of the Romanov dynasty.

ASYA

First published in 1858; this translation is based on the text in
Sochineniya, vol. VII, 1964, pp. 71–121.

100 The Dresden Grüne-Gewölbe was a collection of jewellery made
from gold and precious stones housed in the royal castle. Visits to
the collection were accompanied by supervisory guides and strict
security.

106 *the old-fashioned Lanner waltz*. The waltzes of the Viennese
composer Joseph Lanner (1801–43) helped to popularise the
waltz as a ballroom dance.

107 *Do you still sleep?* The lines are from the third stanza of a poem
by Pushkin (probably written in October 1830 on the basis of a
work by Barry Cornwall) and first published when set to music by
M. I. Glinka (1804–57) in 1834.

108 *a young aristocratic ignoramus*. The reference is to the famous
satirical comedy by D. I. Fonvizin (1745–92), *The Minor*
(*Nedorosl'*), 1782, which exposed the ignorance and hypocrisy of
a family of uncultured Russian landowners. The 'ignoramus'
referred to is Mitrofan, the son of the family.

125 *simple grave*. Asya is paraphrasing lines from Ch. VIII, stanza
xlvi, of Pushkin's *Eugene Onegin* in which the heroine, Tatyana,
reminds Onegin of the country world where they first met and
where her nurse (not her mother) is now buried.

FIRST LOVE

First published in 1860; this translation is based on the text in
Sochineniya, vol. IX, 1965, pp. 7–76.

147 Schiller's play *The Robbers* (1781) was very popular in Russia
during the 1830s and was construed as an attrack on feudalism
and such feudal royal titles as 'prince' and 'princess'.

170 'The Hills of Georgia' refers to a poem by Pushkin of 1829 with
the first line: 'Upon the hills of Georgia lies nocturnal gloom.'

179 *Malek-Adel carrying off Matilda*. The subject of the painting is

taken from an episode in the novel *Mathilde* by Sophie Cottin (1773–1807).

179 *Not the white snows* was a popular Russian folk song first published in 1818; *I wait for you when zephyrs playful* was a song based on the poem of 1816 by P. A. Vyazemsky (1792–1878); Yermak's address was taken from Act V of the historical tragedy by A. S. Khomyakov (1804–60).

185 *Telegraph.* A fortnightly journal published in Moscow between 1825 and 1834. Many works of Russian Romanticism were published initially in its pages.

189 *the young gypsy.* Aleko is the hero of Pushkin's *The Gypsies* (1824). He marries a gypsy girl, Zemfira. Out of jealousy he murders her and her gypsy lover.

201 *From lips indifferent.* A quotation from Pushkin's poem of 1825: 'Beneath the blue sky of my native land.'

KING LEAR OF THE STEPPES

First published in 1870; this translation is based on the text in *Sochineniya*, vol. X, 1965, pp. 186–265.

204 *the Golden Book.* There was no such Golden Book, but it may be that Harlov is referring to the so-called 'velvet book' containing the genealogies of Russian princes and noblemen compiled after the edict of 1682 abolishing what was known as *mestnichestvo* or a privileged order of precedence in the allocation of posts.

228 *Potyomkin's time.* Prince Potyomkin (1739–91), the favourite of Catherine the Great who was instrumental in annexing the Crimea for Russia, must presumably have died at least forty years before the time of the story.

233 Mitrofan (not to be confused with his namesake mentioned in the note to p. 108 of *Asya*) was Bishop of Voronezh and on his death in 1703 he was canonised. Pilgrimages were made to pay homage to his remains. The Optina Pustyn monastery near the town of Bolkhov in the province of Oryol (where Turgenev was born) was founded in the fifteenth century.

269 *the rearrangement of land boundaries.* Arbitration commissions were instituted in 1836 in provincial and country towns to deal with the often thorny question of boundary rearrangement.

THE SONG OF TRIUMPHANT LOVE

First published in 1881; this translation is based on the text in *Sochineniya*, vol. XIII, 1967, pp. 53–75.

283 *whose poem*. The poem referred to is presumably *Orlando Furioso*, composed between 1503 and 1532, by Ludovico Ariosto (1474–1533).

THE WORLD'S CLASSICS

A Select List

Roxana
Edited by Jane Jack

CHARLES DICKENS: David Copperfield
Edited by Nina Burgis

Dombey and Son
Edited by Alan Horsman

Little Dorrit
Edited by Harvey Peter Sucksmith

Martin Chuzzlewit
Edited by Margaret Cardwell

The Mystery of Edwin Drood
Edited by Margaret Cardwell

Oliver Twist
Edited by Kathleen Tillotson

Sikes and Nancy and Other Public Readings
Edited by Philip Collins

BENJAMIN DISRAELI: Coningsby
Edited by Sheila M. Smith

Sybil
Edited by Sheila M. Smith

FËDOR DOSTOEVSKY: Crime and Punishment
Translated by Jessie Coulson
With an introduction by John Jones

Memoirs from the House of the Dead
Translated by Jessie Coulson
Edited by Ronald Hingley

JOHN GALT: Annals of the Parish
Edited by James Kinsley

The Entail
Edited by Ian A. Gordon

The Wings of the Dove
Edited by Peter Brooks

RUDYARD KIPLING: The Day's Work
Edited by Thomas Pinney

The Jungle Book (in two volumes)
Edited by W. W. Robson

Kim
Edited by Alan Sandison

Life's Handicap
Edited by A. O. J. Cockshut

The Man Who Would be King and Other Stories
Edited by Louis L. Cornell

Plain Tales From the Hills
Edited by Andrew Rutherford

Stalky & Co.
Edited by Isobel Quigly

A complete list of Oxford Paperbacks, including The World's Classics, Twentieth-Century Classics, OPUS, Past Masters, Oxford Authors, Oxford Shakespeare, and Oxford Paperback Reference, is available in the UK from the General Publicity Department (JH), Oxford University Press, Walton Street, Oxford OX2 6DP.

In the USA, complete lists are available from the Paperbacks Marketing Manager, Oxford University Press, 200 Madison Avenue, New York, NY 10016.

Oxford Paperbacks are available from all good bookshops. In case of difficulty, customers in the UK can order direct from Oxford University Press Bookshop, Freepost, 116 High Street, Oxford, OX1 4BR, enclosing full payment. Please add 10 per cent of published price for postage and packing.

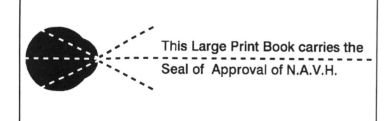

THE SEVENTH WELL

THE SEVENTH WELL

FRED WANDER

TRANSLATED BY MICHAEL HOFMANN

THORNDIKE PRESS
A part of Gale, Cengage Learning

GALE
CENGAGE Learning™

Detroit • New York • San Francisco • New Haven, Conn • Waterville, Maine • London

GALE
CENGAGE Learning™

Copyright © 2005 by Wallstein Verlag, Göttingen.
Copyright © 2008 by Michael Hofmann.
This translation was supported by the Austrian Federal Ministry of Education, Arts, and Culture.
Originally published in German under the title *Der Siebente Brunnen*.
Lines from "Abel and Cain" from *Les Fleurs du mal* by Charles Baudelaire, translated from the French by Richard Howard. Reprinted by permission of David R. Godine, Publisher, Inc. Translation copyright © 1982 by Richard Howard.
Excerpt from "May 24, 1980" from *Collected Poems in English* by Joseph Brodsky. Copyright © 2000 by the Estate of Joseph Brodsky. Reprinted by permission of Farrar, Straus and Giroux, LLC.
Thorndike Press, a part of Gale, Cengage Learning.

LIBRARY OF CONGRESS CATALOGING-IN-PUBLICATION DATA

Wander, Fred, 1917–2006.
   [Siebente Brunnen. English]
   The seventh well / by Fred Wander ; translated by Michael Hofmann. — Large print ed.
     p. cm.
   ISBN-13: 978-1-4104-0784-9 (hardcover : alk. paper)
   ISBN-10: 1-4104-0784-5 (hardcover : alk. paper)
   1. Auschwitz (Concentration camp) — Fiction. 2. World War, 1939–1945 — Fiction. 3. Holocaust, Jewish (1939–1945) — Fiction. 4. Large type books. I. Hofmann, Michael, 1957 Aug. 25– II. Title.
   PT2647.A75S513 2008b
   833'.914—dc22   2008011485

Published in 2008 by arrangement with W. W. Norton and Company, Inc.

In memory of my daughter
KITTY

CONTENTS

7

The seventh well — water of honesty,
Cleansed of all impurities;
Proof against defilement;
Of stainless transparency;
Prepared for future peoples,
That they may emerge from the
darkness,
With clear eyes and free hearts.
— *from "The Seven Garlanded Wells"*
by Rabbi Loew of Prague, died 1609

WALES

ENGLAND

NETHERLANDS

BELGIUM

BRITTANY

Le Havre

Buchenw.
Crawinkel/Ohrdruf
● Salzburg
LUXEMBOURG

Nantes

Paris ● Drancy

Saint-Nazaire

Meslay-du-Maine

Stade de Colombes

FRANCE

Angouleme

Vichy

Pontarlier

Perigueux
(Dordogne)

Lyon

Geneva

SWITZERLAND

Naude

Annecy

Montelimar

Gurs

Toulouse

Lager Agde

Montpellier

Avignon

Le Vernet

Lager Sete

Les Milles

SPAIN

Saint-Cyprien

Marseille

Rivesaltes

Argeles-sur-mer

Perpignan

CORSICA

ITA

FRED WANDER,
EUROPE 1938–1945

EAST
PRUSSIA

Sobibór

RUSSIA

GROSS-ROSEN

BEUTHEN (BYTOM)

GERMANY

rschberg

Auschwitz

▲
Riesengebirge
Mountains

Vienna

HUNGARY

RUMANIA

YUGOSLAVIA

BULGARIA

CHRONOLOGY
FRED WANDER, MAY 1938–JUNE 1945

The Seventh Well is a work of fiction inspired by many of the experiences of Fred Wander during the following years.

EMIGRATION AFTER THE INVASION OF THE NAZIS IN AUSTRIA (MAY 1938–SEPTEMBER 1939)

1938

Beginning of May	Fred Wander flees Vienna via Nauders in Tirol at the border of Switzerland, Austria, and Italy.
Mid-May	Continues through Annecy to Lyon in southern France.

End of May	Arrives in Paris, where he is registered with the authorities until September 1939.

1939

First half of the year	Wander keeps moving; he travels from Paris to Avignon, Montpellier, Toulouse, Nantes, Saint-Nazaire, and Le Havre.
August/September	Returns to Paris, where he lives on rue Saint-André des Arts.

INTERNMENT IN SEPTEMBER 1939, THE BEGINNING OF THE WAR

September	Detained at Stade de Colombes, a temporary camp six miles west of Paris.

14

September 19	Transferred to a permanent internment camp in Meslay-du-Maine through January 26, 1940.

1940

January 26 through early June	Whereabouts unknown.
Beginning of June	Appears in camps at Angouleme, Perigueux (Dordogne), and Toulouse. Makes multiple escapes.
Summer	Captured south of Tarbes at the foot of Pic du Midi-de-Bigorre. Wander is released, makes his way back to Toulouse.
Autumn	Harvests grapes in Toulouse. Flees in the direction of Marseille but is captured en route.

November	Brought to Camp Saint-Antoine (Albi-Tarn).
1941–1942	
	Wander flees and is recaptured several times, imprisoned in several work camps in southern France — Gurs, Le Vernet, Les Milles, Saint-Cyprien, Argeles-sur-mer, and Lager Agde.
June through September 1941	Appears in camps at Montpellier, Lager Sete, and Abbaye de Valmagne.
Until summer 1942	Flight to Marseille. He is recaptured and returned to camp.

August	Attempts to escape once more, heads to Switzerland. He is captured by the Vichy police, then deported to another holding camp.
End of August / beginning of September	Arrives at the internment camp in Rivesaltes.
September 12–16	Held briefly in Drancy.
September 16	Deported from Drancy to Auschwitz, concentration camp in Poland.

CONCENTRATION CAMPS, FROM SEPTEMBER 1942 THROUGH APRIL 1945

September 1942 through May 1943	Wander is forced to work at several satellite camps of Auschwitz near Beuthen.

1943

May	Death march to Gross-Rosen. Transported to several satellite camps of Gross-Rosen, forced to perform slave labor breaking rocks and building streets for IG Farben and its Buna (rubber) factory. At the time, IG Farben was one of the biggest German chemical companies. It was dissolved after the war due to its strong Nazi ties.
Until winter 1944/1945	Gross-Rosen. Death march to Hirschberg and over the Riesengebirge ("Giant Mountains").

1945

January	Transferred to Buchenwald, a concentration camp in Germany.
February through March	Constructs underground shelters while imprisoned at Crawinkel/Ohrdruf, a satellite camp of Buchenwald near Arnstadt.
March	Death march back to Buchenwald.
April 11	Wander is officially liberated by the U.S. Army. His freedom is delayed, however, as he comes down with tuberculosis and spotted fever and must remain in the infirmary at the camp.

June	Return via Salzburg to Vienna in order to find his family. Wander discovers that all except his brother have been murdered in Auschwitz or Sobibór.

■ ■ ■ ■

1
HOW TO TELL A STORY

■ ■ ■ ■

In the beginning was a conversation. Three weeks after the conversation, Mendel died. I didn't know he was going to die, nor of course did Mendel himself. He was already very weak, but still intensely engaged with everything around him. Wherever we were, on the march, or in the timber yard unloading tree trunks, he would deluge us with expressions of bitter contempt, evocations of beauty, dark poetical prophesyings, his word-torrent, his pride. I remember the time when one of the guards emptied a bucket of water over him. (Out of tiredness and weakness, Mendel had fallen asleep on his feet when he was supposed to be stacking wood.) The jackboots all fell about laughing (it was freezing cold that day, they were all bundled up in sheepskins, had cheeks flushed with warmth and big meals). Meanwhile Mendel drew himself up to his full height, his wet gray hair smeared over his brow, and his eyes peered out sharply, not with hate or accusation, but with curiosity. What is driving this man, those eyes wanted to know.

Every other Sunday afternoon (we had just two rest days a month) Mendel would tell stories. Everyone collected in the mess hall. Jews from Warsaw, from Sosnowiec and Krakow, all fascinated by the word. Words had magical powers, they could conjure up an entire beautiful lost world — a richly laid Sabbath table, the winsome loveliness of a Jewish girl, the heady aroma of sweet Palestine wine and raisin cake. It could take just one word to make the men turn pale, make them think, cry, laugh; words lashed them, choked them, made them ache and sweat. And all the time the master of words, the magician, Mendel Teichmann, perhaps fifty years old, tall, gaunt, and burning with an inner flame, stood before them on a bench, talking and waving his arms.

When he took me aside that time to talk to me (they were celebrating Passover just then, hiding in the wash-house, but he, who would have been the high priest of their dreams, happened not to believe in God), we scurried past the barracks so as not to draw the guards' attention, the twenty or so

24

barracks in the Hirschberg camp in the Giant Mountains. Trembling, I blurted out that I would like to learn the art of the storyteller from him. I thought at first he had ignored or overheard my remark, but then he surprised me with a spate of words whose import I would only understand much later. But how am I to reproduce it — in comparison with the force and the splendor of his talk, my report is merely stammering.

"So you want to know how to tell a story? Well," Mendel said, "either you have it in you or you don't. Once, I think it was in Lodz or Warsaw, I had been among friends, telling stories on the Sabbath, and a whey-faced boy came up to me. 'Huh,' he said in embarrassment, the young whippersnapper, but with reproach in his eyes, 'it's one thing if a person's been around the way you have. But what have I got to tell stories about? I wouldn't mind being a writer like you, but I've had no experience!'

" 'I like it when people say that to me,' I answer, and I start asking the young man questions. How can such a thing be, I ask, and where did he live, because so far as I knew there wasn't anywhere in the world where you could hide from life. He lived in an old house, on an evil-smelling street on the edge of a town. He'd lived there from the day he was born, and it was all he knew. A house full of stupid, loathsome people. It could make you sick, the mere sight of them . . . He didn't say much more, my aspiring young man, but it was enough for me — I can see the house before me, I can smell it. I don't even need to go there to look at it.

"The second you walk in, a door opens, and a nosy old man peeps out at you. He's newly shaved, and there are traces of soap still on his cheeks. His braces are hanging off him, and while he finishes buttoning his patched shirt, you get a glimpse of his white scrawny body, the bones and sinews prominent the way they are in people who have worked all their lives. So he sticks his head out the door, and he asks me who I'm looking for, or if I'm lost. Because God knows how rarely a stranger happens by. I say the name of the young man, but the old man shakes his head, no, not known here. Then suddenly, as if he's just remembered, he changes his mind. Oh yes, the little devil upstairs, of course, I had the wrong name for him, his real name was Mottl Leiser but he was sure I meant him, I couldn't mean anyone else. Mottl terrorized the whole house, the house trembled at his approach.

The stranger — me — was surely sent by the welfare department, and better the welfare department than the military, because then it would be too late, if it wasn't too late already. A lad, grown up fatherless, his weak, sickly mother used to beat him until he started beating her back, he shouts, smashes tables and chairs and windows, robs, pilfers, can't keep his hands off the women, and what else can I tell you about him, says the old man, Mottl is a *ganef,* a crook, small as a dwarf, but strong and wicked as the night! He's crazy, I tell you. But who, I ask you, hasn't been driven crazy in this house?

"The old man talks and talks, everything spills out of him like a shower of sparks. And I don't even get as far as Mottl Leiser, but what does it matter, do I need anything more? Of course you notice from the sly and convoluted manner of the old man that he's looking for conversation, nothing more. He tries with all the means he has at his disposal to draw you into a debate, it's as if his life depends on it, that's how much it matters to him. A stranger, too! At long last someone he hasn't said everything to already, you know, who hasn't heard it all before. How often does he have the good fortune of seeing a fresh face? He's not long for this world anyway, the old man, his bones are all crocked. And now he's trapped you, he pulls you into his room, he's wheedled a cigarette out of you, one of your good imported brand, it's a long time since he's tasted anything so good, he shuffles excitedly back and forth, lowers his voice, and tells you everything: because if he knows anything about anything, then it's this house! After Mottl Leiser he starts talking about himself. How he's lived on his own for many years, all alone like a dog. Six children scattered to the winds, oy, what am I telling you, aren't lost children your business? And his wife dying a bitter death.

"And while he speaks, the door opens and closes, faces push into the crack, all consumed with curiosity. The house is alive with noise, it hunches its back like a cat, and it listens. The house is full of murder and mayhem. Its inhabitants all work for a living, and they take it out on each other. A hard lot that forces them for twenty or thirty years to get up at four in the morning to go out into the unforgiving world on the little suburban line that is forever about to break down because of carrying so many people. And in the evenings they come home from soot-blackened factories and damp cellars, come home to their evil-smelling street and their ramshackle old house. They feel nothing anymore, they are exhausted and shattered. How long can you live that way? Eventually they crack. Each in his own way. The men get drunk and beat up their wives. The wives fall pregnant, bury their infants, and before long there's another bun in the oven. And the children, the ones that survive, they grow up crippled inside. The house, they say, that damned house sucked the life out of us! You don't believe it, asks the old man, just look at old Mrozek, a devout Christian, worked all his life, completely dried up from work, like an old stick, four children they had, two died, the youngest turns to crime. Everything they put themselves through on his account! And now? The boy goes out on the highway and commits a robbery. He almost smashes a man's skull. Just to get hold of some money. Not like his honest father, putting aside one zloty after another, over many decades, no, it has to be right away . . . And now he's behind bars, maybe he'll be let out in seven years unless he kills someone else in prison. But wonders are possible as well. Take the daughter of old Kaminska, a common prostitute, a bad woman, how did she deserve a daughter like Nina? A lily, so beautiful, God help her, a pearl, a real pearl

29

of a daughter . . ."

And while Mendel talks in a soft and excited voice, a seeker, a *tsadek,* we've walked round the barracks I don't know how many times (I still dream of it today, the back and forth between barbed wire and watchtowers, back and forth, and when will the end come, when will we get out?), trying to avoid the suspicious glances of the guards, and once spending a quarter of an hour in the latrine.

In front of us on the perch are men puffing and groaning over their sore bellies, squatting in silence or cursing. There's a reek of chlorine, but we don't smell it, we're off somewhere else in our heads. And out we go again, casting a backward glance through the window of the wash-house. Still they're standing there praying, jerking their heads back and forth, striking their hollow chests with their hands. (They have their *taleysim* with them, and I wonder how they managed that, they were frisked four times, the jackboots took everything away from us, how did they manage to hold on to their *taleysim?*) And we walk on, and Mendel is silent. Then he stops in front of the exercise yard, and raises his arms as if in appeal, and breathes deeply and drops them again. The smell is from the cellulose factory. With its halls and chimneys, the cellulose factory looms blackly against the purplish Giant Mountains behind. Sprawled over the slope, it puffs out its yellow smoke, its sweetish toxic jaundiced fumes, into the sky. Inside, in the plant, where the smell is strongest, is where the special brigades, the chosen ones, the rich and privileged of the camp, work: it's warm in there! And we pariahs work outside in the lumberyard, where we are liable to freeze or be crushed by tree trunks. That's why the stench of the factory smells so sweet to our nostrils. It's the sweet smell of the upper class.

"What about the house then," I ask, confused, and to break the silence. "You saw all that in the house where that young man was living?"

Mendel looked at me in alarm. "I see you didn't understand anything. I talk and talk, and you understand nothing. I never was in the place where he lived. Is that so important, the house, the particular house . . . There are hidden strengths in people, but the people don't know it. They wither away, and become crippled, but still life is pressing within them. And since their pores are blocked and their eyes are blind, and they don't know what to do with all that strength, they break out. They break out of their

31

shells, their houses, they break the law, they break out and, yes, they lash out as well . . ."

As he was speaking we were standing by the camp gates, but well concealed so that the guards outside couldn't see us. It was a Sunday and it was raining. Scraps of clouds scurried across the sky. The guards had visitors, their girls. They were laughing and flirting, chatting away happily together. We knew the guards, young beardless men, pink faces bursting with health. German farmers' sons, sons of postmen, railwaymen, and plumbers. And they were murderers. Every one of them was a murderer. They didn't know it, because we were less than human, so they had been told. They had murdered with rifle butts, with bullets, with iron bars and shovels, even with their bare hands. And now they were standing there, flirting and chatting with the girls from the village. And Mendel saw this and he looked at them, and he tried with his sad inquiring eyes, tried to understand, tried to find a phrase, a fitting word that would account for each blow, each humiliation, and each laugh at our torments, each obscene joke at our dying.

It was on one of those days that we lost Yossl. A couple of weeks before, we had received some fresh recruits: forty Jewish boys from Hungary, aged between five and fifteen, and a single Polish boy with them. And Yossl found his brother from Sosnowiec among us! We sheltered the boys, and even so they died under our protective hands. In the very first days after their arrival, some of the children died, and it was true: what were they doing here with us? Then, when Yossl keeled over at his work in the lumberyard, and the sentries shovelled snow over him as a joke, and the little heap of snow stirred and a small hand emerged from it, and they went on chucking snow over him and laughing and smoking cigarettes, and when we dragged him back to the camp that evening, then Yossl was still not yet dead. He was frozen stiff and his face was as pale as marble, and they stood around him at night in the barracks, his brother and his cousins from the little town of Sosnowiec, and they talked to him, cajoled him and flattered him and screamed at him: "Yossl, listen, you must live, Yossl, don't go, your mother is waiting, your father is waiting, Yossl, stay with us, keep us company . . ." And they stroked him and kissed him and rubbed his body with cloths and with snow, they wrapped him in blankets, and they sat him up on the table like a doll, he didn't keel over, he was frozen stiff, but he wasn't yet dead. He was frozen, but deep within him there was still a little ember of life, and they stoked it with their affectionate words, with their prayers and their charms, crying and weeping the while: "Yossl, stay!"

The rest of us, dog-tired, lay on our pallets and listened. Between dreaming and waking, we listened to their lamentations. They had got Rabbi Shimon from the next-door barracks. Rabbi Shimon covered his face and head with his *tallith* and started to pray silently. But Mendel Teichmann took hold of Yossl and shook his head disapprovingly.

"What are you wailing about, why are you crying, are you trying to scare him away with your noise? You should be happy, children, be happy as long as he's alive! Yossl is living his life now, whether it be two hours more or twenty years, what difference does it make, in the scope of eternity? Don't cry, children, cheer him up, Yossl is looking at you!"

Then Pechmann was brought in. He was already asleep, but they yanked him off his pallet and gave him a piece of bread. The western Jew Pechmann, a Vienna boy, he could make music with five fingers on a board. How many times we had called Pechmann, and he beat out a rhythm with his fingers on the table, he was a dab hand at that, and we felt it through and through. With the other hand he would hold his nose and honk like a saxophone. Blues for five fingers on a board. Now he was playing for Yossl. And the rest of us were asleep already, and heard the playing and singing in our dark dreams.

In the morning, as we went to work, they put Yossl in the metal cupboard, all swaddled in blankets, the sweet marble doll, and we trudged out into the morning darkness. In the evening, when we came back, they took Yossl out of the cupboard, and listened to his chest and kissed his eyelids. Yossl Kossak with the marble face. His eyes were just barely open, but they could no longer move. He held his hands folded across his chest, his thin, fine-boned hands, white and shining like bone china. He wasn't dead, they swore he could still hear them. They were quite convinced he could hear them.

Rumors circulated about the Americans, that they were about to open a second front. But when would the second front reach us? The Jews prayed in the wash-barracks, and besought the Almighty, and the Christians joined in their prayer. The summer would come, the long warm days, sunshine and

35

the second front. Mendel Teichmann died shortly after Yossl. He died a senseless and undignified death, let me pass over it in silence. His poems are forgotten, his ashes are scattered over the woods and fields of Poland. Mendel Teichmann, who tried to teach me how to tell a story.

■ ■ ■ ■

2
WHAT KEEPS A MAN
ALIVE

■ ■ ■ ■

A man lugs rocks, lugs wood, cracks lice, fights over a potato, looks for a rusty nail by the roadside so that he can hang up his jacket on the wall at night, sews mittens out of a piece of canvas he has stolen, squeezes his sores, groans, wheezes, prays and weeps in the dark, learns to blow his nose downwind with one finger, wraps his sore feet in rags, roasts a potato after work and chews down his ration of bread. What keeps a man alive?

While he's lugging wood and cracking lice, his humiliated soul retreats into unknown depths. He views his fellow prisoners like a man fallen among wolves, only waiting for them to discover him and tear him to pieces. But inside him he is alive, he is astonished by the noble expression on the face of a dead man, or the beauty of a crystal of ice. He fills his nostrils with the smell of the woods, and he looks about him, looks for the vanished traces of beauty in his life. Suddenly he is looking for a friend with whom he can share these things, and when he has found him, he intoxicates himself with his past, spread out like an oil painting before his eyes. Something in him is driven to yell out: I am human! I have known respect! he wants to cry out. I was loved, I had a home, a wife and children, friends. I have performed kindnesses and not asked for reward. I have seen marvellous things, I know the smell of old cities. I could have done anything, achieved everything, and if I didn't do or achieve, then it was only because I didn't know, I couldn't sense . . . He wants to shout all that, he wants to dazzle, to boast, to talk himself breathless. He can't, he doesn't have the words, he doesn't have the art. But that's what keeps a man alive, the fact that the dream of his lost beautiful life, of freedom and purity of heart, is not yet at an end.

He begins to talk, haltingly, cautiously remonstrating with the other. It might be de Groot, say, who spoke: "You can tell me I lived like a fool, that I was a snob, a bloody stuck-up snob. All right, I tell you, you're right. But I was alive. Deeply alive . . ." He blows warm air into his hands, which are white and half frozen, then he smacks them against his thighs, and he runs back and forth so as not to freeze, the little tailor from Amsterdam. How does he do it, I ask myself, where does he get the strength, this little starved wizened fellow — when I see big strong men fall down every day.

The work is going slowly today, it is bitterly cold. The conveyor belt is empty, there is a mechanical fault in the sawing plant. No guards to be seen anywhere, they are all off sheltering somewhere. We can hear the Red Rooster crowing in the hall. He is shouting and yelling, as if he is pleased that everything has ground to a halt, so he can shout and lash out. Two or three comrades, laden with long planks, come past, listen to de Groot, and roll their eyes. They've heard it all seven times: the lovely Amsterdam afternoons, five o'clock at Kroon's café on the Rembrandtsplein, or Heck's or Huisman's in Kalverstraat. Rikje and himself. She was just as small and tough as him. They could eat and drink whatever they felt like. Delicious chocolate éclairs with cream, or a truffled veal chop in the grill of the Hotel Trianon. They didn't put on the weight. And they smoked like ship's chimneys, cigars, cigarillos, pipe, yes, his wife too. For her fortieth birthday, he bought her a meerschaum pipe on a weekend away

41

in London, at Heester's or Pleester's or whatever the name of the shop was. Then they strolled down the street full of antique shops, on the lookout for an agate ashtray or an old English etching. The worries those people had!

"In the evenings," de Groot continues unabashed, "we would take a constitutional down the length of the Kalverstraat as far as the Dam, then along Damrak to the Central Station, and back to Rembrandtsplein. We could never have enough of seeing the young people, the pretty girls, the young bucks, if you take my meaning. We would drink a cognac at Heck's, before going on to a little restaurant known to insiders, behind the Portuguese synagogue, where people dined on Russian-Jewish, Polish or Moorish specialities in hat and slippers, among humming samovars in candlelight. The curiosity, the plain silly curiosity with which we stuck our noses in everywhere! And the swarms of people in the narrow lanes beside the canals, in the little bars and artists' cafés. How they thronged together, and talked and talked! There's no other way of saying it. Life was beautiful."

They had mingled with a theatre crowd, he told us, with clairvoyants, émigré princes, nightclub owners, and famed assassins on their way to Paris. The talk they heard was royally entertaining; they were astonished by the mental acrobatics of petty adventurers seeking to raise money for some invention or piece of information or other. He and Rikje had no children, they didn't know what worries were.

"All right," said de Groot, "you'll call us blind. Very well, I say, you're right. No, we really didn't have a clue what was going on in the world. We didn't listen to the warnings of our friends: 'Pack your belongings,' they urged us, 'go to America!' We didn't believe the horrible news from Germany, we had always admired and respected the Germans. We thought it was exaggerated talk, as you do, perhaps from people who had something to gain. We were happy. Perhaps we didn't want to see or hear anything else."

"You thought only of yourself," said Chukran, who had come over and joined us. He didn't want to offend de Groot; he said it with a smile. Chukran always smiled, twisted his joker's face into a grimace so that, whatever he said, no one could be angry with him. But de Groot was angry now, or pretended he was.

"What do you mean, I thought only of myself!" he cried. "I gave alms all my life, I

43

must have fed half a dozen writers and artists. Everyone who needed money came to de Groot. What more should I have done?"

"You know what I mean," said Chukran, still smiling. "None of us did what we should have done."

We were stunned, we hadn't heard that sort of talk from him before. "There were people who took steps," said Chukran, "and they're, you know, still alive today."

"But what did they achieve?" asked de Groot. "Nothing!"

"Today we can't appreciate it," said Chukran, "but maybe tomorrow. What they have done or are doing as we speak — our children will see it."

The tailor made a contemptuous gesture and was about to go on. But then the Red Rooster came running up, shouting to us that we weren't to stand around, we had to work, throwing lengths of wood onto the conveyor belt, and sharpish, or he'd show us. The Red Rooster, a so-called ethnic German by the name of Kramer, seventy years old, with a face invariably purple with rage, with spindly limbs in continual hectic movement, twitching or lashing out with a hoarse cry, like the crowing of an old rooster — we laughed at him and were afraid of him, and were careful to look busy whenever he came running up. De Groot from Amsterdam handed me some wood from the great stack the night shift had unloaded. I passed it on to Chukran from Tours, Chukran handed it to Modche Rabinowicz from Krakow, who gave it to Feinberg from Paris, and Feinberg threw it on the conveyor belt, which had already transported whole forests to the chopping plant of the Phrixa cellulose factory in the Giant Mountains, where it was reduced to tiny shavings.

"A Jew can't come to money in Tours," said Chukran, the moment the Red Rooster had turned his back on us to dignify other inmates with his attention. Chukran wanted to get in ahead of de Groot, and tell his own story. "I tell you," said Chukran with a mocking smile, "a Turkish Jew, a *Terk,* who has ended up in Tours, he needs to pack his kitbag with sheets and towels, with silk scarves, aprons and cotton shirts, and try his luck in the weekly markets in the outlying villages. Upstanding Christian men and women live in Tours. People there give each other the time of day, and they ask after the children, and they act respectful, but nothing more. Not that I experienced anti-Semitism there, God forbid, but you have to keep your distance, those are the rules. At least that's what Miriam wanted."

Miriam, his wife, was the daughter of a Jewish baker in Paris, who had emigrated there from his native Poland. The sweet girl had been well brought up, playing the piano and speaking foreign languages. As well as Yiddish, Polish, and French, all of them so to speak her mother tongues, she could speak English and Italian. Chukran explained: "To begin with, she was dead against me. What's a common *Terk,* a peddler Jew, a travelling salesman, to a lady like Miriam? Well, I bided my time patiently. Her father died soon. Her mother carried on the business with three partners, Yids with no sense. Miriam was thinking in terms of a doctor, a gentleman with a degree. Bakers, traders, Jewish tailors and furriers from the street aren't good enough for her. God forbid, am I about to push myself forward? I always came as a friend, a *khaver,* and asked her how she was doing, helped the mother run the business, order the stock, keep the books, collect the debts. I bought wood because they had to extend the shop, I advised on dough-mixing equipment, modern ovens . . . The woman saw how a *Terk,* a coarse and uncultured market Jew, can be a good provider! Well, and Miriam grew accustomed to me. Three years I waited for her 'yes' to come. Then she

46

wanted to leave Paris. She was ashamed of me, because I wasn't refined or distinguished. Every day I drove from village to village in the truck. But then she gave me a son and a daughter, and another son, and Miriam forgot her *khaloymes,* her girlish dreams. But she remained a lady, a bourgeoise! In Tours, I could never go out unshaven, and only in a collar and tie. And not talk business with anyone . . ."

There was another mechanical breakdown in the hall. If we weren't loading the conveyor belt, we still weren't allowed to do nothing; we had to stack the lengths of wood in tidy piles. The Red Rooster had run to the chopping plant on his stick legs. And Chukran fell to pondering for a few moments. De Groot took advantage of the pause to pick up his own thread. Meanwhile, the lengths of wood were passed from hand to hand. Each time we kept hold of them for an instant longer to save strength and not stand there with empty hands, in case a guard unexpectedly showed up.

"Never worked a day longer than five hours," said the tailor. "Four suits a month, one a week, never more! You couldn't get rich on it, well I'll give you that, you're right. But you made yourself scarce, the product rose in value, my suits were like a

47

brand if you take my meaning. Well then, why should I work any harder, and put aside money in the bank? Who for? I'd be a fool. I had the best customers in the Netherlands, and some of them even had crests on the automobiles they drove up in!"

It took protection to get a suit tailored by de Groot. The Duke of Windsor had ordered evening dress from him, that's how far his fame had spread. A suit from de Groot of Amsterdam! Each production a master-piece, fitting a man's profile, expressing his particular quality, his character, his caste, his class. Understatement, dignity, elegance! "I could have employed fifteen assistants," said de Groot, "but then my label would have been finished. I would have become rich, an outfitter . . ."

Chukran laughed aloud, then his laugh turned into a cry of pain. The Red Rooster had snuck up on, and aimed a kick at, the Turk. He was practiced at finding a victim's testicles with the toe of his boot. As the unhappy man rolled around on the ground in pain, the Red Rooster proceeded to kick him in the belly and kidneys. The only thing that helped was to create a diversion; someone had to upset the stack of wood. Then, snorting with fury, the Red Rooster would turn on the new victim. Further tricks had to be employed to draw the devil on further and further down the conveyor belt, into the chopping plant. Those halls were warm, and we thought anyone working there would be well-fed and strong and better able to deal with that madman. For those of us outside, in the cold, in the lumberyard, it meant a couple of minutes of respite, a chance to swear and catch our breath and inhale the pure wood smell, as though the Red Rooster gave off poisonous fumes. You could go and piss behind a stack of logs or hunker down on a tree trunk for a minute, close your eyes and reflect, while a comrade stood watch.

Chukran was pale after his blow. His testicles were already swollen from previous kicks. Thick tears of rage and helplessness dribbled down his puffy clown's face. When he had got over the cramp, he got up, shook his head, and sent a stream of wild curses in the direction of his tormentor. Then he was silent, collecting himself. He stood upright, the strongest among us, a giant, while the rest of us were already Muselmen.[*]

Then he said calmly, in Yiddish: "Why

[*]Concentration-camp slang for a prisoner who is patently doomed.

49

does he beat Jews? What is an old man like that doing here anyway, why doesn't he stay home and drink coffee? What have they done to him? He doesn't know them. Perhaps he knows one who kept a store in his village. Perhaps he knows another one who was a doctor. They only knew the rich Jews. And when he hears 'They're not people, beat them!' he beats them. Because he's stupid. Maybe he felt sorry the first time he did it. But his fear of not obeying is greater than his compassion. If you are fearful and envious, then you will hate the Jews. After he threw the first blow he threw the second, because he knows what he's doing is wrong and he wants to silence that inner voice that says, 'Stop it, it's wrong.' And so he beats and beats. God help him die quickly. The shorter the life, the less the sin."

The silhouettes of two sentries loomed against the evening light. We stacked lengths of wood. Chukran, our best worker, tossed the wood so that it was a pleasure to behold; he wasn't saving any of his strength. The jackboots stomped off, satisfied. I looked at Chukran. You could be years with a prisoner and not know him. The common *Terk,* the peddler Jew, the joker and strong man, the wisecracker and wiseacre, the man of violence and barbarian (if it was a matter of fighting for his survival), had revealed yet another side of himself. The sun faded behind a bank of clouds. We waited impatiently for the end of the working day. Hot soup beckoned. Our pallets and our rest seemed to us all the happiness in the world. But after the end of work we faced the hourlong march back to camp, dragging ourselves along in our sodden clogs, and singing all the while, forever the same Polish songs. Those songs, the smoke from the huts spreading over the white fields, the sadness of the landscape, how beautiful it all was! The hanging heads of our comrades, almost asleep on their feet, immersed in reveries. Hunger and exhaustion had dulled them. But that dullness was a fertile ground for feverish inner pictures. To speak to a man on the march was to shatter the spell. To utter a clear sentence, analyze our situation, or even wring a poem from a dulled brain, to change the words of a song and turn them subtly into something rebellious, who could do such a thing? Never more than a handful of men in each army.

In the middle of our column we carried the sick and feeble back into camp, as we did every evening. This time, among others, it was Modche Rabinowicz. As we marched

51

out at dawn, Modche had sung:

Ot azoy, ot asoy,
Iz gekumen Reyzl's khosn,
Ot azoy, ot azoy . . .*

And then, in Yiddish, almost beside himself, "Children, when we're home again Mama will bless the candles, and Papa will kiss the *hallah* bread . . . We will remember today forever."

He sang and did a shuffling dance, a sudden burst of joy and exuberance spilled out of him. Then, when we got to our place of work, he collapsed and suddenly couldn't breathe, lashed out spastically with hands and feet. We hid him in a toolshed. We looked in on him during our short midday break and were shocked: he had rolled about on the sacks of chalk and was powdered white and ghostly, like a figure from a Japanese legend, a sculpture. When he caught sight of us, he started to cry in a stifled voice, "I'm dying, I'm dying, water, I'm dying . . ."

Someone brought him water, I remember, it was Jacques. And when Rabinowicz started yelling and kicking again it was

*Just like that, just like that,
Reyzl's bridegroom came . . .

52

Jacques who held him tight and said, "What are you shouting like that for, man, why are you making so much noise? You're not dying. We're not going to die, we're going to live. They're going to die . . ."

Rabinowicz was no longer in his right mind, he didn't understand what the Frenchman was saying to him. But we who witnessed it, we understood. In the evening, when we assembled, Rabinowicz was dead.

But now I must tell about Jacques: a Parisian laborer and resistance fighter. A bold character, lovable, cheeky, cheerful, and full of rage. There was a compelling logic about his life story. "When I was fifteen," he used to say, "all I cared about was girls and a hundred schemes for making money." But when he was seventeen, Jacques found himself on the boulevard in a workers' demonstration, and was baton-charged along with the others. The *flics* all but broke his skull; from then on, he attended every rally. When the Spanish Civil War began, Jacques set off for Madrid with the first wave of volunteers. He was wounded several times, and when it was all over he was interned in France. When the Germans occupied the south of France,

Jacques joined the Maquis.[*] His group of partisans were betrayed by a spy, five comrades were shot. It was pure chance that he avoided their fate.

Wherever Jacques went, he gave us lessons in the struggle. One Sunday they got prisoners to unload a wagon. Two strong men climbed onto it, to hand down the heavy slabs of concrete. The rest of us had to carry them to the construction site. Haase, the Kapo,[†] continually urged us to make haste; the guard was new, it was his first time in a camp. We noticed the edginess in his look. A new man was always dangerous. What would he do? The Kapos tried to test him by flattering him and driving us on. We were afraid of the new man, and he was afraid of us, afraid of getting entangled in an unfamiliar situation.

With poorly concealed curiosity he watched us at work. One of the prisoners was too feeble to carry the heavy concrete

*The French Resistance to Nazi occupation, derived from the name for the scrubland of Corsica and southeast France, where some of its early members operated.

†A Kapo (from the Italian *capo*, "head") was the prisoner in charge of a labor brigade. Later used to describe all prisoners given any authority.

54

slabs, so we gave him a wooden pole or a broken-off fragment of concrete instead. Slowly and menacingly the guard approached. Still slightly uncertain, he eyed the unhappy individual. He grabbed the wooden pole from him and pointed to a piece of concrete tubing at least a hundred pounds in weight.

"There, pick that up, you Jewish pig, or else you'll catch it."

The prisoner tried to pick up the tubing, but he couldn't move it.

"Pick it up!" yelled the jackboot, his voice trembling with awkwardness and rage.

The prisoner, a Jewish schoolmaster from Holland, was too weak to stand. He squatted on the ground, with his head hanging in despair. "Pick it up!" screamed the SS man again and again, casting uncertain looks about him. He realized how futile it was, but he couldn't go back. His hand moved to his holster . . .

Then Jacques walked quickly up to the man squatting on the ground, barged him contemptuously aside, and called out, "Fool! No marrow in your bones." We all knew whom he really meant. "Look here, Muselman," he said, "this is the way it's done!"

He shouldered the tubing and carried it

off. The sick man slunk along behind him, while the jackboot stared after them, speechless. Then he grinned foolishly, and stalked off in relief.

Jacques always knew exactly what to do. On the way to work, we heard him singing French and Spanish revolutionary songs, whose magic made us strong and angry. The guard probably sensed the effect on us, but he couldn't understand the words.

"Hey, you bastard!" the guard shouts. "What's that filth you're singing?"

"Filth," the singer replied brazenly, "that's Spanish filth, you sons of bitches!" And added a long and incomprehensible curse. There was a diabolical grin on his face.

The guard, to mask his defeat, ran up and waved his rifle butt at the column. "Wake up, you shitbags, march! I'll show you!"

But Jacques too fell ill and had fits of weakness. Then he would talk little and drag himself along at the end of his strength. Sometimes when we had the sense that he was about to keel over, we were wrong, and he didn't. We heard him emit gruff sounds with every groan and sigh. "Taras, *je viens, tu verras, ne t'en fais pas* . . ." I'm coming back, you'll see, don't worry, I'll be back. Then — Reval — you'll be sorry about Serge, Antonopolo, Maurice . . . He listed

56

the names, even at night in his sleep we heard him listing the names without a mistake: the name of the traitor and those of the victims. Like a prayer.

Jacques saved his strength, never worked without using his sharp eyes to see how much work needed to be done, for this Kapo, for that guard, so as not to draw attention to himself for zeal or idleness. Like me and Chukran and a few others, he sewed caps and mittens from scraps of found or stolen cloth, in the evenings, when most of the men were already asleep. It took effort not to let yourself sink into sleep, but instead to keep your eyes open and make something that the Kapos and the *Prominenten*[*] in the camp would buy, for soup or bread. Jacques kept himself clean, didn't eat grass or trash, kept an eye on his small wounds. It was more than an ordinary vengefulness that made him struggle for each and every breath.

"I don't hate him," Jacques answered once, when I asked him. "Why should I hate him, a cockroach you stamp on . . . But five

[*]Collective term for inmates in positions of authority or who worked in kitchens, laundry, or artisanal workshops; they were often hated as much as the SS.

men on his conscience, you understand . . . I could have prevented it, if I'd been more suspicious. I knew he was weak! And now he's waiting for me. He's afraid of me, he can hardly bear to wait for me. He knows I'm coming for him. He's yelling for me . . ."

His inflamed eyes glittered as he spoke. A vast tiredness and a powerful will were struggling within him. Chukran lived because he wanted to live, Jacques because he had to kill. Mendel Teichmann lived with his eyes, the eyes of the *tsadek,* the wise man, who saw everything. The ones who survived were the fulfilled ones, who wanted to drain their lives to the very last drop — even if it was a cup of poison. The dream wasn't yet at an end.

■ ■ ■ ■

3
BREAD

■ ■ ■ ■

To eat bread, all you need is a little slab of fresh wood. You can find wood like that pretty much anywhere. Wood stands for forest, clearing, underbrush. It signifies house, shelter, comfort. All that's lost. Put it on the ground, on a pallet, on your knee, and you have a clean table. It signals to you that you're at home, where you live. And now the bread: divide it up into three thick slices, break the slices into cubes. Chew each cube long and thoroughly. Taste the grain in it, the rain, the storm. Let the taste of the sun dissolve on your tongue.

Bread is life. He who steals bread from another man steals his life. Kemal the Turk stole bread. Who denounced him? Once, as we were returning to the barracks from work, there's someone hanging suspended. They've tied his feet to the roof beam. Manasse Rubinstein, our youngest Kapo, is standing behind him, swinging the whip.

The criminal makes no sound — is he unconscious? Manasse Rubinstein wears rings on his white fingers, he wears boots, the emblem of the ruling class, and a fantasy uniform sewn for him by Jewish tailors. Is it about the bread? What is the charge against Kemal? Do they, the Kapos, not steal our bread on a daily basis? A lock of Manasse Rubinstein's black hair has slipped down over his eyes as a result of his exertions. Manasse is a handsome man. The angel with the whip. And he metes out the punishment — whatever punishment he is called upon to mete out — coolly, dispassionately. Afterward he washes his hands and lights a cigarette.

Most of the prisoners eat their bread right away. They tear it apart with their hands and gulp down the pieces with the greed of mortal exhaustion. Also, that way no one can steal it from them. There is a loaf of bread between six men, sometimes eight — on rare, good days, one between four! And what governs that? A few scholiasts claim to be able to tell the state of the fronts from the size of the bread allocation. When the allocation is bigger, that means the Allies are advancing and the Nazis are being beaten back, and dreading the rage of the world. Others argue the very opposite.

So the bread comes, the six men crawl into a corner, and go about the sacred business of dividing it up. There are various methods. For example, the drawing of lots. The loaf is quickly hacked into six unequal pieces and lots are drawn for the pieces with numbers on a scrap of paper. It's the same odds for everyone, no one can complain. Whoever has drawn the biggest piece tries to mask his delight, so as not to offend his comrades. He picks it up quickly and disappears under his blanket with it. Whoever has drawn the smallest also goes to bed, but because only sleep can comfort him. It's when you wake up that hunger, cold, and all the Biblical plagues of the livelong day assail you. The normal way of dividing bread is like this: a horizontal piece of wood suspended on a piece of string, two cones on the ends, these are pushed into the bread, and the pieces are elaborately weighed until all the rations are identical. This method has the advantage of taking a long time, which means the bread is still being weighed while others have already eaten theirs. As the bread crumbles in the course of being divided and weighed, everyone holds their caps underneath it to catch the crumbs. Then I still have to mention the masochists, the members of a secret bread cult. They torment themselves with an illusion. They put their ration into a bag they carry with them at all times. The bread, existing outside of their bodies instead of inside, might sustain their imaginations, but it robs them of their strength. They die faster than the others. In the course of working, who knows when, usually unseen by the others, they pull out tiny scraps — their elixir — from their bags, and eat them. Idiots. And then there are the men like Pechmann and others who turn a crust of bread into a seven-course meal, who sit down, produce their carefully treasured piece of board, and feast. Mendel Teichmann laughs at them. Mendel Teichmann the lion tears the bread in pieces and stuffs it in his mouth, at least once a day. As for those other people — ridiculous! That's what squirrels do, rodents, ruminants. Lambs nibble.

A year on, I see him, too, Mendel Teichmann, the *tsadek,* the magician with words, eat up his bread ration with board and knife. People everywhere change their minds, why not here? As Mendel Teichmann feels his strength ebb away, he, once the lion, discovers the small joys of the lamb. Bread. Taste the grain in it, the rain, the storm. Let the taste of the sun dissolve on your tongue.

■ ■ ■ ■

4
A SENSE OF PARADISE

■ ■ ■ ■

For four days the battle had been raging. At night we could see the fire in the eastern sky. The prisoners listened to the sounds with lips pressed together, as if it was the coming of the Messiah. The Red Army had reached Auschwitz, we heard. And then uncertainty and silence and the indifferently falling snow that covered everything. One day, carts and wagons stood outside the camp. Ladder wagons, old carriages, hay carts, even a couple of bright red fire wagons from the days when the fire brigade used horse-drawn appliances. There were no horses.

Rabbi Shimon shook his head. "Surely they won't expect us to . . ." But we pulled the wagons. A thousand prisoners. We pulled them up the snowy mountains as if we had never done anything else. The ice cracked under the wheels. SS Oberscharführer Wenzel, a handsome man, had got hold of a horse from somewhere, and he galloped back and forth, commanding our caravan. What a sight, that strong beast, wound up like a steel spring, picking its way uncertainly over the ice, with taut neck and blood-veined eyes.

Every wagon was being pulled by twenty or thirty groaning Jews. Breath froze in tiny crystals. A few sang, others cried, swore, prayed — no one paid them any attention in the general noise. Lubitsch declaimed French poetry. He pulled on a rope, set one foot in front of the other on the icebound earth, and recited Baudelaire. Rabbi Shimon suddenly came down with cramps. They put him behind a cart to help prop him up. Because anyone who couldn't go on was given a bullet. Feinberg the tailor got his bullet soon, and the little man from Budiach. The Giant Mountains rang with gunshots, the sky was mild and blue. The first dead lay by the roadside, but the march over the mountains had only just begun. On this road, where once Polish armies had ridden against the Turks, there were now Jewish tailors, grocers, and doctors, lying like dummies in strange contortions, only a moment ago they had been moving.

From a farm across the street, a little girl watched the spectacle. The door was open behind her, and swathes of steam came wafting out. Half hidden behind a tree, the girl watched the long column. She had her sleeves rolled up, her healthy red arms were steaming, the trough full of laundry was steaming at her feet. For an instant I was overcome by memories of the various smells of soap and clean shirts, bread and onions and barley coffee. It was good to know they still existed somewhere.

O grandest of the angels, and most wise,
O fallen God, fate-driven from the skies,
Satan, at last take pity on our pain.

O first of exiles who endurest wrong,
Yet growest, in thy hatred, still more
    strong,
Satan, at last take pity on our pain.[*]

Lubitsch declaimed the poem with eyes shut, as though in fever. Perhaps he did have a fever. Rabbi Shimon allowed his head to droop, we knew we wouldn't be able to save him. His nephew, Kalischer, the tiny dwarf Moische Kalischer with the big head that had no clarity in it, who had told me everything while we were working in the

*Baudelaire, "itanies de Satan," trans. James Elroy Flecker.

71

lumberyard, all about their beloved little town of Sosnowiec where they had lived, about his mother and seven brothers, and their miserly uncle — now he pressed himself against his uncle, because he was the only one left, while all the others were rotting in the ground. And Moische Kalischer cried. He too had cramps. Many had sudden cramps. All who had eaten potatoes that morning, fighting over them just as we were setting out, hot potatoes boiled in stinking water, they all now came down with cramps. And Kalischer stepped aside to void his bowels. That's where he got his bullet. The shot felled him like a blow from a club. Meanwhile, the world still contained little girls with pink cheeks and steaming hands, who washed clothes and knew nothing about anything, and who hid at the sight of us. It still contained rooms with wood-paneled walls in old farmhouses, where the good smell of fresh bread, onions, and barley coffee had taken refuge.

Race of Abel, eat, sleep and feed,
God is pleased;
grovel in the dirt and die,
Race of Cain.
Race of Abel, your sacrifice
flatters the nostrils of the Seraphim;

Race of Cain, is your punishment
never to know an end?
Race of Abel, your fields prosper,
your cattle grow fat;
Race of Cain, your belly clamors
like a famished dog.[*]

I knew the lines. For years I had listened
to Lubitsch declaiming them. He said he
knew seven hundred lines of poetry by
heart. Lubitsch came from an old Jewish
patrician family that owned several sugar
factories and large estates in Slovakia. He
could speak French better than any other
language, and that was before he had emigrated to France. Before long, he had found
a very good job there. There was no better
qualification for a job in Paris, he had told
us, than a mastery of French. Lubitsch was
a pederast, but who cared about that. He
accepted the greatest sufferings and tribula-
tions with a stoicism that no one could
understand. His world was poetry and
higher mathematics. He rarely met with
anyone he could talk with on equal terms,
so on free days he would look for a piece of
paper and fill it with rows of figures and
mysterious formulae. His strength was fad-

[*]Baudelaire, "Abel et Cain," trans. Richard Howard.

ing, his face and hands were disfigured by swellings. But he still refused to acknowledge the evil in the world.

There was a sharp turn in the road. Several carts had come to grief there, crashing against old trees below. Crates and sacks lay scattered about, some had come open and spilled their contents. We could see silver Sabbath candelabra, copper kettles, samovars, furs, piles of damask linen, even a spinet. The jackboots yelled at the prisoners to gather up the boxes and sacks. But all the carts were already overloaded, and every jackboot was looking after his own booty. There they were now with their crates and their sacks, the robbers, biting their lips. There were dead bodies among the ruined carts as well. Thin streams of purple colored the snow.

The paper cement sack I wore against my skin creaked with every step. I had turned up the collar of my striped jacket and pressed my cheek against it. It was warm there. If Pechmann had still been alive, he would have gone flitting from man to man, whispering, "Keep going, children, not much longer. The Germans are frightened, believe me, I know. There are partisans waiting on the Czech side of the border . . ." Blinking nervously with his naive eyes,

74

which brightened at moments in fits of confused hope, he would have tried to encourage us and himself. Ever since we had known him, he had picked up on every rumor or report that promised any turn in our fate. Perhaps like all of us he could see the catastrophe looming, but he didn't want to see it. Till the very last moment, he was waiting for a miracle. Even in death he had a smile on his thin blue lips and a childish expression of surprise, as if he didn't quite believe it.

But Pechmann was no longer with us. Nor was Chukran, the strongest of us, the Turkish-Jewish trader from Tours in France. I was lying at the time in the sick-barracks, because I was spitting blood. Almost all my comrades in the sick-barracks were spitting blood. That morning, Chukran was still joking in his familiar way, making us laugh with his grimaces — not without its dangers if you were spitting blood. One of us choked to death from a hemorrhage incurred from laughing. That night, Chukran's best friend Lemberger had died. We had all been waiting for it to happen. Lemberger had stopped eating several days previously; his salivary glands had failed, he was no longer able to swallow. But Chukran was still eating, and no one thought he could die.

Well, early in the morning, the prisoners' doctor and Karel, the nurse, were looking at the dead man. Chukran pulled his broad joker's face. "You'll see, doctor, it's my turn next!" The doctor and Karel grinned and shook their heads. Toward noon, Chukran got quieter and quieter. As it grew dark outside, he lay down flat on his back, pulled a leather wallet out of his tattered shirt (none of us still had anything like a wallet — how had he managed to pull that off?), took out a photo of his wife and four children as well as a couple of letters and mementos, looked at them calmly, put them back in the wallet, handed it to his neighbor, Jacques, who was convinced he would see Paris again when it was all over, and said, "Send this to my wife." And then his face turned black.

The road wound its way among precipitous drops, through ancient forests smothered in snow. Clinging onto the carts were men who no longer had any sensation in their feet, and were hoping merely to extend their lives by an hour or so. But they kept dropping to their knees behind the carts. The jackboots would grab them like so many sacks of potatoes and drag them to the roadside. A bang and an echo and nothing else, not even a scream. The sun sank in thick mist, mist tinted pink, then red, orange, and blue. More mountains loomed in front of us. A Jew next to me by the axle, a man I didn't know, large, bony, and stooped, his face extinguished, kept murmuring with every breath, "How much longer? How much longer? How much longer?" He kept his eyes shut, his hands, which were ripped and bloody from the axle, kept pulling the wagon, we all were pulling the wagon, the wagon was our life, the wagon was a game, whoever succeeded in getting it across the mountains had won.

Then it got dark, and the banging from the rifles stopped. Now they just pushed the victims over the edge, and left them to die of cold. We spent the night in an erstwhile sawmill. Suddenly, miraculously, the old building loomed out of the fog. We collapsed onto mounds of fragrant sawdust, as into a lovely feather bed. Outside the open window casements, bullets hissed by to warn us. The men screamed in their sleep, groaned with twisted mouths. A couple of dozen men failed to get up in the morning. The groans had been their last. Their sleep, their deep sleep, had dragged them down. We couldn't help them; we envied them.

During the descent on the Czech side, the

wagons began to slide. Dragging them uphill had been torture, but downhill was infernal. Not until four or five wagons had gone over the side did we learn how to brake them. We looked out thick branches from the side of the road. Whoever was still with us might have a chance. In front of us lay the valley, the column of vehicles made its way downhill with a deafening din. The soldiers yelled, swung their rifle butts at the heads of the prisoners if progress was too fast and a cart threatened to go over the edge. Their faces were purple with rage. Others, who had already seen their vehicles go, walked on empty-handed and no longer yelling. Silently they trudged along behind us, sensing illumination.

"Get back, away from the axle!" yelled one of the men who still had some strength into the ear of a weakling. "Hold on, Litvak, hold tight, the road's going to get steeper!"

Litvak's name was Sasha. The fact that the eastern Jews in the camp called him Litvak was a kind of acknowledgment of his Lithuanian origins. But he came from Brussels, and who he really was, and what was going on within him, only I could guess. I knew him from the transport, and from the platform at Birkenau. The doors had been opened, and the SS men yelled out, "The men out! All the men out!" There was wild confusion in the car, as women and children clung tearfully to their men. A few half-drunk jackboots broke it up with swinging fists and revolver butts. "All the men out!" Sasha gently loosened the hands of his beautiful wife from his neck; the children — adorable little fair-haired angels — he firmly and tenderly prised away from his legs. It had to be. Outside, one of the Germans had already slaughtered a child, and was laughing with hard eyes. I was down on the platform with the other unmarried men, looking up. It seemed to me I had never seen such a beautiful woman. Then Sasha was standing beside me, stepping up to the martial sound of a tango. The music of the prisoners' orchestra drowned out the cries of the children. Slowly the train rolled on, in the direction of some tall chimneystacks. Sasha watched it go. He didn't know what would happen there. We all didn't know, though we feared the worst. And now, years later, there he was staggering behind a cart, almost in his death agony. He didn't complain, he had never talked that much anyway, his eyes were directed within. I knew what they saw. Only I, who had watched before, knew.

In the evening hours, we saw the town

below us. Lily-white was the sky above, lights dotted about the slopes like occasional stars. The outskirts of Reichenberg. Snow-flakes began to fall, and muffled the noise. Men stood on the road like statues, not moving. I looked back at Sasha. But Sasha was no longer there.

■ ■ ■ ■

5
THE SEVENTH WELL

■ ■ ■ ■

The men no longer talk. Almost a week ago, in the Giant Mountains, when there was still food, a loaf of bread each and a can of meat, which we gulped down, and snow to moisten our lips, then you could still hear the croaky voices. Now their lips are dried. They talk only to themselves, in fever, in death agony. A few have come home, and are talking to their loved ones. They tell them stories, ask questions, soothe, and sweet-talk. When the train moves, the murmurs and death rattles are drowned out by the clattering of the wheels.

The train has been going for several days now. Sometimes it stops overnight on a siding near a bridge that civilians hurry across, casting nervous glances down at it. Open wagons stuffed full of men, bent double with cold. Only when they die do they stretch out in something resembling dignity. There lies Meir Bernstein, half rigid, but his eyes are open and staring intently. What does he see? Not Perez and Berkowicz at his feet, waiting for him. Because he has good shoes, the farmer Meir Bernstein, and a warm jacket of cellulose. What does a dead farmer want with shoes and a jacket? They bide their time.

Meir Bernstein looks past them. He sees his wife Chanah, and he sees the five children. They are sitting at the festive table, the mother has lit two candles, and covered her head with a white cloth. She closes her eyes to pray, then she *bentsches,* she blesses the candles, the fragrant honey-colored *hallah,** which they are about to break, blesses the heads of the children, and Meir Bernstein smiles in delight and he thinks, Chanah, he thinks, Chanele, I am back on the Sabbath, I knew I would be back with you by Passover. So he thinks. How do I know? Because he often used to talk about Sabbath at his house, the rich farmer Meir Bernstein. All eastern Jews like to talk about holidays. But they are not talking now. They are dreaming. No more true stories from a life that will never come back, no more Hasidic sophistries, *bonkes* and memories; this is a train in which there are nothing but

*Sabbath bread.

84

dreams, fever dreams, crazy dreams till a man's dying breath. A dream train rolling through the dark forests of Germany. Dreams from melancholy-bold Warsaw and sun-baked Provence, dreams from Vienna and Paris, and from the black coal pits of Charleroi. I know the stories of the dead who lie on the outer platform of the wagons. I know the stories of Meir Bernstein, he told them many times. His lips are moving, he is whispering something. Perhaps a prayer in thanks? "Thank you, Almighty," he whispers into the cold air, "thank you for letting me see my Chanah and the children once more, thank you, *reboyne-sheloylem.*"

Then the train rumbles over a set of points, disturbs his dream. It brakes with a shrill squeal. It will come to another stop, in the middle of nowhere. The sentries will leap out onto the embankment and stretch their legs and laugh with gruff voices and call out to one another. The locomotive will whistle and demand to be allowed to pass, but it will have to stay there for a long time and puff and snort, like a captive giant. Just like yesterday, close by a German station, when suddenly Chaim Jitzchok swung himself over the side, little sixteen-year-old Chaim Jitzchok, and started running. Silly boy, why don't you think before you act?

First, it's all quiet, we hold our breath and listen, then there's banging and popping from all sides. They're playing with him, like a cat with a mouse, pretending to let him go. Chaim must have lost his mind, now he's offering them a pastime. Again, we hear the sadistic soldiers' voices, they're driving the victim to his death. Chaim Jitzchok is running across a boggy field, he creeps behind a spindly birch tree, which is immediately cut down by bullets, he runs on, the rope round his waist comes undone, his pants slip down; he falls in a puddle, the ice breaks with a ring like a bell. Thunderous laughter. The train slowly moves off, there is no more time, they give him a bullet in the neck. Silence.

Today too the locomotive snorts and puffs, it makes an almost human wail, the sentries stamp their feet on the sodden sleepers. Two or three prisoners reach over the boards to try and pull a bit of snow off some fir twigs. The jackboots yell, "Get down, you Jew pigs, or we'll shoot you!" And the men jump back. Never again will they feel moisture on their lips. They die silently. Only Meir Bernstein raises his head, angry and a little astonished. Perez and Berkowicz are waiting at his feet, they seem almost to be listening to his thoughts.

Those plebs always listened in a kind of numbness when Meir Bernstein told his stories — with the pride and condescension of a rich farmer who has fifty cows in his sheds, and who rules over vast acres. And Meir tells his stories with artful embellishments, almost like Mendel Teichmann and others who have been persecuted for centuries, and who have learned to live by the word.

"Hert mikh oys," Meir Bernstein likes to begin, *"vel ikh aykh dertseyln a mayse* . . . I want to tell you a story: It was on a Sabbath, and everyone knew that the Sabbath is a holy day, a *yontev,* in the house of Meir Bernstein. Now, Meir Bernstein was never one of those Jews who stuck to the letter of the laws of the Talmud. Devout, yes, but the spirit, not the letter! Because God lives in me and you and every shrub and tree, and is bigger than a letter, so I too am bigger than a letter. But Shabbes is Shabbes. No light is lit by my hand, horse and cart remain in their stable. Then on Friday evening a peasant comes by, a Christian. Not a bad man, but he's had a bit to drink, and he wants to prove to me I'm a *meshumed* and no Yid at all! 'Meir,' he says to me, 'Meir, get your horse and cart and come with me. The weir is closed, and it can

hardly hold the swollen stream, and if you don't open the gate, the meadow will be flooded.' I go out to fetch the farmhand. But the farmhand is sprawled out in the straw, drunk on schnapps. I put the horse to, and we ride out to the weir. Ignoble people gave schnapps to the farmhand, and shut off the weir. I open it with my own hands, the goy watches me, surprised I don't ask him to do it for me. Then as we're riding back through the village, he says, 'Come in and have a drink with me.' Well, he's deserved a drink, because he came to get me. The bar is full of peasants and the smell of schnapps. A few are shouting and banging on the table and singing rude songs. 'Well,' says the peasant, 'what did I tell you?' He points to me, and everyone laughs. They offer me plum brandy and *treyf*. I drink, but I don't touch the meat. One of the goyim says to me, 'If you've put the horse to, and ridden out on your cart on the Sabbath, then surely you can eat unclean meat as well?' They laugh and laugh and they mop their faces. I remain serious. 'The Sabbath — today? There must be some mistake, my friend. Tomorrow is the Sabbath. Whoever comes to Meir Bernstein to make a mug of him, he must be from yesterday. Get the landlord, young man, ask him what day it is, the Sabbath or no?' The landlord, to whom I lent a thousand zlotys, he doesn't want me to come and mortgage his tables and benches and his horses, and he looks at the peasants, and then he looks me in the eye. 'No,' he says, 'today is not the Sabbath, tomorrow, if God wills it, is the Sabbath.' The peasants laugh and shout. Outside, Gallach walks by, the Catholic priest. 'Call him, tell him what's happened, ask him what he says!' Gallach looks in their faces, which are wet and red, the eyes dimmed from booze. He shakes his head. 'If Meir Bernstein has laid hands on the horse's collar and turned the screw on the gate, then Meir is right, it can't be the Sabbath!' "

Perez and Berkowicz have given up, because another man next to Meir Bernstein, who also has shoes and a coat, has died faster, and now they share the inheritance and creep under the canvas. For evening is drawing in, milky white fogs are dotted about on the slopes and over the forest, a swarm of black crows flies up almost noiselessly, the air is damp. Someone has brought along a piece of canvas, the size of a blanket. They spread it out, and under it lie some twenty men, pressed together like herrings. Whoever lies under it can hardly breathe, but at least he's warm. On the first night I lay under it, but tonight I'm not lying under the canvas. All around sit the old and the feeble who don't go under the canvas because they would die there, and who don't lie down but remain seated because they know that the light goes out when you sleep, that you fly away without a sound, like the crows. And they want to stay alive. But why?

I could sleep, but tonight I'm not going under the canvas, because I've taken a decision to flee. I'm going to try it at night, not stupidly, like Chaim Jitzchok. Long after midnight, when the jackboots are asleep on their feet, slumped over the sides of the cars, not moving, that's the right time. The train puffs through the night. I wonder where we are now, there's no light, no little gleam of hope. I carefully go over the plan, my blood-starved brain needs hours to arrive at a clear thought: it must be dark, I say to myself, no snowy fields, only woods and bushes will give me cover. I hunker by the side of the car, freezing, my eyes falling shut. To sleep under the canvas and not be cold seems the greatest happiness in all the world. Why torment myself? To try to flee in this country may be certain death. But no more than staying here with the others, who one after another stretch out. What to do? The men are all dozing or asleep, not one is awake, they are not suffering. Condensation mixed with soot settles on their skin. One of the two sentries, at the front, in the corner of our wagon, is still smoking a cigarette, but he's almost falling asleep over it. I drill my nails into my palms to stay awake. The wooden planking of the cars is creaking and singing, the iron jangles, whines, and moans, it's a bitterly cold night. If I fall asleep, I'll freeze, if I make my break too soon, they'll pick me off with their rifles. I need to stay awake and be patient and endure my thoughts. Meir Bernstein will be dead by now. Perhaps he'll move his lips once more, an angel will fly past his eyes in death. God the Father, whom one may not see, is waving with a palm frond from behind a picket fence, and Meir Bernstein calls out to him, "I'm coming, old man, I'm coming," he calls, "wait just a moment longer, I'm coming. Because life is so sweet!"

"Don't sin," Meir had said to a Christian during the march over the Giant Mountains, who had wanted to make an end and run into the line of fire. "Don't sin. Everything else you may give away, but life itself is not yours to give. Only God may take it from you, and none save only Him."

And now it's time: the train is puffing its way up a hill, the sentries are slumped over the sides like sacks. I pull myself up, slowly, because each movement could wake them. And then I look over the side, see the countryside, flat and snowy, a great expanse of white . . . It's decided, the country doesn't want me. I slump back, I fall on the canvas, beneath which the sleeping bodies stir and kick, and someone curses me. That's the voice of Lederer from Charleroi, the coal miner, he seems to have strength left, the way he hacks at my back through the canvas with his knees and elbows. Or perhaps I'm suffocating him . . . In the morning they'll drag him to the front of the car, where the dead go. They'll put him with Meir Bernstein, and take his shoes off him.

He had come to our camp in the fall of 1942, Meir Bernstein, having lost everything, his fields and his animals, his wife and children and the last of the gold pieces that were sewn into his jacket, which was torn off him. For a long time he kept silent. Only later did he begin to speak. Through his own words, for the duration of two years, he lived his life over again, got everything back — to lose it again, piece by piece. First of all, his beloved daughter. She died on a sunny day, in the middle of summer. She was playing in front of the house when the hay wagon tipped over and crushed her. Meir didn't complain, didn't wail like Job, didn't argue with his god. All he said was, "Recha, my little Recha, she was happy and innocent."

Erich Pechmann, who could make music with his five fingers, interrupted Bernstein. "God takes the happy and the innocent to himself."

Meir Bernstein despised western Jews, and Pechmann was a western Jew; what was he doing blathering about God? "Quiet," Meir Bernstein hissed at him furiously, "don't talk about things you don't understand."

"But look," the other persisted naively, "she died happy, God spared her sufferings like ours . . ."

Meir Bernstein shook his head. "Recha should have lived. She would have accepted suffering with open hands. Living, living is everything, suffering is nothing!"

I remember another conversation, following a day off work, in the darkness of the barracks. Meir Bernstein and Mendel Teichmann had taken it in turn to tell stories, had gotten drunk on words, had evoked the scent that dwells in the narrow lanes on *yontev,* outside the houses of wealthy Jews, drawing the poor, who stand by the door waiting for presents. The aroma of roast veal and fishes, of onions and wine vinegar, raisin cake and oranges. The shining eyes of the little ones, singing and laughing, and the peals of girlish giggles. Then there was a break in the storytelling, and Meir Bernstein's voice suddenly cracked. "Sinner that I was, damned conceited sinner. Thinking I was rich and out of reach of misfortune, for all time. That my blood would triumph in my children and my children's children."

And out of the dark barracks, where the tired men were listening, the voice of Mendel Teichmann: "The curse on us is like the water of the seventh well. Do you remember the words of the great Rabbi Loew? 'The seventh well will wash away what you have collected, your golden candelabra, your house, your children. Naked you will be left, as from your mother's womb. And the honest water of the seventh well will cleanse you, and you will become transparent, like a well yourself, made ready for future generations, so that they will climb from the darkness, with a pure and a clear eye, and a light heart.'"

I did fall asleep after all, and I didn't freeze. When I awoke, the train had stopped. The dead lay piled up on the front platform of the car, as on a heathen altar, one on top of the other, and Meir Bernstein on top of all. He lay chill and stretched out, his bony face almost black, mouth and eyes shut.

On another track, not far from us, recruits for the front were being put on trains. They were very young, not much more than boys. Horses whinnied, the young soldiers bantered and laughed. What was it that had dulled their senses so that they were able to laugh? The morning sky was a bright, poisonous pink. The buildings on the slope were a muddle of shadows. People lived there, ate, drank, slept in beds. The men in front of me, both living and dead, ragged as tramps and gypsies — silent, frozen tramps — how miserable was their ignorant suffering.

Slowly the train moved off. The busy streets of the town seemed somehow stony, empty and dead. People stood around in them fascinated, unable to move. A railway-crossing attendant, a policeman, a man on a ladder cleaning streetlamps. He looked down in our direction, his shoulders hunched around his face, a twisted expression on his mouth, as though he were saying, "Peace to your ashes." Or else, "Go to hell!" It could be either; we weren't to know.

That morning Bertrand Lederer from Charleroi died and Abram Larbaud from Montpellier, Efraim Bunzel from Prague died and Samuel Wechsberg from Lodz, and others died in the cars on either side of ours, whose names we never learned. A religious man was praying next to me: *"Shma Yisra'el, Adonai Eloheinu Adonai ehad . . ."* Praised be your name, Eternal One, who has chosen us from among all the peoples . . . His eyes had a dull gleam like copper. There was no longer enough warmth in his body or moisture to make his breath cloud like that of those people in the streets. The train was picking up speed, it clattered over the points, it shook us about, causing the odd man to wake up with a groan. The sky became steel-blue and deep, and only scattered little pink clouds smiled down, like innocent children.

■ ■ ■ ■

6
KAREL

■ ■ ■ ■

His close-set little eyes, always looking strained, offended, surprised, a little dismayed, gave him a certain resemblance to a monkey. The only time he used his glasses was for reading and operating. Then, looking calm, concentrated, and merry, he cut open the boils of the sick. A long time ago, he had taken a couple of semesters of medicine, but then, as he said, he had hit the town. His parents, well-off carpet merchants in Lyons, had spoiled him. "I was a boy genius," he said self-mockingly, "a prodigy. Studying was no harder for me than eating cookies. I read a book a night. Passed all my exams with distinction. So smart, it could make you sick. What for would I be a doctor? With my brain, I could do anything that took my fancy."

His father, a little Russian Jew, was a martyr to hemorrhoids and a boggy prostate. He hoped his son would one day save him the expense of doctors' fees and heal him, whereas those leeches of specialists only made things worse. What was a sick Jew good for? A milch cow for the medical profession. But then his father died. His mother went to Tarnopil to stay with her sister, whom she hadn't seen in twenty years. All alone in Lyons, Karel (his real name was Charles, but here in the camp everyone called him Karel) gave up his studies, invited prostitutes into the apartment and a bunch of new friends he barely knew. They stole whatever wasn't nailed down, or else broke it.

"I always had high standards," Karel would quip. "First it was a book a night, now it was a different woman. I discovered women in a big way. I was as ugly as a pickled cucumber, but the little honeys of the rue Mercière went for me all the same. The red-light district in Lyons isn't very big, so before long I was a prince there. Well, I was throwing money out the window with both hands, as they say. God forbid that a Jew not be able to manage money! Ten Jewish misers couldn't extort as much as a single spendthrift can put other people's way. And do you believe I ever regretted it, you fool," he would ask anyone who happened to be listening. "What did you miserable flea-flickers ever do with your lives? Always crippled with worries and fears that there might be bad times ahead? And now?"

Anyone who took issue with him would get a dose of his sarcasm. He didn't spare even his patients. Mostly they were so shocked by what he said that they kept perfectly still and forgot their pains for a few minutes. Once, a Muselman came to him with a hand as puffed up as a swollen liver sausage. Karel told him to sit down and lay his hand flat on the table. The boil was flush on the wrist, he had to operate immediately. He got out the basin for the pus and the rusty scalpel. There were no anesthetics and nothing to cleanse a wound with, beyond a little potassium permanganate. Karel said calmly, "We'll soon kill that little porker for you." Then he turned angrily to the patients, who were groaning and raving and arguing on bunks round about. "Quiet!" shouted Karel, and added a long string of blasphemies. "Open the window, the stench here is foul enough!"

The new patient had beads of sweat on his brow. Karel sat down serenely opposite him, felt the swelling and, with his alarmed and offended expression, looked into his eyes.

"How old are you, *khaver?*"

"Twenty-one."

"Where are your parents?"

"Gassed."

"How do you know?"

"I was told."

"Any brothers or sisters?"

"A brother and a sister, both in the camp."

Karel prepared his instruments, then he said, "Perhaps they've already been shot or hanged. And you, you're afraid of a little cut with a knife. Keep still!"

The patient held out his hand, and Karel sliced open the swelling with a single cut. A second cut across, and the pus flowed into the bowl. The young man didn't move or make a sound. Now it was all over, it was Karel who had beads of sweat on his forehead. He laid a strip of paper bandaging over the wound. "Whew," he said, "you've got some nerve." For a moment, the patient saw the traces of extreme concentration and pain in Karel's features. But already he was turning to the next one.

Karel found the Jewish songs that were often sung on days off unbearable, because they were so often performed with tearful voices and heavy sighing. It was only the comic songs from the ghetto, which were in the minority and full of disguised bitterness, that he liked. He said, "Sentimentality is a Jewish disease which you have to shake off. The Germans are exterminating us, and they're sentimental as well."

All his activity, his inexhaustible energy, went into masking his feelings. He squirted poison like an adder. And yet he spent sixteen hours a day working with the sick. Fetched water, boiled shirts and cut them in strips, gave a dying man a mouthful of soup, settled differences over a piece of bread, ran through the barracks hunting for a man suspected of carrying typhus or prisoners who couldn't get up in the morning and were already half-frozen. The actual prisoners' physician and Karel's superior, Dr. Levin, a tall handsome man, already tired and resigned, or perhaps grown a little indifferent, was no longer astonished, no longer shook his head at Karel as he had done to begin with. "We don't have any medicines," he had used to say, "what are you running around for, making everyone *meshugge?* Let them die quietly." Now he let Karel get on with it. He was almost infected by the mania of his assistant. He no longer seemed to be so indifferent in the face of death, he listened with more patience to people's laments, no longer moaned when someone called him out at night.

On one occasion, they brought him Alek. The boy had fallen off some scaffolding, and lay there brokenly. The Kapo brought him in in a wheelbarrow. His limbs hung crookedly over the edge of the barrow. Alek remained alive for another half an hour. Dr. Levin and Karel fussed over him, cut his convict's clothing off his body, gently, carefully washed him, talked to him. Alek breathed heavily and unevenly, made incomprehensible gurgling sounds and kept his eyes stiffly open. We all knew his story: Alek was born in Tunis, had lived in Brazil, had moved with his mother to Paris and Grenoble when she lost her husband, had been to school on three continents, could speak five languages, had married at the age of twenty — and enjoyed the best days of his life in the camp of Rivesaltes at Perpignan, near the Spanish border, wrapped in a blanket with his Nadja. The prisoners lay on the ground in the barracks, or on straw and paper and blankets. Their blanket was their honeymoon suite. They lay there in a silent intimate embrace, respected by all. The honeymoon voyage was to Drancy, and then on to Auschwitz. There they were parted, and it was over.

Karel pleaded with him aloud: "*Khaver,* you know Nadja's on her way to you," he said, "don't worry, she's coming . . ."

"What are you doing, you idiot," cried a sick old man from his bunk. "Why are you lying? It's wicked to lie to a dying man!"

"Am I lying?" Karel retorted coolly. "What makes you so sure I'm not telling the truth?"

"But he can't hear you," wheezed the old man, "he can't hear you anymore!"

Karel spun round, with his astonished expression on his face. "Why are you shouting like that, and making a fuss? What business is it of yours?"

The old Jew tore at his hair. "You should talk to me, talk to us, he can't hear you."

"You know?"

"I know."

"Quite sure?"

The old man rolled his eyes. The others followed the quarrel, grinned, sniggered.

"What do you mean sure," asked the old man stubbornly. "Nothing's sure in this world."

"In other words, you don't know whether he can hear, or if he's already deaf," said Karel. "Well, I don't know either, and that's why I'm talking to him, so that he doesn't feel all alone, wherever he is now . . ."

Two hours later, another young Jewish boy fell off the same part of the scaffolding. He was dead on the spot. And the Kapo trundled him into the camp in the wheelbarrow too, which was white with plaster dust, spotted with red. We were stunned when we saw it. Was it coincidence? Murder? Someone whose hobby was throwing Jewish boys off the scaffold, and was able to indulge himself? We never knew. No one asked any questions.

We had sunrise and sunset in the camp too. Some days bleed dry like a discarded bunch of narcissi. And then there are glowing, sputtering evenings. Mornings when a sun comes up bloody as out of a battle. I remember one red Sunday morning. The sun hid behind veils of haze that glowed a milky red and then lilac, like the cheeks of our consumptive brothers. It was icy cold, steam clouds vomited out of the doors of the kitchen barracks. We envied the kitchen personnel, striding through the camp gates with their sleeves rolled up to show off their muscular arms, not freezing, back and forth between the kitchens and the supply room, the *Prominenten* of the camp. But there was greasy smoke also from that part of the barracks where the artisans lived, the camp cobbler, the tailor and others. They were frying a cat there, you could smell it a mile away.

I'm talking about a time when Pechmann was still alive, when Chukran was setting the comrades on fire as he did every other Sunday with skillful descriptions of delicious dishes, when Mendel Teichmann was sitting on the foot of his bunk, meditating aloud, and ten Galician Jews were saying *kaddish* in the washroom. The old actor Baer had just recently lost his mind. He was talking wild stuff, gesturing like on stage, and strutting about proudly but somehow brokenly. When one of his old friends spoke to him, he smiled a lofty tragic smile, swayed, didn't understand, and was obviously weakening by the minute. Karel was called. Karel addressed him: "*Khaver,* it's bitterly cold, what are you doing out of doors, have you lost something? You'll catch cold standing here. Go to bed, don't go to work today. If you take it into your head to go walk about, they'll come for you."

Baer seemed to be standing in the midst of a gathering of councillors and worthies, that's how puffed up he was. "Gentlemen," he said contemptuously, "when I was twenty-five years old, I played King Lear in the Arts Theater in Krakow, you can't expect me to make a fool of myself, and moreover . . ."

Karel could see it was no use talking. He gave a nod to one of the kitchen staff. The fellow picked up Baer in his arms like a big doll and carried him inside. Applause and laughter could be heard from the kitchen barracks. The kitchen boy, an eighteen-year-old giant from Kalisch, swaggering and unimpressed, grinned. Karel tried to wrap Baer in blankets. Baer struggled and wept like a child. He scolded softly to himself, but in powerful oaths. Philistines, without a clue who he was. He ended up crying himself to sleep. Schloime, his nephew, a dirty stupid young man, abjectly devoted to his uncle and terrified that he might die (because every day Baer got a liter of soup on the strength of his reputation, which was the highest accolade the camp elders had to give), and then where would he get a helper from? Ever since Baer had lost his mind he no longer touched his free soup, which he had previously shared with Schloime. Schloime tipped it greedily down his own gullet.

Men were pulled in every day to the wagons, at night and on Sundays too. Wheels had to roll for victory, we could read the writing on the side of the cars in white letters. There were always pipes to be unloaded, concrete parts, wooden beams, planks, and bricks. That morning too they had selected thirty men to do the unloading. The Kapos darted through the barracks and chose: dirty, lousy, and feeble men, but also strong men who didn't enjoy protection from any of the *Prominenten.* No one knew by what criteria the Kapos made their selections. For sure, they lit on people whose faces didn't fit. Anyone who had been selected once for Sunday duty lived in fear, did everything not to attract attention during the week, and tried for all they were worth to ingratiate themselves with the Kapos. But often it was all to no avail. Not to have a day off after fourteen sixteen-hour days was often the end.

When the Kapo got Altschul out of his bunk, he sobbed and acted weak and ill. He was weak and ill, and it wasn't hard for anyone to appear still weaker. And sometimes the Kapo would have mercy. But he needed to present thirty men within ten minutes at the guard post. If he spared one Muselman, that meant punishing another, whom he would have to take instead. In this way, the Kapos soon became immune to feelings. Altschul had to go. We watched the thirty men march off into a light blizzard, while we sat around and hunted lice in the barracks. Altschul's lanky form brought up the rear. The guard gave him a vicious kick that sent him sprawling in the dirt. He didn't get up again. The jackboots strolled up to him, and they would certainly have made him get up in a hurry. But instead his comrades grabbed him and pulled him away.

He was a little middle-class boy from Dortmund, a bloody western Jew. His parents had given him the Germanic name of Kuno. But nothing had helped, not the blue eyes, the straight blond hair, the tall Nordic form — a Jew was a Jew. He was a good-looking boy, all right, our Kuno Altschul, but not very smart. He failed to pick up the tricks and ruses, the cunning we needed to survive. At work, he quickly burned up his energy, instead of using his eyes and only applying himself when it was really necessary. In turn, he would draw attention to himself through being tired when it was essential to prove one's vigor. He didn't understand that. It caught up with him when he was unloading bricks, he was caught between the buffers as a wagon silently came up behind him. He screamed the entire way as they carried him back to the camp. Karel ran to the camp elder, begged him to ask for morphine from the

110

SS Oberscharführer Wenzel. The elder shook his head. "I know what Wenzel will say. 'What do you think this is, a sanatorium? There's a war on. Morphine is for soldiers, not for Jews.' That's what he'll say."

Karel ran back. Altschul was lying on the wooden table with a crushed pelvis, screaming. All the patients who could so much as crawl left the infirmary. The camp elder, Dr. Levin, and Karel stood by. They should have been able to knock the poor man unconscious, but not even that was possible. For the first time, Karel lost his nerve. In the cubbyhole he slept in with Dr. Levin, one could hear him cursing: "If anyone had come to me back in Lyons and said, 'You dirty Jewish bastard!' I'd have finished my studies, and my eyes would have been opened . . ." Then nothing was heard for a long time, just brief groans of despair. And then the voice of Levin: "All right, *khaver*, and if you'd finished studying, how would that have changed anything today?"

One morning, a couple of hundred prisoners were standing in the yard. Wenzel was reading from a piece of paper, the orderly was writing down names, and the Kapos were combing the barracks, looking for men. But they weren't looking for the sick

111

and the feeble, the Muselmen, as usual when there were offers of "rest and recreation" at Auschwitz (through the chimneys, as everyone knew who no longer believed in fairy tales). The two hundred were needed for a new factory somewhere near Gliwice, where — just think of it! — they would work indoors, in rooms. Everyone who was chosen was jubilant. I snuck out of the sick-barracks and stood in line among the chosen ones. But Wenzel and the elder walked down the lines, grabbed everyone by the scruff and gave them a shaking. The feeble ones sagged at the knees, and were rejected. I wept when I saw them leaving the camp, wept with rage. And Karel — at the very last moment, they got Karel too. He had pulled on a medical orderly's satchel and run along after the unit.

A couple of weeks later, we heard there was an outbreak of spotted typhus in the new camp. We didn't believe it, because they brought Karel back to us, along with some writer called Berger, a political prisoner, whom they still needed. Then Berger came down with spotted typhus too. He was delirious and was shut away in a separate section of the barracks, along with Karel, who was assigned to look after him. The door was nailed shut, and Karel was given what he needed through the window. We were told how in Gliwice they had nailed up the doors of the prisoners' barracks, yes, and the windows too, even though not everyone was infected, not by a long chalk. They were just left to starve. They didn't need any of them, seeing as there was no shortage of manpower from Gross-Rosen and Auschwitz.

One day the writer was dead. Karel remained quarantined for four more weeks. We saw him running back and forth in the room like a caged animal. No one else returned from the other camp. Karel was the only survivor. There was sadness and bitterness in our camp. A father had lost his two sons — and he had been so proud that they both had been taken! There were still cousins, brothers, friends. At night we could hear muffled songs of grief, groaning and complaining in the barracks.

"Did you know my Zikmund?" I heard a Jew asking the man in the next bunk to him. "No, you didn't know my Zikmund, because he was not himself when he came with me to the camp. Because he lost his mind when he saw them killing his mother. A heart like a glass bell, a light crack, and it doesn't ring anymore . . ."

It was dark in the barracks, the only light

through the window was from the search-lights mounted on the towers over the barbed wire. Another voice said, "Lord, our King, we call on you from the depths, take us to you!"

Most of the men were sleeping, groaning, snoring. "It cost him his mind," said the old Jew, still talking to his sleeping neighbor, "it cost my Zikmund's mind. And us? How much more will we have to see? Why don't you take away our sense as well, Lord, please, I beg you, take away the yoke and the knowledge from my brow!"

"Because the world is beautiful," I could hear Mendel Teichmann reciting in a soft tender voice, "and the dew wets your tired eyes, which never cease to be astonished at your beauty. O dawn, smile upon our night-mares . . ."

"But when I go back to Chelmno," a Galician Jew lisped in his fever, "what shall I say? How will I look, standing there all alone? The windows will no longer be lit up for Shabbes, with the candles and the children's eyes. When I get back to Chelmno . . ."

"No one will go back to Chelmno," snapped another Galician Jew. "Chelmno is no longer in this world!"

The day Karel came out of quarantine was

the day Pechmann died, as already related. Karel acted as though he had never been away. He immediately took charge of the infirmary, ran around, exhausted himself, fetched water, boiled shirts, God knows where he managed to get hold of them, cut them into strips and made bandaging. He sliced open boils — "just like Mamme dividing the fish on the Sabbath," one of his astonished patients remarked — he scolded, reviled, poured scorn on everything that moaned and wept in self-pity. With his hands that gave out strength, he helped a dying man by holding his head and dribbling water onto his chapped lips.

I had been visiting Pechmann (I was no longer lying in the sick-barracks). Pechmann was stretched out on his top bunk, barely moving anymore. His large eyes burned like coals, he could hardly speak. Someone owed him for his margarine ration. Jankele from the fifth barrack, who had been swapping with him for a week, margarine for bread, because Pechmann could no longer swallow, his salivary glands had failed, and he was surviving on soup and margarine. For two successive days Jankele had failed to bring him the margarine, even though he had already got Pechmann's bread. His daily ration of margarine, the size of a child's thumb. And I went to Karel and demanded that he call Jankele and extract the margarine ration from him. But Karel didn't even listen. I couldn't understand him, I lay in wait for him, forced him to listen to me. Then Karel shook his head, glanced across at Pechmann who was lying perfectly still on his bunk, only his eyes moving. Outside the door, Jankele was dealing, trading the margarine ration that he owed Pechmann to another invalid who couldn't swallow. "No," said Karel, "leave Jankele his margarine. Maybe he can use it."

I didn't understand. I hated Karel, I couldn't believe he was capable of such injustice, that he had given up on Pechmann. Just like that. And now, when, as we heard, the Americans were advancing and the Red Army all but had Germany in its grip. Then, when I went to visit Pechmann the next evening, he wasn't there. It was August 4, 1944. The Allies continued their advance.

But now back to the place I had got to: the beginning of 1945. We had crossed the Giant Mountains, and had the long journey on the open cattle cars behind us. The train was chugging up a long slope, through thick forests. Next to the tracks, a road wound in and out. "The road of blood," said one of the comrades in our car, he knew the place. There were long lines of prisoners marching, trucks were pushing their way through the crowds, also cars carrying officers who stared expressionlessly through the misted windows. SS sentries bellowed, from time to time shots were fired. The mountain seemed to ring with a vast industry. The name Buchenwald lodged in our bones like a fever. Of the sixty prisoners in our car, perhaps a dozen or so were still alive. They sat hunkered dully on the bare boards. The jackboots up on the running boards between the cars got ready for arrival, gave youthful shouts, called coarse words to other jackboots on the road, smoked or crammed the rest of their journey rations into their mouths.

Just as we reached the top, the sirens sounded. The sentries leaped off the cars and hid in the forest. The train went into a siding and stopped. Nothing more to be seen: no human being, no uniform. A small station building, various camouflaged barrack buildings. Where was the main camp? There on the slope, on the other side of the peak, surrounded by forest. Then we heard the all-clear. The jangle of the heavy iron bolts on the wagon doors. But not the usual guttural voices gruffing, "All right, all the men out!" Only the metal sliding of locks and bolts. When it came time for our car to be opened, a couple of pale faces peered in, before going on to the next one. Whatever was alive crawled to the opening and dropped down. The snow was too old to break anyone's fall properly, and some who had got that far remained lying on the ground where they were.

Everywhere lay the harvest, in and under the cars, on the tracks, on the roadside ahead. Only a few had the strength to stand up. When they did, they stood in wonder: women, with shopping baskets and push-chairs! A film gone insane. Instead of the main camp with bellowing SS men, instead of the craven, sadistic, noisy Kapos, always intent on promulgating fear and discipline wherever they were — this silence. An eerie small-town idyll. Women emerging from an air-raid shelter, hurrying back to their hearths, their pots and pans, carrying bread, milk bottles, apples, beer. Children, with knitted blue-and-white-striped caps. A sky overhead in forget-me-not blue and white clouds over the tops of the trees, delicate as Brussels lace. The women and children had to go right past our halted train. But they didn't look at the train, didn't see the curious figures tumbling out of the cars (was it a scene they were too familiar with?), crawling along the ground, twisting silently this way and that, trying to get to their feet. Then one young woman fainted. Someone caught hold of her pushchair to keep it from rolling down the hill. No one spoke. The young woman lay on the path. She had seen us. The only one.

And then we saw too: on the edge of the road where the wives and children of the SS men were going shopping were great stacks of railway sleepers, a long row of them, each stack built up of criss-cross layers, four and four and four, to a height of six feet. Only they were dead bodies.

There were women and children on the Ettersberg. Shops that sold meat, bread, and apples. There were houses with beds, carpets, and laid tables. There were radios, glass-fronted cabinets full of knick-knacks, and pictures on the walls. I looked at the train. What were these tumbling figures? Were they human? I saw Karel. He had slung on his medical orderly's bag. His close-set little eyes, which always looked straining, offended, surprised and a little dismayed — they had the coppery luster of

119

death. A smile was welded onto the shrunken face, mocking, a little embarrassed. He dragged himself from one man to the next, as if to ask, Can I help you? But he didn't ask, he no longer had the strength to get out a single sound. When we were marched through the camp gates I no longer saw him. All over the frozen ground were bodies lying, squatting, jerking. I saw other prisoners wearing thick mittens starting to collect up the bodies and stack them under the commands of a jackboot, like railway sleepers, carefully, layer upon layer crosswise, four and four and four.

■ ■ ■ ■

7
EZEKIEL — AND THE CITY

A city of a hundred thousand inhabitants. What city? Precinct of Paris? Or Warsaw? Of Brussels? A melting pot of two dozen different nationalities. By the end, the only way even SS officers dare to go in there is with drawn revolver. The Red Army washes over the camps. Auschwitz is liberated. Hundreds of cars loaded with human freight roll toward Buchenwald. Later, whole trains full of corpses will be found somewhere on the tracks outside Dachau and Terezin. The sons of Europe will be found in gullies and forests beside the principal marching routes. Mown down. Assembled on the exercise yard in Buchenwald are the sorry remnants from the camps to the east, evacuated before the arrival of the Red Army. They are led to the pen in front of the effects room. There they are stripped of their rags, deloused and shorn, and for the first time after the long journey given a piece of bread and a plate of soup.

"Give me my pants, murderer!"

"You'll get your pants, with pretty zebra stripes on them and all." Haase, the camp elder Haase, a man with black hair, with thick lips, stands there naked, shaking with cold. Dethroned. Haase, the camp elder from the little camp of Hirschberg in the Giant Mountains, used to go around in patent leather boots, nicely fitting breeches, a sort of uniform tunic, and a white shirt. There were diamonds sewn into the front of his pants (does sir dress to the left or the right?). You wonder how much he managed to extort from the Antwerp jewel merchants. His eyelids are trembling. Prisoners go by either side of him to the counter, where they hand over their bundles of clothes. Then they are dunked in baths of disinfectant, move on under hot showers, submit to the electric clippers. Then they stand there, newly born, squeaky clean and steaming, nothing on their bodies, not so much as a louse. Only camp elder Haase still has his full complement of lice. "My pants!" he screams. "Murderers! Give me back my pants!"

Outside Block 16 in the quarantine camp (the first wooden barracks up on the Ettersberg were built in the thirties), a thousand new arrivals are waiting to be admitted. All are wearing clean pajama suits, all are shorn. Only Haase and a few other Kapos have been allowed to keep their hair — as a sign, as it will transpire. A topsy-turvy organization here, who was to know? They'd have done better biting it off! One of them was hanging upside down by the barracks door. "Are you a Kapo?" a couple of burly fellows ask. "Yes." They spun him round in a steel grip, feet up, his head disappeared . . . Only when we at the back reached the barracks door did it dawn on us. Next to each entrance there was a tiny concrete sink in which to rinse off wooden clogs. My my, they were thorough with their delousing here: bloodsuckers large and small!

Four weeks in quarantine, on a hundred and fifty grams of bread per day. Five men in a rack, four levels high. They are let out just once a day, when the barracks are scrubbed clean. A pedantic SS officer, with a couple of men to back him up, inspects the block. The block elder reports: one thousand one hundred and sixty prisoners, twenty-eight sick, nineteen fatalities! The jackboot writes it down on a piece of paper, baring his horsey teeth. It looks like an attempt to smile, but it's nothing but a reflex. As he takes down his details, correct to the bone, oh, so correct — so many living, so many dead — he stands there in soldierly pose, at ease, chest out, teeth bared. Nothing escapes his trained eye, not a crumb on the damp wooden floor, not a straw on the lousy tubercle-ridden pallets. The living are shivering outside in the icy rain. The dead are in their bunks. The jackboot growls, "Why haven't they been removed? A disgrace!" The block elder says he has several times made his report, but the prisoners at the crematorium had too much to do . . . The men on room duty take the dead and stack them neatly by the door. The pedant grimaces; order in all things.

The scrubbing of the long barracks takes four hours, even five. All that time we stand outside between the blocks in rows. No movement, not a word is permitted. Even so, amidst all the noise of the big camp, the pattering of the rain, the clatter of the columns marching past in their wooden clogs, a few dare to exchange whispers. Next to me a boy, sixteen years old, is crying, with his head on my shoulder. Manasse Rubinstein, inmate of the camp from the age of twelve, beautiful as an angel. That was his salvation, his curse: a Kapo at fourteen!

High boots and a rawhide whip. He prefers whipping old men. He whips them dispassionately, with a calm and cold heart. As if he knew any law other than violence. Now he's crying, a boy again. Manasse Rubinstein is washing his stone face and his hands, his bloody hands, with his tears. I see Lubitsch, whom I supposed dead, standing in front of me, and Feinberg the tailor, I see Perez and Berkowicz, familiar figures left and right in the ranks of prisoners. They look at me as I cradle Manasse Rubinstein's head. Do they expect me to push it away with disgust? They don't expect anything, they don't feel anything.

Only one man has pity for Manasse: the magician who took refuge with us in our ranks. On that first day, four men took refuge with us. Buchenwald has its social strata, its hierarchy, its illegals. Three Jehovah's Witnesses and a Frenchman, probably a political, had slipped into quarantine the way one might slip into the catacombs. Will the SS demand their deaths?

The oldest, who carries pages from the Bible concealed about his person and quotes from it incessantly, the oldest, with his magician's face, marked and scored like the ice of a glacier, he doesn't know Manasse

Rubinstein's past. He sees a Jewish boy crying, a lost child. He nods affectionately, he wishes he could stroke him. Instead he quotes from Jeremiah: "If ye will still abide in this land, then will I build you, and not pull you down, and I will plant you, and not pluck you up: for I repent me of the evil that I have done unto you. Be not afraid of the king of Babylon, of whom ye are afraid; be not afraid of him, sayeth the Lord: for I am with you to save you, and to deliver you from his hand . . ."*

A commotion in the ranks causes the magician to stop. Jackboots march by. An old Jew standing next to the Jehovah's Witness sinks silently to the ground. Everywhere there are prisoners lying in puddles, no one pays any attention to them. Later, when we are dismissed, they'll be collected up like fallen leaves. Does the magician really believe the words he recites? He carries on, and we all listen in silence: "And I will show mercies unto you, that he may have mercy upon you, and cause you to return to your own land. But if ye say, We will not dwell in this land, neither obey the voice of the Lord your God, saying, No; but we will go into the land of Egypt, where we

*Jeremiah 42:10–11.

128

shall see no war, nor hear the sound of the trumpet, nor have hunger of bread; and there will we dwell; and now therefore hear the word of the Lord, ye remnant of Judah; Thus sayeth the Lord of hosts, the God of Israel: If ye wholly set your faces to enter into Egypt, and go to sojourn there; Then it shall come to pass, that the sword, which ye feared, shall overtake you there in the land of Egypt, and the famine, whereof ye were afraid, shall follow close after you there in Egypt; and there ye shall die."*

As we re-entered the barracks, soaked and chilled to the bone, and lay down on our boards, bodies close together, seeking warmth, we heard the call: "Camp elder Haase to the office! Manasse Rubinstein to the office!" Manasse went green and started to shake, as he always did when the call went through the barracks, which happened several times a day. Haase got up from his bed, determined this time to make an end. His comrades held him back. In the box over the door from which the voice came there was a crackling, a whistling, and then we could hear scraps of a conversation in the SS office, from where orders were

*Jeremiah 42:12–16.

relayed by loudspeaker all over the camp. Haase had vomited. There was silence in the barracks. All eyes were on Haase and Rubinstein. Two of the earlier Kapos had obeyed the orders right after their arrival — not knowing any better. The SS murdered the Kapos from other camps. They were careful to destroy their helpers once they were no longer needed.

At night, Block 16 trembled, snorted, simmered. The prisoners slept a light, barbarous sleep. But it would be a lie to say there were no little joys in Block 16. Curiosity, wonderment, thirst for knowledge. So I listened to the Jehovah's Witnesses disputing among themselves in the dark of the night. I saw the old man with the magician's face hold a page of the Bible up to his eyes. "He that is far off," he read, "shall die of the pestilence; and he that is near shall fall by the sword; and he that remaineth and is besieged shall die by the famine: thus will I accomplish my fury upon them. Then shall ye know that I am the Lord, when their slain men shall be among their idols round about their altars, upon every high hill, in all the tops of the mountains, and under every green tree, and under every thick oak, the place where they did offer sweet savor to all their idols. So will I stretch out my hand upon them, and make the land desolate, yea, more desolate than the wilderness toward Diblath . . ."[*]

Whereupon the second Jehovah's Witness read: "Go ye after him through the city, and smite: let not your eye spare, neither have ye pity: Slay utterly old and young, both maids, and little children, and women: but come not near any man upon whom is the mark!"[†]

The third Jehovah's Witness said: "Is that God's voice, speaking through Ezekiel? Are those not human thoughts? Only man is vengeful and vain, only he would create God for himself in his own image!"

And then Lubitsch. Here in Block 16 in Buchenwald, he no longer quoted Baudelaire. Still erect, though only a shadow of his former self, he sometimes walked between the rows of four-tiered bunks, his eyes full of restlessness and distraction. What was he looking for? I remembered Perpignan, where he had also wandered distractedly through the barracks. He was probably the only man in the whole camp at Perpignan, at the foot of the Pyrenees, to whom it had

[*]Ezekiel 6:12–14.
[†]Ezekiel 9:5–6.

occurred to found a club. Its members were five or six educated men. I can still see the indulgent or mocking faces of the other prisoners listening to the conversations of the club members. They sat on crates and bundles in a corner of the stifling barracks, and one of them said, "You're wrong, my friend, Madame de Renal was never un-happy, not even when Julien shot at her, even that sent her into ecstasies, if you've read your Stendhal properly! To die by Julien's hand — what more could she hope for! As for comparing her to Madame Bo-vary, that's ridiculous. Bovary's a dwarfish figure by comparison . . ."

"What I should like to ask you," wheezed another one of the gentlemen, ever at pains not to get any stains on their good suits, "what I should like to ask you" — address-ing Lubitsch, who, as they all knew, was a pederast — "is which of the ladies you would have preferred, I mean, for yourself?"

Lubitsch missed the barb, and continued on with the discussion. The conversational-ists chortled, and debated the virtues and aptitudes of Mesdames Bovary and de Renal. (They did so in an exquisite French, too.) Another time it was the turn of Balzac to go under the microscope, then they waxed eloquent on the nobility and corruption of Rastignac. They debated the complicated relations between Volkonsky, Rostov, and Trubetskoy in *War and Peace,* raved about Natasha, Anna Karenina, and Kitty, racked their brains to try and remember an entire scene of *Hamlet* without mistakes or omissions, or interpret one of Lear's great soliloquies, only then to fall into a renewed argument as to whether Cousin Pons or Colonel Chabert was the more successful repository of Balzac's own sense of failure and resignation. The captive audience in the barracks sometimes complained, or they kept up a bitter silence, full of ominous presentiments, or they mocked those self-infatuated snobs. Outside, long trains were loaded with people being sent to uncertain destinations. Was there really nothing else to talk about? Lubitsch, I am sure, sensed the angry atmosphere, and regretted it, but remained the chief spokesman for the group. A demonstration against barbarism? Who can know.

Even here in Buchenwald his innermost being was still rebelling. Tall, gaunt, mighty bones, sunken cheeks, eyes buried in their sockets, a prominent hooked nose — restless, frittering away precious energies, he mooched about here and there, muttering inaudible spells like a shaman. What were they? Still poetry? Or mathematical formulae or music: last efforts at ordering the chaos that surrounded us?

A man I had never seen, but who seemed to occupy part of Block 16 with his powerful voice, would sometimes start declaiming in French either after rations had been given out or in the middle of the night. To all of us who were able to understand him, it was clear that this was an intellectual or artist who had served as a tour guide in the Louvre while still a student. It sounded a little like this: "*Mesdames, messieurs,* here you see Géricault's *Raft of the Medusa.* His masterpiece, if you like. A group of shipwrecked survivors on a raft, the living and the dying together . . . Géricault's source for the subject? *Mesdames, messieurs,* Napoleon had just fallen, a world was going down! See how the artist painted these bodies, glazed and glistening with brine. Classical forms, through a sheen of Romanticism. This magical light, a glorification of death, or of life, if you prefer. And the hope for salvation, in the form of that group at the back of the painting, those men who have caught sight of a sail on the horizon. But the question remains, will their ship ever find them?"

There was a tumult in the barracks. Not that they understood him, or were provoked by his sarcasm. Hardly anyone was listening to him. But the strong sonorous voice, and the sheer obstinacy of this madman, excited their anger. "Shut your dirty gob," one of them yelled in exasperation, close to tears. A few groaned with pain; then, with a loud crash, a bunk collapsed. The loudspeaker creaked, and shrilled with a deafening whistle, as the office passed on ghostly communications that were not intended for our ears. They listened, cursed, coughed. It stank in the barracks, miasmas of pus and rotting flesh. But the madman got to the end of his monologue:

"You see before you here, *mesdames, messieurs,* the *Massacre at Chios* by Eugène Delacroix, an atrocity perpetrated by the Turks in Greece. See the victims lying in the foreground of the painting, waiting for the *coup de grâce,* no complaints in their faces, no fear. Unavoidable, the fate that is approaching them. What was Delacroix's message to us — that we shouldn't care? The Romantic in him called for empathy, feeling, but only in the onlooker, *he* was to feel dread and horror, while the victims themselves . . ."

"Ta gueule!" cried a solitary voice in the

darkness, shut your mouth! Fresh tumult, shouts, curses, also laughter. Then quiet.

Suddenly the madman begins afresh: "Or *The Lady in Blue, mesdames et messieurs,* if you'd kindly follow me, surrender yourselves to these colors, this intoxicating blend of feeling and inner loveliness, *The Lady in Blue* by Jean-Baptiste-Camille Corot . . ."

One night, we are woken by a voice. Suddenly, out of malodorous darkness, a song lifted light and magical, an Italian love aria carried by a light tenor. It could only be Antonio! I had come across Antonio before, in the camp at Perpignan, and in the limbo of Drancy. Many awoke and listened spellbound. The tenor was singing exquisitely — perhaps with the last of his strength.

A shout broke in: "Stop it! I can't bear it. Stop it, you're driving me crazy. Stop, stop . . ."

The outburst of that unfortunate ebbed away in a fit of loud, desperate sobbing. Block 16 became deathly quiet, only the rough breathing of many inmates and the sobs of the unknown man — bursting his chest, choking his throat — were audible. Then the singer ended his song. *"Addio* *amore."** It was like poison, like a drug, it drove the blood into our hearts and choked us. A glimpse of paradise. The Jews on the mountain, in the valley below the promised land of Canaan, behind them the desert where they were to wander for the next forty years.

In the morning I looked for Antonio. I headed in the direction from which I had heard the singing in the night. I walked down the long rows of plank beds, with men lying in them. Something had sharpened my vision, allowed me to see faces otherwise than before. Disfigured faces, faces swollen with wounds, with scurf, with purulent sores, but faces that had still somehow retained some of their individual character: pride and self-respect, comfort, and a last shimmer of better days in the past. Someone poked his head out, the head of a saint, taking in everything with naive curiosity. Someone hunkered down, his long and shockingly thin limbs strangely twisted, to pray with closed eyes, rocking back and forth ecstatically, and pounding with his fists against his chest. There someone lay quite still, only his hands moving, as though

*Puccini, *Turandot,* Act II, sc. 1.

137

making signals to an invisible spirit — the convulsions of death. Someone else was in a waking dream, with a painful smile playing about his lips. Death was all alone among a great number of men. Some lay there stiffly, eyes open, anonymous and despised, like deserters: deserters from a remarkable existence. Then I found Antonio, but he was no longer living. A little man, with dark skin and dark eyes, that even as they faded wore a wistful expression of regret, the last flinching of someone who had seen much that was beautiful. A Mediterranean type, with sores on his legs and a grotesquely swollen head on a neck like the stem of a flower.

■ ■ ■ ■

8
BLUES FOR FIVE
FINGERS ON A BOARD

■ ■ ■ ■

Along with the Jehovah's Witnesses a political had come to us, a Frenchman, as already mentioned, who went by the name of Pepe (certainly his cover name). "Why are we still talking," Pepe scolded us, "what are you moaning about all the time? Because we don't have any rifles? All the time we're talking, comrades are remaining silent in the cellars of the Gestapo. They laugh in the Nazis' faces, knowing full well that their laughter is going to cost them everything, the highest price! The Russian Revolution made the Fascists blind with rage."

His rants were not poetry like the speeches of Mendel Teichmann, they were revolution. The word "revolution" burned on his lips and in his brain. To Pepe the concentration camp was a test he had to pass. Whoever failed was not fit for the revolution. He approached the study of his situation and the people around him with childish zeal: "Tell me about yourself," he would say. Or: "Tell me about Pechmann. What was he like? You keep referring to Pechmann. Was he in the Maquis?" No. "Well, what then," he would mutter crossly. As far as he was concerned, someone who wasn't in the Maquis wasn't worth bothering about.

"Listen to me," I began. "You know what Mendel Teichmann said about Pechmann on the day Pechmann died?"

"I'm not interested," said Pepe, "about your Pechmann and that . . . whatever his name is . . . Cowards, amateurs, what's the point?"

"Listen," I insisted, "your revolution, when it comes to pass, let's say in ten years, all right? What then? Who will live in the world where your revolution has prevailed, only Maquisards?"

Pepe reflected for a while. "Everything will live then," he replied. "Dogs, cats, whatever has lived to see the day!"

"Well then, and now I want to tell you what Mendel Teichmann had to say about Pechmann: that he was an attempt on the part of nature to make a good man. There are a million such attempts. Inexhaustible Nature is patient in its inventions. That's what Mendel Teichmann said."

"Yech," said Pepe, bored, "we can't use

142

good people right now. What we need are heroes, fighters, executioners, knife-grinders, desperadoes."

"You will need all sorts of people," I said, "when the revolution has taken place." I gasped — it wasn't me speaking, it was Mendel Teichmann speaking through me. What had Teichmann done to me? What had Pechmann done to me? And what would Pepe do to me?

"Where did you first come across Pech-mann?" Pepe now asked me. He had nibbled.

I said, "In Perpignan, on the Spanish frontier."

"Yech," said Pepe in surprise, "where exactly?"

"In Perpignan, in an old army camp, presumably left over from the First World War," I explained. "In 1942 they collected prisoners and put together long trains for the deportees that finally took them to Auschwitz. At night they had the biggest campfires I ever saw. Why, have you been there?"

"I was born there, but my parents moved to Paris. I can remember the mountains on the horizon, I can almost see them some days, like a purple wall . . ."

"They broke up the old barracks," I went

on, "and lit vast fires. The wood was moldy, it was as light as cork, you could crumble it between your fingers almost to dust, and it burned like tinder, the flames were thirty, forty feet and more. The young people danced around them in a ring. They danced a *hora* and sang wild Jewish songs. When someone got tired, he left the ring and lay down somewhere, and someone else took his place. All night, the boys and girls were stamping round and round the fire. A cloud of smoke and dust loomed above the camp like a mountain, underlit by the flames. The prisoners sat and watched in their thousands, and then went to sleep in the barracks where they were eaten alive by sand fleas, were woken up by the singing and chanting, and went back out and stared in the flames."

"What did the guards do?"

"Watched. Same as us, same as the prisoners, stared at the fire and the dancers. One or two of the young men were kept busy collecting wood from the old barracks, to keep the fire going. Glowing embers flew up and scattered in the air like fireworks. The people went gray, their heads were covered with ashes, their faces were scorching. And the chorus sang all night at the top of their voices. They held hands and danced

144

round and round in a circle, like dervishes."

"What did Pechmann do? Did he dance as well?"

"He was one of the wildest dancers."

"What about you?"

"I watched."

"Why?"

"I don't know. I had to see everything. If I'd been in the midst of it, I'd only have seen a part."

"That's not true," said Pepe, "you should have danced too. You don't know what they were feeling. You didn't experience their intoxication. If you weren't in the thick of it, you don't know."

"Maybe you're right," I said. "At any rate, Pechmann was. He fell in love with a Jewish girl called Mariana. She was very beautiful, and he was a good-looking man. I couldn't take my eyes off them. By day they sat exhausted in the lee of a wall somewhere, on the yellow sand, holding each other tight and kissing."

As I talk, at night, in Block 16 in Buchenwald, the pictures return to me and my throat goes dry. Perpignan: a large camp, perhaps twenty thousand souls. A sandy desert, with those gray, rotted barracks. In the harsh light of the Mediterranean sun,

145

the termite-riddled wood of the barracks has a silverish sheen, like slate or malachite. There are people here from all over France. Men and women, old people and children. The camp is divided up into silos, and the different silos separated by barbed wire. In the morning a group of officers of the Garde Mobile sit down at tables under the white sky and read out names. Whoever's name is called has to go over to Silo 20, and that's where, everyone knows, the transports go from. The French officials don't exert any pressure. The people leave voluntarily. Why do they not put up a fight? Sometimes, when members of a family are called, but other members of the same family not (maybe their turn won't come till the next transport, the day after tomorrow), there are cries, laments, even protests. The officials are cool and unmoved. It's an order, they say, the Germans provide us with the complete lists, it's nothing to do with us.

The people stand around, staring at the officers, trembling in case their names are called. Then, once they have been called, they are quiet and they go. That's it.

They come from many European countries. They have emigrated to France, a country they expected to shelter them, and which is now collaborating with the Germans. Persecution, uncertainty, the specter of being transported, have made them soft. They have left fathers behind, mothers, sisters, brothers. Their brothers and sisters may already be "there," in Germany, in Poland, some say in the ghetto, or in Auschwitz, as a few whisper. (It's the first mention of Auschwitz, in the south of France.) Where they are, think the Jews, I can be too. When fate has spoken, they adjust to it. Better an end with horror, than horror without end!

Only a few rebelled: "Why don't you put up a fight? Why do you run meekly to your destruction, like sheep?" Pechmann is among the rebels. He negotiates with the French officials, there are no Germans to be seen. He talks to representatives of the Red Cross, who come to inspect the camp but are unable to do anything. He fights to prevent families being torn apart, tries to stop a mother who's lost her child in the confusion from being sent away. He shouts, swears, pleads, comforts. And at night he dances with Mariana. They hold each other's hands, they stare into each other's eyes, as if they meant to drown.

One day, Mariana's name is called. Pechmann holds her back. "Wait," he says, "don't go, don't step forward, they won't find you here in this crowd! I'll talk to the officials, I'll get you off, I'll try and secure a reprieve, I know influential people here. We'll run away together, to the mountains . . ."

She lays her hand over his mouth and smiles sadly. "No," she says, "let me go, I must."

He knows why. She's told him a hundred times. Her mother is there, and her father, and three brothers. She goes. And from that day forth, Pechmann is no longer rebellious. A week later, when his name is called, he passes quietly through the gate to Silo 20.

There was singing not just round the bonfire. There was a barrack building where young people met up at night. They told stories, sang French, Polish, Yiddish songs. Mostly French citizens, secretly hoping not to be sent away, thinking the mediation of influential friends might secure their release. But one never knew, suddenly when people went missing — were they on transports, or had they actually been released? This is where Antonio sang, where many sang whose names I have forgotten, and Pechmann sang too, and played jazz. Antonio was Italian by birth, grew up in Marseille, fought in Spain, a veteran of the notorious

French camps of Saint-Cyprien and Gurs. Antonio sang in Italian and Spanish. The listeners were amazed that there was a man here who could sing so beautifully, in this desert, in the camp at Perpignan. But then why should they be amazed? There were university professors in the camp, surgeons, psychiatrists, actors, writers, and virtuosos. A few may have been released, but all the others were put on transports.

With Mariana's leaving, Pechmann had changed. His gray-blue eyes had a feverish glint. He walked with a slight stoop, as though looking for something in the dust at his feet. In the evenings, he sought company, he beat out a rhythm on a board with his hand. With fingers he played the drums. With his other hand he pinched his nose and mimicked the saxophone. He played the blues. Everyone fell silent when he played. He magicked up an entire band — a one-man band, without instruments. Girls wept silently. Two or three couples danced. Pechmann burned, he was infectious, there was power, sorrow, and poetry in his music. Before long, everyone was humming along, moved to his rhythm, burned with him, in a delirium, unable to stop. Pechmann must have been thinking of Mariana. He couldn't wait to go to where Mariana was, every day he wanted his name to be called. But he was cheerful, and had a soothing answer to every worried question.

"What will happen?" asked an old Polish Jew. "They say they want to wipe us out!"

Pechmann smiled. "Can you work?"

"What do you mean, can I work?" the old man protested. "I'm a painter and decorator! My whole life I've worked, with my own hands. Here, feel, they're hard as stone!"

"Well then," said Pechmann, "they'll find work for you. The Germans are at war, they're sending their own men to the front to fight. But behind the lines, they need people to work."

"But they say they want to kill all the Jews, get rid of us all."

"That's not true," said Pechmann, but he knew he was lying. "If you're fighting a war and you want to win it, you can't afford to kill people who would otherwise work for you. We will work, therefore, and we will survive."

Wherever Pechmann went, he calmed frightened people. He played and he trumpeted: blues for five fingers on a board.

While I was talking, in Block 16, Pepe studied the faces of the men who were lying or squatting nearby, dozing or listening.

Pepe kept his eyes open: all these impressions would come in useful sometime, everything was valuable material for his single purpose.

A prisoner came in and fetched Pepe. When he returned, he pulled out a piece of hard, dry bread from under his shirt, broke it in pieces, and gave them out. He wasn't, it seems, completely anonymous; his comrades knew where he was hiding. The Jehovah's Witnesses also received supplementary rations from their illegal camp organization. After we had ground up the hard bread between our teeth and swallowed it most appreciatively, Pepe said, "Now go on, what happened in Perpignan?"

"It was the time of the wine harvest," I said. "Trucks drove into the camp, selling ripe grapes. Whoever had no money was given some by the Red Cross. The grapes were delicious. Everyone could eat as much as he wanted. The wind blew the smell of the sea into the camp, at other times there were warm waves of scent from the plain: lavender, rosemary, and mint. Sometimes there was a sweetish cadaver smell mixed in too. Thousands of rats had made a home for themselves in the deserted barracks. We observed their battles, their campaigns to secure the garbage mounds behind the barracks. In the evenings, many prisoners hung about on the perimeter of the camp, in the hope of getting a breath of fresh air. Sometimes an officer of the Garde Mobile would come along. A tall, impressive-looking individual, with an old-fashioned mustache with turned-up ends. He took off his military cap, rested one foot on a rock, pressed his left fist against his hip, and in his magnificent pose surveyed the prisoners. An operetta character, cool to the core, a winning smile, slick and smooth. Of course, many people clustered round him, because he had news for them. He talked about the great theaters of the war, and of the latest transports. While he spoke (and one learned everything and nothing from him), he eyed the young women pretty shamelessly. This time, his eye lit on a girl who was standing by the barbed wire a little to one side. Her mother, a thin and wizened old woman, saw his interest and moved nearer. I saw her making her way through the crowds, to be nearer to the uniform. For a long time she stood at his side, a misty smile on her creased face. The officer, who had several times seen the old woman with her daughter, must have guessed immediately . . . He smiled back at her, even nudged her with his elbow.

"At last, night had fallen, he called everyone nearer. 'I'm in charge of the transport tomorrow,' he drawled with friendly condescension. 'I want to give you some well-intentioned advice: don't make any trouble for us, and don't try and escape from the train. As of today, we have permission to shoot. Anyone attempting to flee will be shot down without warning.' He said this not at all menacingly, but quietly, in a mild and kindly tone of voice.

" 'Excuse me,' a prisoner spoke up sarcastically, 'I don't want to make trouble for you. But you hand us over to the executioner, and you complain that we make trouble for you?'

"The officer shifted a little. 'I'm only carrying out my orders,' he said, a little thrown by the intervention, 'that's my duty. Don't imagine organizing these transports is a pleasure for me. But what can I do about it? Nothing. If I don't run a transport, someone else will do it instead. This is an occupied country. Just think . . . I need to put my family first. I'm sure you understand that.'

"Silence all round. He hadn't expected an effect like that. They stood there as if turned to stone. One could hear the rousing singing of the young prisoners around the campfire, the crackling of the embers in the air, yes, even the whistling of the rats was audible. Now the officer began to feel awkward. The cool silence went on for longer than he could stand. He put his cap back on and made a clumsy movement in the direction of the gates. Once more he turned back to face us. 'What if I refused to carry out my orders, what good would that do? Someone else would come along, and take a harder line. At least I try to be humane, so it's to your advantage . . .'

"As no response was forthcoming, he left. No one said goodbye to him, as they had usually done before. At the gates to the silo he turned back. This time his glance was not for us, but for the girl. He didn't want to miss out on his victim tonight. Everyone was pale after his last words, which told us how things stood. Even the old woman pandering her daughter was hesitating. But then it went through her like a bolt of lightning. She looked round discreetly, and crept off after the officer. That night I watched her with her daughter. She talked long and insistently to the girl. Now flattering her, now scolding her. Her daughter listened to her with large, naive, uncomprehending eyes. In the morning, the place where the two of them had been encamped was empty. Miserable remnants of straw. No one asked where they were. Most probably didn't even remark on their absence, as there were more names called out in the early morning. People got up stiffly from their beds. The dirt, the dust, the stench made them dull. The children were crying. Grandfathers and grandmothers squatted exhaustedly on bundles, among open suitcases, discarded clothes and clay-soiled worn-out shoes left behind by those already deported."

I talked for a long time. All round me everyone was asleep in Block 16, in Buchenwald. Two or three comrades complained, they wanted quiet. Pepe, however, could not get enough. He crept up closer to me, almost pressed his ear to my lips, and asked, "What happened afterwards? Where did you see Pechmann again? Did he find his Mariana?"

"No," I replied in a whisper, "he never saw Mariana again. I saw him in the outcamp at Gross-Rosen near Beuthen. They were building a power plant there."

"But . . . Pechmann," Pepe pressed me, "something's missing . . . you're not telling me something, his character . . . I can't quite imagine him."

"Yes," I said, "probably you're right. He was an average guy, like all of us. There was nothing out of the ordinary about Pechmann. Only . . . how to put it . . . things seemed to get into better perspective when he was around. As if you'd suddenly understood something important about your life."

Pepe shook his head, yawned. My answer hadn't satisfied him. He slid over, down a level, to his bunk.

■ ■ ■ ■ ■

9
THE SMELL OF OLD CITIES

■ ■ ■ ■

Without ever having been to Odessa, to Granada, to Riga, Lemberg, or Kursk, I had somehow encountered the smell of the old cities in the night-black barracks, put together from odd words, melancholy confessions, declarations of love to a place, a street in some outer precinct, a narrow back yard with a pear tree growing in it, a mossy flight of steps, a little house. O destiny of the Jews: when they do settle, they, so widely-traveled, cling with such desperate love to a chance patch of ground. When they lose their home through force of others or fault of their own, they inconsolably carry around the yearning for it wherever they go. Strangers everywhere, they have a pronounced sense of rootedness. At every window, in every doorway they sniff the familiar smell of a little piece of home, even if it is the home of others.

■ ■ ■ ■

"I was born in Poltava," said Feinberg, "but I lived for forty years in Paris, in the rue des Rosiers, a little Jewish street, just like in Poltava, if you like, or Baranovici. A little lane full of miserable dreamers, who'll scold you if you don't treat them like proper bourgeois! Full of *meshugeners* and thieves, just like all old cities: fantasists, naive businessmen, who, if you're a stranger there, will try and sell you the blue out of the sky and are deeply offended if you question their honesty. They're little *nebbish* scoundrels, not even real scoundrels, because the real ones are already rich and distinguished, and have moved out of the little Jewish lane into a part of town where no one knows them. A lousy lane, the rue des Rosiers, where Moische Kuhn sells fish and Chaim Silberstein sits outside his basement and nails shoes, and the old junk dealer Jitzchok Lemberger bundles old paper. No, he's no longer bundling it, he's no longer selling empty bottles and scrap metal in his back yard. What's that — he passed away in the night? But I only just saw him . . . The neighbors are standing outside the house, waving their arms and talking. Only last night they were calling him an old scally-wag. Now they're honoring him, and expressing amazement: What, he had a son? A doctor, well really, a professor even. Where? In Philadelphia. Sent the old man fifty dollars a month, nice and regular. He's alive still, and in good health, a fine man! Once he came here to visit, quiet and modest. He wasn't ashamed of his old father, but walked along the street at his side and across the square, with arms linked. He gave money in the synagogue, he paid for new velvet curtains, even though he's no longer of the faith. Well good luck to him, Amen! And then he went away. And the father went back to bundling paper and sorting bottles. Well, what's he to do with himself all day, an old Jew. A dreamer, a fantast. Always with the big speeches telling everyone what's what. *Khokhmes.* He chased his son away long ago, because he wouldn't wear sidelocks and sort bottles. A ne'er-do-well, the father said, and look at him now . . .

"A street full of craziness, full of sorrows and tiny joys, where there are still one or two little pale-faced Hasidic boys with sidelocks and black-burning eyes hurrying to synagogue, where women lug home heavy bags full of shopping in time for Shabbes, and the yards are full of steam from the kitchens and the smell of roast goose from over there where a rich man lives, full of the yells of children and the scolding of mothers. The tradesmen stand around in the little square, talking and wheedling and making deals under the open sky, or over a cup of coffee with schnapps. Other men are chatting outside the synagogue, praying, or telling stories with self-important expressions. Foolishnesses. But all the same, what a Jewish quarter like that is capable of producing! It's like a hothouse, stifling, rich humus, wild shoots, but also rare blooms: a mathematician, a doctor, a virtuoso, a poet . . .

"If you walk down a Jewish street, don't be bothered by the superficialities, the noise, the smell, the traders tugging at your sleeve, the pale disturbed faces with wild eyes, the enigmatic imprecations, exaggerations, imaginings — the surface of the sea is wild, but you need to go to the deeps! Hidden away in the Jewish quarter live quiet, modest, hardworking people. We had someone living next door to us for years, few people knew him, he didn't attract any attention. A watchmaker, shy and kind and helpful. He worked ten hours a day, put his savings into a fund for an invention. For many years, he put each free hour he had into his construction. The children were neat and nicely turned out, the wife was a good, quiet woman. One day, they were jubilant, the invention was a success. But the man was mortally ill. I knew a poet once, who never published a line. A quiet, industrious man. He made his living as a nurse in the Jewish hospital. On holidays, he read his poems to the patients, told stories, I've never heard stories like that . . .

"The Jewish street, with its noise and bustle, don't be thrown, don't get tangled up in useless talk about what a bad place the world is, go by, go round the corner and drink a *bromfn* in a bistro in the rue du Roi de Sicile or the rue de Turenne, where you'll find a couple of old trees as well, with benches under them, and by way of background the façade of the Musée Carnavalet. Sit on one little bench and watch the other. It's a mirror. What will it show you? Early in the morning, there'll be a *clochard* lying on it, a tramp. You can watch him get up to begin a new day in that wonderful God-given life of his. He scratches himself a long time, groans, eyes still closed tight, takes a pull from a bottle of red wine under the bench, and rinses his mouth out with wine! Then he draws a deep breath, stretches, shakes the cold out of his limbs, belches, and potters off into the city. Tomorrow he'll wake up on a bench somewhere else, in a Metro tunnel, or in the Jardin des Plantes. At ten o'clock, the local philosophers will come down to the park, the old guard, a former assistant of the Préfecture, or a retired police inspector and an old cloth seller from the rue Ferdinand Duval. An employee of mine, he tells them, with a pompous gesture, imagine, gentlemen, a *schlemiel,* who's spent half his lifetime selling coarse linen, dimity, lining silk, thread, trouser buttons, in a word costermonger's things, is learning Shakespeare, he knows twenty parts off by heart, a *meshugener,* he can recite *Hamlet* for you all day long! While the *grisettes,* the little girls from the nearby tailors' workshops, are rummaging around in the drawers full of ribbons and shoulder pads, he regales them with "To be or not to be, that is the question." Or some completely inappropriate passage from *As You Like It.* And what happened? You won't believe it: thirty-nine years old, not a hair left on his head, a wife and four little ones, he goes along and auditions, speaks the parts like a stripling of seventeen. In the Théâtre des Gobelins, in front of the director. And yesterday I saw his name on a billboard, like a great famous star actor. He's made it, he's become a comedian, makes a whole city laugh, that sad figure, a Jew, a nobody, if you'd seen him. Well . . . so what do you say now?

"But to get back to the bench. The philosophers have been relieved by the workmen from a nearby building site, who have their lunch here, passing around a bottle of wine and cutting up their bread and meat, every morsel nicely bite-sized, all done with care and enjoyment. Then along come the young mothers with their infants, pretty young women, they sit and knit and sun themselves, their infants scramble over the rails, the policeman wags a good-humored finger at them and makes sure nothing happens to them. Then in the evening, courting couples sit on the bench and cuddle. One couple next to another, and sometimes an old geezer in between, who doesn't see and doesn't look, doesn't bother the couples, just sits and reads his newspaper in the fading light. It might be cold and rainy, but the couples won't be put off. They will sit there till the clock strikes ten, and then the girls will get a little nervous. They get up, and then along comes a *clochard,* lies down on the bench, stows his half-empty bottle of wine underneath him, has a good scratch, and so ends the day, his big, solitary, God-given day.

165

"I sat on that bench too, it was 1917, the war wasn't yet over, and I wasn't a grown man, I didn't have a beard, my locks made me look older, but my girl loved me anyway, just the way I was. And now I sit on the bench in the evenings, opposite the Musée Carnavalet, and who's kissing and cuddling with her young man? My daughter Germaine! For a while I watch her in bewilderment. Then I creep away. But Germaine sees me, she comes running after me, red face, eyes full of tears: 'Papa, are you spying on me?'

"She trembles with shame and rage. I stroke her cheeks awkwardly. 'No, my darling, I'm not a spy. I was here by chance . . . Remember, I used to come and sit here with your mother. But her father knew, and my mother knew who we were with, there were no secrets in those days in families.'

"And then she cries and stands in front of me, and stares at me like a stranger. And I see: my own daughter knows nothing about me. And what do I know about my daughter?

"But when I get back," says Feinberg, in Block 16, at night, "if I should be spared to see the ground-floor apartment in the rue des Rosiers again in my life, I will just stand

166

and listen, and the walls will speak to me: 'This is where you lived,' they will say, 'this is where you brought up your children, where are they now, did you look after them properly?' And I will reply, 'I believed, I put my trust in God. I was happy,' I will say. 'Every day I was happy. I had my worries, and I quarreled sometimes with my family, with my wife, with my children, and I cursed, and I committed sins of every kind, I lied, I told thousands of little lies, that was my life. But still I was happy, they were my best years, with my children, with my wife, all of us together . . .' But the walls will demand an accounting, and they will ask, 'Here you sat, and frittered away your time. You were a dreamer. You daydreamed. You knew nothing. And what happened, where are they now?' 'I don't know,' I will say. And then I will cry. But the walls will be implacable with me: 'You are crying now, because you have suffered misfortune. But did you cry then? And yet the world was full of misery. Did you not see it?'

"I will cry, and not understand. One can understand the sorrows of others, one can find words of comfort for others, even those who have lost everything. One's own sorrows one cannot understand. Nor find comfort or advice for. And the people who offer advice, because they don't know and haven't suffered — you should flee from them. You should run away and hide. Speak to the walls. Only they know. But because they know, they will remain silent."

■ ■ ■ ■

10
WHAT DOES THE
FOREST MAKE YOU
THINK OF?

■ ■ ■ ■

This is the story of Tadeusz Moll. Cold and hunger and a powerful army of tubercles and typhus germs had knocked great holes in our numbers. But every day new transports came up the Ettersberg, up the road of blood. Humans came and went. The now uncertain hand of the executioner no longer knew its business. Like beasts to the slaughter they drove the prisoners out to the assembly point, and loaded them onto trucks and trains.

I don't remember anymore how I came to be on one of the transports. All at once I heard the singing of rails under me again, and the rhythmic clatter of iron wheels. No one knew where we were going. At any rate, it wasn't far, the land was being squeezed between the first front and the second front, Allied tanks were advancing from both sides. The train stopped somewhere in open country, and then we marched through the dense silence of the Thuringian forest. A remarkable camp under tall fir trees took us in. No barracks this time. Shallow bunkers in the ground, into which we descended, like Odysseus into Hades. Bunk beds stacked all round the damp walls. There were men lying there already, the few survivors from a transport that had got there a couple of hours ahead of ours. From the half-dark of a corner into which I was facing, I beheld the flickering eyes of a boy.

"Where have you come from?" he asks.

"Buchenwald. And where you?"

"Auschwitz. I was working in the gas chambers . . ."

He has little time, he has to take the first listener, a father, or stand-in father. He trembles as he talks, it chokes him like vomit, in spasms. I am terribly tired, my eyes are falling shut, my consciousness is flickering like a lamp on the last drop of oil. I see a boy I must listen to. Things we had often heard and never properly taken in, things we thought were exaggeration, and that someone was now telling me he had personally seen (for a long time to come, I will have the feeling that my diseased imagination has played a trick on me, some Homeric jest): they got undressed, hung their clothes neatly on numbered hooks, and then went in, to bathe, as they were told. Behind them the iron gates were shut. The gas was switched on . . .

"Sometimes we had several transports a day," stammered the boy, "we could hardly get through it. When we opened the chambers, the bodies pressed against the doors tumbled out, knotted together, wet with tears and blood. We carried them in wheelbarrows to the ovens. And we knew: one day it would be us going through the chimneys."

Tadeusz Moll was the name of the boy from Auschwitz, and Petrov was another man who comes into the story, a Red Army man. The former well-grown, contemplative, pale. The other had a foot injury, which he had to keep secret — if you wind up in the hospital here you'll never get out. Tadeusz Moll, pain made him tough and silent, it was etched into his face like a mask of wood. In spite of his torments, in spite of his horrible rags, his dirt and scurf, he couldn't quite keep the Sunday child out of his demeanor. He was a healthy and attractive specimen, there was lightness in his blood, a cunning twinkle in his narrow eyes, a bright friendly smile on his strong mouth. (That very first morning, I'd given him a

173

coat, a long blue army coat without sleeves that I'd organized, and didn't need; he was moved to tears, and remained devoted to me.)

Tadeusz Moll's mother was a pianist, his father a lawyer. Three days after the Germans had marched into Lodz, they picked up his father. Already waiting in the car outside the door was the elite of the street: a couple of secondary schoolmasters, an old retired professor, a dentist, a newspaper editor . . . When Moll talked, he tucked his head between his shoulders, and his face creased up. A child, an old man, Moll was somehow both. In spite of everything he had been through (not long after they'd picked up his father, shots rang out in the park), one could tell he was a pampered boy from a good family. His mother had idolized him. ("Tadeusz, don't run like that, you'll sweat and catch a chill! Tadeusz, my gold, take your time eating, put your book away and sit up straight!")

Already at thirteen, Tadeusz was a little gentleman. He looked down on people in the street. His papa was a good lawyer. Papa was famous! (Shortly after the gunshots in the park, Mama became rather strange, she didn't cry, she was just not there anymore. Or, she had always been strange, and now she took refuge in madness.)

"Where did they pick you out . . . Did you work in the gas chamber?"

Tadeusz Moll scratches his forehead, his rough, wrinkled forehead that gives him such a strangely vexed appearance. "I don't know," he says, "it was in the big yard where they were all standing and waiting. Mama was talking, odd stuff I didn't understand. A couple of men came up, prisoners. They looked at me and said, 'Come and shovel coal with us, you can have a bath later.' They stood me by an oven. It took me a while to realize what sort of oven." ("Swing that spade, swing that spade, faster!" ordered the guard, and then he laughed. "Do you know what that stench is, sonny boy, it's pure Jew fat!")

Tadeusz's hands were soon bloodied from work. He got used to it. And how did he get out of there? He's not able to say that either. He got sick. Usually when someone got sick, they were fed to the gas. But he didn't get put in the gas chamber. The two men smuggled him out with the bundles of clothes from the dead people.

"Who were they, people you knew from Lodz?"

"No idea."

"Did they come on the transport here with you?"

"Haven't seen them. I think they're all dead."

The first morning in Crawinkel, we saw there were Russians, Jews, French, and Poles in the bunker. In twos or threes they pressed their rigid bodies together under a blanket, to get some warmth. Tadeusz Moll, Petrov the Red Army man, and I smiled at each other as we woke up. At four in the morning they chased us out into the cold. Steel stars blinked at us from behind shreds of cloud, the wind ruffled the firs. Kapos hustled us through the bunkers to the gate: "Faster, this way, you idiots, get in line, count down, and get a move on!" The scrape of thousands of wooden clogs, shrill whistles, brutal cries somewhere in the forest. We heard no one complain. Whoever couldn't go on anymore just dropped. One word was handed on from rank to rank: this is hell, *dos Gehennem, ç'est l'enfer!*

Crawinkel was the name of the place near the camp. (Did Goethe not mention some idyllic Krähwinkel somewhere in his oeuvre?) The camp did not offer that practical amenity called a gas chamber. Under the tall firs, bodies were turned to ashes in huge pyres. Swathes of toxic smoke hung sluggishly about the tree roots, and covered the tangle of dead bodies like blobs of cotton wool. At the camp entrance where the prisoners assembled, and were counted and assigned duties, a band played notorious ballads: "O Donna Klara" or "Wiener Blut."* On a stage ten feet up from ground level, musicians, prisoners of course, scraped and tooted and banged on their instruments. The allocation of tasks took two hours. Kapos and jackboots strode along the ranks of prisoners, grabbed each one by the chest and gave him a push or a shake. Whoever collapsed didn't have to work, but he got no bread either. Whoever got no bread was dead the next day. And each time a work gang headed out, they played us out: *Muss I'denn, muss I'denn zum Städtele hinaus.*† The jackboots barked, "Two three four five, two three four five, get a move on, you shitbags, or I'll kick your asses!"

The apex of the forest echoed, the tips of the firs swayed transfigured. As we filed past

*Popular tunes by Strauss and Offenbach. "Wiener Blut," in English, is "Vienna Blood."
†"Must I, must I leave the shtetl, whilst you, my darling, stay behind."

the stage, we saw, tied to a pole underneath it, a young man. A strikingly well-formed boy with broad shoulders and long, slightly curving thighs of steel. He was dressed only in a thin convict's uniform, without a coat. With his head lowered, he watched us on our way. In his stone face there was a wild and stern expression that none of us, at that first sight of him, understood. We didn't yet know what was about to happen to him.

Outside, a little factory railway awaited us. A dapper little locomotive on narrrow, damaged rails, setting up a jingling as of cowbells and shaking up some hundred frozen bodies, almost breaking their bones. The prisoners stamped and roared in the icy wind, beat their bodies, swore and yelled. The sound of the clattering cars, and then the echo of the walls of the gorge swallowed our noise, turning everything into a crazy symphony. What were they looking for in the deep defiles near Arnstadt? We drilled holes into the chalk, loaded rocks onto freight cars, dragged concrete tubes and iron props through the deep forest.

Do you remember the forest of Vincennes? And the hot wind in the low shrub woods of Avignon and Orange? The metallic rustle of old burdocks, explosions of lavender and thyme. Have you still enough juice in your brain to picture this: the summer of 1941, after the first few months' internment in the forest of Mayenne? You rolled around on the forest floor when you were allowed to leave the camp, remember? With your hands you pulled up moss and earth, you rubbed your face on the good dusty trunks of thousand-year-old beech trees, as one might rub one's face on a beloved's breasts. And later on, that night near Toulouse, in a tractor barn: traitor moon, someone saw you. The face of a young woman through the crack of light at the door, her soft call: *Qui est-ce . . . ?* Who was she waiting for, her brother the Maquisard? Then she sees you, and she looks you fearlessly in the eye. She goes. You think she's gone to fetch the men. But she comes back with a blanket, a warm blanket that smells of horses, half a bottle of wine, and bread.

Or the flight to the Swiss frontier, you had already covered twenty-five miles through forests and over mountains. And now a light at the edge of a clearing. Your thirst is tormenting. The light from the inn draws you inside. I walk in, ask for a drink though I've got no money. The landlord doesn't ask me for money, doesn't ask, who are you, where have you come from? He leads me out across the yard. Now, I think, he's throwing me out. Leave, he will say, get lost, I can't do anything for you. But he opens a door. He opens the door to his own quarters. His wife looks me in the face, and she understands. They don't ask, they don't demand any explanation, they see and they guess, and it's enough. You are given something to eat. They sit respectfully by. Make up a bed for you. Watch over your sleep. At dawn they wake you. When you vanish into the forest, your pockets are full of precious things: bread, meat, sweet grapes. Your hands are still wet with their tears. They begged your forgiveness for the injustice that is being done to you.

Every morning we went to the gully outside Arnstadt, where we unloaded sacks of cement or dragged concrete tubing up the mountainside. All over the hilltops, along the edge of the gully, vertical air shafts are being drilled into the rock. An army of slaves ripping deep holes in the flank of the mountain, to what end? Why the gigantic exertion? The war was lost, any child could see that. The fronts were clamping together, the air shook with incessant bombardments. They drove us on like crazy to work faster and faster, as if there was something they could do. Subterranean factories for missiles? They didn't need them anymore. Even the ack-ack gunners had stopped dobbing their little white powder puffs of clouds into the sky. Glittering in the sun, airplanes skimmed unmolested down the valley, drew dawdling little circles, dropped a bomb or two on a station, just for the hell of it. Carefully they dropped their little bangers into the valley so as not to hit any of us prisoners. Those were our little breaks — when the air-raid alarms went off, or when they were dynamiting holes in the rock. Then the jackboots would scuttle off, and the prisoners had half an hour to themselves, began to talk and gesture, time enough for their hearts to lighten a little.

Five or six men get together in a sunny spot. Petrov forgets his pain, and lays an imaginary table. Clumping here and there with his stiff leg, miming the officious expression of a waiter, he ushers the guests into his restaurant. Tadeusz Moll joins in right away. He produces the man of the world, the cosmopolite pampered wherever he goes, he's good at that. "I'd like caviar with white bread and butter, and a white Bordeaux!" The waiter nods at each order from the guest, guaranteeing that everything is available and of the expected quality. Then he rolls his eyes with delight at the gentleman's exquisite taste. The spectators are helpless with laughter. The waiter serves, sweats, brings imaginary steaming dishes which he passes around and uncovers for the discriminating nostrils to sniff at. Tadeusz Moll eats, drinks, dabs his lips, his face, his neck, stuffs the food down his gullet with wild comedy.

I wonder at the inexhaustible resources in such a young person. How could a sixteen-year-old survive the gas chambers without being damaged? Tadeusz caught my eye. Later he came up to me. To cheer me up, he played another scene, in Yiddish: *"Oy, a tepele kave, oy, a glezl bromfn, oy, hob ikh gekholemt a zisn troym. Oy, hob ikh gemakht a shmaytz op di noz, a fargeign!"** He wipes his mouth appreciatively, rolls his eyes with a blissful expression. Then, with no connection, he asks me, "Have you read about the wandering of the soul through the seven skies? You don't know anything about the streams of light and fire and water before the sixth heaven! And the angels call to you:

★"Oy, a cup of coffee, oy, a glass of schnapps, oy, did I have a sweet dream. Oy, how I blew my nose, a pleasure!"

'Unworthy man, can't you see with your own eyes? Are you one of the children who kissed the Golden Calf, unworthy of seeing the king in his splendor?' "

He stands there in silence for a while, looking serious, introspective. The men all stand there silently. The station building is in flames. A few uniforms start crawling out of the shelters. In a moment they'll start yelling at us again, and making us work. But the sun shines, the sky is blue. Tadeusz Moll blinks at me. "The body suffers, the soul soldiers on. Comfort her, give her a kind word from time to time. When the body suffers, the soul should laugh! That's what Baal-Shem taught us."

We could work out what it meant: five more minutes' break. We wished we could embrace them, the bombers. Their sky-writing spelled victory: sit tight, children, life is beautiful! The prisoners stood fear-lessly under the open sky where already the Allies were unchallenged. They talked, they warmed themselves with their words and with the noise of the front. But there were also days when the front went silent. Then the inner fire would die down, our lips freeze, everything listened quietly and waited in apprehension.

183

■ ■ ■ ■

Petrov didn't moan, but his ravaged face was white with pain. Every upsurge of courage or exuberance was dearly paid for. After each session in the sun, his leg swelled horribly. He would be left hanging onto the car, shuffling along after it into the mineshaft and out again, because that was the only way he had of disguising his limp. He was always able to find two or three Russian comrades who were willing to take over his part of the work. They would give him cover, one on each side. If a guard or a Kapo came along, they would start yelling and pushing each other to work faster, and push the car so that it struck sparks. Not one glance was to fall on their sick comrade. If anyone happened to notice his swollen leg, that could only mean a bullet for him.

Another time, as once again a couple of British reconnaissance planes swooped past and our guards had disappeared like rats into their holes, Petrov called me over, produced a couple of carrots from his pocket that he must have picked up going after some farmer's cart, scraped them clean with his knife, and shared his precious find with me. We crunched them up with delight,

184

and smiled at each other. We weren't able to converse much, but the difficulty gave a universal character to such communication as we did have. He would fire off a string of fierce oaths, and then say, "Tomorrow Nazis kaputt! We go home!" And I asked him, "Do you have a wife and family?"

He laughed, held his hand three times at different levels between knee and chest, and said the names. In his narrow eyes was a lust for life. He's as strong as a bear, Petrov, I thought. I could picture him striding through the streets of his little Ukrainian town, with the supple-kneed walk of an experienced rider, a little scorn in the corners of his eyes, and appetite quivering round his slightly upturned mouth: appetite for everything, food, drink, laughter, love. His face was as changeable as a sky in March. With barely detectable movements of his mouth, eyes, nose, he could really say everything. When he laid his hand silently on my shoulder sometimes, it needed no words.

Tadeusz Moll and Petrov are together pushing freight cars, the day is gray and long. The stones are no lighter when it's Moll and Petrov doing the pushing. The comrades see that something must be done. Chukran comes into my head, there was someone who had a solution for every problem. We organize several caps, and then I take Moll and Petrov to the latrine. There's a lot of traffic there. God knows there's nowhere else the men can go, to have a little breather every so often! The guard knows it too. Every ten minutes the guard walks by the latrine. He barks and swings his rifle butt. Better not to take any risks, think the men. A blow with a rifle butt, in this place . . . A couple of unfortunates were sent sprawling into the ditch. That's why everyone hops away at the guard's approach. The guard curses at them from a distance. Why wouldn't he curse, the way they look. He's had it dinned into him, anyway, that they're not human beings. They'd squat there all day if you let them. The guard is sick with nausea and contempt. The later in the day it is, the more irritated his curses, the harder his blows.

"You just sit here till we come for you," I say to Tadeusz. To Petrov I pass on Chukran's nugget of wisdom: "The trick is to pluck out the Cyclops's eye, but without him noticing! Each time the guard comes, you have to be a different person, someone he hasn't seen there yet. Turn your cap round, put on a different one, don't squat in one place, pull faces, change your posture, be upright, then slump again. If the guard sees through your act, then good-night. And keep an eye out for Tadeusz, it's dangerous if he goes to sleep."

Tadeusz Moll is young, he's never been in love, he has no one waiting for him. He doesn't have the cunning to keep himself alive. But is it not possible he has the wisdom of his forefathers? When I go to the latrine after a couple of hours to check up on them, they're squatting side by side on the pole, chattering away. The guard's just been and gone, now they've got a few minutes' respite. Moll talks Russian with Petrov. He can speak Polish, Yiddish, He-brew, Russian, French, and German. ("Mama wanted me to go into business, like her brother in Paris. A cosmopolitan, equally at home in Paris as in Lodz or Warsaw. Papa reckoned I was a born lawyer. I learned a bit of everything, but nothing really. What I liked reading best were the old writings, Maimonides, the books of Rabbi Israel Baal-Shem. Grandfather was a Hasid, who taught me to read and sing . . .") When I went back after another two hours, it wasn't Moll but Petrov who had gone to sleep. I let him doze on a while, the guard was nowhere in sight. I could hear Moll reciting sentences in Hebrew. Leaning way forward on the pole, his head sunk between his shoulders, eyes shut, Tadeusz Moll was reeling off sentences:

"God took me out of the midst of the people of the Flood and bore me on wings of wind to the highest Heaven and brought me to the great palaces at the top of the seventh heaven Araboth, place of the throne of Shekhinah and the Merkabah, the hosts of anger and the armies of rage, the Schi'anim of fire, the cherubim of torches, the Ofannim of fiery coals, the servants of the flames and the seraphim of lightning, and he set me to serve the throne every day . . ."

At this point an old Jew interrupted him from the far end of the latrine pole (between them squatted other men, straining or groaning or talking to themselves). "No," the old man said severely, "the words are not 'to serve the throne every day,' but 'to attend the throne.' "

Tadeusz showed no emotion on his pale face. He thought for a second or two. "No," he replied, "it's what I said it was: 'and he set me to serve the throne every day.' "

The old man shook his head in astonishment. "I only meant to test how well you knew it. How old are you, *khaver?*"

"Seventeen."

"You are very learned for one of your age. But you are arrogant, my son. Arrogance leads you to look down on the ignorant. But God is in the ignorant as much as in the lettered!"

I had dropped my guard: at that moment the sentry appeared in the doorway, he hadn't alerted us as usual with his curses, but snuck up on us silently. He picked up a rock and slung it furiously at Moll, who ducked and let it crash against the wooden partition. Then he got up, did up his pants and stomped stiff-legged, on numb feet, but erect, past the guard. The soldier had puffed himself up, his face was purple. He had drawn breath for one of his terrifying tirades. But he remained silent. He stared in his rigid pose at the Jewish boy as he climbed, none too quickly and with not a sign of fear, up the slope, to where the freight cars came out of the mountain to be emptied. The cars scraped and squealed on their terrible rails, the drivers barked, the air trembled with noise. The guard seemed not to notice as a dozen other occupants of the latrine whisked past him. Even Petrov hobbled quickly past.

I have often thought about this scene in later years. Tadeusz had a guardian angel,

189

no question. The story of the two unknown men who twice saved him from death in the gas chambers had something inexplicable about it, but it was not a lie. Or was the explanation quite simply his baffling stoical-naive attitude? And was such an attitude the result of absentmindedness and awkwardness — was Tadeusz clueless in the face of danger, or did he despise it? Did he lack the cunning with which to survive, or was his calm in fact a sign of higher cunning, developed over hundreds of years of persecution? In his beardless, still not fully formed features there was meekness and a note, striking in one of his years, of irony. The guard must have heard a little of the conversation, though of course without understanding any of it. And his disgust at these alien people, who were capable of spending hour after hour squatting on the latrine and conducting learned disputes at the same time, that disgust had been supplanted by surprise. Or had he by some miracle felt disgusted with himself?

That evening, as we swung into the square in front of the office, to the jolly rhythm of the band ("*Wir sind vom K. und K. Infanterieregiment*"), to be counted, searched, and humiliated, we saw: the lad on the post underneath the band was not alone. There were six posts, and three of them were now tenanted. Very young men, milksops, mother's boys. As with the first, their caps and coats had been taken off them, and they stood there shivering. Or rather, we couldn't see whether they were shivering, what they were going through. On their faces lay that stiff spectral earnestness of certain death, an expression far more gruesome than the expression of death itself. At last we heard what this exhibition of prisoners under the bandstand was about. Comrades told us, the ones who had seen it before: "Just wait," they whispered, "see how many posts are still unoccupied?"

We were not frightened. Each of us had witnessed various dazzling scenes of the great *son et lumière* of terror that the officials of dictatorship liked to put on for themselves. Besides, we were each of us preoccupied with our own piecemeal execution, we could hardly stay upright with fatigue, we were greedy for our bunks, for warmth and for a couple of hours of sleep. Even the sight of the living Satan in all his pomp with a great retinue, against the background of hell, where men were simmered in great pans, even that would not have fazed any of us. It was the hour of sleep. We had a right to sleep! A bitter brief

191

and sweet night lay ahead of us, filled with dull delirious visions of food, drink, and a sight of a beloved face. Once we had drunk our bowls of stinking beet soup, we threw ourselves down on the boards and fell into a trance. A bunker like ours full of prisoners must dream up a whole universe! It was a cauldron of helpless desires, creaking like a ship as it takes in water and sinks. Only a few still had the strength to remain awake and converse.

Tadeusz, half asleep, was murmuring something to himself. When the three of us were pressed together under one blanket, a blanket stiff with filth, dried blood, and pus, Petrov and I and Tadeusz between us, we could hear a rushing murmur in our ears: a mechanism, a *perpetuum mobile,* that ran on nothing but life itself and was trying to prevent its own dissolution. At that time, Tadeusz Moll was in a dangerous condition, torn between the desire to live and an ever-increasing yearning for peace. To throw in the towel! To give up and let yourself drop! At that stage, everyone developed a little array of reflexes: one man moved his fingers, his toes, his shoulders; another would nod his head, blink his eyes or move his lips, pray, whisper names or some secret charm. When one's will broke and the reflex snapped, the struggle was over. The man then wanted only to die. And there was nothing easier than that.

In the black solitude of the bunker, Tadeusz Moll was murmuring: "His servants sing to him and confess the power of his miracles, as Lord of Lords, surrounded by thrones, ringed with the peoples of the lords of glory. With a shimmer he wraps the heavens, and his splendor shines down from the heights. Abysses flicker in his mouth, and firmaments sparkle forth from his form . . . But Mama," he interrupted himself in a tenderly mocking voice, "how should I greet the king without bowing? What use to me is my blind pride now . . ."

Roused from my sleep, I eyed him curiously. There was an expression of peace on his childish mouth. He was fantasizing with half-open eyelids, through which tears were oozing. But his whole countenance was in the form of a question, an unanswerable sarcastic question.

What does "forest" make you think of, sleeper, you . . . The aroma of a forest, the sight of a forest, peace in the deep woods, the rustling of the crowns, the majestic nodding of treetops in the wind . . . For all time the smell of forest for me will be mingled with the smell of burning and the image of toxic white puffs of smoke on the naked bodies of the dead of Crawinkel. But also the memory of warm afternoons of childhood at the foot of the Kahlenberg in Vienna, tired and drunk with color and light. The buzzing of wasps in the tall grasses, the angry drone of horseflies on their quick flight, their escapades around some tiny disintegrating corpse, half-buried under ferns. The metallic glitter of their wings and carapaces, lulling hum of crickets, and in the distance, also productive of a pleasant drowsiness, a scrap of conversation under the burning sun, the laughter of maids and mowers in the fields, a stifled gasp of pleasure. The world is still at peace. Above the steaming earth is a profound harmony. But also the memory and the taste of your bitten lips, the kisses of that girl in Saint-Nazaire, who died shortly afterwards under the Germans' bombs . . .

Sleeper, do you hear me? The world no more at peace. But I — I will live for ever. I will be happy. I will be drunk with pleasure and love. I will be strong and prevail. The aspect of the forest will never be unmixed for me. Forest, peaceful silent machinery, storing rainfall and sipping from streams; turning life to rot and rot to life; plenitude and emptiness; microscopic life and eternity in a dewdrop, you will never make me forget this picture: a stage in the middle of the Thuringian forest, set on six thrusting young trees, musicians on it, droning, scraping, banging, and underneath the young men, the attractive sons of anxious mothers, young know-it-alls, light-footed scramblers over wall and fence, toying with danger, opponents of a hierarchy of deadly laws, barbed wire, watchtowers and trenches, testers of God — and Tadeusz Moll among them! (The gibbets too, the broad gibbets of good stout oak, on the exercise yard, a rectangle cut out of the green fir wood of Crawinkel, the gibbets also had six hooks. What morbid joker thought that one up? Just wait, the comrades had whispered, until they're all taken. How many posts does the stage have?)

The day had begun quite well. It was no longer so intensely cold, a diseased copper-colored sun came peeping through the gray scraps of clouds. There was a different sentry on guard at the latrine. So again we were able to send Petrov and Moll into exile. Petrov's leg was less swollen, but he had a temperature and needed rest. It was certain that one of them would fall asleep, and that was risky. We organized our roster. Every hour a comrade was to look in on them. But then it wasn't possible to go to the latrine whenever one wanted to. The times when someone was allowed to go were determined by the guard at the rock pile.

Tadeusz made a particularly cheerful impression that morning. But it was a confused, almost drunken cheerfulness, which made me suspicious. By ten in the morning, he had disappeared. We looked for him all over but could find him nowhere, and the more time passed, the more worried we became. Petrov said he had only closed his eyes for a few seconds. But he had noticed that Moll got anxious each time the guard came by, in spite of their practiced use of disguise. And then he was suddenly gone. Was he planning to flee? No one could get out of the closely guarded gully. But that evening, we were sent home fully two hours late. Assembled in front of the works office, where the little railway stopped, we were counted over and over again. The jackboots were frantic. A dozen of them went searching with dogs. They told us that if they didn't find the runaway, we'd spend all night outdoors. Then they came back, with Tadeusz in their midst. He had been asleep, nothing more. Had lain down in the cement hut and covered himself up with empty sacks, so that no one could see him. He was coated with cement dust from head to foot, his rosy face, after a long and restorative sleep, shone through a layer of gray powder. But the dogs had already marked him with their teeth and claws, his clothes were ripped, and his hands were dripping blood. He looked round in glassy-eyed astonishment, still half-asleep. Did he understand the seriousness of the situation? Not to be present for roll-call meant attempted flight as far as the SS were concerned. Flight was punishable by death. And indeed, a moment later, Tadeusz Moll was led down the steps, his hands cuffed, his expression already that of a lost man. The delinquents were no longer with us. Not yet there, but not here either. What's the name of that strange land on the edge?

At night, as Petrov and I lay under our blanket, without Tadeusz, we could still see the scene. "Strip!" the duty officer had ordered. Tadeusz took off his clothes in front of the assembled work detachment. "Faster," ordered the officer. Out of regard for his comrades, Tadeusz moved faster. The officer — a strongly built, good-looking man in a smart uniform, holding a little bamboo

197

cane in his hand — rolled complacently back and forth, heel and toe, heel and toe, in his big boots. He might be a schoolmaster in civilian life, or a post office employee. A cheery disposition, rosy complexion, wide jaw, white teeth. He didn't snap, didn't let himself get carried away, unlike some of his inferiors. Nice and easy was his watchword. When Tadeusz had taken off his shirt, his cement sack appeared. (Almost all of us wore cement sacks next to our skin, a cement sack gave you warmth and moral fiber.) The officer picked the cement sack to shreds with his little cane. The young sentries laughed: what a card! Then Moll was allowed to pick up his jacket and pants again. The officer gave him a prod with his cane and so directed him stylishly to the pole. A jackboot stood ready to tie Tadeusz to the stage, but the officer smilingly told him not to bother. It really wasn't necessary here. There was no point in running away. After ten paces he'd be downed by a burst of machine-gun bullets. (Two watchtowers stood over the place.) The officer gave a signal to the musicians standing up on the stage: "A waltz, gentlemen, if you please," he cried out jovially. Mechanically the musicians started to play. Night all around, searchlight beams passing over the forest, the barbed wire, the footpaths between the bunkers. "Wiener Blut," played the band. Our breath is frozen. "Dismissed!" calls the officer in a bright, sonorous tenor, and the troop of half-dead men returns to the camp.

A restless night. Petrov groans with fever, sometimes he talks to himself out loud. As far as I can understand, he's talking to Tadeusz Moll. Once, he grabs hold of me and seems to mistake me for Tadeusz. I call out to him: "Petrov!" Gradually his eyes become sighted. Then he rolls onto his back, breathing heavily. I too cannot stop thinking of Moll. Between waking and dreaming, I have visions of Tadeusz Moll at the stake.

In the morning at roll-call and as we march out, we are astonished to see him standing there just the same as last night. So it is possible to survive a night hungry, freezing, without sleep. Only now did I notice that just one of the men was actually secured to his stake, the first of them, a French partisan by the name of Nicolas. The rest (there were five in all by now) merely had their hands tied behind their backs. How long could they stand it? Nicolas had been standing under the bandstand now for four days and four nights. The young men stood in the snow erect and seemingly unbroken. Why didn't they charge at the wire? A bullet would bring release. Maybe the fact that they weren't made fast to the poles constituted a certain challenge, even a humanitarian impulse, on the part of the executioners: Go and run at the wire. In five seconds it'll all be over.

But if one of them did that . . . Would the others then not have to suffer for even longer? And Nicolas was tied, he couldn't get away. So perhaps that last humanitarian impulse was actually nothing but a last fiendish provocation. Oh yes, that was something they shone at, such refinements of physical and mental torture.

Why didn't they run away, Tadeusz and his new mates? Was it a form of desperate solidarity, or was it another inhibition of a sort hard to gauge? Did they want to die in full consciousness of their martyrdom? Why did a man insist on draining the cup of his life to the last drop, even if it was only humiliation and torment? Or did it have something else to offer after all? Did it have some value of which the rest of us were not aware? I have thought about these questions a long time. There is no answer. No one standing beneath those gallows was able to leave report, not so much as a word.

But perhaps there is an answer after all. A

fictional answer: Do the men under the gallows think? Of course they think. Do they talk to one another? Perhaps at night. What do they say? What goes through their minds? What do they see with their eyes? One thing one mustn't forget: hunger and exhaustion have certainly diminished their ability to think and feel. But perhaps life, compressed into that tiny remaining time, sharpened by barely imaginable sufferings, perhaps life has become distilled to some quintessence of itself . . . No, we won't presume that the hours spent standing under the gallows raise one's consciousness of existence. That would be water on the mills of the despisers of life. Let's take it at face value: dying means dying.

"Listen," the first delinquent, Nicolas, could have said to Tadeusz Moll, "don't stand there so still, otherwise you'll freeze. Move. Shift your weight about continuously, that helps. From one leg to the other. Tense your muscles, then relax them, tense, relax . . ."

Tadeusz made no reply. His eyes seem to say, what's the point? But he does it anyway. He shifts his weight from one foot to the other, then from the heel to the ball of the foot and back. After a while he notices that he is feeling the most varied relief. He starts to move his whole body. A rhythm of circular motions from neck to shoulder, to his torso, to his thighs . . . A strange clarity becomes his. What a good thing to feel his muscles, to drink in the air, the cold, clean air. What will happen? Does Tadeusz still believe in the possibility of rescue? No, this time is for real, he thinks, with a fleeting spasm of nausea. Didn't even Jesus tremble on the eve of his crucifixion: "O my Father, if this cup may not pass away from me, except I drink it, thy will be done . . ."

Tadeusz feels his feet turning numb. In his hands, which he can't move, he feels a thousand needle-pricks, but then his hands too go numb. It's no good, the cold is entering him. But he doesn't give up. He looks at his comrades either side of him, each lost in thought. Then Tadeusz smiles. Not from pity or sympathy with these men, or with himself. Tadeusz Moll no longer exists as such. There is only his spirit. ("When the body suffers, the soul ought to laugh!") Man lives in the universe, on this planet, in a country, in a house — in himself. The last resource is love. Whoever doesn't know love will not find anything else, not the tiniest chamber in his breast where he may warm himself. ("Why am I thinking of Jesus, am I a Christian?") He is no Christian. He doesn't believe in God, or in miracles. ("I read all those stories of massacres of Jews in England, in Spain, in Germany. Stories of wise and steadfast rabbis who with their own hands killed women and children rather than let them abandon their faith. Stories of the ending of whole communities in conflagration. But the story of the Jew Jesus — he preached love! Didn't the Hasidim also talk of love? The all-powerful and omnipresent love of God, equally present therefore for Jews and Christians and atheists!") He doesn't believe in miracles. But isn't this life a miracle, this body he will shortly quit? (He has already quit it. Tadeusz means that he has stepped outside himself and is now contemplating everything calmly.) His blood is still circulating, his heart is beating lightly and evenly, his whole edifice is calm. Like an ecstasy, his understanding of his body overcomes him, as though he could slip into its capillaries and witness its continuous creation. This body is a crystal, formed over millions of years, a mystery and a part of the world. He feels the ground under his feet, the curvature of the earth as if it could breathe, this heavy, warm, extraordinary spinning mass, whose orbit he feels, this racing orbit through space, which at the same time is rest, unrest, likeness. Substance, the connectedness of all things. He doesn't see the forest, only shadows against a pale sky. The moon is hidden behind clouds. Only the posts he can see, made of untreated fir, the beams of light and the shadows of men in furs and boots, plodding sleepily back and forth over the snow. He loves the fir trunks and the beams of light, he loves the air, the cold, the lonesome moon, because all of them together make up life. Tadeusz feels the touch of the air as a mother's tenderness, he can feel the fir trees there in the night forest, as if he had long invisible arms. He embraces the trees and kisses them, in his mind he wets his lips with pure white snow, he breathes in the scent of the needles and the dry bark, a cloud of smoke from the barracks under the watchtower, carried to him on a puff of wind, a breath from his comrade Nicolas, who is staring out into the darkness as if he can see a light in it.

"Forgive me!" Tadeusz hears one of the delinquents whisper.

For a while there is silence, and then his neighbor replies, "You shouldn't have done it. There was no point, the dogs were quicker. Dogs have good noses."

"I'm sorry . . ."

"I shouldn't have followed you. I felt right

away, this is a mistake. It just wasn't the right moment. We could have waited."

"It's over."

"I was a fool to follow you. I trusted you."

"I hope your mother doesn't curse my name."

"It was a terrible mistake. It would have been right to stay with the others. It's always better to stay with the others."

"We are with the others, if you care to see."

"Yes."

"I'm sorry. Forgive me."

"Forgive me too. We're going to join our brothers."

Tadeusz Moll smiles when he hears that. He says to Nicolas, "I read in the work of Rabbi Loew . . . do you know who I mean?"

"No."

"Anyway," he says. "The king and the beggar are worth the same. When the king's time comes to die, he says to the beggar, 'Give me a year of your life, and I'll give you my kingdom!' "

The Frenchman laughs. Tadeusz goes on, "And in another of the old books you can read: 'The stone lives for ever, he suns himself, he bathes in crystal waters, all the splendor of the earth is his forever. Does he know? He doesn't know. But man knows, and he pays for his knowledge with his life!' "

The other laughs.

"Why do you laugh?" asks Tadeusz Moll.

"I don't read books," says Nicolas. "Take off my handcuffs, and I'll bite through the throat of that guard standing there. That's why they handcuffed me. I fight back. But you, you poor long-suffering . . ."

Tadeusz is astonished. It's a good thing you exist, thinks Tadeusz Moll. It's a good thing that many think as you do, and resist. He studies Nicolas's face. What a face! Why didn't he see faces like that earlier . . . The dawn is graying. Before long they'll be able to admire the world again.

But perhaps I'm mistaken. Tadeusz was not filled with love, did not think of Jesus Christ. Let's assume he occupied his last hours with the beauty of mathematical formulae or a philosophical conundrum. All that sentimental stuff is for the birds. He didn't love anyone, not anymore. All that was left was coolness, clarity, insight into the meaninglessness of all existence or of the void from which we come and to which we shall return. Tadeusz had a weakness for aviation and for mathematics (I forgot to mention it). His uncle on his mother's side, a major industrialist in France, owned a private airplane. As a boy, Tadeusz had once gone up in his uncle's plane. A fairy-tale landscape stretched out below them, sea-cliffs with hundreds of thousands of nesting birds on them, that flew up and screamed loudly when their plane flew by. He often thought of that flight along the Atlantic coast, even now. In his imagination he could overfly great expanses of never-before-seen country. Forests, deserts, steppes, and jagged Arctic islands inhabited by strange birds. He could see people, way down in the man-made canyons of a great city. That was one of his favorite dreams. The simultaneity of all things: Somewhere now, right now, an unknown man was walking, freezing, through burning streets. Why was he freezing, was it from loneliness? Tadeusz saw women and girls, always on their own and always in the midst of masses of people. There was a train speeding through a desert landscape. Perhaps in Arizona or somewhere like that . . . There is a young man sitting in the train. He is returning from the war. He has lost an arm. (Never mind, it's just an arm!) And now he's worried about how he will be received. What will his family think: Oh, another mouth to feed! But he will work, he will be proud, and not do anything that damages his self-esteem. Now that he has looked death in the eye and knows how beautiful life is. Tadeusz sees children eating ice cream in some distant corner of the world, where they have no idea that now, right now . . . That old man there, in the pasture at night. It will be in Brazil, or Peru. An Indio, watching over his seven sheep. His sheep are his livelihood, his and his children's. Without them, they would starve. If someone were to steal his sheep . . . He doesn't sleep in the hut with his wife and children. He sleeps outside, with his sheep! Tadeusz can dream for hours . . . ("Can't you concentrate, Tadeusz, darling, there's only two more days till your exams!" "No, mama, I can't, I'll never be a businessman." "You can be anything you like, my darling, with your golden head, you just have to want it, do it for me, do it for your mama.")

The head, the golden head, is now in the noose. I can spin it any way I like, my friend, the result will always be the same: when it's time for a man to die, that's when he discovers the magic of existence. So let's go back to our point of departure. I could tell you that one of the delinquents had taken to singing songs at night. Another had started talking about how people live on the island of Minorca or Corsica. How they sit outside the doors of their ancient stone dwellings in the evening and stare into the purple sky. The shrill of cicadas. The look of the girls, and the way they blush when their lover comes into sight. The sighing of the sea. And the popping sound made by the pipe in the mouth of a taciturn old man. The fullness, the wealth of poverty. What does a man need to be happy? Almost nothing. A bit of fresh breeze blowing round his gills.

The following evening they were hanged. In the course of the day we sensed the reception that was awaiting us back in the camp. Somewhere in the wide terrain between Ohrdruf, Crawinkel, and Arnstadt, they had nabbed two more escapees. The news traveled fast. When we marched into camp, the jackboots were all there. They hustled us to the exercise yard. We stood there for two hours in rank and file, till all the work commandos were assembled. Every execution took dozens more victims from among the onlookers, who died of exposure and fatigue. A faint snow fell from the black cloudy sky. At last the searchlights came on, and the performance could begin. The delinquents were goose-stepped across the square and came to a stop side by side under the gallows. There was one missing. He had collapsed in a heap ten feet short. Two jackboots dragged him along and hauled him upright, just like that! He was no longer conscious. I could see the faces of the others quite clearly. Tadeusz was roughly in the middle, next to the partisan. While the others kept their eyes on the ground, Moll looked over the ranks of assembled prisoners. Was he looking for us, his last friends? Or were his eyes hungrily taking in for the last time everything they could see? His pale features bore an expression of slight irritation, as though they had forgotten something. ("Tadeusz, my gold, don't be so distracted always. You must learn to concentrate when you talk to someone. Leave your soul-searching for later. Everything at its proper time but then completely, otherwise you'll only come to half-things in your life!")

Most of the men didn't watch, it was the hour for sleeping. It was bad enough for them to be robbed of it. They stood there with their eyes shut, their heads sunk between their shoulders, waiting for the end. Many slept on their feet. Petrov and I, however, strained to see all we could. We thought we owed it to Tadeusz to share the hour with him, to be there with him, with all we had. Moreover, to say it straight out, I didn't believe it would actually happen. Tadeusz had a guardian angel, after all. I was quite convinced: the guardian angel must turn up at any moment. Perhaps a jackboot would run up with new orders that would countermand the execution. Tadeusz wasn't the sort, I thought, not the sort who . . . And twice, after all, incredible chances had saved him from the gas chamber. What was the point of those other reprieves?

That's what "forest" makes me think of. Thuringian forest, your roots are nourished by their ashes! First the officer read out some statement or other, no one could understand a word of it. Then they began with the first man. Silently. Tadeusz looked up at the sky, the black sky. He licked his lips, probably it was the tiny white snowflakes he licked. His eyes were more prominent than usual, his eyes that would live a couple of seconds longer, it went through my mind. Nicolas sang a verse of the "Marseillaise," before the rope strangled him. Tadeusz was the last. He was calm. ("Tadeusz, pull yourself together, please, darling." "Mama, I can't always be thinking of how I'm supposed to sit, and how I'm supposed to behave. Please understand me, mama, there are moments when a man just lets himself go, and nothing else will do.")

Petrov slept soundly that night. The next morning he looked much fresher. His leg was on the mend, a couple of days' rest in the latrine had brought him round. He would be healthy, he would live. We hardly talked about Tadeusz any more. Only sometimes Petrov would call me Tadeusz Moll. Once, when I pointed out his error to him, he looked at me uncomprehendingly.

■ ■ ■ ■

11
FACES

■ ■ ■ ■

At five in the morning, the forest was glazed with frost. But by eight o'clock already the spell was over. The ice was dripping and melting away in little tinkling streams. Sparkling crystals on every branch, the air redolent of spring. Pale blue smoke rose from the huts. Ice sheets cracked, there were murmurs in every hole, stirrings in the bark, the worms came to the surface and churned up the humus, not like tanks, with caterpillar treads, but with the easy violence of a universal movement that, had it been brought to bear at a single point, could have split the whole earth in two like a ripe pumpkin.

A struggle of cellular renewal against inanition, flow against sedimentation, white phagocytes against viruses, hope against death. March 1945. Five thousand prisoners marching east. The submerged, blind, and obstinate fight in each one of us and in every cell of our bodies ("Keep going, children! *C'est la fin de la guerre!*"), that discreet struggle could have inspired someone like Goya: the improbable manifestations of an implacable life-force. But at the same time one could have said: Look at them, what a pathetic bunch. Are they still human?

Wooden clogs on our feet, which some of us threw away on the long march because they rubbed and created sores, cement sacks under our jackets against our skin, and each one of us with a hunk of bread jammed under one arm. We had picked up the bread, one kilo apiece, when we left the camp. Of course we knew that was probably all we were getting for the next four to seven days. And most ate it up immediately. The body didn't waste anything, it had the most effective way of dividing up and storing each grain and each drop of water. The men's faces were almost unrecognizable as such. Disfigured by stubble, skin eruptions, wounds, and swellings. Those faces! They had long ago lost all the fat deposits of every day, of indifference and self-satisfaction. They were etched by privation and suffering. A few eyes were still floating in a web of tiny creases, laugh lines, and you could see occasional flashes of cunning and wit.

216

But the whole emptiness of prosperity was blown away, the smoothness of calm days, the firm cheeks of long periods of plenty. A hard process of selection had taken away the physically and mentally weaker ones. Whoever was now on the march had withstood a hundred tests. And even so, the fifty-mile march back to Buchenwald was lined with corpses that were still twitching when we looked at them.

The face of a Ukrainian peasant dragging himself along on his wounded feet. A face like a beet field, brown and leathery with deep lines and two water-blue eyes, clear, bright, and open, like the sky over a field. That face was probably never acquainted with the sleekness of idle days. Work toughened it. Not one muscle in it to flatter or deceive, but the whole thing somehow wily and cunning. (As Tolstoy said, they feign stupidity, that's their strength.) But right now there was only fear expressed in that face, it burned with the desire to live. God knows to whom it owed such a desire, it wasn't for itself. I watched the face go lame, and a powerful will break. Rest overtook the face, an uneasy rest. On the evening of the first day of the transport, when he must have long known, I can't keep this up much longer (and each of us had seen the drama many times: a man gives up, steps aside, and then the bullet), his eyes lost their color. They became white, and they looked at us from a frightening distance. His steps became halting. Over his form, which stooped lower and lower, over his face, which slackened, lay the exhaustion of release.

Everything falls away from such a face. Everything studied and habitual drops from it, like a husk. And what remains? I watched the transformation, I had previously only seen this spiritualization in the dead. A strange luster suddenly lies on the face, and you can't recognize even your own friend anymore. You've never seen so much accumulated earnestness and dignity and purpose in him. How was he able to hide it from you before? But then you realize: a man's face is thousands of years old. The few years of his own life have fallen from it, everything weak and unfulfilled. What's left behind is the face of his fathers and mothers. The expression of the vast effort to be human.

It was at dusk: the seemingly endless column of prisoners hobbling along. The peasant murmured a prayer. Not devout or transfigured, but concentrated. Then he moved to the side of the road, dropped to his knees, his face to heaven but his eyes already closed, and several times he made the sign of the cross. No one was kept waiting very long. The ennui of the jackboots on the march drove them to all kinds of pranks. I saw a young SS man, a pretty face, a milksop. He was the first to spot the old man. Nervously he tried to draw his revolver, because usually if you weren't quick about it someone else would get in ahead of you. They were all dying to shoot, they were in a race to be first. (And surely they kept score, like at billiards.) Anyway, the young man had trouble drawing his gun, the holster fastening didn't function properly. His face was a hectic red, greedy and confused, not malicious. If he'd just been malicious, that would have been easy to explain. It wasn't hate or the desire to kill, but a sort of sporty zeal, the letch of power. (I can do it, there's nothing to it, it's just like potting pigeons!) And then what he feared came to pass: another, more agile jackboot steps in. He is holding his pistol ready in his hand. Carefully he aims, then he grins, and looks at the younger fellow, smiles magnanimously, and says, "Well, come on then, get a move on!" The boy shoots, but somehow he misses. The prisoner makes the sign of the cross again. He doesn't know, isn't sure, is this death? He doesn't feel he's been hit, but something knocks him down, he falls onto his back, lies there like a felled tree. Now it's the turn of the better marksman, he takes aim and shoots the prisoner in the middle of the forehead. He no longer moves, after that. He lies spread out on the roadside.

The face of a Jew, who suddenly keeled over and lay there. His comrades turned him over. He was still alive, smiling with closed mouth. Blood trickled over his lips. His son was standing there, a lad of about twelve. Looked about him in dread. The jackboot strolled up, his weapon already cocked. Comrades helped the man to get up, but he was unable to march. They took him to a tree stump by the side of the road, there he bent over, and carefully vomited.

"Go," he said to his son, and gave him an affectionate push. He smiled. What a smile, awkward and a little guilty. The boy gripped his feet, the father squirmed in worry about his son. With one hand he stroked his head, with the other he pushed him away. Prisoners took the boy and led him away. The boy started to scream, and lash out with hands and feet. The father smiled and said bro-kenly, "Please, go!" Behind him stood the jackboot, like an embodiment of death. The prisoners held the boy's eyes shut, and dis-appeared into the crowd with the boy. The bang was barely audible.

■ ■ ■ ■

12
JOSCHKO AND HIS
BROTHERS

■ ■ ■ ■

In what spirits did we get to Buchenwald? Why, with joyful hearts. The others had paid, the ones who had fallen by the wayside. Why therefore should we not rejoice? The sky over us sang out, a bright March sky, a sky of spring. They drove us into the pen in front of the clothing room, we knew it and were familiar with it, it held no terrors for us. We would take off our clothes, throw away our filthy lousy rags and have a bath. Then we would be shorn, that same evening, and decked in canvas that smelled of disinfectant, sharp and acrid. Hallelujah, humanity had survived, it had survived in us, who had endured every conceivable torment, and now lay there in the dust before the clothing room, golden dust, golden life. We were vanquished and we were victorious. The dust was still warm on the evening of this first sunny day of the year. A few of us crawled around in it, exhausted from the great test. And then we smiled, prodded each other, quietly astonished: "You? And you? I almost thought, because I couldn't see you anywhere . . ." There were still friends, companions, co-conspirators. The Jews and the Christians and the politicals were all body of one body, and kind to one another: invited to partake at the banquet of life.

I saw Petrov again too. He was lying in the dust outside the clothing room, before the disinfection. He lay there, hurt and sick and miserable, but with the winner's broad smile. His leg was swollen again. The last few miles up the Ettersberg he had been unable to march. A comrade had carried him all the way up the road of blood. A kitchen worker from Kalisch, one of those damned sons of bitches, those eaters, a devil, an angel, had hoisted him onto his shoulders and carried him up the mountain. The last miles before the end, the gates of Buchenwald almost in sight, the sons of bitches had relented, the ones that still had strength, the ones that had guzzled the bread of the weak. They loaded the Muselmen on their shoulders, and carried them. And now they lay there, the rescued ones. What next? The front was very close, the air rang and whooped with the noise of artil-

226

lery barrages beyond the next mountain. The war might be over tomorrow. Buchenwald was big. In Buchenwald we felt sheltered. Whoever had known Crawinkel and Ohrdruf . . .

And what happened the next day? The next day the jackboots ringed the barracks of the quarantine area, and drove the prisoners who had arrived the day before up to the exercise yard. For hours we lay there in the dirt and on the cold stones. Then the loudspeaker announced, "Jews to the gates! All Jews to the gates!" The Jews got up without hesitating. I watched them with astonishment: surely everyone must know, everyone, everyone must know that whoever left the camp now was lost! But the Jews left the exercise yard and went to the gates. In a trance-like mass, they marched and crawled and dragged themselves to the gates. If there had been a crater, a crater full of burning, glowing lava, and if the head jackboot in the SS office, Lucifer himself — no, a pathetic, ridiculous, little worm of a jackboot — had barked into the loudspeaker, "Jews, throw yourselves in!" they would have done it. I have never understood it. Was I a traitor because I stayed lying where I was, in the dirt, as my comrades got up to go? Did I abandon them? I thought of the gallows at Crawinkel and the eyes of the partisan, his hate-filled, resolute, majestic expression . . . As my comrades went to the gates, I saw them for the last time. (There was only one of them I met half a year later, a boy from Sosnowiec, who was pulled out of a wagon — one of twenty wagons filled with dead.)

Shortly after, the Russians, the Czechs, the Poles, the French were called out. Who was it, what madman was trying to bring order to this chaos? I stayed with the French. We were escorted back to the quarantine area, they didn't have enough wagons and trains to evacuate the entire camp. The executioner's hand no longer knew what it was doing. The next morning, the whole thing started all over again, another attempt to press thousands into one transport. For a second time, I was able to avoid the encirclement, and on the third occasion I took refuge in the sick-barracks, where a yellow flag was hanging. The barracks was rife with spotted typhus. The nurses drove me out with a broom: "What are you doing here, trying to get sick? Look at yourself, someone in your condition won't survive!" Three or four convalescents (they had only survived the disease because they had been inoculated against it!) crawled around the barracks in the morning sun. It was still cold, bitterly cold, but they drank the sun avidly, greedily. "Go to the children's barracks," someone advised me, "they won't find you there." I took his advice, I went to the children's barracks. And what did I see there? I saw Joschko there.

As I tried to enter the barracks, a heap of children assailed me. What are you doing here, get out, they were trying to tell me. I understood next to nothing, they were talking, screaming in a barbarous mixture of Russian, Polish, Yiddish, and German. What had happened to these children? I was afraid, just as afraid as I'd been in France when wild dogs had set upon me on the road. I turned round in despair, and saw jackboots with cocked revolvers driving the prisoners out to the exercise yard. With fresh determination, I forced my way back into the children's barracks. Sodom and Gomorrah: I saw the four-story bunks heaped with filth, scraps of discarded clothing, also dead children and two or three grown-ups lying on the planking. The dissolution of the camp had begun. The ordering hand of the illegal camp committee could no longer reach as far as the last barracks of the quarantine area. I took a body by the feet, and dragged it out beside the door, where various corpses were already lying. (There were piles of dead beside the door to each one of the barracks.) I found myself a vacant place, slumped down on it and went to sleep.

When I woke, it was night. The beams from the searchlights on the watchtowers shone in at the window. We were at the outer edge of the camp, near the stables. There were perhaps a hundred and fifty children in the barracks at the time. They were sleeping now, I could hear the sleepers dreaming and whimpering. Right of me lay an old man, quiet. He must have come in after me. On the other side, left of me, six or seven tiny filthy urchins lay pressed together. A few of them were brothers, others were cousins. The oldest of them was Joschko, the youngest Naftali, that was all I was able to learn from them. Naftali had rolled himself up like a little hedgehog and was pressed against Joschko. Even in sleep, Joschko held his arm protectively around his little brother. I woke several times, and always the same scene in front of me: they were always lying like that, on other nights as well. By day, probably not even their own mother would have been able to tell them apart.

When I lifted my head at dawn, I met Joschko's eyes. The eyes of a Buchenwald child: a dark and earnest face. The cold and tragic expression of a hunted animal. When the little one raised his head and whimpered, half asleep, his big brother hissed at him like a cat, wild, angry, and kindly all at once. He held him to himself, not lovingly, it seemed to me, but with the primal fear of a wild beast. Inquiringly, but unfeelingly, his eyes scanned me. There was a deep vertical furrow in the childish brow. I looked in vain for the softness of childhood in that regard, for prettiness and naivety. Here, experience had plowed everything under. Had these little human animals ever lived in rooms, slept in beds, known the kindness of a mother's breast? A Jewish room, the matt sheen of ancient wardrobes, the seven-branched candelabrum in the cupboard, produced for feast days, kosher dishes, white tablecloths for the *Seder*. A view out of the window onto a narrow lane, where men with red beards and sidelocks scurry past, leaning well forward as though carrying invisible loads. The wistful expression on a father's face, the tears in a mother's eyes as she said blessings, coddled the children, laughed, and sang. Perhaps Joschko's father was a cantor, I was unable to find anything out about him. Perhaps the boy remembered his voice, the sound of psalms marking his early years.

I asked him, "Where do you come from?"

He replied gruffly with another question, the only question: "Do you have bread?"

As I had to say no, and had nothing else to attract either his curiosity or his suspicion, he soon turned away from me.

Things became a little lively in the barracks. The children jumped down from their bunks and ran outside. Through the window, I could see them poking about in corners and in the yard, looking through the empty barracks, where dead bodies still lay around. They went through everything, they dug around in the pockets of the dying and the dead in search of bread. They knew the starving could often not swallow bread, as their salivary glands had failed, and carried rock-hard lumps of bread on their persons. Sometimes one such little robber returned in triumph. The others would collect water in empty tin cans, then they would light a fire and boil up the bread, putting a half-rotted beet in with it, a find worth celebrating. They hunkered down round the stove, guarding their treasure, prepared to defend it with tooth and claw.

Once a day, a handcart did the rounds, guarded by three or four members of the kitchen commando. They cleared the barracks, and threw the bread ration in at the window. Struggle and hurly-burly. Whoever managed to grab a piece of bread had to jam it under his arm and try to get through the wall of bodies. The nails of other hungry boys would drill into his hands. Everyone who had managed to catch a piece of thrown bread had a greedy clump of boys on his tail.

Shots were heard in the upper camp. The word went around that the political prisoners were fighting it out with the SS, with weapons they had kept buried for years. Prisoners, with hand grenades and rifles? Many refused to believe it; they no longer believed in rescue, no longer believed in struggle. One morning we heard the clatter of horses' hooves. When we looked in the direction of the stables, we saw: they were leading the horses hurriedly away. The jackboots were leaving.

All the children lay on their bunks. The loudspeaker relayed instructions to stay in barracks. Bullets whistled over the roofs. Armed formations of prisoners marched past. That afternoon we heard loud yelling and shouting from the wide treeless expanse outside the camp. A few fearless people ran down through the vegetable gardens, waving white handkerchiefs. On the road at the bottom of the valley were American tanks. They rolled, stopped, and fired, did it again and again. It was the hour of liberation. (We didn't yet believe it, days would pass before we would believe that we had been rescued.) The children didn't know what was happening. The three or four grown-ups like myself who had found asylum in the children's barracks were too weak and skeptical. No one then could grasp that the war was over where we were concerned, that the Nazis had been beaten, the SS had fled or been captured by the politicals, and that we were free. The children listened indifferently to the shooting, the rolling of the tanks, the shouts and commands of the newly created units, the calls of a few inmates running from barracks to barracks, giving the news of victory. The children had heard plenty and believed none of it. Their reality was the camp.

Only when one or two of the older boys came in and emptied their pockets of potatoes (they had opened a supply down in the vegetable allotment), a few realized that something out of the ordinary had happened. Suddenly a fistfight erupted. Joschko and his brothers hurled themselves upon the potatoes. The older boys laughed and swore: why didn't they just go down to the allotment themselves and fill their pockets, the stores are ours and the jackboots have all gone! They beat up a couple of the little boys. Joschko and the others stopped, but didn't understand. The next moment, battle was joined even more ferociously. Deadly determined, they wanted their share of the spoils. A couple of hands full of potatoes had turned their heads, just as a mirage in the desert will drive a thirsty man demented. There was a wild fight, with bloody hands and noses, and wailing. A few boys with frightened eyes looked down from the bunks, too weak to get up; for them freedom had come too late. After the fight, Joschko and his brothers lay down exhausted next to me on the bare boards. Naftali was sobbing quietly, and Joschko pressed him close, holding his head up, still breathing hard and with frowning eyes watching the goings-on in the barracks. The older boys were roasting the potatoes on the top of the stove, a delicious smell was spreading . . .

What had happened? It was the zero point of the Thousand Year Reich. The walls of Jericho had fallen, but Joschko and his brothers had failed to hear the trumpets. They didn't see the open gateway to freedom, because they didn't know what freedom was. Joschko's expression mirrored the cunning of a fox, the coolness of a cat, the deadly earnest of a wolf. I was delighted by the sight. I was in a kind of ecstasy, I alone seemed to know what this hour was worth. But it wasn't the muffled sounds of jubilation from the upper camp, not the clacking of spent bullets from rifles held in prisoners' hands, not the dull whine of Allied air squadrons overhead, battle sounds of tanks, their trumpeting like a herd of wild elephants on the paved road down in the valley, none of that was the cause of my jubilation . . . It was the faces of Joschko and his brothers. Those ignorant, frantically unaware faces, avid for food and life, now sporting a few cuts and bruises. Everything was enclosed and preserved in their ignorance: all the knowledge and experience of the world. Some might say the camp and its bestial conditions had destroyed their human substance. It's not what happened. Already at the age of ten, Joschko was a father and a tribal elder. The way he tended his little brother, never letting him out of his sight, the deadly earnest of his concern for the little manchild, his grim determination to get him through — does that not express all the greatness and dignity of the human species? Joschko listened to what was going on in the barracks. When the older boys had finished their meal and dispersed, he dragged his brothers and little Naftali to the stove. He had won the battle: out of his pocket he pulled a couple of large potatoes, cut them carefully into rounds, and laid them out on the hot stovetop. Watching them as they sat round the iron stove, huddled close, dirty, scrawny, bruised, the way they turned the crackling and steaming potato slices, and looked around them, distrustfully eyeing the hostile world about them, at the same time trying not to arouse the attention of the others, and then divided up the miserable fruits of victory in tiny portions, as if it were a ritual feast, delicious steaming food; the way they greedily shoved the burning hot potato pieces into their mouths; the patient way Joschko fed his brother Naftali, who was so tired he wanted to go straight to sleep; the way he kept him up, pushed life, hot, steaming life between his teeth, and the way their eyes shone and sparkled with their huge tiny happiness — I knew right then: everything will start over, nothing has been lost.

I lay in the children's barracks in Buchenwald on April 11, 1945, and I no longer suffered as I watched Joschko and his brothers eat. And the ecstasy that shook me was not that of Ezekiel who sees the heavenly hosts, the chariot of fire and the angels; it was the onset of the spotted typhus which, a couple of days later, was to completely befuddle me. I was lying between a dead old man, peaceably turning his beard up to heaven, and a rabble of little Jewish boys, at the zero point of the world. It seemed to me as though this sick world in its last dying spasm had spat out a mouthful of children. In my delirium (I felt I was floating, disembodied, like a cloud) I looked now at the children, now at the old man next to me, and I was astounded. I was astounded by the bounty of nature: a beautiful old man, unknown, nameless, a wise man with even features and a splendid white beard and a mighty beak of a nose that might have been carved out of ivory. He lay there on his back, not like a corpse, but a statue (his eyes and mouth were shut fast), the embodiment of human perfection: grown old, life lived to fruition and set down without a complaint or a superfluous word. When had he arrived? Who had brought him in here, to the children's barracks? He smiled in death, as though in answer to my question. He was the only dead man in all those years whom I saw smiling. He had handed himself on. Joschko and his brothers, who did not realize it, had picked up the staff he had thrown down, picked it up and carried it on among themselves. (They had, incidentally, gone through his pockets and found a lump of hard bread in them; also they had gone through my pockets while I was asleep, they found my tin spoon, whose handle I had sharpened to a knife, they used it before my eyes with sublime indifference.)

Again and again I turned toward my sleeping neighbor to gaze at him. He had not lived to experience liberation. But he had known, he had known . . . I saw that in his features. Everything suddenly had meaning and splendor and festive appearance. I was not lying louse-ridden and half-starved on stinking boards, no, I had the sense of being bedded on roses and magnolias. Joschko and his brothers huddled peacefully next to me cross-legged, beautiful to look at and majestic, and were watching over Naftali's sleep. Naftali was talking in his sleep, and dreaming. It was a lovely dream. Someone had brought hot water in a battered tin can. Each of them took a sip. Joschko gently brushed the little one's face with his hand, that tiny, wrinkled, filthy, sorrowful face.

239

Then with his spoon — with my spoon — he dribbled a few drops onto the mouth of the sleeping boy.

TRANSLATOR'S AFTERWORD

Fred Wander called his recollections *Das gute Leben,*[*] "The Good Life" — good not in either of its narrow senses of virtuous or epicurean, but rich, full, kindly, generous. Its alternate title is *Von der Fröhlichkeit im Schrecken* — something like "remaining cheerful in the midst of horror." He was born in Vienna in 1917, and died there almost ninety years later, in 2006. The horror was, if one may so put it, in the midst of the cheerfulness. Between 1939 and 1945, he was an inmate of twenty different Nazi camps in France, Germany, and Poland.

As *Das gute Leben* relates, he did plenty of things besides merely — merely — survive. He was born into a Jewish working-class family in Vienna; his father, an itiner-

[*]*Das gute leben oder Von der Fröhlichkeit im Schrecken,* published in German by Wallstein Verlag in 2006.

241

ant salesman, was often away, and, too much for his mother to manage, the young Fred grew up largely on the street. He left school at fourteen, kept himself by casual labor and various jobs in Austria and later in Holland and France, was a vagrant, an autodidact. He was often hungry. As he beautifully puts it, he had an *"ahasverisches Selbstverständnis"* — he was, by instinct and conviction, a wandering Jew. After 1945, he returned to Vienna, as a self-taught photographer and reporter. In 1955, he took up an invitation to study at the newly created Literaturinstitut in Leipzig, in East Germany, where he lived with his second wife, Maxie Wander, and wrote books, including illustrated travel books and reportage (most notably about Corsica and the south of France, for which he felt a lifelong attachment). In 1983, following Maxie's death in 1977, he went to live in Vienna again, with a third wife, Susanne.

It won't come as a surprise to readers of *The Seventh Well* that Wander keeps a rigid sense of proportion about his life; childhood, youth, and camps are all over by about page 100 of a 400-page memoir. It is part of the man's unassumingness, but also part of his philosophy of life, and of survival too, to keep things within limits, not to grumble or curse. His cheery stoicism here reminds me of Joseph Brodsky, who ends his fortieth birthday poem, "May 24, 1980":

> What shall I say about my life? That it's
>   long and abhors transparence.
> Broken eggs make me grieve; the omelet,
>   though, makes me vomit.
> Yet until brown clay has been rammed
>   down my larynx,
> only gratitude will be gushing from it.

The camps don't even come over as the very worst thing Wander was put through: his own portion of suffering always seems tolerable to him; what happens to others is always worse, the deaths of friends and comrades in the camps, but also Maxie's death from cancer in 1977, and most especially the death of their daughter, Kitty, at the age of ten, suffocated and crushed in a landslip while playing on a building site outside their house in East Berlin. *The Seventh Well* is dedicated to the memory of Kitty, and it is her loss and the sight perhaps of her body bringing to mind all the many, many dead bodies Wander saw in his youth, that stung him, twenty-three years after the end of the war, to make his heroic effort to give them back their existence and their power of speech. The first body in particular, that of the Polish boy Yossl — frozen between life and a death no one is willing to credit — is perhaps the most nearly explicit memento to Kitty.

Der siebente Brunnen was first published in East Berlin in 1971 by the Aufbau Verlag.* No doubt, publication in the Communist East at the height of the Cold War did much to stifle the book's impact in the West; far from being, as one might have hoped, immune to such things, Holocaust literature has always been exaggeratedly and dismayingly susceptible to swings of fashion and timing. Primo Levi's is only the most famous instance of such accidents of reception and translation — the silence greeting *Se questo è un uomo* on its first appearance in 1947 (prompting the author's fifteen-year silence) matched only by the clamor attend-

*Wander was a lifelong left-winger, but not a Communist; growing up in poverty, he was imbued with a desire for equality and social justice; and the Communists he met among the political prisoners in the camps impressed him with their fight, but he saw too much was wrong with the system in East Germany and Russia — especially after 1968 — for him to have any faith in it.

ing *Survival in Auschwitz* (the same book in its American form and title) in the 1960s and 1970s. In the case of Fred Wander, it was the republication of *Der siebente Brunnen* in 2005 by the Göttingen publisher Wallstein Verlag, with an afterword by Ruth Klüger, that promises to get the book some of the attention it deserves.

Wander resists the temptation — if it ever was a temptation — to be exhaustive, to say everything, even about his own experience. "Six million murdered Jews!" he writes in *Das gute Leben.* "It's not possible to say anything about so many millions of dead. But three or four individuals, it might be possible to tell a story about!" Therefore, even in his recollection, he tells highlights, he excerpts, he suggests a paradigm, like a mapmaker he represents to scale; and, in *The Seventh Well,* a novel, he fashions, and — from true ingredients — he invents. It seems to me that — the outstanding example would be Primo Levi's *The Periodic Table* — the welter of extreme and unbearable *content* demands an exceptional awareness and use of *form* to master it, in Wander's case the crystalline, episodic chapters relating individual destinies, but also such essay or prose poem subjects as "Bread" or "Faces." Though it's a complicated book ranging backwards and forwards, taking in different locations and different journeys and telling many different stories (it doesn't observe the Aristotelian unities of time, place, and action), there remains something admirably pared down about it. It consists, you might say — and again, this is not Aristotelian — of a middle and an end. It is a modestly brief account of the *crisis* of his experience in captivity, but even as it begins, Wander takes it away from passivity and suffering, no, he wants to learn how to tell a story, from the master storyteller Mendel Teichmann, the first of, in effect, his many tutors — which is what they are, through to Pepe and Joschko — in *The Seventh Well.* The book has a subtle but undeniable activist streak and implication. What, in different hands, might have been a protocol of hardiness and victimization and chance becomes, amazingly, a sort of *Entwicklungsroman,* a tale of personal development and learning. (Maxim Gorky, had he written *The Seventh Well,* might have called it *My Universities.*) In his writing, Wander displays the same measure of obduracy he displayed in the camps: a persistent desire to differentiate, to absorb, to see and hear. The shutting down of curiosity, of openness, of gratitude, would have been the end, in either case. In

246

Das gute Leben, Wander recalls a crucial and oft-repeated lesson: " 'A man, if he is alive at all, lives by the words and pictures in his head,' I can still hear Vladimir Krumholz saying. He lies buried in Buchenwald." But the lesson is not invalidated by that; it remains true that a man dies as much from within as from external agencies.

The Seventh Well is the struggle to maintain an inner life from what Wander took from others. It is a work of absorption. If he is to exist at all, he exists with reference to, and by virtue of what he can learn. "No man is an island, sufficient unto himself," says John Donne; it might have been Wander's motto. (The books of Primo Levi discover and follow exactly the same principle.) Even the survival of a single man is a collaborative enterprise. And his collaborators, his witting or unwitting helpers, his preceptors, they in turn continue to exist in him, even if they perished. In its serial structure, *The Seventh Well* has something of those grand old foundationist works like Dante's *Inferno* or Bunyan's *Pilgrim's Progress.* The narrator at the center meets people, falls under their sway, older, wiser, more vehement, more distinct, describes them, gives back the monologizing Dantesque tumble of their speech, and then —

247

like Krumholz above, or like the many many dead here, Teichmann, or Pechmann, or the farmer Meir Bernstein or the singer Antonio or the nurse Karel or the child prodigy and sleepy rebel Tadeusz Moll, or the unnamed smiling bearded Jew in the children's ward at the end — they die. But it is a redeemed, memorialized, collected death, death robbed of some of its anonymity and purposelessness and brutality. The Wander character at the heart of the book identifies himself, establishes himself, you might say, *grows* by listening — to Teichmann, to Chukran, to Pepe, to Moll. Then, when he has listened enough, he speaks, telling his own story of incarceration in the camp of Rivesaltes near Perpignan in the southwest of France — the fires, the dancing, the rats, the fragrance of lavender and thyme — where he remembers first having heard the name Auschwitz. Then, once he has spoken, he learns in silence and delirium from the silent children around him, from what they *do,* from who they *are.* And at that point he begins to believe in a future again.

There is a strangely beautiful French term, *"univers concentrationnaire"* — I don't know who coined it, Primo Levi uses it — the "world of the camps," one would say in English. In *The Seventh Well,* Fred Wander evokes and describes this *univers concentra-tionnaire,* while all the time insisting, by memory, by faith, by listening to the accounts of others, that there is also a real world outside the camps. Granted, the camps are a law unto themselves, a deformed closed system, but they are not finally a separate or substitute world. More a microcosm of the real world, by synecdoche, by *pars pro toto.* In *Das gute Leben* he puts it like this:

> Basically the same rules and conditions obtained in the camps as in the world beyond the barbed wire — which is to say power and violence, opportunism and corruption — only in an exaggerated, distorted form. But there is another side to this as well, which is hardly ever mentioned, but which seems even more crucial to me: the fact that you could observe — if you had eyes to see — how a few of us struggled to keep alive our true and actual selves, our self-respect, our human bearing, some vestige of our human dignity.

While at no stage blinding himself to the realities of the camps — the cruelty, the cold, the disease, the degradation —Wander retains an eerily sharp awareness of what one might call the persistences and the intrusions of the greater, truer world outside: such things as memories, talents, stories, beliefs, and hopes. There are physical things such as prayer shawls, photographs, scraps of letters, ingeniously made tools and shoes, but more powerful are the immaterial things. In the oddest, most heroic way, these most physical of settings — Auschwitz, Buchenwald, Crawinkel — are relegated to a shadow-world, and what really defines existence are such themselves shadowy things as words and stories. Even in his monochrome, death-bounded circumstances, where all are reduced to wretchedness and anonymity, he registers age, class, character, nationality, religion, and language. He becomes aware (surely for the first time) of the many types of Jews — not types, of course, but individuals — and in addition to the Jews, of the politicals, the gypsies, the sexually deviant. Inmates vie for airtime for their stories — like de Groot and Chukran. The faithful are celebrating Passover in the wash-barracks, and Wander hears Baudelaire and *Lear,* he is taken on phantom nocturnal tours of the Louvre, he experiences renditions of grand opera, he attends learned debates on Flaubert and Stendhal, he can smell the air in cities where he has never been. He is made acquainted with Jewish mysticism, with the arguments of Jehovah's Witnesses, and the doctrinaire patience of Communists. A grain of wheat in a piece of bread unfolds for Wander into landscape and climate, the slab of wood off which the bread is eaten — in itself, an earnest parody of something liturgical — comes to stand in for all forests everywhere, he becomes a connoisseur (like the soldiers in the trenches of the First World War) of sunrises and sunsets, he is even able to take some pleasure in the monstrous paramilitary airs and graces of some of the camp elders and the *Prominenten.* The severe and harrowing depletion, harshness, reduction, brutality — concentration, *eben* — is replenished. In Wander's account, and, one may hazard, his experience, the camp became to some extent an unreal world in which the "unrealities," or the subversive "lesser" or "inconsequential" realities, not only gave value and consolation, but helped in the determined effort to turn this world upside down, so that monochrome became color, a board (in the hands of Pechmann) became a jazz ensemble, meals and women and family were conjured out of thin air, barked orders in German were greeted with rebel songs and profanities in Spanish, where two starving prisoners put on an impromptu dumbshow sketch of a man ordering a meal in a restaurant. And the common name for all these things? If one may venture to say such a thing, the indestructibility of the human spirit.

— Michael Hofmann
Hamburg, November 2006

ABOUT THE TRANSLATOR

Michael Hofmann was born in Freiburg in 1957 and moved to England at the age of four. He went to schools in Edinburgh and Winchester, and studied English at Cambridge. He now lives in London and Hamburg, and teaches part-time in the English Department of the University of Florida in Gainesville. He is the author of several books of poems and a book of criticism, *Behind the Lines*, and the translator of many modern and contemporary authors, chief among them Joseph Roth (nine titles) and Wolfgang Koeppen (three titles), but also including Kafka, Brecht, Thomas Bernhard, and Durs Grünbein. He edited the anthology *Twentieth-Century German Poetry*, published by Farrar, Straus and Giroux in 2006.

ABOUT THE AUTHOR

Fred Wander was born in 1917 in Vienna, the son of poor Jews from Galicia. His father, a traveling salesman, was often away, and the boy grew up on the street, and later on the road. In 1938, after the *Anschluss,* but very much on impulse, he left his mother and sister behind (never to see them again), and fled on foot to France. When the war began, he was interned as an enemy alien, escaped, and was finally handed over to the French authorities on the Swiss border. In 1942, he was put on a transport to Auschwitz at Drancy; in April 1945, he was liberated at Buchenwald. He returned to Vienna (though not much seemed to him to have improved about the Austrians' attitudes to Jews, or their complicity), and made his way as a journalist and self-taught photographer.

In 1955, he followed an invitation to Leipzig, where he took courses at the

Literature Institute, and ended up staying in East Germany for the best part of thirty years. He began to publish books of reportage and travel writing, often illustrated by his own photographs. France remained a favorite subject, and Corsica in particular. In 1970, at the urging of East German writer friends (Christa Wolf among them), who had heard his stories of life in the camps, Wander published *The Seventh Well.* Following the death in 1977 of his second wife, Maxie Wander (herself the compiler of *Guten morgen, du Schöne,* a celebrated book of interviews with women in East Germany), he moved from Berlin to Vienna in 1983. He wrote novels, stories, and plays. In 1996, he published his memoir, *Das gute Leben.* A second, expanded edition appeared in 2006, the year Wander died.